SUPREME JUSTICE

Also by Gary Hardwick

Double Dead
Cold Medina

SUPREME JUSTICE

GARY HARDWICK

A Novel of Suspense

WILLIAM MORROW AND COMPANY, INC. / NEW YORK

Har

Library of Congress Cataloging-in-Publication Data

Hardwick, Gary.
Supreme justice / Gary Hardwick. — 1st ed.
p.   cm.
ISBN 0-688-16513-3 (acid-free paper)
I. Title.
PS3558.A62368S86   1999   98-56008
813'.54—dc21   CIP

Printed in the United States of America

First Edition

1   2   3   4   5   6   7   8   9   10

BOOK DESIGN BY BERNARD KLEIN

www.williammorrow.com

*To my brothers, Willie James Hardwick
and Jeffrey Dean Hardwick, who were
killed . . . without knowing*

Justice is the end of government.
—James Madison, *The Federalist, No. 51* (1788)

"Where is Abel thy brother?"
"I know not. Am I my Brother's Keeper?"
—God and Cain (Genesis 4:9)

The key to life is the light of a child.
—Joe Black (1998)

SUPREME JUSTICE

Prologue: A Fight

The circle of kids moved in unison on the old neighborhood street. The crowd kicked up dust as the two boys fought in the center. The combatants punched and shoved, and the tight circle moved to accommodate them but never letting them outside the circle.

The fighters were twelve or so, and about the same size. One wore a bright red shirt, and the other a white T-shirt, stained with dirt and blood.

The crowd of boys cheered on their chosen fighter. They stayed close together, locking arms, to keep the ring intact.

Lost in the crowd, among the bigger bodies, was a skinny, white kid with red hair styled in a buzz cut. He was out of place in the all-black crowd but held his own, jostling and shoving with the others.

The fighters battled on a dead-end street with a playground adjacent to it. Beyond the dead end was an abandoned field, filled with trash and old, junked cars. It was midday, and the sun washed the area in hot light.

A fierce pickup basketball game was going on at the playground across the street from the fight. The basketball players played their game, oblivious to the battle in the street. These were bigger boys, sixteen to twenty years old, and basketball was serious business to them. The sweaty men elbowed and shoved one another as the game drew to an end.

The fighters were in a clinch and punched at each other, trying not to let go. The boy in white wiped at his nose, which was bleeding.

"You fucked up this time, boy," said the boy in red to his opponent.

"You stole my bike, you punk ass," said the boy in white.

The boy in red pushed his enemy away from him, and landed a blow on the side of his head. The boy in the white shirt swung wildly and missed, almost losing his balance. The boy in red moved in closer and tried to hit the other, but missed. His opponent punched him in the belly and heard him yell loudly.

"Kick his ass, Moses!" yelled a fat kid to the boy in the red shirt.

"Move, move, Marshall!" yelled the white kid to the boy in the white T-shirt.

The two fighters circled each other, looking for an opening. Moses faked a jab, and Marshall jumped back defensively. Moses smiled.

"How many times do I gotta beat you before you leave me alone?" asked Moses.

"Not this time," said Marshall. He lunged at Moses and caught him in the chest, knocking him on his ass. Moses quickly got up and ran at Marshall, kicking. Marshall sidestepped, and the kick missed. Moses moved in closer, throwing blows at the other boy.

Across the street, a tall skinny boy slam-dunked a missed shot, and the pickup basketball game ended. Players cursed and talked trash as money changed hands.

One of the players saw the commotion in the street, and ran over to watch the fight. Soon, the others followed.

"I got five on my man in red," said one of the bigger boys.

"Shit, I'll take that," said another of the big boys. *"What they fighting about this time?"* he asked the white kid.

"Moses stole Marshall's bike and sold it to Steve Collins and them," said the white kid.

"Damn," said one of the big boys. *"Gimme five on Marshall. Whip his ass, Marsh. You can't steal a man's ride."*

The big boys made bets and laughed as the fight continued. Marshall landed a solid blow on Moses' chin, and the crowd cheered. Moses dropped to one knee holding his jaw. He tasted coppery blood.

"Give?" asked Marshall.

"Fuck naw," said Moses who stood up. *"You ain't never beat me."*

Moses waded back into the fight and grabbed Marshall in a headlock. Marshall fell to the ground, taking Moses with him. The two boys rolled for a moment, then Moses pushed away and got to his feet. Marshall stood up only to be hit in the stomach by Moses. Marshall doubled over and Moses kicked out his leg, knocking the other boy over. *Marshall fell hard to the ground with a loud groan.*

"Yeah!" yelled Moses as he punched the air.

In the crowd, the big boys cursed and exchanged money.

"Marsh, your mama's comin'!" yelled the white kid.

The smaller boys ran away as a big woman approached the fight scene. The skinny white kid stayed behind, helping Marshall to his feet. The woman looked angry as she stomped her way toward them. Moses didn't move. Marshall held his stomach. He was covered in dirt and still bloody.

"He started it, Mama," said Moses. The words were hardly out of his mouth when the woman smacked him hard in the face.

"You forgot who you was talkin' to, boy. I know you." The other boys laughed. "Y'all want some too?" asked the woman.

The boys were all silent. Some snickered, but made sure the woman didn't hear it.

The woman went to Marshall. "Both of you get your asses home right now, before I beat you all over this street!" She looked at the white kid and said: "And you, Danny, you get your narrow ass home before I call your mother."

The white kid looked at the woman with fear, then ran off without a word.

"Come on," said the big woman. She walked off, and the two boys followed her. "I swear," the woman continued, "all the boys in the neighborhood, and you fight your own damned twin brother."

The brothers walked toward their house as the big boys laughed and high-fived behind them. Some of the boys called out to the brothers, teasing them about being picked up by their mother.

The brothers walked along barely hearing their mother yelling at them. They just glared at each other with hatred.

Part 1

SIGHTED JUSTICE

1

Masonic

"No Douglas! No Douglas!"

The crowd chanted loudly outside of Masonic Temple in Detroit. A few snowflakes fell from the winter sky, adding to the white blanket that covered the area. It was January, and the cruel Michigan winter was in full swing. People held their signs and placards high as TV cameras panned the crowd.

The protestors had come out for Farrel Douglas, associate justice of the United States Supreme Court. Douglas had won his seat on the Court by a narrow margin in a politically charged congressional confirmation.

Douglas was a black conservative, a badge that he wore with pride, but many in the black community hated him for it. Groups from all around the country had bitterly opposed his appointment. And since he'd been sworn into office, Douglas had consistently voted against affirmative action, minority districting, anti-discrimination laws, and every other liberal measure. He'd also voted for just about every conservative cause that came up to the court. He even wrote the majority opinion in a case that stopped black medical schools from using race in its admission policy.

The signs in the crowd illustrated a singular dislike of Douglas. Some showed Douglas as a lawn jockey, others showed him with a "mammy rag" tied around his head, still another pictured him in a KKK hood.

BLACK RACIST, TRAITOR, UNCLE TOM, the signs spelled out the hatred and disgust of the crowd.

Douglas was set to speak at the winter commencement of Wayne State University Law School in Detroit. It was a controversial choice that had brought national attention to the city as well as to the law school. Many other schools and institutions had turned Douglas down for speaking engagements, but WSU's dean had not relented to the pressure. She booked Douglas for the event and had not backed off, despite tremendous opposition.

Police patrolled the area, keeping the protestors at a legal distance. Secret Service and FBI agents were strategically posted, holding their earpieces and talking into hand microphones.

On the street, beyond the auditorium, a TV news team interviewed a tall man with a thick black beard. He was dressed in a big overcoat and wore a hat made of African kente cloth.

". . . So, we are here to protest this Uncle Tom in black robes!" said the tall man. He eyes were narrowed, his mouth in a snarl, and white smoke puffed out at his every word. "Farrel Douglas is nothing short of a race traitor, a modern-day Judas. We are appalled that anyone would bring Farrel Douglas here to Detroit, where we have a black majority."

"Why is there so much hatred for Douglas in the African American community?" asked the reporter, a pretty Asian woman. "Doesn't he have a right to his opinions as a judge?"

"Farrel Douglas is not a judge, he is a plague, a vile sickness on our race. He has helped our enemies destroy us, and for what? He wants to be accepted by the white race. But they will never accept him. They are just using him to destroy us."

Suddenly, there was a loud murmur within the crowd. Several people pointed to the street. A long white limo rolled toward the auditorium. It was led by a police cruiser. Another police car followed behind the limo. The crowd began to yell obscenities and moved toward the white limo. Police tried to hold them at bay.

Douglas had turned down offers to sneak into town. He'd said on a news program that he was going to walk right in the front door of Masonic Temple. When asked why, Douglas had stated: "I won't take the back door for white people, and I sure as hell won't do it for black people." This comment had only put more fuel on the fire.

The security men pushed the crowd back as the limo's door opened.

Farrel Douglas got out. He was a tall, regal-looking man, with a tangle of thick salt-and-pepper hair.

The crowd booed loudly and threw debris at the justice. Douglas looked at them with disinterest. He set his eyes on the doors to the building, and started toward them as if he were headed for the promised land.

The security men flanked Douglas, then enclosed him in a tight circle. They pushed and shoved their way through the crowd to their goal.

The air was filled with yelling, profanity, and chanting. Flashbulbs exploded, and the TV cameras' hot lights poured over the spectacle. Douglas and the security officers moved slowly, but steadily, toward the big wooden doors.

Halfway to their destination, a small black man broke through the security circle, and spit on Douglas's coat.

"Fuckin' Tom!" yelled the man.

A big FBI man pushed the smaller man back. The crowd screamed its disapproval and rushed toward the justice. The security circle started to break. The security men began to talk into their mikes all at once, then pushed Douglas faster to the doors.

The crowd was now a mob, and it pursued the justice. The agents fought the crowd, inching their way to the auditorium. Douglas showed no fear. He never took his eyes off the big auditorium doors as he moved.

Finally, Douglas and the agents arrived at the landing to Masonic Temple's entrance. A female FBI agent opened the doors. The crowd backed off a little, still yelling insults. Douglas started into the building, then stopped. Without warning, he turned on his heel and faced the angry mob. He stood there a moment, his face still expressionless. Then he smiled, and raised a fist.

"Power to the people," he said. Then he walked back inside.

The crowd exploded in screaming and cursing. Debris landed on the big doors as they closed with a loud clang.

High in the dark rafters of Masonic Temple, a soft alarm sounded. A sleeping man awoke suddenly and turned off the mild beeping of his watch. He turned on his back, his eyes wide open and alert. He checked the watch again. The blue light on the illuminated dial threw dim light onto his face, making him look ominous, ghostly. Below him, music played, and he heard the muted voices of a crowd.

The man reached to his side, and pulled a case toward his body. He opened the case, and switched on a small light inside. He checked the contents, then turned back onto his stomach and peered out of an opening facing the auditorium's stage. A large crowd was assembled and people in green robes filed in. He scanned the stage, and saw that it was decorated in green and gold. He closed one eye, and squinted. He had a clear view of the speaker's podium.

The man turned back onto his back in the cramped space and reached into the black box. He pulled out the stock of a high-powered rifle, and began to assemble it.

The graduation ceremony was about to get under way. The graduates and their families were seated. The crowd buzzed with anticipation. All over the auditorium, TV cameras lined the walls. Reporters practiced their lines and interviewed graduates and their families. In the background, the security men were on watch.

The crowd grew silent as the music swelled. People quickly hustled to their seats. The dean of the school and other dignitaries marched out to the stage in their robes adorned with ornate sashes. Douglas walked in the middle of the procession, a stoic look on his face. In the audience, there were audible ''boos'' mixed in with the applause. Douglas seemed unaffected by the jeers. He took his place of honor as the keynote speaker next to the dean of the school.

The ceremony began as planned. One dull speaker after another went to the podium and said his lines. The crowd and the media sat patiently, awaiting Douglas.

Douglas himself seemed to enjoy the festivities. He sat quietly, listening politely to each speaker. But he seemed to tense as the dean started to announce him.

''. . . and in today's legal world, there is no mind as keen, no heart as courageous as our keynote speaker. Graduates, faculty, parents, and family, I give you Justice Farrel Winston Douglas.''

The audience applauded loudly. Still, the jeers were there underneath the politeness of the moment.

Douglas calmed himself, his face settling into a jurist's unreadable gaze. He rose and smiled graciously, then reached down to shake the hand of the dean, who was much shorter.

The crowd rose to its feet; some graduates and parents did not stand. Douglas reached the podium, and shuffled some papers. He cleared his throat.

"If I had known this many TV cameras would be here, I would have worn my *good* robe," Douglas said. The crowd laughed politely and seemed to settle. "I promised myself that I would not talk about myself today," Douglas continued. "But I will say this. Thirty years ago at Harvard, a white man spat on me for having the nerve to become a lawyer at this nation's most prestigious school. Today, a black man spat on me for having the nerve to be a judge who votes his conscience."

The room was silent at this. Douglas took a drink of water from a cup that had been placed on the podium.

"Graduates, future lawyers," he continued. "It takes courage to be in our profession. And that is what I want to talk about today. We may debate issues and ideologies, but one thing will never change. Throughout history, lawyers, black and white, have answered, and will continue to answer, the clarion call for justice."

The audience broke into loud applause. Douglas seemed surprised at this. He allowed himself to smile a little. Photographers seized the chance to take pictures.

Suddenly, Douglas was struck by something. He grabbed at his chest as a spray of blood flew from the wound. Douglas was shocked, his eyes wide with surprise. He stumbled back a little, bringing both hands up to his chest. The crowd gasped. Douglas's mouth opened, but no sound came out.

Then, his forehead exploded.

Douglas fell backward. His arms flailed out from his body and up in an arc, like a bird spreading its wings. Blood flew from his head and neck, rising in an arc, spreading and falling with the body of the wounded man.

The dais on the stage dispersed in a frenzy. People in the audience screamed, and police rushed the stage. One FBI man pointed up into the lights.

Another shot hit a man sitting behind Douglas. The man fell off his chair onto the stage, grabbing at his lower back. There was no report, no sound from the shots. Still another shot came, hitting the stage floor and splintering the wood.

The audience bolted for the doors, knocking over TV cameras and reporters. On the stage, an FBI officer and a police detective stood over Douglas's body.

"Ambulance!" yelled the FBI man.

"The rafters!" yelled the detective. "The rafters!" Men and women from the security force ran toward the exits that led to the stairs.

On the stage, Douglas's body lay in a pool of blood and tissue. His eyes were wide open, one filled with blood.

The people around the body stayed away from it for a moment, then after they were sure the shooting was over they huddled around Douglas. A doctor checked for a pulse and yelled for everyone to move away. Douglas's body jerked and shook a moment, then it stopped.

In the upper part of the building, a mixed squad of local police and Secret Service burst into the area. Adrenaline pumped as the men and women looked around the area, their guns out in front. The area was dark and musty, like an old attic. It was also deserted. No officers were there.

''Who's covering this area?!'' asked Don Bathers, the Secret Service leader. Bathers was a chunky man about forty with a thin mustache and glasses. He was breathing heavily and staring at each of his men with intensity. He went to the area where the shot had come from, a crawl space at the left wall. He stooped down and looked inside. The gun in his hand trembled and he lowered it to his side.

''Collins and Deavers,'' someone quickly answered.

''No,'' said a female officer. ''Collins and Deavers had street duty. They brought Douglas inside. I saw them.''

''Who the fuck authorized that?!'' asked Bathers.

An FBI agent ran into the area. ''Sir, we got a man with a gun downstairs!''

''Let's go, now!'' yelled Bathers.

All of the officers quickly hustled back down the stairs into the main building.

On the ground floor, several officers chased a young black man of about twenty through the bright hallways. The man was dressed in jeans, a T-shirt, and a hat with African designs on it. In his right hand was a big black 9mm gun.

He ignored the officers' calls to stop. One cop fired a warning shot that slammed into a concrete wall. The young man kept running as if he had heard nothing. He slammed into the front doors and ran outside.

''He has a gun!'' said a local cop to Bathers as the latter got on the ground floor. ''He was told to surrender and he ran. He made it outside. It's a foot race now, sir.''

''Get everyone on him!'' said Bathers. ''I want him alive!''

On the street, the three law enforcement groups chased the running man. The suspect ran toward Cass Corridor, a bleak, rundown part of the city. He turned on Second Avenue and tried to pick up his pace. His hurried breath made puffs of smoke in the cold air. His hat flew from his head, and long dreadlocks tumbled out, bouncing as he ran.

The suspect stopped cold as he saw a Detroit police car turn a corner. The siren blared and the cherry lights flashed. He quickly ran to an old, vacant house. He tried to pry the old door open, but it was nailed shut.

"Stop!" yelled a local cop behind the man.

The suspect stopped. He was a dark and smallish man. Dreadlocks covered his face, making it difficult to see his features. He still held on to the gun.

The cop was even younger. He was white and had the fresh face of a kid.

"Drop the weapon and put your hands where I can see them," said the young cop.

"I got you, Vic," said his partner behind him, a black man about thirty.

The suspect wheeled around at the sound of the voices behind him. Absently, he raised the gun.

Vic fired, hitting the suspect in the chest. The man fell backward. He hit the door, then fell forward onto his knees. He knelt there a moment, looking tired. Blood spread across his shirt, soaking the bright pattern. He dropped the gun he'd held in his hand.

Vic went to the dead man and checked his pulse. "He's gone, Lenny," he said to his partner. "Shit, why did he do that?!"

"It's okay," said Lenny. "It was clean." Lenny helped his young charge put his gun away, then he took a closer look at the dead man. "Jesus, that's not a gun."

"What?" said Vic absently.

"This is not a gun. It just looks like one. It's a piece of black wood."

Vic began to panic, but his partner calmed him down. Bathers and his men got to the scene a moment later. Bathers was speechless for a second as he looked at the corpse on the cracked concrete of the decaying house.

"Who shot this man, dammit?!" Bathers yelled.

"I did," Vic said. "I had to."

"It was clean," said Lenny. "We heard an armed suspect was being pursued. He had what appeared to be a gun in his hands."

Bathers looked at the dark wood by the dead man's hand. "That's not a damned gun," said Bathers.

"I only had a second," said Vic.

"It was clean," said Lenny.

"Take these two into federal custody," Bathers instructed an FBI agent. The agent took the young cop's gun and escorted him and his partner away.

"This is bullshit," said Vic. "He had a gun."

"Wait," said Bathers to the officers. "Did he say anything to you. Anything at all?"

"No. He just turned with that thing in his hand," said Lenny.

Bathers looked at the sidewalk. A crowd of officers were on the street now. An ambulance rolled slowly toward the scene.

Bather's face registered shock for a second, then he grabbed his radio and began to yell into it. "This is Bathers, secure the auditorium! You hear me, get every available man and lock that damned place down!"

At Masonic Temple, the tight line of security had been broken during the chase. Crowds of people stood around buzzing with fear and excitement. The media groups made the circuit, greedily lapping up anything they could get on tape.

As the law enforcement team came back in numbers to secure the building, a man ambled casually onto the street out of a back entrance, made his way to a parked car, and drove away unnoticed.

2

Federal Case

Marshall Jackson was not happy to be in jail. He nervously paced the narrow confines of the little cell, cursing under his breath. He had far better things to do than be here.

Jail was unforgiving, he thought. It fed off the freedom of men, and did so without remorse or humanity. He believed this, even though he was not a hardened criminal, but an assistant United States attorney.

Marshall was in jail for contempt of court. Judge Clark Langworthy's decision to sanction him was hasty, and occasioned by very unjudgelike anger over the cross-examination of a witness. Judge Langworthy had asked several questions of the witness, interrupting Marshall's momentum. Marshall took verbal exception to this, and the judge shipped him off to the holding cell.

Marshall loosened his tie and sat his tall frame down on the old bench that was the holding cell's only furniture. He was the cell's only occupant. In fact, he was all alone in the wing. The regular criminals awaiting court dates were in another area. This area was reserved for special guests of the government and victims of evil judges.

He heard footsteps coming his way. The holding cells were just off a long hallway. The hallway was dark at his end but illuminated by a light at the other. Soon, Marshall saw the elongated shadows of people coming his way.

"About goddamn time," Marshall said in a low voice. He'd been locked up for over a half hour. More than enough time to learn his supposed lesson. The judge had obviously surmised that and sent a court officer to let him go.

Marshall stood up and put on his suit jacket. He walked to the cell door, and was surprised to see Judge Langworthy himself approaching the cell. A large bailiff followed Langworthy, dwarfing the judge.

Langworthy was a short, squat man of sixty-eight. He was appointed by Jimmy Carter and in the ensuing years had become the chief judge of the district. He was a noted liberal, which made him a fierce opponent of the government. He stopped at Marshall's cell door.

"You picked a bad day to mess with me, Mr. Jackson," said Langworthy.

"With all due respect, Judge," said Marshall, "if you're looking for an apology, you've come to the wrong man."

"This I know." Langworthy gestured to the bailiff, who opened the cell door. "I guess I should have said *we* picked a bad day. There is a situation that makes both of our egos unimportant today."

Marshall stepped out of the cell. "What situation?"

"I've been told not to say right now, but the building has been closed, and we are told to conclude our case. You and brother counsel will do your closings, and I will send the jury out."

Langworthy turned and left abruptly. Marshall looked at the bailiff, who just shrugged. Marshall walked toward the exits, not knowing what awaited him in the courtroom upstairs.

Marshall waited patiently for his opponent to finish his summation in court. Langworthy sat and watched dispassionately.

The gallery had been cleared. Before Marshall had been jailed, it was about half filled, mostly with ATF officers and the families of the victim.

The defendant, Lewis Quince, had allegedly shot and wounded an ATF officer while transporting illegal guns. Quince had a reputation as an important gun dealer who serviced an illegal drug clientele. He had a long and violent history on the street and was apparently the man to see if you wanted any weapon, from the Saturday Night Special to an illegal assault rifle.

Marshall wondered how many young black kids were dead because of Quince's enterprising nature. So many times a gun would be recovered at a murder scene and there was no way to trace it. If they could follow the trail, they'd probably find Quince. The ATF had been after him for a while but so far had never gotten this close.

Quince had made incriminating statements to officers. Statements that he alleged were elicited by a beating. After all the motions to suppress, evidentiary hearings, and yelling, Langworthy had played Solomon and thrown out roughly half of Quince's statement.

The defense attorney, Ivan Stahl, was a veteran defense lawyer. He was fifty or so and looked like a saintly priest. Marshall had tangled with him before, and he was always formidable. Stahl's strategy had been to trash the government, making the actions of the ATF agents and federal prosecutors seem suspect.

Stahl finished his closing. Marshall rose and faced the jury. Marshall, a tall and good-looking man, was always an imposing figure in court. He walked across the courtroom gracefully, making sure that he passed by his opponent, whom he looked at with mild disgust so the jury could see.

"I'm sure you've all heard the expression: 'Don't make a federal case out of this.' It means don't make a big deal out of something. Federal cases have always been those that are more important to the nation than ordinary state matters. But what separates a regular, garden-variety crime from a federal one? Well, we do, ladies and gentlemen. Only those crimes that affect the peace and security of the entire nation become federal cases like the one you are sitting on. And we give the government its power in making that determination."

Marshall moved closer to the jury. Most people thought the government was mysterious and distant. It always helped to put a face on it.

He quickly went back through the facts of the case. He told how Quince had been surprised by the officers, and how he had wounded one in the chest. He laid out all of the evidence and danced around the fact that the gun had never been found. But he knew these things didn't win cases. Juries were always swayed by strong, familiar emotion, no matter where it came from.

"My opponent has taken great pains to bash the government in this case," said Marshall. "He says that we forced a confession, manufactured evidence, and tried to railroad his client into prison. Isn't it funny how people always try to get us to distrust our government? They want to exploit our belief that something is wrong with the government, that it doesn't work anymore. Well, that is a lie, people. The government isn't perfect, but it does work."

Marshall moved even closer to the jury. He was making eye contact with them. His stare was intense, unwavering. He'd practiced it for a long time.

"Not long ago, a black man couldn't even become a lawyer legally. More recently, I would have had to enter this building through the back entrance, if at all. But now I stand here before you, an attorney, with the power of the United States federal government at my side." Marshall lowered his voice, as if telling some great secret. "We made this possible. We did it because this is our government and it does work." In his normal tone, he said: "This defendant shot one of our federal guardians, a man with a wife and family whose duty was to protect you and me from the violence assisted by men like Lewis Quince. And now, it's our job to get him. So, let's do it. Then we can all go home."

Marshall walked back to his table confidently. He noticed Stahl had a pissed-off look on his face. Marshall knew why he was angry. He hadn't played the race card, but he had shown it. He'd used his race to get the jury emotionally invested. Now, they all felt better about themselves and the government because a black man had the right to be a federal prosecutor. If the government could overcome prejudice, then maybe it *did* work.

Stahl was upset and Langworthy didn't seem to like it either, but Marshall didn't care. Race was a powerful theme in American life. It was one of the few things about which everyone had strong emotion. Race had worked against him many times, so he would be damned if he wouldn't use it to work for him.

Langworthy charged the jury. Marshall sat uncomfortably. He had argued bitterly with Langworthy about the jury instructions. Langworthy had taken every opportunity to give instructions that would make it easier to presume government misconduct and result in an acquittal. Langworthy abhorred police brutality and government coercion and Marshall was paying for it.

When Langworthy finished, the jury was led out of the courtroom. Quince was taken away. Now the waiting would begin. Marshall walked over to Stahl and politely shook his hand.

"Nice closing, Marshall," said Stahl. "I wasn't aware that government misconduct had been vitiated by civil rights."

"It was in all the papers," said Marshall with a smile.

"Langworthy should have kept you locked up."

"Sorry, but you know we don't like it when one of our ATF officers catches a bullet. The gloves come off."

"How about a deal?" asked Stahl. "My guy says he can give you some of his clients. One of which I'm sure you'll be interested in—your brother, Moses.''

Marshall recoiled at the mention of his brother's name. He hadn't thought about him in months. He remembered the line from the movie *The Ten Commandments* when pharaoh forbade anyone to speak the name.

''I don't know how you feel about that,'' said Stahl. ''But if it was my damned brother, I'd jump at it.''

''Okay,'' said Marshall. ''Quince does fifteen to twenty-five on the charge, and he gives me a list of all his clients, and he testifies against them.''

''Shit,'' said Stahl. ''How about we just shove a shank into his heart right now. You know he can't do that.''

''That's what I thought. Then we can each sweat out this verdict.'' Marshall closed his briefcase. ''So, do you know why Langworthy decided to spring me? He said something about a 'situation.' ''

''He wouldn't say,'' said Stahl, ''but I do know there's been some kind of shooting. The building was cleared and several cases adjourned. Unfortunately for us, we were close to finishing.''

''Excuse me, everyone,'' said Langworthy. ''I'm letting the jury go with instructions to finish their deliberations tomorrow.''

Marshall was about to object. He felt that a quick deliberation would mean a guilty verdict.

''This morning, Supreme Court Justice Farrel Douglas was assassinated,'' said Langworthy. ''He was shot at the commencement program for Wayne Law. The city is on alert, and a manhunt for the killer is under way. I will inform counsel when the jury reaches a verdict.'' Langworthy got up and walked to his chambers.

Marshall was stunned. He just stood there for a moment, looking at the federal court seal. Then he saw Stahl hurrying from the courtroom and shook himself back into reality. Marshall gathered his things and walked into the antiseptic hallway of the federal courthouse. Normally, the building was busy, filled with lawyers and court staff, but now the halls were empty. Marshall's footsteps echoed as he walked toward the elevators.

He moved to the end of the hallway. He got to the elevator and found it filled. A large group of people waited for the next car. Marshall walked to the end of the hallway and took the stairs. He was headed back to the U.S. attorney's office, and he knew the place would be on fire.

3

······························

Dark Holiday

Marshall walked into the U.S. attorney's office building on Fort Street in Detroit. The huge building had once been a bank, but was now home to the feds. With its imposing stone body, tall glass windows, and spacious lobby, it still looked like a business office.

Marshall rushed in, flashed his ID at the security men, but found that they stopped him anyway.

"Sorry, Marsh," said one of the security guards. "We have to search everyone today. We're on alert."

"It's okay," said Marshall as the guard passed a detector wand over his body.

Marshall quickly passed by the guard station and got on a crowded elevator. He pushed the button that read "23." The car started up.

Marshall felt himself breathing hard. His heart was beating rapidly under his chest. He realized in that moment that he'd run all the way over.

"I heard his head was blown off," a man behind Marshall whispered.

"He won't get any tears from me," said a woman. "He got what he deserved."

"A man was murdered," said another woman, in a blue suit. She was standing in the front of the elevator. "I don't appreciate your statement."

The elevator doors opened and the woman in blue walked out with several other people. Marshall turned and looked behind him. The couple that had spoken were both black, but he knew that already. Black people hated Farrel Douglas. Douglas was not his favorite legal personality either. He didn't like any of his decisions and felt that Douglas tried too hard to be the ultraconservative that everyone said he was. But he did not hate the man. He just didn't understand him.

The elevator made another stop, then reached the twenty-third floor. Marshall stepped off and moved to the hall guard, who searched him again. Marshall moved on. The seal of the U.S. attorney's office greeted him on a wall.

Marshall rushed in to find the office quiet. He expected the place to be in a frenzy. The area was mostly deserted. Only a few assistants manned their posts. Marshall walked over to Jessica Cole, a pretty young secretary who was fond of long, painted fingernails.

"Where is everybody, Jess?" asked Marshall.

"In the lounge, there's some kind of conference on TV about the murder," said Jessica. She smiled at him, and her gaze lingered. Marshall remembered that Jessica had a crush on him. He'd heard about it second-hand but was aware that she found him attractive.

"Thanks, Jess."

"You're welcome, Marshall," said the young girl.

Marshall walked off and was aware that she was watching him as he left. He tried not to think about the young girl. He was a married man and he already had enough problems at home. He walked to his office, tossing his things inside.

It was unusual for the place to be so quiet. The federal government was a constant in the world, a place where there was always some kind of work to do. Then Marshall remembered that national incidents like Douglas's assassination were dark holidays, times when the government, and probably everything else, stopped normal business.

Marshall made his way to the lounge, where a crowd was crammed into the small room. It looked like everyone from his division was there.

He worked in the Capital Crime Division, a department where the best and brightest ended up. They prosecuted only major federal crimes. Every incident of murder, hate crime, and drug offenses in the region ended up at their doorstep. It occurred to Marshall for the first time that the assassination of Douglas was one of those cases, and might be assigned to his office.

"Can you believe this shit, Marsh?" asked a portly man about thirty. He was Walter Anderson, a lawyer who'd come into the office about the same time as Marshall. Walter was a chubby, round-faced black man with a quick laugh and keen instincts. He was a good lawyer and Marshall's best friend in the office. They socialized in and out of the office, and had done several cases together.

Walter was a good man and a fine lawyer, but he'd had some serious problems with drinking and gambling that had almost gotten him kicked out of the office. But Walter had made it through the hard times, the divorce, and therapy. He was better now but still had to take it one day at a time.

"No, I can't believe it," said Marshall. "What do we know so far?"

"Douglas was blasted by a pro," said Walter. "High-powered rifle, the whole bit. Messed him up pretty good, I hear. A retired lawyer named Wendel Miller caught one, too."

"I heard they chased a suspect, a black one," said someone.

"Yeah, but he got himself killed," said Walter. "Committed suicide is more like it. This fool turns on a cop while holding a piece of wood. Well, of course the cop shot him dead."

"Who was the dead guy?" asked Marshall.

"Don't know yet," said Walter.

"The boss have anything to say?"

"You know old Nate, nothing. He's waiting to see where the dust settles, then he'll spring right into action. So, who do you think is gonna catch it?"

"This?" asked Marshall. "I'd guess that they bring in an outside hitter, someone from D.C. This is big, like Oklahoma City. I guess he'll assign Deacons, then." John Deacons was Marshall's boss and the head of CCD.

"Shhh," said a heavyset woman with blond hair. "I can't hear. Toby is about to comment."

"Sorry, Roberta," said Marshall. Roberta Shebbel was one of the best lawyers in the Capital Crimes Division. She'd received more offers from law firms to leave the government than anyone else in the place, even Marshall.

They all watched as Helen Newhall, the United States attorney general, came onscreen. Newhall, called Toby in private, was a modest-looking woman with a head full of short, dark hair. Toby walked up to a podium crowded with microphones.

"I have spoken with the president, who will make his address to the nation in a half hour," she said. "But he has told me to express his deep sorrow at the loss of a great American jurist.

"The Justice Department will be coordinating with law enforcement to apprehend the suspect. At this time, we are still investigating the crime scene, and hope to have leads soon. I will be flying to Detroit after this conference to head the effort myself."

Toby descended the stage as questions were yelled out. She waved them off, and made her exit.

The lounge exploded into conversation. The attorneys and staffers understood that the investigation would center in Detroit, and that meant they all were in a position to see some action on the case.

"Well, I'm done for the day," said Walter. "And it looks like a lot of judges will be adjourning cases in the coming week in order to go to Douglas's funeral."

"You sound happy about it," said Marshall.

"I like it when judges let me go home early, Marshall. Besides, I hated that damned Douglas. It's sad, but that's what you get when you do what he did."

"And what did he do?" asked Marshall.

"He betrayed his people," said Walter. "He's like those black men who used to round up freed slaves and sell them back into slavery."

"That's a little harsh, don't you think?" asked Marshall. "Douglas was a judge, not some turncoat in a war."

"Really? Tell that to my cousin. He didn't get into medical school because of one of Douglas's rulings. After all the struggle we've done in this country, the best we could get on the court was him? I don't think so."

"The man had a family, Walter, kids."

"I know and I feel more sorry for them, but I can't lie. I despised the man."

Marshall said good-bye to Walter then walked to his office. It was a small but sufficient place. On his wall hung pictures of Dr. King, Mandela, and Jesse Jackson. Next to them were pictures he'd taken with federal judges Thurgood Marshall, Damon Keith, Leon Higginbotham, and Stephen Bradbury, all of whom he greatly admired.

Marshall's door was open, and the chatter from the office was loud. He was restless. Even though he played cool with Walter, he was already thinking that he wanted in on the Douglas prosecution. Maybe Deacons would assign him to the team.

Marshall had only a few years in the office, but he'd prosecuted many capital cases and had an impressive winning record. Farrel Douglas was not his idol, but no one could just kill a federal judge and get away with it. It struck him as a little corny, but it offended his sense of justice. Also, he knew that if he were ever going to become a federal judge, which was his goal, he was going to have to prosecute cases like this, something more noteworthy than a wounded ATF officer and a scumbag like Lewis Quince.

Marshall sat down but couldn't keep still. He jumped out of his chair and was headed for the door when he noticed that the chatter had stopped. He looked up to see Nathan Williams, the head of the U.S. attorney's office, walking into his doorway.

Nathan was a fiercely intelligent lawyer and a good friend. He'd been in office for five years or so. The U.S. attorney changed when the president changed, so there was always a new man coming. But Nate had held on for a while and was rumored to be going to Washington. He'd made headlines after he helped solve the murder of Harris Yancy, the Detroit mayor, with the help of a state prosecutor named Jesse King.

Nate walked into the office. He was normally a spit-and-polish kind of guy. But today he was disheveled, his tie was undone and coat rumpled. Then Marshall remembered that Douglas had been a mentor to Nathan when the latter was just a young lawyer. They were friends, and he was probably feeling all of the pain you felt when someone was taken before his time.

"Sorry about your loss, sir," said Marshall.

"Yes. He was . . . a great man," said Williams. "We were actually scheduled to have dinner tonight. I'm expecting my first grandchild soon. We were going to celebrate."

"I guess the court will be in mourning for a while."

"Yes, but I've already heard rumors of replacements for him."

"Jesus," said Marshall. "What's wrong with people?"

"It's just business, Marshall. There are several important cases coming to the Supreme Court. They need a full bench. If the president doesn't start now, his enemies will undermine him." Williams looked sad for a moment. "Toby is coming late tonight, Marshall. I think you should meet her."

"Yes, sir. If you don't mind my asking—"

"She's bringing a lawyer from her staff," Williams cut him off. "But his job will really be to observe and keep Toby in the loop. The man who was shot could not have done this alone. When we find his accomplices, they will be prosecuted out of this office—and you're going to do it."

Marshall was shocked into silence. He took a breath, then said: "Thank you, sir. But what about John Deacons?"

"This is big, but it's not for him. You're the man for this job."

Deacons was white, and Marshall wondered if that was what Nate meant. He wanted to ask him but didn't want to risk offending Nate. It was not often that a black man rose to Nate's position in the legal profession. He had probably suffered all manner of insult to his intelligence and competence in his time. Marshall didn't want to add to it by questioning his decision. It would sound ungrateful.

"I'm very flattered and pleased to take the assignment, sir," said Marshall.

"You get to pick the rest of your team. Just two others. Any other people will be behind-the-scenes support. Get ready for an all-nighter. Toby will be in at midnight."

Williams walked away. Marshall followed him out of the door and into the bull pen. Williams was not the kind of man to sit on a decision. He was already prosecuting the case, and the killer hadn't even been caught yet.

Suddenly, Marshall noticed his colleagues staring at him. They had apparently been watching his office all along. He knew that they knew. Walter Anderson quickly moved over to him. His face was flushed with excitement.

"You got it, didn't you, you sonofabitch?"

"Yes." Marshall headed for the door.

"I'm putting in my bid right now," said Walter. "I want on the team."

"I need some air, man," said Marshall. "Excuse me."

Marshall walked out of the office, and headed for the elevator.

"Don't forget about your friends when you choose the team," Walter called after him.

The office din seemed louder as he walked to the elevators. His head was spinning. He had just been tapped to prosecute the biggest case of his career, and despite the terrible tragedy involved, he felt like dancing.

Marshall walked slowly to the elevators and got on. He turned, and saw his colleagues still watching him in awe. The elevator doors closed, and the last thing he saw was the seal of the United States, finely etched in glass.

4

....

Side Hustle

LaShawn Reid counted out his money carefully. The bills were new, and they tended to stick together. He smiled and smelled the newly minted bills. Nothing smelled as sweet as new money, he thought. He quickly finished. It was all there, five thousand dollars. Pretty good for some little damned pieces of metal, he thought. He didn't own a computer, but he knew the chips were worth a lot of cash.

LaShawn, his partner, O.T., and the buyer were standing in an abandoned auto body garage on the east side of the city. The floor was littered with old scrap metal and broken tools. The sun was out, but it was a January morning, and the garage didn't provide much shelter, so it was cold inside.

LaShawn was a dark, thin man with a shaved head and goatee. His partner, O.T., was squat, with a shaggy beard and a buzz cut. O.T. wore a big gold stud in the side of his flat nose.

The buyer was a young, white man named Tommy. He had sandy blond hair, freckles, and stark, green eyes. Tommy looked over the microchips with a big magnifying glass. He closed the plastic case and looked at LaShawn.

"Nice, very nice," he said. His breath turned into pale smoke from the cold.

"Nothing but the best," said LaShawn. "Check it out. My shit even made the news.'' LaShawn held out a newspaper. On a back page was a story about the theft of a case of computer chips from a local warehouse. ''Shoot, I'm damned-near famous—''

''I didn't know that,'' said Tommy nervously. ''Doesn't that kind of thing bring a lot of trouble? I don't need trouble. I already got people on my ass.''

''Take the knot out of your dick,'' said LaShawn. O.T. laughed softly. ''It's just a little newspaper story. You are the scariest damned man I know.''

''It's just that this is delicate, that's all. Each of these processors is catalogued with a serial number. It takes a lot for me to erase the trail. I have to create new numbers, then intermingle them with legitimate ones. If someone got nosy—''

''Nobody knows shit, all right?'' said LaShawn.

LaShawn heard a noise from outside. O.T. heard it too, and pulled a Cobra .38 and went to the old metal garage door.

''Hey, what's with the gun?'' asked Tommy worriedly. He clutched the chips to his body unconsciously.

''Gotta be careful, that's all,'' said LaShawn.

Tommy was using the chips to build computers on the cheap, and then sell them to public schools via a government contract. A nice hustle, thought LaShawn, but it was a white man's hustle. He wasn't interested in elaborate scams. All he wanted was the money. His deal was one hundred percent profit.

''Shit's okay,'' said O.T. ''Nobody out there.''

''I might need some more of these next week,'' said Tommy.

''Can't do it,'' said LaShawn. ''I barely got away with these ones. My people don't like side deals. I gotta wait until the time is right.''

''I can pay fifty percent more in a week,'' said Tommy.

''Ain't worth it. I'm fucked if I get caught by my crew. You can't put no price on that.''

''Look, my contract has got to be closed. After that, we can get a better schedule. It's all crazy now, and they want the shit yesterday.''

''Sorry, can't help you,'' said LaShawn. ''We out, man. Beep me in a couple of weeks or so.''

LaShawn and O.T. started toward the door. LaShawn passed some money to O.T., who stuffed it into his pocket without counting it.

''Okay, double,'' said Tommy from behind them. ''I'll have to fudge my numbers a little, but at least I'll make the deadline.''

LaShawn and O.T. stopped walking. "Well, that changes everything," said LaShawn. "Maybe we might have to take more of a chance at them prices."

"Good," said Tommy. "I'll need Pentium II chips like these or better, and if you can get some of those Zip drives or writable CD drives, I'll pay ten percent more."

LaShawn tried to quickly calculate what that meant. He wasn't good at math, but he understood *more*. "All right," said LaShawn. "A week." He slapped five with Tommy.

When LaShawn turned to leave, a man with a sawed-off shotgun burst through a door in the back of the garage.

O.T. went for his gun, and the man fired, hitting O.T. in the meaty part of his thigh. O.T. fell to the ground, screaming and dropping his weapon.

LaShawn dropped the newspaper he was holding, and turned to run, only to find a woman holding an S & W shorty .40 coming through the metal garage door.

"Don't think so, my nigga," said the man with the shotgun. He turned the weapon on LaShawn. "Don't move, or I'll have to cut you down like your boy there."

"LaShawn, LaShawn," said the woman. "Whazzup, boy?" She had an evil smile on her lips.

"Dake, Nita," said LaShawn. "This was for the crew, I swear . . ."

Dake lowered his shotgun and kicked O.T.'s gun away from him. Then he went to LaShawn and Tommy and searched them for guns. He removed LaShawn's gun, a 9mm.

"White boy's clean," said Dake. O.T. groaned. Dake kicked him in the face. "Shut the fuck up," he said.

Dake was a stocky man, about twenty or so. He had medium-length braids that came to his ears and a baby face that seemed out of place on his frame. Nita was an angular woman with long black dreadlocks. She had a pretty face, marred only by a nasty scar on her chin.

The metal garage door creaked again. LaShawn turned to see another black man walk in. The sun reflected off the snow outside, framing the man, making him look like a long, dark shadow. He was dressed in a black leather trench coat and a black leather hat. He stepped into the garage, surveyed the scene, then motioned Nita and Dake to lower their weapons.

"Will somebody tell me what's going on here?" said Tommy. He took a step but was knocked down by Nita.

"Stay your ass down there," she said.

"No need for that, Nita," said the tall man. "Let him get up." His voice was a smooth baritone.

Tommy stood as the man in the leather coat walked toward them.

"Moses, man," said LaShawn, "this was legit for real. I was bringing Tommy here into the crew."

Moses Jackson glared at the smaller man and said nothing. He took a few steps, and picked up a rusted monkey wrench from the dirty floor in his gloved hand. The old tool was broken, and covered with some kind of green fungus. The open doors had let in the cold air from outside. It ran along the ground like a snake, moving around the people inside.

"Time," said Moses. "I'm losing time just being here having to deal with this shit." Suddenly, he moved to O.T., raised the wrench, then brought it down into his head, killing him.

Tommy screamed.

Dake clamped a hand over Tommy's mouth. "Too late for screaming, my nigga," he said. "You in the shit now."

Moses walked away from the dead man, back to LaShawn and Tommy, who both looked at him with terror. Moses pulled off his hat, revealing a head of short, wavy black hair.

"I don't wanna hear no more shit about how this deal is for me, LaShawn. You tried to fuck me. All hustles go through the crew, you know that."

"Moses," said LaShawn, "I was gonna—"

Nita smacked LaShawn hard in the side of the head with the shorty .40. LaShawn reeled to the side, almost falling over. "Don't talk while the man is talking, muthafucka," she said.

"What's your name?" Moses asked Tommy.

"I didn't know anything about your business," said Tommy. "I just needed these chips, man. Please, let me go. You can have all the chips back, I don't care." He was shaking now. The case with the chips vibrated in his hands.

Moses walked over to Tommy and put a hand on his shoulder. "If I wanted to hurt you, you'd be hurt by now," said Moses. "Now, who are you?"

"Tom Delaney. People call me Tommy."

"How much did you give my man here for those chips, Tommy?"

"Well, we kinda dealt on a per case basis—"

Moses dug his fingers into Tommy's shoulders. Tommy yelled out in pain. "Five thousand," he said. "Five thousand."

Moses took his hand from Tommy's shoulder. "This is why you don't run the crew, LaShawn. Those chips are worth twice that on the street."

LaShawn looked at Tommy with anger. He was about to say something when Nita grabbed his face.

"Dumbass," she said. "This white boy fucked you on the hustle." Nita pushed him away, then faked a punch. LaShawn almost tripped trying to duck it. She laughed at him.

"As you can see, Tommy," said Moses, "this man works for me. Normally, I get pissed off when white people cheat the brothers. But I'm gonna ignore all that history. LaShawn here brought all this down on himself. You can have those chips you cheated away from this fool. You earned that. But from now on, the price is ten."

"Okay, great," said Tommy. "I gotta be going—" Tommy quickly moved for the door. He was pulled back by Dake.

"I don't think the man is finished," he said.

"You will deal with my man Dake here from now on," said Moses. "If you go to a competitor, we'll come looking for you. If you go to the cops, we'll come for your family. You can leave now."

Tommy moved to the door on shaky legs and left. Moses turned to LaShawn, who was trying desperately to look brave. "So near as I can figure," said Moses, "you been side hustlin' for over two months now. How much have you made?"

"Moses, please—"

"How much, dammit!" Moses yelled.

"About fifteen thousand," said LaShawn. "Moses, I'll pay it all back, I swear—"

"You would have made five thousand off this hustle if you had brought them to me like you were supposed to. Ten thousand lousy muthafuckin' dollars. That's the price you've put on your life."

LaShawn took out the money. "Here, take all of it. O.T. had some, too. I'll get the rest. Then we're cool, right?"

Moses walked over to O.T.'s dead body and took the money from his pockets. Then he picked up the bloody wrench.

"Come on, Moses, don't do this." LaShawn backed away.

"Put your boy in that metal Dumpster over there," said Moses.

LaShawn walked over to the body. He tried not to look at his friend's decimated face. Wispy smoke rose from the body's warm blood. LaShawn picked up the body and placed it in the Dumpster. When he finished, his clothes and hands were bloody. He looked at Moses, whose face showed no emotion.

"Those pieces too," said Moses.

LaShawn trembled as he lifted the small bloody pieces of his partner's head from the cold ground.

"Damn, I guess that nigga's head wasn't as hard as I thought." Nita chuckled softly behind him.

LaShawn put the fragments in the Dumpster. He had to shake some that clung to his hands. When he turned around, he saw Moses, swinging the broken monkey wrench at him. LaShawn threw his hands up over his face.

The wrench's jagged head hit LaShawn in the right knee. LaShawn yelled out, his breath turning into a stream of smoke. He fell to the ground, hitting it hard.

"No!" LaShawn cried, holding his broken knee. The wrench had cut his leg above the knee, and warm blood seeped between his fingers.

Next to Moses, LaShawn saw Dake walk up, holding two large plastic containers. He had not even seen Dake leave to get them. He knew what was in those containers. He panicked, begging for his life.

"No honor among thieves," said Moses. "But there is principle. Nita, hold him."

Nita held LaShawn as Moses broke his other knee with the wrench. LaShawn's eyes rolled into his head from the pain. Nita slapped LaShawn's cheek hard, trying to bringing him back.

"Let him pass out," said Moses. "No need to be nasty about this. Lift him in there."

Dake and Nita picked up LaShawn and put him into the metal Dumpster. Moses took the plastic container and poured gasoline inside. Moses took a small metal cigarette lighter and flicked it to life. The blue flame wavered in the cold air.

Moses peered into the Dumpster. He saw LaShawn, lying next to his dead partner. "The only thing more important than time is principle," said Moses.

He dropped the lighter into the Dumpster. Yellow flame shot up from inside. The crackle of the fire was loud in the big garage. Dake began to throw debris in the fire to help it burn.

"Shit's gonna smell," said Dake.

"It's okay," said Moses. "Make sure to burn all the bloody spots on the floor. "Don't make it easy for the cops.""

"Damn, I needed some heat," said Nita. She held out her hands to the flame.

"Heartless-ass woman," said Dake. He laughed.

Moses watched as Dake set fire to the blood on the cold ground. He poured gas in the area, then set it on fire with a butane lighter. They looked like little bonfires, flickering in the chilling draft on the dirty floor.

LaShawn's disloyalty had stopped the planning on his next job. In his occupation, he needed to deal with traitors quickly and ruthlessly. Leading a crew of thieves required timing and precision, and there was no place for men bent on independent stealing.

"Damn, Moses, check this out," said Dake.

Moses looked in his direction. Dake was holding out the front page of the newspaper.

"I was going to burn this, but look who it is," said Dake.

Moses took the newspaper. On the front page was the smiling face of his fraternal twin brother, Marshall. Next to the picture was the headline:

FEDERAL PROSECUTOR NAMED IN DOUGLAS ASSASSINATION

"Nigga ain't bad looking," said Nita. She laughed. Moses cut it off with a hard glance.

"You gonna tell him what you know?" asked Dake.

"I don't deal with that muthafucka," said Moses.

Moses took the newspaper from Dake and looked at it with disgust. He'd been running his crew for a long time, and it was rare that he was reminded of his former life. His brother, the golden boy, was once again in the limelight.

"Dake, pour the other can of gas in there after a few minutes," said Moses. He crumpled up his brother's face and threw it into the fire. "I don't want nothing left but ashes."

5

....

The Screaming People

Toby Newhall had blown into town late the night before and had not stopped talking since her plane set down at City Airport. She rarely, if ever, came to the city, and it seemed as if she wanted to get out as soon as possible.

Marshall had stayed up all night waiting for her. Nate had sent him home, only to call him back in at 6 A.M. Since then, it had been the Toby Show. She talked endlessly about the case, stopping only twice to take calls from two senators in D.C.

Marshall sat and listened to Toby with Nathan Williams and Toby's assistant, a straight-arrow lawyer named Robert Ryder. Marshall didn't like Ryder's looks. He was too clean, too handsome, too blond, too— good. Lawyers were all at least a little dirty. It was an occupational necessity. Ryder seemed more priest than lawyer, more Boy Scout than snake. Perhaps Marshall's cynicism was peaking, but Ryder's lack of negativity was downright unsettling.

Toby, on the other hand, was a real lawyer. Tough, ambitious, and earthy. She was the kind of person who even as a little girl probably showed that she was destined to run things—organizing the doll parties and sleepovers, manipulating the prettiest girls and their parents to do what she wanted. She was a natural-born leader.

Toby was a former army colonel and CIA staffer. She was also a former D.A. out of Colorado and had a reputation for being hard on her subordinates. She was neither a Republican nor a Democrat and was widely rumored to be a serious political candidate in both parties.

Nathan looked tired. He'd gone for a day without sleep, and one of his best friends had been killed right under his nose. Marshall felt sorry for him. Nathan was a private man, not usually given to public emotion. Marshall had seen him preside over all manner of human nastiness without ever losing his cool, reserved fed-face. But this murder had crippled him. He looked like he needed a hug.

"The president wants this shit put to bed as soon as possible," said Toby. "The people want to know the government avenges its own. I've authorized everything you'll need to catch this fucker, whoever he is. Bob here will keep me posted on everything you do, but other than that, it's your show, Nate. So, what do we have?"

"Don Bathers from the Secret Service was head of security," said Nate.

"I know him," said Toby. "A good man."

"He said after the shots that killed Douglas were fired," Nate continued, "a man was seen running from near a door to the rafters. He appeared to have a weapon. Said man was pursued and killed. We didn't find the murder weapon on him or at the scene."

"I know all that," said Toby. "Who is he?"

"We don't know," said Nate. "His prints don't match anything we have. He had a wallet, but the ID was phony."

"Wonderful," said Toby. "I'll tell that to Douglas's family. Your husband was murdered by a man with no gun, and he has no damned identity." She took a second, then: "I apologize for that. I'm feeling the stress."

"All's forgiven." Nate smiled a little. "But I know your frustration. We can't tie the man to anyone who helped him, now that he's dead. And having no identity only makes it worse."

"He was obviously a planned distraction," said Toby. "The question is, who was he a distraction for?"

"The CIA is working on his identity," said Ryder. His voice had a tinge of Kentucky in it, and he seemed eager to join in. "The cop who shot the suspect is going to be cleared."

"The killer was in a crawl space close to a door," said Nate. "The man with the gun broke security and allowed a window for any accomplices to escape."

"My Lord," said Toby. "Does the media know about that?"

"No," said Nate, "and I don't think they will."

"What else do we have, Nate?" asked Toby.

"We found the place where the shots came from," said Nate. "The killer was holed up in a little area that's used by servicemen. That whole area is being swept by our people. If there's anything there, we'll find it."

"How did he get in?" asked Ryder.

"We don't really know," said Nate. "The building was swept before the ceremony. I've seen all the reports. Nothing was missed on our end."

"He got in during the ceremony," said Marshall.

Toby turned to Marshall, as if she had just noticed he was there. Her left eyebrow was arched, as though she didn't believe he was capable of speech. "Someone report that?" she asked.

"Just a feeling," said Marshall.

"Oh, really?" Toby turned her full attention to Marshall. She had steel blue eyes, and an expression that made her look like she knew everything that you didn't. Marshall could see Williams shift in his seat a little. Ryder leaned back in his chair, waiting for what was coming.

There was tension in the room now, but Marshall remained cool. Toby and her kind loved to intimidate, but he already knew that if he was going to work his way up, he'd have to stand his ground.

"A feeling?" said Toby. "Did you know that no major American assassination case has ever been closed satisfactorily? Mr. Jackson, we're gonna need hard evidence to end this matter. Many people, especially your people, hated Farrel Douglas. There may have been a great many reasons to want him dead. Feelings won't get me a conviction."

"I know, ma'am," said Marshall. "And I'm sorry if I spoke out of turn, but we've looked at all the security reports. The killer had to have walked into that building, and somehow slipped up to the rafters."

"And the gun?" asked Toby.

"My working theory is that it was already there, or he brought it in concealed as equipment, perhaps. I think this thing was planned out months ago, when Douglas announced he was coming here."

"You would make a good FBI man, Jackson, but these conjectures don't make for good lawyering," said Toby.

This was a direct assault to Marshall's competence. If she was to respect him, then he could not back down. Toby had a reputation for admiring strength, and not taking any shit from her people. The ranks of her assistants had turned over twice since she'd taken office. He had to go at her before she sensed weakness.

"Sorry if you feel that way, ma'am," said Marshall, "but that's the way I work."

Toby seemed to wince a little at these words. Williams was openly nervous now. Toby stared into Marshall, as if she were reading something in his eyes.

"If you're gonna win this case for me, Mr. Jackson, you can't ever let anyone deter you from your instincts—not even me." Then to Williams she said: "Good choice, Nate." Toby motioned to Ryder, who pulled out a large, brown case. "This is the information on all the major political assassinations in the country since Lincoln caught one on his night out. Study them, Jackson. Powerful men don't die quietly. They always leave people screaming."

Marshall took the case and opened it. Inside were about twenty CD-ROMs. They were stored chronologically. From what he'd heard and read, assassination investigations were always massive, labyrinthine undertakings that usually led to nothing. So far, this case didn't seem as though it would be any different. There was a lot of data to digest, but he vowed that if there was a bottom, he'd get to it.

"Thank you, ma'am," said Marshall.

"Now, I have to meet with all of the local law enforcement people," said Toby. "Your FBI point man on this will be Bill Webber; he's assigned a senior agent, Chris Sommers, to head the investigation."

Toby got up and went to the door. Over her shoulder, she called Nate. Nate went to her dutifully, leaving Marshall and Ryder alone.

"Well," said Ryder. "Looks like we have the ball." He had an expression on his face that was too smug to be a frown, and yet too hard to be a smile.

"Yes," said Marshall. "I'm going to bring on two people from my office to assist us."

"No problem," said Ryder. "As long as they know it's our case."

Marshall didn't respond. Ryder was getting territorial early, and with good reason: this was going to be a national case of epic proportions, and if they won, they'd come out of it with glory, TV appearances, and the capability of going into any of a hundred high-paying jobs.

Marshall walked to the door, when Jessica stepped into view. She smiled sweetly at him and handed him a note.

"Marshall, I have a note from Judge Langworthy's court," she said.

"Oh," he said. "It must be my verdict in the Quince case. Thank you, Jess."

Marshall took the note and looked at it. It seemed that despite his winning closing, Quince, the gunrunner, had been acquitted.

"Bad news?" asked Ryder.

"Yeah," said Marshall. "A gunrunner I prosecuted got off."

"Sorry," said Jessica. "You'll get him next time." She walked away. She was wearing a short little skirt and high heels. Her behind swayed, and Marshall thought that she was putting on for him just a little. Ryder watched her walk away with interest.

"Pretty girl," said Ryder.

Marshall didn't answer. He looked away from Jessica and stared at Langworthy's note.

"You okay?" asked Ryder.

"Yes, I just hate to lose," said Marshall.

"Me too," said Ryder. "That's a good quality to have when you work for Toby."

"Come on," said Marshall. "Let's go to the crime scene. Maybe we'll find one of Toby's screaming people."

6

....

Danny Boy

The score had been easy, they'd hit a little check-cashing and party store at noon, the same day the government checks came in. As expected, the store had been stocked with cash, stockpiled to steal money from the poor bastards who didn't have bank accounts to cash their dole. They'd hit the place hard, wounding the security guard, and scaring the living shit out of everyone there.

The three men divided up the cash quickly on a table. They were holed up in a little house on the near east side of the city. A big shotgun lay next to the score. The job was smooth, but the store owner had a silent alarm. The cops had come, and the bullets flew. They had run and lost them around the Davison Freeway.

The robbers were all black and in their twenties. One was a stocky man with brownish hair. The other two were brothers. Rael was lanky with light-brown skin. His brother, Paul, was fat with a mess of un-combed hair.

"Hurry the shit up," said the stocky man, named Noon. "I gotta get on. I got bitches waiting."

"What bitch would wait for your fat ass?" said Rael. His brother laughed.

"Yo' whoring-ass mama," said Noon. "Think I'll ass-fuck her today."

"Just count the money, nigga, and don't fuck it up," said Rael.

Paul counted the big pile of money faster. Check-cashing stores always had a lot of small bills. After their customers cashed their checks, they usually bought liquor and food and the store got it all right back. He didn't know who was worse, the damned store owners, or the lazy-ass, nonworking people they serviced. He was a robber, but at least that was a job.

"And don't fuck up the count, Paul," said Noon. "Yo' dumb ass was never good in math."

"You made me forget where I was, nigga," said the fat man. "Now, I got to start all over."

Paul's brother, Rael, laughed. "Both of y'all need to be on TV. Dumb asses."

"Damned cop fucked up my car," said Noon. "Did you pitch them plates?"

"Yeah, I told you I did it three times," said Paul. "Damn, you a scared-ass nigga."

"I set this shit up," said Noon. "So I gotta worry about stuff. Unlike your triflin' tagalong ass, I think about what I do. If we was in a company, I'd be a watcha call it? A CEO and you two would be them muthafuckas carrying my shit to the airport."

"How the fuck do you figure that," said Rael. "I got all the guns and shit together. I would at least be a vice president or something."

"Both of y'all need to quit," said Paul. "The white man ain't gonna let y'all run no damned company. That's why we gotta do what we did today. Damned shit is all against a muthafucka from birth. We ain't never had a chance to get ahead."

Noon and Rael echoed agreement to this commentary. The men could agree on nothing but the well-worn notion that omnipotent men controlled their destiny, made them unfit for decent society, and drove them to their desperation.

The men went back to counting their cash. Paul's lips moved as he counted, struggling to keep the numbers in his head.

Suddenly, the door to the room flew open. A big, uniformed cop swung in the door, holding a 9mm Glock in one hand, and a .45 revolver in the other.

"Wha'sup fellas?" he said. "Gettin' yo' party on up in here, I see."

For a second, the three men were stunned. The voice sounded like that of a black man. The depth, the cadence of it, was unmistakably black. But the face it came out of was white, a handsome Irish face under reddish hair.

The tension in the room was electric as Officer Danny Cavanaugh stood before the robbers, guns out in front, his eyes darting among the three men. Behind him was a black woman in a uniform with a riot gun aimed at them.

"Okay, fellas," said the woman. "You know the drill—"

Paul reached for the shotgun that was on the table. He was fat, but he moved with quickness and fluidity. Paul was swinging up the weapon when Danny shot him in the forehead with the Glock in his left hand. As Paul's body fell, the shot from the .45 in Danny's right hand hit him right in the ear almost at the same time.

Rael pulled out a gun, getting off a shot that missed the two cops. The woman cop fired the riot gun, and the left side of the table exploded, sending wood splinters and money flying into the air.

Danny yelled something and opened fire on the two remaining men. Rael caught one in the stomach from the Glock, then another in the leg from Danny's .45. Noon fell to his knees, and was raising his hands in surrender.

Danny fired another shot that missed Noon. He was about to fire again when the female cop pulled Danny's gun down, causing him to fire the Glock into the floor.

"No, Danny!" she said.

Danny looked dazed for a moment. Then he lowered his guns. "Call an ambulance, Vinny. And take your time," he added.

Officer Venice Shaw left as Danny kicked the guns away from the wounded men. He walked over to Noon, who was trembling with fear. Danny put the .45 away and knelt beside Noon.

"I sent my partner out so I could kill your monkey ass," Danny said calmly.

"Come on, man," said Noon. "Look, you can take all that money over there. Just turn and let me go."

"You know who I am, muthafucka?" asked Danny.

"Yeah, yeah I know."

"Say it!" Danny shoved the big gun at him.

"You that crazy white boy, Two Gun, killed some homeys."

"That's Danny Two Gun, you bitch, and it was *three* homeys. So, you know what's gonna happen if you fuck with me. Now, I got a question and I want an honest answer. If I even think you lyin' to me, we can cancel Christmas for your ass."

"I didn't shoot that guy at the store today!" Noon almost yelled. "My man here did." He pointed to Paul, lying in a pool of blood.

"I don't care about the damned camel-jockey you shot, lard-ass nigga."

"What you want? I said take the money."

Danny cocked the 9mm and put it to the man's head. "You know why I carry two different guns, my brotha?"

Noon didn't answer. He just looked at Danny with fear and hatred in his face.

"Well, I'll tell you," Danny continued. "See, guns have different weights, balances, you know. A nine millimeter is a precision thing, evenly balanced, controlled, but a revolver is front heavy, off kilter and shit. That's me. Sometimes I'm cool and other times—" Danny suddenly smacked Noon hard in the face with his free hand.

Noon's head snapped to the side, then he tried to grab Danny's gun hand, but Danny moved it, and swiftly hit him in the side of the head with the butt of the gun.

"Be nice. Okay, I know you muthafuckas been doing these party store jobs 'round town. I'm interested in the one you pulled last week. You got real lucky and found some drugs in the safe. About two keys. I want to know who you sold them to."

"I can't tell you that man, you know I'll be—"

Danny hit him again in the head with the butt of the gun. Blood trickled from the wound, running down Noon's meaty cheek.

"Damn! Fuck!" Noon yelled. "Okay, we dropped it on Onion, that nigga from the west side. He drive that yellow Mustang."

"Okay, you gonna meet some brothers from narcotics, and you gonna cooperate with them. 'Cause I'm gonna tell them what you told me, and I'm gonna get credit when they use you to bust Onion. If you fuck me, you'll be dead before the end of the day. Now, I know as soon as your lawyer gets here, you're gonna tell him what I said, and start acting like a punk ass—"

"No, no I ain't gonna punk out."

"Yeah, I know you ain't now, not while I'm here with this big-ass Glock in yo' face. But sometimes you forget about that shit when the lawyer show up. So, when you feel that urge, remember this—"

Dan lowered his gun and shot the stocky man in the thigh. Noon yelled and fell over backward.

"Danny! Shit!" yelled his partner, Vinny. "You promised me!"

"He went for my gun." Danny stood up. "The bullet just grazed him. He ain't hurt, but he'll remember it." To Noon, he said: "Won't you?"

The wounded man just screamed, holding his thigh, trying to stop the blood.

"Why did you do that?" asked Vinny.

"You know why. I'm working toward my goal."

"This ain't the way to do it, Danny, and you know it."

"If I had wanted a preacher for a partner, I would have requested one."

"Everyone's coming," said Vinny. "Clean your shit up. I'm not backing you up on this one if it gets hot."

"That's cool," said Danny. He stepped away from Noon, who was rocking back and forth and wailing like a child. Danny looked at his partner and smiled, his face suddenly turning softer. "You know, you lookin' fine today," he said.

7

Crawl Space

Marshall looked up from the auditorium stage into the rafters of Masonic Temple. At his feet were dried bloodstains, and the outline of Farrel Douglas's body. The shots had come from high up, and the blinding light had probably hidden any movement that might have been detected. The killer had been perched in a perfect place to do the job. And apparently, he had completely evaded the tight security surrounding the event after he killed Douglas.

This troubled Marshall. He'd seen the security plan for the event himself. How could someone get through the net, and get up there? The answer was, they could not, not without a lot of planning.

"Accomplices," he thought out loud.

"You say something?" asked Robert Ryder. He was standing not too far from Marshall on the stage.

"Just talking to myself," said Marshall. "A bad habit." Marshall focused his attention on a smallish man in a dark rumpled coat. He was Serrus Kranet, their ballistics expert. Serrus was good, the best by most reports. He spoke with two other men, who chatted feverishly.

Marshall walked over to them. At the sight of him, the men all stopped talking.

"Problem, Serrus?" asked Marshall.

"No . . . well, I don't know," said Serrus. He was fifty or so and was balding badly.

"Let's hear it," said Marshall. "Better I know about it now than in trial."

The other men stiffened and seemed to back away from Serrus. He was the leader, and therefore, the one who ultimately got all the shit.

"Well," said Serrus. "The trajectory shows that the shots came from up there, in a little crawl space by the left wall, but we are in the margin of error."

"Are we beyond the margin?" asked Marshall. He understood that if they were, then the shots had come from somewhere else.

"No," said Serrus. "We are within the margin, but barely."

"Margin of error is acceptable as evidence. The defense, if there ever is one, will attack it, but juries tend to hold on to this kind of scientific data like gospel. Is that all?"

Serrus was quiet for a moment, and Marshall thought that whatever was coming was not good. "Well, we were going to run a test on the bullets that killed Douglas, but something happened—there were no slugs."

Marshall was shocked for a second, and he knew that it registered on his face.

"What the hell do you mean, no slugs?"

"The bullets were .308 cartridges. Nothing strange there, but they left only fragments, the bullets shattered on impact, both of them."

Marshall was not a ballistics expert, but he did know the basics. A bullet contained a lead projectile and a powder charge. The firing pin ignited the charge, which sent the bullet along its merry way. But there was always a slug in the corpse, unless it passed through. Bullets were known to shatter, but what were the odds that two of them would?

Serrus answered this question before Marshall could ask it.

"The odds are astronomical that two ordinary bullets would shatter like that."

"So, if we catch the killer and get his weapon, we won't be able to get a match."

"Not to those slugs," said Serrus. "But that lawyer, Wendel Miller, has a slug in him. It hit his spine, but if we try to get it, he'll probably be paralyzed. The fourth shot went through the stage and ricocheted off several metal beams. It's pretty beaten up. Probably no good for a match."

"Shit," said Marshall. Reasonable doubt loomed already without the ability to match the bullet. "What are the fragments from the Douglas bullet made of?"

"It's lead, of course, but they shattered in a way that I've never seen," said Serrus. "You could say they exploded."

Marshall flagged this as a potential problem. If they couldn't explain the ballistics results, then the defense could color it any way they wanted to. They certainly couldn't match a gun to a shattered or severely damaged bullet, and that might be the end of the case right there.

"Get me all the reports tonight," said Marshall. "And you know the drill—no leaks to the press."

Marshall went over to Ryder, who was talking with Christine Sommers, an FBI agent whom Marshall was acquainted with, though he could not remember the case.

"Chris," said Marshall. "Good to see you again."

"Same here," said Sommers. Marshall remembered that she was a nice-looking woman. She was medium height but for some reason seemed taller. She was graying, and it became her. Sommers looked tired. As a senior agent, she was probably catching a lot of hell.

"I want to check out the shooter's position," said Marshall. "And you and I have to talk about the ballistics reports, Robert."

"It's Bob," said Ryder. "Chris here says that they've been getting a lot of calls on the murder."

"Right," said Sommers. "We got the usual crackpots, Oswald did it, and shit like that. But there are some things that might turn into leads."

"Such as?" asked Marshall. He didn't really need to know right now, but he always wanted to know the caliber of person he was working with.

"We've got your Douglas haters," said Sommers. "Black fringe groups and black militia; yes, they do exist. Also we're checking into anyone who has made a threat against a public official in the last five years."

"Great," said Marshall. He was satisfied for the moment. Sommers rattled off the answers like it was second nature. The sign of a pro. He glanced up at the rafters. "Shall we?"

They stood outside of the small crawl space as the lab men continued to work. The crawl spaces were above the second balcony and circled around the heart of the room. The killer had chosen one by the wall because it was near the door. He shot Douglas, then quickly ran out of that door and down the stairs. In the commotion with the mystery man and the fake gun, the killer had gotten out of the building.

Marshall could see down to the stage and all around the first twenty or so rows of seats. The space had a good vista. The killer had picked his place well.

"The security team did a sweep of these the day before, and the day of. They found nothing," said Sommers. "So far, the lab guys have no prints or anything. And I suspect that they won't find any. Our boy was smart."

"We're getting all of the TV tapes from that day. Maybe he was caught by a camera," said Marshall. "And maybe he talked to someone we can ID."

"You think he'd be that stupid?" asked Ryder.

"Not stupid, unlucky," said Marshall. "There were so many cameras, maybe he got caught in a sweep."

"Never thought of that," said Sommers. "It's a good bet."

Marshall was reaching, but he'd done a lot of cases in his years as a lawyer, and sometimes after all the hard work, fancy procedures, and high-tech shit, you just lucked up into something.

"Does the FBI have a package for me?" asked Marshall.

"Yes indeed," said Sommers. "And it's big. We're still putting it together, but I'll swing by your place later if you don't mind."

"You gonna swing by my place, too?" asked Ryder. The flirting in his voice was unmistakable.

"Sure thing," said Sommers in a very businesslike tone. "You get one too, sir."

That was the end of Ryder's fantasy, thought Marshall. Sommers had nary a hint of amusement in her face as she looked at him. Ryder smiled a little anyway and seemed to back off.

Marshall regarded the crawl space. It was small, but large enough to accommodate a man. Whoever had gone in there did so with great passion and determination. They would need to be just as tenacious in the investigation if they wanted to catch such a man.

"Got something!" yelled a man from inside the crawl space.

"Gordon's got something," someone said.

All eyes turned to a tiny man with brown hair as he slowly pulled himself out of the hole. Marshall went to the man and helped him up.

"Careful," said Gordon. "I'll drop it." Gordon was a small man with a rather large head. In his hand was a pair of forceps.

''What did you find?'' asked Marshall.

''Well, I was looking at the inner wall, which would have been to the killer's back,'' said Gordon. ''But I thought, what the hell, you know? Then, I saw the tip of a nail and there was something on it. I had to work it out carefully, but I got it all. Look there.''

Marshall examined the tiny nail fragment. On its tip, he could see a small strand of black hair.

8

....

Marshall

Marshall was exhausted as he pulled into the driveway of his home in Palmer Woods. He'd been going for twenty hours straight, and wanted only to see his bed. He got out of his car and lifted the heavy files that filled his backseat.

They were all excited by the find of the hair in the crawl space. A call had gone out to Toby and the president. Nate Williams had almost jumped for joy. But the elation was short-lived. They compared the hair they'd found to the hair on the mystery man they'd shot, and it did not match. Douglas's assassin was not the man who had been killed. Still, they had hard evidence. That was always a good thing.

Marshall was less excited than the others. In the age of the *Simpson* case, DNA and its evidentiary value could be made questionable. But he had to admit that it was a good break, so he didn't let his cynicism get the better of him.

He went inside his house. The home was huge, like all the homes in Detroit's affluent Palmer Woods and Sherwood Forest. He walked inside and heard his heels echo on the cold marble of the foyer.

"Chemin," he called. "You home?"

No answer.

"Good," he said to himself.

Marshall moved into his office and set his things down. He reclined on the soft leather sofa in his office and loosened his tie. He noticed his answering machine light flashing. He wanted to just let it wait, but he had to know if any news on the murder had come in.

The messages were mostly from his coworkers, congratulating him and sucking up for a position on the prosecution team. He already knew that he wanted Roberta Shebbel. She had the best legal mind in the office. If any messy issues came up, he'd need her wisdom. Walter Anderson had left three messages, each more desperate than the one before. Walter was begging for a chance to be on the team. Marshall wanted to give him a shot, but he was afraid Walter would crumble and go back to his old ways of drinking and dereliction. But he was a friend, and with Bob Ryder in the mix, he might need loyalty on the team.

Marshall took his 9mm out of his desk and took off the trigger lock. He never liked to have the gun locked while he was at home. Chemin had made him buy the lock out of her deathly fear of guns. But he hated the thing. If you needed the weapon, an intruder could kill you before you got the damned thing off. He took the gun, the black steel was cold in his hands. Marshall unlocked it and put it back into his drawer.

He stretched out on the sofa and tried to sleep, but he was too wound up now. He was excited by the Douglas case. He couldn't manage a straight thought, but he needed a clear head. When he got like this, there was only one solution. Marshall put on his workout gear and went into his makeshift gym in the basement. The room was dark. It smelled damp and musty. Crates and boxes were lined up against the walls.

Marshall turned on a light. He walked over to the old workout bench he'd bought and picked up his old boxing gloves, and started out on his heavy bag. He threw a straight right, and dust flew from the gray bag. More punches followed, and soon he was sweaty, breathing hard, and his head began to clear.

Marshall was born five minutes before his fraternal twin brother in an unusual labor that lasted over a day. Their mother, Beatrice, was a strong, exuberant woman, who loved her children and guarded her family dearly. She was a serious woman who fancied big hats and Sunday church. She loved to cook and sometimes made meals for the other families on the block.

But she was also a very emotional woman who was always under siege by the fierce world of the inner city. Beatrice seemed to live and die with each tragedy of the neighborhood.

When her adopted mother, a thin, cheerful woman everyone called Little Ma, was killed in a robbery, Beatrice had gone into a panic that necessitated a visit to the hospital. But mostly she was a solid, good woman who any kid would have been proud to call Mama. Marshall treasured her and couldn't imagine how his life would have been without her.

Marshall's father, a big autoworker named Buford, was a loud, happy man and father. Good to his family and friends, he made it his duty to minister to his two sons, teaching them simple and important lessons of life.

Marshall's memory of his father was a big booming voice, hearty laugh, beer and sweat smell, and big hugs on a stubbly face. Their home was a haven in their rough neighborhood. With so many of his friends fatherless, Marshall and his sister Theresa felt special to have a dad in the house full-time and even more blessed for him to be such a positive force.

This didn't sit quite well with Moses. It was evident early on that the fraternal twin boys were opposites. Moses was as bad as Marshall was good. Moses stayed in trouble, and even Buford's tough love couldn't stop him. Moses cut school, disobeyed his parents, and was a relentless thief. He stole anything and everything, sometimes he stole just to see if he could do it. It was his passion from early on. Buford and Beatrice always had their hands full with the boy.

Moses and Marshall were, nonetheless, inseparable. They both cut school together, ran the streets, playing basketball and hanging out with their friends. The twins were thick as thieves then. They supported each other, lied for each other, and made their parents' life difficult. Moses was definitely the leader of the two. Marshall just thought of his brother as a fun and uninhibited person, and he admired his strength.

One summer night, Marshall and Moses had been chased off the local basketball court by a group of bigger boys. They'd hung around for a while, when a boy they called Ducey decided to play what they called simply ''cars.'' They'd stand on a street corner, covered in darkness, and throw rocks at the cars that whizzed by on a busy street. The nicer the car, the better. It was a silly and dangerous game, and that made it all the more attractive to the young boys.

Marshall and Moses stood on the corner that night with three other black boys, their pockets filled with stones. Mostly, they missed. It was hard to hit a moving vehicle. But suddenly, a slow-moving car came their way. It was an Eldorado, a red one. It drove by, and the rocks flew. Marshall saw the back window shatter, and they all cheered. Then the Eldorado screeched to a halt. The young boys immediately broke into a run.

"Black bastards!" the car's occupant had yelled.

The other three boys split up, but Marshall and Moses, as usual, ran together. They'd run about a half block, when they heard the shots behind them. One bullet hit a tree, taking off a big chunk of bark. Marshall saw his brother run into a backyard and hide. He, however, was still on the street, and in full view of the shooter. Another bullet whizzed by his ear as he ran through a vacant lot.

Marshall jumped a fence, his heart racing in his chest. He hid among a row of garbage cans in the backyard of a man named Hudgens. He sat there on the warm ground, thinking that he might die. They'd played the game many times, but no one had ever stopped and shot at them. Suddenly, the consequences of his actions fell upon him. It was wrong what they had done. It was supposed to be fun, but he had never thought about the man in the car. Now, it was too late. The shooter was after him, and he knew if he caught him, he'd never go home again.

Suddenly, he heard footsteps and the sound of metal hitting the ground. The shooter was reloading his gun.

"You're dead, motherfucker!" yelled the man.

A white man, thought Marshall. At least, he sounded like he was white. He was even more afraid now. Any white man who would run into the 'hood like that was crazy. Marshall tried to push himself down farther behind the cans without knocking them down and giving himself away.

Marshall heard the old gate creak as the shooter entered the backyard with him. He was about thirty feet or so away. The yard was dark, and Marshall prayed the shooter couldn't see him.

The man moved in Marshall's direction. As he came closer, Marshall saw that it was not a white man, but a black one. His dark face turned, looking around the yard. He looked Marshall's way and lingered for a moment.

Marshall shifted and knocked one of the cans into another one. The clang sounded like thunder to him. The man raced toward him as Marshall jumped up and tried to run away. A strong arm caught him by the shoulder. He was spun around right into the one-eyed stare of the shooter's gun.

For a moment he thought he was done. There would be a flash, then darkness as he was carried from this world.

"You're just a kid," said the shooter. He was wearing an expensive silk shirt, and Marshall realized that he could be a criminal, a player, as they used to say.

"I—I'm sorry," said Marshall. "We didn't mean it."

"Jesus Christ," said the shooter. "What the fuck—?"

"I'll never do it again, please don't kill me, please." Marshall was crying now. He looked into the black man's face, searching for compassion.

The man's look of surprise turned into deep anger. He brought the gun closer to Marshall, resting it on his nose.

"This is what fools get in life, boy," said the man. Then he cocked the gun.

Marshall shook with terror. He felt warmth run down his leg as he pissed his pants. An eternity passed as the man held the little boy at bay. Marshall understood the other side of the street now. He'd only seen the side where all things were possible, where the consequences of your actions were left behind as you ran to safety. This was the real aftermath of bad behavior. Violence, fear, and death.

"Get the fuck away from me," said the man as he released Marshall. "Go home to your fat-ass mammy."

Marshall was paralyzed. He told his legs to move, but they did not. Then the man's arm shot out and knocked him backward.

"Move, goddammit!"

Marshall ran faster than he'd ever run. He heard the man laugh behind him as houses and cars whizzed by his frightened face.

The next morning, Marshall got up early and thanked God for sparing him. He made a promise then and there to straighten up. This drove his brother away from him. Moses was dedicated to mischief and was hurt when his brother rejected him. They began to argue and fight constantly. Soon, one twin's purpose in life became the eradication of the other. Each wanted to kill that part of him that had dared to become uncooperative.

Moses became the bane of Marshall's existence. Twins, even fraternal, are tied to each other from a young age. They were dressed alike, and received all the normal dual presents on birthdays and Christmas. He shared a life with him, and therefore had to love or hate him sooner or later.

Moses became obsessed with getting his brother back. He bribed him and tricked him into staying out late, getting into all manner of trouble.

One night, Moses seduced his twin into waiting for him while he broke into a nearby house. Theresa had warned him not to go, but Marshall was led to believe he was waiting for his brother to have sex with a local girl. A job that no man worth his balls would turn down. But Moses was really breaking into the house to steal a little color TV he'd seen. When Marshall discovered that it was a robbery, he normally would have gone home, but he didn't. Years later, he would think that maybe he missed his brother a little and wanted them to be friends again and stop fighting. So he stayed as his brother handed him a small TV through a window. He took it and waited for his brother to come out.

Marshall waited, but no Moses. Something had gone wrong. Moses had fallen inside and hit his head, or was trying to take something much too big to fit through the little window. But after a while, Moses came wiggling out of the window full of life and smiling like it was Christmas.

They fought all the way home, and Marshall vowed never to do anything with him again. Moses just laughed off the threat and ran away to sell his stolen goods. Marshall would always remember that walk home. He had walked out of his brother's life for good that night. Moses tried incessantly to get him back, but Marshall remained resolute. Soon, Moses gave up and started to build a life without his twin, a life filled with disobedience and grief for everyone in the home.

Buford and Beatrice argued even more than normal as a result. Beatrice wanted Buford to magically make the boy behave. And Buford didn't see how he could when he worked so much, so of course he blamed Beatrice for not being firm enough.

Marshall saw his father stay out later and later. Not wanting to fight with his wife, Buford just spent more time away from his family. He didn't see how this only made matters worse.

Then one night, Buford didn't come home. Marshall tried to get to sleep but had stayed awake. Lately, he couldn't sleep until he heard his father's voice booming as he came through the door. Hearing them argue was better than what he heard that night: silence.

The police came the next morning. He remembered his mother wail as she fell to her knees at the doorway. Buford had gone to a card game, where a fight had broken out, and Buford had been shot. The other men had all denied that they were the shooter and no gun was found.

Murder. Marshall had heard about it and saw it touch people he knew, but it didn't seem like something that could ever happen to his father, who was more than human. But he was gone.

Marshall blamed his brother. Somehow, this was all Moses' fault. If he had just not been so foolish, his father might have been home that night. He wanted to tell himself that it was the random violence of life that caused it, but it felt better to blame Moses. He was something that Marshall could see, talk to, hit if he wanted.

Beatrice ended up in the hospital, shaking violently and unable to speak. Marshall sat in the waiting room, fighting off the urge to kill his brother.

They had a funeral for Buford in a ceremony that Marshall thought would surely kill his mother. She survived the ordeal physically, but something in her had been buried with Buford, something that she had never gotten back.

The murder investigation went on for three weeks after the funeral. A cop named Robert Cavanaugh was assigned to the case. Cavanaugh was a former autoworker and a good friend of Buford. He broke the silence of the suspects and arrested a man named Percy Vane as the shooter.

Marshall remembered the day he came into their house with two plain-clothes detectives, who seemed nervous to be in a black household. But Cavanaugh lived just a few streets over, and so he did most of the talking. He and Beatrice talked for over three hours about the case. Percy had killed Buford, but he'd try to get out of it by pleading self-defense.

A week later, Cavanaugh came over with his son, a quiet little boy named Danny. Marshall and Danny hit it off right away. But Moses didn't like the strange boy and stayed away from him. Cavanaugh told Beatrice that he wanted to help the family as much as he could. He also wanted his son to have friends in their neighborhood. He was skinny, weak, and always the only white kid around.

Buford had actually helped Cavanaugh get a job at the Chrysler plant before Cavanaugh had become a cop. Before then, Robert Cavanaugh's life had been crumbling. His wife was leaving him, and he wrestled with alcohol. The Chrysler job stabilized him, and saved his family.

Robert Cavanaugh had bright red hair, twinkling green eyes and a thin Irish brogue. He eventually quit the plant and became a cop like his father before him.

Marshall and the family anguished as the trial dragged on, and Percy's lawyer, a brilliant young attorney named Frank D'Estenne, almost got Percy acquitted. Marshall watched in stony silence as the lawyers worked, manipulating the truth and bending lies to look like truth. All through the ordeal, he stared with hatred at Moses, who seemed unaffected by the trial.

Marshall knew then that he wanted to be a lawyer, to help present the truth in the public forum. Percy was convicted and sent to prison for thirty years. The family had cheered the verdict of guilty of manslaughter. Cavanaugh and his family had sat through the entire trial with the Jacksons and seemed just as happy.

The conviction brought closure to the family. It was the end of a nightmare. Marshall shut the door on his father's life and faced the uncertainty of a world without him.

Beatrice caught the weight of Buford's absence and bore it for the rest of her life. She worked full-time at a public school cafeteria and did cleaning work on the weekends. But she could not stop the natural force of a missing husband and father.

The home seemed empty and insincere after that, and the Jackson siblings began to mutate into children of loss. They became wild, aimless, and took to the streets as a replacement for the man they had lost. Suddenly, the danger of the neighborhood invaded their house and twisted their lives into ruin.

Marshall's older sister, Theresa, started drinking, and drugs soon followed. She moved from one stupid boyfriend to another, until she got knocked up like the rest of her friends. Beatrice and Theresa fought bitterly about the unborn child, and Theresa moved out of the house and got on welfare. She came back when her daughter was born with a mental defect that would render her handicapped for the rest of her life. Theresa didn't understand that you had to stop taking drugs when you were pregnant. The baby, little Fiona, would forever be a reminder of that mistake.

Marshall became a regular visitor to the Cavanaugh home during this time, going there to escape the darkness that had fallen on his own home. He and young Danny soon became best friends.

The Cavanaughs were one of the few white families who stayed in the black neighborhoods, in part because the city had a residency requirement for its police officers, but mostly because they liked the people there. They were God-fearing Catholics and believed that each man was their brother.

The Cavanaughs were a good but troubled family, just like Marshall's own. Danny's older brother had been in jail for most of his life. And even though a good job had helped Robert Cavanaugh, he still drank too much and argued terribly with his wife, an amiable woman named Lucy. But they were lucky in that despite their dysfunction, no one had died because of it.

Marshall and Danny shared their lives in the black neighborhood.

Danny had already picked up the lingo and rhythms of the street and at times seemed more at home than Marshall. There were a few white kids who got locked into the community and culture and in effect became just as black as their friends. Danny was one of those kids. Sometimes Marshall would hear him talking and not even know he wasn't black until he saw his face.

They were ostracized by their friends for their friendship but held on fast to each other. Soon, Marshall looked at the little Irish boy as his brother.

This drove a bigger wedge between Marshall and Moses. Jealous and alone, Moses' resolve to do wrong deepened until it became his philosophy. He became worse, getting kicked out of school, fighting and stealing everything in sight. He was a monster devouring the happiness and hope of his family.

Beatrice was pleased with Marshall's transformation, but like so many mothers from the inner city, she felt her work was done with him, and concentrated on the bad son. Moses got all her attention and compassion, even as Marshall excelled in school, graduated with honors from Pershing High School, and enrolled in Wayne State.

Marshall's relationship with his mother soured and he was off in the world on his own. He did well in college but dropped out and joined the marines. Danny Cavanaugh went against family tradition and joined with him.

Beatrice was angry and heartbroken. She did not know what the service held for a black man in America. But Marshall wanted to be as far away from her and Detroit as he could get. So, he joined the service and went overseas. He didn't write or talk to his family for months.

In the service, Marshall learned to be strong, tough, and resilient. He learned his way around a gun and vowed never to be without one at his disposal.

Danny Cavanaugh excelled as a marine, going through boot camp as one of the sergeant's favorites. He was also the best shot in the camp. Little quiet Danny became a kick-ass soldier. He thrived on the machismo and the violence. He lifted weights and gained twenty pounds of muscle. Marshall watched the transformation with astonishment. The little kid who he used to protect from bullies was now fierce enough to eat them all alive.

They were assigned to a platoon and sent to Europe as the Soviet Union crumbled and long-brewing ethnic hatreds erupted. They assisted a UN peacekeeping force in Eastern Europe. Marshall soon learned that what peacekeepers really did was to kill anyone threatening the peace.

Marshall and his battalion fought in the cities and countryside and drove the violently hateful rebels back. He had shot at many men but didn't know how many men he had hit. But Danny had kept count. He had six notches on the butt of his rifle, but Marshall was sure it was an exaggeration. Marshall was amazed by the depth of the hatred between these white men who looked so similar to one another.

The armed service was not his salvation, but it pointed him toward it. He learned a sense of justice and respect for his country. He had a lot of problems with America. It certainly had a history of mistreating his people, but after going around the world, Marshall felt that America was the best deal going and it was up to individuals to help themselves, using their own power and resources.

Not long into their service, Danny's father had a heart attack, and Danny reluctantly left the service and enrolled in the police academy. It seemed that the Cavanaugh tradition was going to be upheld through another generation.

Two months later, Marshall started to miss America and his friend. He grew tired of the service and decided that he had to go back home and finish the life that he'd started.

Marshall returned to Detroit. He was now a man, and saw the city as a place of great opportunity. His people were in power and ruled the city. He'd always wanted to be a lawyer, and now he had the money and courage to try it.

Marshall became reacquainted with his mother. Beatrice's life was now in a shambles. Moses had milked the family of all resources and love, and Beatrice had depleted herself trying to save him. Marshall was furious and vowed to drive his brother into the dust if he had to.

But Moses was now a full-fledged criminal king in the neighborhoods, feared by people, and wanted by the law. He ran with killers, drug addicts, and prostitutes. He used his mother's house as living quarters for his friends, and a station for his activities. Theresa had married and moved away with her daughter, fearing the violence her brother brought home with him each night.

Marshall confronted his brother and, with the assistance of rookie police officer Danny Cavanaugh, drove him and his element out of his mother's life, by moving her away. Beatrice lived with him for a while, then decided to move into a retirement home with people her own age.

It had been hard for Marshall to forgive his mother for his belief that she had emotionally abandoned him, but he had to. He was alone in this world that was now so new to him. He needed the strength of his family to set the foundation for his life.

Marshall received his degree in criminal justice at Wayne State. He later enrolled in Wayne State Law School and graduated with honors. He joined a small law firm specializing in criminal defense but soon grew tired of the game. Defense lawyers rode a sharp edge of denial. He needed a job where the lines were more clearly defined.

So Marshall wrangled a job working in the city's legal department. While defending the city on a big police misconduct case in federal court, he impressed the presiding judge, Stephen Bradbury, who recruited him as one of his clerks. That job, added to his trial experience, got him into the U.S. attorney's office. It didn't hurt that Bradbury got bumped up to the Sixth Circuit Court of Appeals, and that he was friends with Nate Williams, who was appointed U.S. attorney soon thereafter.

He kept in touch with Danny all through this time on the legal fast-track, renewing his friendship. Ironically, as Marshall grew more educated and refined, Danny became more rough and streetlike, a result of his job as a cop. In a world dominated by stereotypes, they were a paradox: the white man was black, and the black man was white.

The day he walked in the U.S. attorney's office Marshall remembered what the man had said to him the night he almost died. *"This is what fools get in life, boy."* Marshall had survived the dangers of the street, and did not get what fools got. He looked up at the seal of the United States and knew he had found his professional home.

Marshall stopped his workout. He was dripping with sweat and breathing hard. The tension he'd felt was gone now. Immediately, his mind went back to the case. Whoever had killed Douglas had to be organized and perhaps part of a group of conspirators who hated Douglas too. A lone-gunman theory was bullshit, a beautiful lie told to people who didn't know any better.

Marshall ascended the stairs from the basement and hopped into the shower. The hot water felt good on his tight muscles. The hair they'd found was definitely from an African-American, and he already knew the motive. Hatred. The FBI was already checking out all local and national black militant groups that might have wanted Douglas dead. To his surprise, there were a lot of them.

Marshall was struck by the irony of his case. For so long, blacks in America had been targets of violence, discrimination, and murder. But now they had truly arrived. They were doctors, lawyers, and heads of state. And it seemed they were also engaged in the weighty business of political assassination.

9

Chemin

Marshall finished his shower and put on fresh clothes. He went back into his office and started taking out the forensic reports on Douglas. There wasn't much to tell. The cause of death was two bullets in the body. One in the chest and another in the head.

He waded into the sea of paper when the doorbell rang. Marshall stopped his work. It couldn't be his wife, he thought. Marshall's hand went for the 9mm he kept in his desk, then he thought better of it. Prosecutorial paranoia. He got up and answered the door.

He looked out the peephole and saw Agent Sommers standing in front of the door, checking out the house.

"Hey, Marshall," said Agent Sommers as Marshall opened the door. She had a big package at her feet. "I've got all the reports from my office and the TV tapes. Damned TV news guys gave us shit about it too. Speaking of which, they're all saying the man who was shot was the gunman, so they don't know what we know yet."

"Good. They don't need to," said Marshall. "We don't want any conspirators to know what we do." He suddenly remembered the case he and Sommers had worked on. It was a postal worker who was shot and robbed on her route. Sommers had been a dogged investigator, tireless and methodical. He was suddenly glad to have her on his side.

"Wanna come in, have a beer or something?"

"Do I ever," said Sommers. "But I'm on the clock. I'm still checking out leads."

"Call me if you get anything," said Marshall.

"I will," said Sommers. She lifted the package into Marshall's waiting hands, then turned and walked off.

As Marshall watched Sommers leave, he saw his wife's car rolling down the street. His stomach tightened. He could not remember when he began to dread seeing his life partner. Things were not rosy for them these days, and he knew the Douglas case would only make matters worse.

Chemin Harris-Jackson was a bright, big-eyed beauty who was funny, intelligent, and full of energy, the kind of woman who enlivened just about everything she did.

He remembered the first time they met, how she had taught him to say her name. It was at a state bar association. He couldn't remember why she was there, but he remembered that she had been radiant, charming, and very funny. Men had lined up to test her favor, and for some reason, he'd won out.

"Sheh-men," she had said, teaching him her name. "Not Shaman. They use magic. I do it the old-fashioned way." She was sexy, playful, and very confident. He had followed her around all night like a lost puppy, captivated by her.

Chemin worked for a company called Hallogent, a big consulting firm that sold information on consumers and companies. They also followed buying and investing trends on a global basis. She was an assistant vice president and proud of her position.

Their courtship had been almost like a fairy tale. Romantic evenings, passionate sex, and bonding in that way that added layers of richness to a relationship. They shared everything about each other. This was normally the period when you decided that the other person is not right for you, but it only seemed to draw them closer.

Even then, Chemin was an unusually strong and independent woman. She never complained and was always ready to fix any problem herself. Marshall liked that, up to a point. A man wanted to feel that his woman needed his help. And as much as he tried to lie to himself, Chemin did not need him. But he loved her, and that was all he could see. Everyone walked on air when love hit them, oblivious to what lay below their dangling feet.

They were married two years after they met. Danny Cavanaugh stood as best man, and Marshall could have sworn that he saw his brother leave the service early even though he was not invited.

Marshall thought that his life could never get any better. The first few years were just an extension of that otherworldly courtship. But soon things started to go bad. He realized that people changed after marriage, or perhaps the way you perceived them changed. To be a girlfriend was one thing, but to be a wife was a different, more powerful thing. He didn't know exactly how or why it happened. All he knew was that the woman he married was different from the one he was now married to.

Chemin was a great person but an unhappy wife who escalated the stress of his already pressured life. And the worst thing was, he knew why. Children. She wanted them. He didn't. Chemin was about to turn thirty, and she felt that it was time to start a family. Marshall, however, was unsure. He'd had such trouble with family. The idea of starting one terrified him. She stopped using birth control and screamed at him when he bought condoms. These days, they did not have sex at all. She refused to do it with him as long as he did not want kids. So they both suffered. Mad and sexually frustrated, they were having a standoff of epic proportions.

They fought constantly about everything, and through bouts of reconciliation, he felt the trouble deepen to critical. Now they just stayed out of each other's way, too in love to get a divorce, and too proud to change. The strong, independent woman he'd married was now a fierce, and beautiful, enemy.

Marshall pulled the box in the door and waited. He didn't want to close the door while she was outside. Chemin would think of that as some kind of negative action. So he waited for her. Chemin parked her car and got out. Marshall's heart quickened as he saw her long legs extend from the door. Her skirt was short and tight, and for a second, he remembered the passion he had for her.

Chemin got out of the car. Her eyes were large, light brown, and always seemed to have something behind them, some mystery that you might never know. Her hair was black, and cut short, and she had a dazzling smile, when she did smile, which wasn't much lately.

Chemin glanced at him, then took out her cart. Because Hallogent sold information, Chemin always carried around a little handcart filled with papers, computer disks, and videotapes.

''Hey,'' said Marshall, trying to break the ice.

"Didn't expect you to be home," said Chemin. She walked to the door. Marshall moved out of her way, and she stepped inside. She was wearing perfume, something new.

"I needed a rest," he said. "The case—"

"Yes, I know. The case is taxing you, you're tired, stressed. I know the routine, honey."

"Can we have a *minute* of civility?"

"Sure." She walked into the kitchen.

Marshall turned toward his office. This was where he usually locked himself away. Or he went out to see Danny, but he knew he had to do something about this. The Douglas case was going to be a bitch, and he did not need trouble at home.

"I think we need to talk about this some more," said Marshall as he entered the kitchen.

"Why?" said Chemin. "We're diametrically opposed. I want a baby, you're still maturing."

That was another thing, Marshall remembered. Chemin had a cutting, sarcastic sense of humor. She knew it, and she used it whenever they argued. It was part defense mechanism, but it always stung.

"There's no need to be insulting, Chemin. I know where we stand. But I think we can compromise. As soon as my case is over, we can explore this."

"No," said Chemin, turning to him. "I've put off jobs, vacations, and friends for your cases. I am not going to put off life for it. No more, Marshall."

"Then, I don't know what to do." He shrugged and walked off to the other side of the room, looking out of a window.

"We need help, Marshall. We should go to that doctor I told you about."

"No," said Marshall, almost yelling. "I'm not going to some stranger to solve my problems. If we need a third party to talk to each other, then maybe we shouldn't be together."

"You're so afraid that she'll think you're wrong, aren't you?"

"You'd love to get me in a room with another woman, so you two can gang up on me, wouldn't you? Well, it ain't happening."

The counseling issue was their latest battlefield. Chemin was convinced that marriage counseling would save them. Marshall detested the idea. He had always been a man who fixed his own problems. Buford had always said that. "A man takes care of his shit."

To Marshall, it was like admitting defeat, like he was not a man any more, but some whiny, henpecked fool who couldn't control his woman or his life. The very thought of it made his blood heat up.

"This is not about women ganging up on you. It's about what we mean to each other, if anything."

"No counselors. You can sign up, but you'll be sitting on the couch by yourself."

"I already am, in case you forgot. My psychologist told me to seek help—with you."

Chemin had been seeing a shrink for about half a year. She was a strong woman, but also had a bad temper. After so many fights at home, she had gone to a shrink and things had gotten better, for a while. Now, it seemed the psychologist was trying to get him into therapy, too. That's all they knew, he thought. That was their answer to everything. From death to a hangnail, the solution always cost a hundred bucks an hour.

"Let's just talk, you and me. That's how we got into this relationship, why can't we fix it the same way?"

"Because you're unreasonable, Marsh. You don't listen to me."

"We don't need other people to solve our problem."

"Okay, you want to fix this between us. Fine. Either we get pregnant, or it's over, we divorce."

Her words stung him for a moment. She stood before him with her arms folded defiantly in her smart business suit. She never looked more beautiful, and that made her statement hurt all the more for some reason.

"You don't mean that."

"What did we get married for, if we're just going to live without a family? We're just dating and fucking with wedding rings on."

"We're wearing rings, but we ain't fucking. Not for two months now."

"You don't get any unless you mean business," she said. "It's hard on me too, women do like it in case you haven't heard. But I'm fighting for something bigger than us, so if we have to go without, so be it."

"Is that all our commitment means to you, that you can be so callous to me?"

"Apparently, that's all it is, Marshall. Unless you want to make it more. A baby makes it more. It's on you now." Chemin's eyes narrowed a little, and her face took on a determined expression.

He knew that look. Chemin was the type of woman who liked to draw lines in the sand. She had given him a deadline on proposing to her, and had told him to warm up his cold feet two weeks before their marriage. When she drew one of her lines, she meant it.

"Our marriage is more complex than that, and you know it," he said.

"Fine, then I'll just have to do what I have to do," she said. She turned on her heel. And in a lower tone, he heard her say: "Like always."

Chemin walked out of the room, and Marshall could hear her footsteps as she ascended the stairs. He felt a weight lift from him. This was not what he had hoped for when he got married. How could he tell her that he couldn't go to counseling because he feared starting a family, that the uncertainty of life was terrifying to him?

He'd had too much hardship in his own family to jump into one. Beautiful, innocent babies grew up to be evil children who broke their parents' hearts and drove them to an early grave. Or they were born retarded, like his niece, a testament to the folly of trying to have them.

He could not shake the feeling that his family was doomed, destined to end in this generation.

Chemin could not see this because her family was perfect: parents with a forty-year marriage and close relationships among all her siblings. She had no idea of the poison he carried inside of him.

Marshall went back into his office. He ripped open the box Sommers had given him, and looked at the collection of tapes. He picked up the one marked CNN first and popped it into his VCR. There were twelve tapes in the box, and he'd probably be up all night searching them.

He looked at random footage. People in the crowd scenes, preparations for the commencement. He went through tape after tape, and then he saw it.

On the cameras of a local station, he saw a man who looked like the one who had been shot. He stood in the overflow in the lobby of the building. People randomly blocked his vision, but he could see that after the commotion started when Douglas was shot, the man had a case. He then passed it to another man, who disappeared from sight.

All of the men were black.

"Yes!" Marshall cheered quietly. This was something. He was going to check the tapes for more images. Maybe someone caught some faces.

He picked up the phone and called Ryder, Nate, and Sommers. He filled them all in. Each of them sounded happy, except for Nate, who immediately talked about doing video enhancement.

He heard the doorbell. He was going to get it, when he heard Chemin come downstairs. He heard female voices that didn't belong to his wife.

Marshall peeked out of his office door and saw Chemin and two other women. One was tall and pretty with brown hair. The other was chubby with a head of long black hair.

"Oh, shit," he cursed. It was his wife's friends Rochelle and Devonne. Chemin had gotten into the habit of having them over a lot lately. He hated them. Both were single. Rochelle was divorced and Devonne had never been married. They all sat around and talked about men. He knew Chemin had told them all about their situation, everything they did and didn't do. He could already feel his ears burning.

He had to get out. He packed up his things and headed toward the back entrance. He was in the kitchen when Rochelle stepped in.

Marshall saw her eyes flash when she looked at him. She knew, he thought. She knew everything.

"Hey, Marsh," she said in her husky voice.

"Hello, Rochelle," he said.

"Leaving?"

"Yes, I have some work to do at the office."

"Kinda late, isn't it?" she said. The look on her face was positively evil.

"Yes, but us feds are always on the clock." He wasn't fooling her, but it was all he would give her the satisfaction of hearing.

"Oh. Well, you gotta keep busy."

He walked out of the door and got into his car. He saw the blinds on one of the windows swing to the side. They were watching him. He cursed. Thrown out of his own house. He drove away. He reached down and dialed his cell phone. He'd page Danny and meet him at a bar. He definitely need a stiff drink or two.

He headed toward the Lodge Freeway. All the way, he kept seeing his wife's hurt eyes, and the men on the tape, handing off a case just big enough to contain a high-powered rifle.

10

Among Thieves

Moses was a little nervous as he clipped the red wire. He didn't go out himself much, but this was a special job. The electrical wires were inside a long pipe running on the side of the house. The alarm wires looked like a water pipe, and most people would have mistaken it for such, but not Moses. He knew what was inside: the keys to yet another kingdom.

Moses separated the ends of the wire, then cut the last one. The lights on the alarm box inside the house flickered, then went out.

"All right," he said. "We can go in now."

Dake and Nita were behind Moses as he moved over to a pair of big glass doors. They were all dressed in black, and their faces were covered. There were security cameras, but when he disabled the alarm, the camera system went off too. Stupid move on the owner's part to connect them.

Moses carefully cut the window to the large back door of the big house. He reached in and lifted the latch. Then he removed the steel rod that was placed at the foot of the door to stop it from opening. He tried the door, but it still wouldn't open.

"Top latch," said Dake.

"Fuck," said Moses. He reached into his black bag and pulled out his glass cutter. Then he cut another hole at the top of the glass door. He reached inside and found a long metal rod had been placed between the sliding doors. He pulled it out and then slid the doors open. They went inside.

The mansion was dark, but he could tell it was spacious and ornately furnished. Big pictures hung on the walls, and in the middle of the room was a spectacular glass chandelier.

"We should get a truck for all this shit," said Nita. She laughed softly.

Moses passed all the lovely decor, going to the stairs. "This is it," he said to Dake and Nita. "You two see what else is in this place we can use, while I go upstairs and find the safe. Don't turn on any lights, don't take anything big, and don't take off your damned gloves and touch anything."

"Cool," said Nita.

"We got the shit covered," said Dake. "It's all under control."

Moses moved quickly up the stairs to the master bedroom. It was even more beautiful than the living room downstairs. Moses looked around, then went to a crude-looking stump on the floor by a fireplace. A fireplace in the bedroom, thought Moses. Some people had it all.

Moses took out some tools and began to open the safe. He had the combination, but he needed to make it look good. The big Grosse Pointe home belonged to Arnold Brown, a wealthy banker and financier. Arnold's son, Ernest, was a typical rich boy, arrogant and rebellious. Ernest was dating a black girl and doing a lot of drugs. He'd gotten in deep with a local drug dealer named Wiz, and his parents were not going to bail him out again.

Moses found out about Ernest's situation and bought out his debt. In return, Ernest supplied him with the combination to his parents' safe. It was a fair trade, he thought, and Mom and Dad were probably heavily insured.

Moses took out a crowbar, and lifted the face off the safe. It made a loud noise. He stopped and reached in his pocket and took out the paper with the combination. Suddenly, he heard an electronic beep. It was muted and distant. He looked around nervously, and waited. Silence. He started to go and check on Nita and Dake, but thought better of it. Probably just a digital clock, he thought. He quickly started on the safe. He punched the code into the keyboard and the door hissed open. Inside, he saw four thick stacks of cash, papers, and five jewelry boxes.

"Damn," he whispered to himself. He was excited and tingled all over. God, he loved stealing. It was like making your own Christmas. And he'd always loved the holiday. He and his brother always had to share presents, though.

He felt anger as he thought of his family. His father's murder had devastated the family. But he and Marshall had not been thrown closer together by it. Moses had loved his father, and the pain of losing him drove them both to the street. But Marshall had abandoned him, left him for a skinny white boy and his so-called better intentions. Soon, his love of family was replaced with a love of taking what was not his.

Moses pushed the faces of his family out of his mind and grabbed the cash and stuffed it into his bag. Then he started on the jewelry boxes. They went into the bag. He sifted through the papers to see if anything else might be of use. But it was just stocks, bonds, the usual nonusable crap. It took some extra time, but a good thief is thorough. In a house like this, something innocent-looking might be worth millions. He carefully looked through everything in the safe. Then he saw a gun inside the safe at the bottom. It was a silver-plated .22. He took that too.

He got up and left the room, leaving the safe open. He hurried downstairs. He got to the foot of the stairs, but did not see Dake and Nita.

"Fuck," he said. They were the dumbest people on the planet. They had to move.

Suddenly, Moses heard a sound from behind him. He turned and saw a figure standing in a shooting crouch.

"Dake? What the f—"

The figure yelled something Moses could not understand, then fired.

The shot went wide and Moses dodged, falling to the floor. He pulled out his own gun and returned fire. The dark figure ran behind a table.

"Police!" a man's voice yelled.

Moses did not recognize the voice. It was not Dake's or Nita's voice. It was a cop, but how? He must have fucked up the alarm, he thought vaguely as he hid behind a sofa in the living room.

"We got you hemmed in!" said a voice.

This voice was different from the first. There were two of them now, he thought. Moses' mind raced. He was clean just a moment ago, and now there were two cops right on his ass.

Suddenly, Moses saw one of them move, and a glint of light flashed from a torso. A badge, he thought. That meant a uniformed cop. There were probably only two of them, then. Normally, the uniforms were the first on the scene. He knew if he didn't get out now, the place would be crawling with cops soon.

Dake and Nita were probably outside, handcuffed in a police cruiser, he reasoned. It pained him, but it was part of the job. They knew the score. His job now was to get out in one piece. If he went back to prison again, it would not be good for him. His rap sheet was long, and today's judges were all unforgiving bastards.

He stood up and ran for the door. He fired at the shadows in the big room as he sidestepped to the door. One of the cops fired a shot that missed. It hit a big grandfather clock, shattering its face. Another shot rang out, and Moses felt his shoulder explode in pain. He was thrown back and fell into the big glass door, breaking it into pieces.

He landed outside on the hard pavement. His head hit first, and he saw a flash of light. He heard footsteps, and soon the cops were above him. Moses' head snapped to the side as one of them kicked him in the side of the head. He tried to get up, but more blows crashed into his body. He felt blood from his shoulder run down his arm as he was kicked hard in the abdomen and fell to the ground. His head hit the pavement again, and he slipped into blackness.

11

The Swirl

Marshall watched Danny Cavanaugh walk into the bar at Fishbone's in downtown Detroit. The place was packed, and the smell of Cajun food filled his lungs. Danny was a big man. Six four and about two twenty. His red hair literally shined in the light of the bar. He moved around a patron and made his way over to his friend. Marshall sat at the bar with a full beer and a big tray of Fishbone's specialty, alligator voodoo, fried alligator meat.

"Danny boy!" Marshall called out to him.

"Wha'sup, my brotha?" yelled Danny.

As usual, a few people, black and white, looked shocked to hear the black voice coming from the face of a white man. Marshall was used to it. He smiled as Danny walked toward him.

"Party started without me, I see," said Danny. They hugged, and Marshall felt better already.

When they were younger the other black kids made fun of them, called them "The Swirl," which was the name for chocolate and vanilla soft-serve ice cream swirled together on a cone. It was also a slang for a black and white couple. The young boys hated the name, and had had many fights because of it.

Years later, when Danny's wife left him, he moved in with Marshall for a while. They kidded each other about the name. The Swirl had made a comeback.

''How's Vinny?'' asked Marshall.

''Still in love with me,'' said Danny.

''Only God understands that.'' Marshall laughed. ''Isn't it dangerous to be dating your partner. I mean, you piss her off one day, and bam, she shoots you?''

''Never happen. So, what's the problem?'' Danny ordered a beer.

''Man can't have a drink with his best friend?'' said Marshall.

''Not on a weeknight. Not when he's got the hottest case since the mayor got smoked. How's that goin'?''

''You know I can't talk about it.''

''Well, I say good riddance to that muthafucka Douglas. He never did the brothers any good.''

''Not your kind of brother, huh?'' Marshall laughed.

''Goddamned skippy,'' said Danny. ''That old fart Douglas was just a puppet for rich folks and fuckin' everybody else.''

Marshall was silent for a second, then: ''Chemin and I got into it again.''

Danny lowered his head, then looked at Marshall with compassion. ''Jesus, you are a pussy! Back in the old country, we'd feed her a couple of her own teeth, and she'd shut the hell up.'' He laughed.

''Yes, but in *this* country, you do that, and a big muthafucka like you crashes the party.''

''You got that shit right.'' Danny's beer came, and they clinked glasses.

A pretty black woman walked up to the bar and placed an order. Danny caught her eye, and she smiled.

''Excuse me,'' Danny said and he was off to the races. He returned a moment later, folding a cocktail napkin into his pocket.

''No fuckin' way you got her number that quick,'' said Marshall.

''Yes fuckin' way. You forget, I ain't some married muthafucka like you.''

''So what you gonna do with it? You live with Vinny. I know she don't let you date.''

''I ain't gonna call the woman. I'm just keepin' my shit sharp, you know what I'm sayin'?''

''Damn, I miss that,'' said Marshall. ''I used to love women.''

"Be happy," said Danny. "You got a good life. Chemin is a hard woman, but a good one. Trust me, I know."

"Yeah, but I'm about to lose her," Marshall said. Even he could hear the tinge of sadness in his voice.

"Look, you know I love Chemin, but don't let her run your life. She's got to know that you the man, you know?"

"Spoken like a divorced-ass loser," said Marshall, laughing.

Danny downed his beer and ordered another. "Okay, I know we're supposed to be all sensitive and shit nowadays, but unless something wrong happened, you still got a dick."

"Well, I haven't been using it lately."

"You know what I mean. It's the law of nature. You gotta rule. If she can't handle that, then let her go find another man who'll put up with her shit."

"You tried that, and ended up losing half your shit."

"Damn, that was hard," said Danny. "True, but hard. But it's still a fact someone has got to rule; if it ain't you, then it's got to be her."

Marshall took this in. Danny was a little crude, but there was always wisdom in his words. "As usual, your logic is all fucked up, but ultimately inescapable."

"Well, I may not be a rich-ass lawyer like you, but I know me a couple of things here and there."

"Shit, I ain't rich. In fact, you're picking up the tab tonight." They laughed again.

"So, I made a good bust today," said Danny. "I think it's gonna help me get that detective's shield."

"What about your record, did you take care of that yet?"

Danny averted his eyes a little. "Well, that shit's still following me, you know."

"Dammit, Danny, you can't keep breaking the head of every guy you arrest."

"I got a job to do, and I only know one way to do it, you know?"

"But no one's gonna make you a detective when your IAD file is as thick as the Bible. You need to stop feeding the Narcs and Homicide guys all your leads and collars, and rehabilitate your image."

"Fuck that. I want to be a detective, but I'm not gonna be some faggot in a suit."

Marshall visibly bristled. "Is that what I am?"

"I never said that." Danny took a long drink of beer.

Marshall stood up and looked Danny in the eye. Both men were big, and several people at the bar noticed the tension.

"You always go there with me. You're still upset that I became a lawyer instead of going to the police academy with you."

"Hey, I admit I don't like it, but I've made peace with the shit, all right?"

"Don't insult me because you can't control your violent streak."

"You know I hate that!" Danny slammed his beer glass on the counter. Suddenly, he realized what he had done, and the irony of it. "Look, man, I'm sorry," he said.

Marshall sat back down on the bar stool. "It's okay, I was out of line too."

The two men looked at each other and their history seemed to pass, then they hugged and ordered more beer.

Marshall always marveled at his times with Danny. There was still a lot of racial strife in the country, and yet they had bypassed all of it and never questioned their friendship. Maybe it was because they had been thrown together in family turmoil, or because they'd served together under stress in the marines. It seemed there was always something bigger than their differences to hold them together. Whatever it was, he wished he could give it to everyone, because he loved his friend dearly.

"Okay, I'll take your advice," said Danny. "I can do some of that goddamned antiaggression training shit the bosses like so much."

"That's a good start. Great. Let me know if you need any help." Marshall thought a moment, then: "And I'll take your advice. I'll just have to get to the bottom of this thing with Chemin and let the chips fall, you know."

"Now you talkin' like the nigga I know and love." Danny smiled.

The bartender, a slight black man, frowned when he heard Danny's statement. Marshall caught his look and quickly shot back: "Yeah, he said *nigga*. But you see, he's a nigga, too."

"That's right," said Danny. "I'm what they call a high yellow." He laughed.

"See, he's black, he just don't show it. It's in here." Marshall pointed to his heart.

"And here." Danny pointed to his crotch. They laughed loudly, and the bartender smiled with them.

12

Vengeance

The tapping at Marshall's door was light as always. He always found this a curious quality of Judge Stephen Bradbury. Bradbury was an ordinary-looking man. His bland features and balding head made him seem even more unremarkable. But Bradbury was in fact a brilliant man. The average person would look at him and see a bus driver or an accountant. Marshall saw only greatness.

"Come on in, Judge," said Marshall.

Stephen Bradbury walked into Marshall's office with a big smile on his face. He was elegant in a charcoal gray suit and blood red tie. Bradbury was approaching sixty, but he didn't look it. He was a former track star at Yale, and he still kept himself in great shape.

"Well, so you finally caught a big fish, huh?" said Bradbury. His voice was deep and soothing, the kind you might hear from a disc jockey late at night. He sat down across from Marshall.

"Yeah, I wanted to call you when I got it but—"

"I know." Bradbury took a seat. "It gets crazy. I used to be in your shoes. So, how's it going?"

"Slowly, unfortunately," said Marshall. "These kinds of cases are always tough. So, how's your family?"

"Oh, everyone's fine. Claire says hello, and the kids are okay too. Although Yvonne had the flu for a while. Jonathan just got a promotion at GM."

"That's good. And you look well. I swear, you're getting younger instead of older."

"Thanks, you liar," said Bradbury.

"I hear the Supreme Court docket is on hold until another justice can be named."

"Yes," said Bradbury. "And the backstabbing has already started. I hear I'm on the short list."

"That's great," said Marshall. "Congratu—"

"Not yet. It's only a rumor. I'll let you know if it happens. Look, I just wanted to say congrats, and if you need me, I'll be around. This is a big moment in your life, son. The great future I always knew you'd have is probably tied to this. As a friend, I want you to come to me if anything goes wrong." Bradbury stood up. He and Marshall shook hands.

"I appreciate that," said Marshall. "You know, I do need something right now."

"What's that?" Bradbury turned around.

"I'd like to know your opinion on the case. I know you and Douglas were enemies."

"Not enemies, adversaries. There's a difference." Bradbury sat back down. "Farrel and I were not friends, but we liked each other. I have to say that I was not surprised at what happened. He was asking for it."

"You think so?" asked Marshall, who was suddenly aware that his former mentor was upset.

"The man was dishonest, in the worst way. He was intellectually dishonest. He used his color to get the job, then turned his back on everyone who fought to get him there. There was no love lost between us, that's for sure."

"But you are upset about it?"

"Yes, I'm upset." Bradbury shifted in his chair. "I didn't agree with the man's philosophy, but he was black, and he had an obligation to be smarter than to start all the trouble he did, then go out in this crazy world. His family—" Bradbury stopped for a second. "Didn't deserve this. Our people suffer quietly these days, Marshall, but we continue to fight. His political choices hurt us, and now in death, he hurts those of us he left behind."

Marshall was surprised at his old boss. He had never heard him say a kind word about Douglas, but now it seemed that he was saddened by his departure. Marshall guessed that no one liked it when one of their peers died. It was too close to home and raised terrible thoughts of mortality.

"So, you think his views killed him," asked Marshall.

"That happened a long time ago," said Bradbury. "He was shot because he was hurting people, his people. You just can't do that. A Supreme Court justice speaks and moves mountains. He was killed because he was killing hope, and that is the only thing that keeps many of us going." Bradbury grew quiet. "Listen to me, I've started making a speech. I should be leaving. You take care, son."

"Good-bye, sir."

Bradbury walked out of the door. If his old friend was right, then Douglas could have been killed by just about anyone. Marshall was hard-pressed to think of any black person who liked him except Nate Williams. But his experience told him this killer didn't engage his occupation on a whim. Whoever killed Douglas had a reason beyond mere hatred.

Marshall checked his watch, then left his office and went into the conference room down the hall. They were all going to watch the tape of the commencement and try to ID the mystery men they'd found.

Marshall joined his newly assembled team and watched the videotape over and over. The FBI had assembled a collection of all the tapes showing the men. So far there seemed to be only two of them. The black man who was shot appeared with a case and walked through the crowd, then he handed it off to a taller man, and that man disappeared.

"How in God's name did he get in with that?" asked Roberta.

"No one knows," said Marshall. "The place where the assassin shot from was covered from the floor, but not above. No one can seem to explain why. The FBI is investigating, but already everyone is running and covering their asses."

Walter Anderson chuckled softly. He was happy to be on the team. Marshall had made the call, but he was still unsure about it. Walter's past substance abuse problems made him a risk, but he'd been on the wagon for a long time. Still, he'd told Walter to be on his game or else.

Nate Williams was in Philadelphia, Douglas's home, attending the funeral. Marshall was clearly in control of the case. It was a little scary, but he was filled with positive energy. This was his opportunity to run with the ball.

"The FBI is coordinating a list of men from the records of the school and the auditorium,'' said Marshall. ''All men who fit the description of the two men on tape will be on it.''

''That cuts it down to about a half million suspects,'' said Roberta Shebbel with a laugh. She was already in her evidence analysis mode.

''Yes, but we'll cut it further when the FBI matches that description to all known subversives and black militants in the area,'' said Marshall. ''Everyone read the updates and report on your assignments to me later today. Nate will be in Philly for the next two days. Bob, anything from Toby?''

Bob Ryder looked as if someone had awakened him. ''No, but I'll be hearing from her today. She's in Philadelphia, too.''

''Okay, people, let's do it—''

Marshall was cut short by a man in the back of the room. As the team dispersed, John Deacons, head of the Capital Crimes Division, walked in the door. Deacons was Marshall's boss and probably felt that he should have gotten the case. Nate had bypassed him, and Deacons had disappeared. The rumor was that he was quitting the department. Deacons was a medium-size man, slightly balding with stark blue eyes. He was a good lawyer, known for his trademark bow tie. Deacons walked over to Marshall, smiling a little.

''John,'' said Marshall. ''How are you?''

''I'm resigning, effective today,'' said Deacons.

Marshall stiffened, knowing that this was just the beginning of Deacons's anger. ''I'm sorry to hear that,'' said Marshall.

''I don't think so,'' said Deacons. ''You're the new golden boy.''

Marshall tried not to flinch at the use of the word *boy*, but he knew he betrayed himself.

''Look, John, I'm sorry for how this all went down, but I have to do my job.''

''I trained you, Marshall,'' said Deacons. His voice was filled with anger. ''This should be my case.''

''Nate made the call,'' said Marshall, knowing what was coming next.

''I know,'' said Deacons. ''Nate, the benevolent father. You two are so tight. And I suffer because I'm not black, and I can't get as close to him as you.''

''You know Nate is not like that. He made a professional call, and that's all there is to it.''

''Is it professional to have your buddy Walter on the team? The man almost drank himself out of this job.''

"Walter's better now, and you know he's a good lawyer. Hell, you've said so yourself many times. Look, I'm sorry you're leaving, and I wish you the best."

Marshall was getting mad and he knew he should leave. He took a step and was surprised when Deacons' arm shot out and stopped him.

"This is bullshit and you know it. If you had any decency, you would have demanded that I be given this case with you as my second. You know this is unfair, but you'd rather step on my corpse than do the right thing."

Marshall moved Deacons's hand from him. "The right thing?" he said incredulously. "How many times have black lawyers been forced into second-string roles when they've deserved the first chair? How many times have you and your friends knowingly favored one another out of friendship and loyalty? This is the way it is, John. The ones with power make the rules, and everyone else gets with the program, but as soon as that power is in the hands of a black man, you want to change the rules."

"If you weren't black, you wouldn't have this case," said Deacons.

"If you weren't white, you wouldn't care," said Marshall.

"Toby wanted him," said Bob Ryder.

Marshall and Deacons turned to see Ryder standing not far from them. Marshall was so angry at Deacons for his assertions, that he'd forgotten that Bob was still in the room.

"Toby called and talked to Nate as soon as Douglas was killed. She gave him a description of the man she wanted. Williams and Toby agreed that it was Marshall."

"So, Toby wanted a black man?" asked Deacons. He seemed shocked at Ryder's statement.

"No, she wanted a *good* man," said Ryder. "Marshall, I'll get on that FBI coordination right away." Ryder left the room.

Deacons turned back to Marshall. He seemed upset and embarrassed. "I—I don't know what to say," said Deacons. "I guess I'm just disappointed for not getting the case. I'm sorry."

"You're a living example of what's wrong with this country," said Marshall.

"I said I was sorry," said Deacons.

"We've worked together for years, yet my conviction means nothing to you. But one word from Bob Ryder, and you're sorry."

"It's not like that," said Deacons. "It had nothing to do with him being white."

"Like hell it didn't." Marshall was pissed. "You've walked around this office, pretending to respect Nate Williams and me, but all this time you've never believed that we earned our positions. People like you, harboring secret prejudice, keep all the decent people in this country apart, suspicious, and distrustful of one another. Well, fuck you and your bullshit attitude, John. The world is moving too fast to care about you and your kind. We've got a job to do."

Deacons looked like a child for a moment. His shoulders slumped, and he looked away from the taller man. Marshall stepped around him and walked out of the room and into the hallway.

He was going back to his office when he heard a commotion behind him and voices yelling his name. He turned to see Agent Sommers, Bob Ryder and several other men running down the hall.

"Marshall!" yelled Bob Ryder. "A man says he's the killer and—"

Ryder was cut off. Several people all started to shout at him all at once. Marshall quieted them down and looked at Bob Ryder.

"Bob, what is it?" asked Marshall.

"A man is outside on the steps of this building with the press, confessing on TV."

Marshall rushed into the crowded conference room. On a TV monitor, Daishaya Mbutu commanded a throng of reporters as he spoke on the steps of the federal building. He stood with two men who held a large flag with two black fists on it. Emblazoned in red underneath were the words: THE BROTHERHOOD. There were about six black men with Mbutu in all. They wore military fatigues and hats wrapped in African kente cloth, a colorful fabric accenting blues, reds, and yellows. There were at least fifteen reporters crowding the area. Security guards could be seen, but they took no action. Several FBI men were already on the scene as well.

Mbutu was an imposing man who commanded attention. His long dreadlocks hung down on his African shirt. His features were sharp and were probably once considered handsome. Now they looked mean, punished by years of anger. His eyes were a deep shade of brown, fired with his emotion.

". . . again I say, I took care of Farrel Douglas!" said Mbutu. "He was a traitor to his people and an enemy of the state. I am a revolutionary in the cause of justice, and I have taken the first step toward freedom for my people."

The reporters yelled questions at Mbutu. He ignored them. Mbutu's men raised the banner high.

"Mr. Mobutu—" said a reporter.

"The name is Em-boo-too," said Mbutu slowly. "Em-boo-too. A name that people will remember for a long time to come."

The men with Mbutu clapped at this statement and admonished the reporter for his ignorance.

"Sorry, sir. Mr. Mbutu, did you kill Farrel Douglas?" asked the same reporter.

"I am here to challenge the FBI, CIA, Justice Department, and all of the powers that be. I am here, and I defy them."

"Who was the man who was shot fleeing the assassination?" asked another reporter.

"He was obviously a man willing to die for what was right," said Mbutu.

"Did you know the man?"

"I know what was in his heart," said Mbutu. "He was filled with anger and passion for his people. I am sure that whatever he did, it did not justify him being killed. That man was executed by a white cop. Another casualty of the war being fought between the races in the god-forsaken country we call America."

The men behind Mbutu clapped loudly and encouraged him to go on.

"There's a black prosecutor on this case," said a small male reporter. "What do you think about that?"

"He should be shot too," said Mbutu. The other men with him laughed loudly.

Marshall watched with detached emotion. All eyes were on him. Mbutu was the leader of the Brotherhood, a local black militant group. He was a brilliant and charismatic man, given to fiery oratory and stinging humor. The Brotherhood was a force in the black community, and Mbutu was a legend. He had impeccable civil rights credentials, and had been a Black Panther and advisor to several national leaders. Whatever he was up to, it was big. He was embarrassing the department, daring them to arrest him.

"Should we pick him up?" asked Sommers. "My men are ready."

"Yes, but let's let him hang himself a little more," said Marshall. "Let's see what else he's got. He hasn't said the magic words. He hasn't said he killed him."

"Right," said Roberta. "All he said was 'I took care of him.' "

"But in reference to Marshall, he said 'He should be shot, too,' " said Walter. "Isn't that an admission that he shot Douglas?"

"No," said Marshall and Roberta together. They both smiled a little.

"Mbutu would need to say something direct about his involvement. Let's just see how stupid he is."

"Well, my men are ready to grab him on a second's notice," said Sommers.

Marshall wondered if it could be true. Mbutu certainly had a reason to kill Douglas. They were opposed on every issue. Marshall remembered what he had read in Toby's materials on assassination. An assassin always killed his victim as a symbol of something else he wanted to destroy. Farrel Douglas was a symbol of conservatism, and worse for Mbutu, black conservatism, which in Mbutu's mind meant a weakening of militarism and an end to his reason to live.

". . . Where's the big, bad government?" asked Mbutu. "I'm here, ready to do battle."

"What proof do you have that you're involved?" asked an Asian reporter. "You won't admit to killing Douglas, but you're here trying to get arrested. Give us all something we can use."

Mbutu smiled at the reporter. "Okay, my Asiatic sister, I will give you all something. I have played this game long enough. Black people are still hostages in the country. We were taken by violence and subjugated by violence. We were forced first to work as slaves, then later to live as subservient citizens, supporting the country's elite. We limp along in America, desperately looking for the humanity in the inhuman ruling classes. We are lost, but I am here to lead us to a new promised land. The only thing that America understands is violence. It is the basis of everything this country has and will have. And only by violence will political and social change come. That is why I took action." Mbutu gestured to one of the men. He reached into a duffel bag and pulled out a long black case. Mbutu opened the case and lifted out a rifle. It was a short black gun with a big scope. "This is my sword."

Mbutu held the weapon high over his head. The FBI men pulled their weapons, training them on Mbutu and his men. The reporters recoiled, moving away from Mbutu. A cameraman tripped and fell. Man and equipment tumbled backward onto the hard ground.

"Justice is mine," said Mbutu.

In the conference room, an audible gasp could be heard. All eyes turned again to Marshall.

He tried to ignore the stares of his team as he thought. He could almost feel the tension and energy coming from Sommers. She was ready to take action. The investigation was dragging along, and for whatever reason, this fool had fallen right into their hands.

"Okay," said Marshall. "Take him down."

13

....

Militant

Marshall faced Mbutu across the table. To no one's surprise, Mbutu had waived counsel. He had been arrested right in front of the Federal Building and had not put up a fight. Marshall was playing into his hands, but once he saw the rifle, he could no longer let Mbutu command the spotlight.

Mbutu was a handsome man beneath his ragged dreadlocks. He was about sixty and looked a little tired. This was understandable. He had just half-confessed to murder, and given them the probable murder weapon.

Marshall was in the room alone with the suspect. The interrogation room was small, sparse, and claustrophobic. One wall was dominated by a mirror where the litigation team watched in the adjacent room.

By now every major news group in the country was running the story. Nate Williams and Toby had both called from Philadelphia and were updated. Each of them expressed their desire to either prove Mbutu was the shooter or eliminate him as a suspect as soon as possible.

The news organizations had learned that the mystery man who was killed was not the shooter. Marshall was angry about the leak, but knew it was only a matter of time before it would have gotten out anyway.

Mbutu had refused to talk to any FBI men. He wanted Marshall. Mbutu was known to be an expert on the law even though he had never gone to law school. Marshall could see that Mbutu wanted to match wits with him. And the prospect angered and excited him at the same time.

"Quite a show," said Marshall. "I knew you were given to theatrics, but I never thought I'd see you do something like this."

"I had to," said Mbutu. "It was only a matter of time before you'd come looking for me or someone in my organization. I know how to play the media as well as the next person."

"Better, I'd guess," said Marshall. "So, who was the man we shot?"

"Come on, Counselor, you don't think it's gonna be that easy, do you?"

"Why not?" asked Marshall. "You came here voluntarily, trying to embarrass us."

"And I succeeded."

"Maybe, but still we have you here in custody. You haven't demanded a lawyer. So, why play games? Tell me the man's identity."

"Sorry, you know that if I know him and he can be linked to the killing, then so can I. Find out the best way you can."

"That little rifle you had, it's called a Wagner .308WIN. They make them in Germany. It's very expensive and illegal. Where did you get it?"

"At Wal-Mart. They had a sale." Mbutu laughed.

"Okay, then how about this one. Did you kill Farrel Douglas?"

"He killed himself," said Mbutu. "With his traitorous political agenda and disdain for his own people."

"So, you killed him because of his legal opinions as a judge?"

"He died because he was a threat to black people. America has tried everything to stamp us out of existence. Douglas was just the latest invention."

"You haven't answered my question," said Marshall. "Did you do it?"

"You're testing the gun I had. Let science make that determination."

"Why the game? Either you did or you didn't. If that gun matches, do you know what will happen to you?" Mbutu had no way of knowing that they couldn't match slugs from the gun. Marshall was trying to scare the truth out of him.

"I know. The attorney general made it clear that she will seek the death penalty, even though Michigan doesn't have one."

"This is a federal crime," said Marshall. "The federal statute allows capital punishment."

"Hmm," said Mbutu. "I need to brush up on my law."

"I know you, Mbutu," said Marshall. "You never do anything without a reason. What do you hope to do by this? Media coverage, a platform for your views? Your organization is still powerful, but recently, you are less and less relevant to the people.''

''I am as relevant as ever.''

''No, you're not. We know your organization has been losing membership. As the black middle class grows, more and more of them and their children move away from your kind of radical views and toward more conventional forms of protest.''

''They are lost black people who've forgotten their tradition and heritage. I will reeducate them.''

''Even the downtrodden brothers are leaving you. Many of them embrace Islam and other religions as a way of dealing with their problems. Old, broken-down militants are a thing of the past.''

''The people need to be led!'' Mbutu slammed a fist into the table. ''They don't know what's good for them. The white man's plan has always been to separate and disable us psychologically. I will change all that.''

''Your day is over. Admit it!''

''My day is just beginning. That's why I—'' Mbutu stopped, collecting himself. He smiled at Marshall, shaking a finger at him. ''I see you're smarter than I thought, Counselor. Yes, my efforts have been appreciated less by our people, but when they see what I have done, they will know that my way is the only way.''

''Are you trying to start a race riot or something?''

''I'm starting a race *revolution*,'' said Mbutu with a smile. ''There's a difference. I don't necessarily want violence. But I do want change.''

''So you want black people to kill anyone who is opposed to what they want?''

''White America does it. Lincoln destroyed the South and bang, he caught one. Kennedy wanted to change society, and stop Vietnam—bang. Dr. King, Malcolm X, Robert Kennedy, bang, bang bang! This is our country, brother. This nation was built on the bones of millions of Native Americans and black slaves. Genocide as social progress. Who's the real assassin here, me or your bosses?''

Mbutu's words cut deep. Marshall could not divorce himself from the truth in his words. Undeniably, there was violence in America's birth, a violence that had shaped society and changed the course of human history. And one man's patriotism was another man's bloodbath. But reasonable men understood that this was a matter of humanity, not politics, race, or philosophy. Men were violent, and no one race had a monopoly on that savagery.

"Your soapbox is old, Mbutu," said Marshall. "Our people are past believing that our problems are some kind of personal hate crime. We are all part of this country, good and bad. I'm the good; the question today is, what are you?"

"I'm your conscience," said Mbutu.

Marshall had made a mistake. Mbutu battled with words and ideology, and he'd moved Marshall onto his turf. If this interview was to yield anything, then he would have to get back to the business of lawyering. Mbutu was an intelligent man, but his rage and his love of black people were his weaknesses.

"Okay, I will agree with that," said Marshall. "You believe a lot of things that many of us have abandoned, perhaps against our better interest. But someone killed a black man, a man who had risen to the top of his profession, a man who marched with Dr. King and served on the board of the NAACP. Whatever else he may have been, he was one of us, and now he's gone."

"He was a traitor!" yelled Mbutu. "He used black people to get those jobs, hid amongst us until he saw his chance to cross over and use his knowledge to help hold his people down."

"Even if that is true, he didn't deserve to die."

"Oh yes, he did. I was not going to let him live another moment as a symbol of our failure." Mbutu trailed off. He knew he had said too much. His eyes were wide and angry, then he smiled. "You are my brother, Counselor, and yet you seek to crucify me with my own righteous anger. I will no longer talk to you. Either charge me, or release me from this prison."

"You can count on being charged," said Marshall, rising from the table. "And don't ever use the word *crucify* in reference to yourself. You are not Jesus. You are a murderer with a big-ass mouth."

Marshall ignored Mbutu's cynical laughter from behind him. He walked out of the room and joined his team, who had been watching behind the mirror.

"Clever man," said Roberta. She wiped her glasses.

"He didn't cop to anything," said Ryder, "but he's in this somehow. I can feel it."

''Mbutu has always been a showman,'' said Marshall. ''His method has been to embarrass the establishment and add followers to his cause. Up to this point, murder has not been his thing.''

''But you said it yourself, Marsh, his day is over,'' said Walter. ''Something like this could bring back his organization.''

''Maybe,'' said Marshall. ''Let's wait him out. The gun will let us know what game he's playing.''

''But we can't match it,'' said Ryder

''We live in the age of technology,'' said Marshall. ''We're going to put the slugs back together and see if we can match them to that rifle.''

''Jesus, can that be done?'' asked Walter almost to himself.

''We're going to try,'' said Marshall. ''And if we get any kind of match to that weapon Mbutu had, we'll hang him.''

14

Hustler's Hustle

Moses rubbed his bruised ribs and tried to breathe steadily. The wound to his shoulder was bad enough, but each breath stretched the bruised muscle around his rib cage and brought even more pain. The cops had worked him over pretty good. He'd been apprehended inside the house and arrested. He had screamed abuse, but the judge was buying the resistance theory promoted by the police. Moses had fired shots at the cops, so it was all justified in the mind of the court.

He'd been arraigned and entered a not-guilty plea. The judge had set a high bail, a half million dollars cash, based on his prior record and the shots fired at the officers. He could raise the money, but it would take time. Dake and Nita had not been taken down with him, but they were nowhere to be found. Only those two could get to the money. Moses wondered if the cops had killed them and disposed of the bodies. But that didn't make any sense. Why would the cops have spared him?

He heard a guard coming. He listened to the catcalls and professions of innocence of the other prisoners. Then the guard, a man named Dean, stopped at his cell.

"Your lawyer's here," said Dean. "You got a half hour."

Moses was taken to the meeting area. His lawyer, Ted Walker, stood with a grim look on his face. The guard left them, and they sat at a wooden table.

"How are you?" asked Walker.

"Fuck the small talk," said Moses. "What you got?"

"The reason why you're in here," said Walker. "I've talked with the prosecutor, and he says that the cops were called and that's why you got caught."

"I know that, muthafucka," said Moses. "I fucked up the alarm, and the signal went on when we opened the door."

"No," said Walker. "They were called from a phone. A cell phone."

Moses was shocked into silence. He remembered hearing the distant electronic beep while robbing the house. The kind a cell phone would make.

"Dake and Nita," he said in a whisper.

"Yes," said Walker. "I don't have the cell phone number, but I'd bet it was a number stolen by your people."

Moses was silent. He understood the gravity of his situation. Dake and Nita had set him up on the Grosse Pointe job. They had called the cops and then left him to be apprehended. They knew the response time in the affluent neighborhood was less than ten minutes. He'd told them that fact himself.

Dake was Nita's lover, and the fact that Moses had been her boyfriend first had not mattered to Dake. But apparently, they both had reasons to want him out of the way. If they had killed him, the crew would rebel and take them down. This way, he was dead cleanly. He knew that he had to watch his back in prison now. County was a place where a hit could be purchased cheaply. Even now, dressed in the orange jumpsuit and chains, he could not believe it. His two right-hand men had betrayed him.

"Get me out of here," said Moses.

"That's going to be hard," said Walker. "I'll need money."

"Get the bail reduced," said Moses.

"I can't," said Walker. "Didn't you recognize that judge? She's the one from your last case. The court has a system now that keeps putting you back with the same judge. She is not about to reduce your bail after convicting you before. You got a weapons charge, burglary, assault on an officer, and attempted murder."

"You just do what you can," said Moses. "I'll work on my end."

"Look, you have a retainer, but it will run out soon."

"Don't you talk to me about money, nigga!" said Moses. "I paid for your damned house and your bitch's condo. Don't fuck with me. Just do what I tell you. I'll get the money."

Walker was silent. He stood up and collected his briefcase. "I'll do what I can," he said.

Walker left the area, and Moses felt there was a good chance that he'd never see the lawyer again.

Dake and Nita were smart. They had planned this thing good, and he had never seen it coming. Moses was in jail, and under the crew's rules, he couldn't deal his way out by turning on anyone, even the people who had betrayed him. Moses would bet anything that Dake and Nita had found his stash of money and taken that too.

But if they thought he would die here in county jail, or go quietly to prison, they were mistaken. They were hustlers of the highest order, but he was a hustler's hustler. And he had more tricks up his sleeve than even they knew.

Moses got up and went back to the door leading to the cells. Dean, the guard, came to him and pointed him toward the back. Moses smiled as the guard approached him.

"Something funny?" asked Dean.

"Yeah, something's funny as hell," said Moses. "I need to make a phone call."

"Why? You just saw your lawyer."

"I need to call another lawyer. I want to place a call to the U.S. attorney. He's my brother."

15

The Message

"Fuck you, you punk-ass cop!" yelled the black man to Danny Cavanaugh. "That's right, white boy, I'm talkin' to you!"

"Sir, please, step back and let me do my job," said Danny calmly. His fist was clenched, and his jaw tight as he faced off with the black man.

"Your job? Suck my dick! Fuck you and your bitch-ass job! You ain't nothing but an overpaid rent-a-cop, come in here tryin' to push a nigga around. Kiss all of my natural black ass!"

The man raised a hand as if to hit Danny. Danny stepped back and raised his nightstick.

"Sir, if you don't cease from the aggressive behavior and abusive language, I'll have to take action," said Danny.

"Action? Go on muthafucka, take action on me! I'm ready. See, I know the law, you can't do shit to me as long as I don't do nothing. I'll sue this city's ass right off and I'll have your job, you badge-wearin' faggot!"

Danny took a step toward the man to show that he meant business. "Sir, this is the last time. Move out of the area and let the officers do their job. You are impeding an investigation, and I'll have to lawfully remove you, if you don't stop the—"

The man lunged at Danny. Danny easily evaded him and caught him in a headlock with one arm. With his free hand, he brought the nightstick down toward his head and pulled it back just before it hit.

"Great," said a thin white man in a police officer's uniform. "You can let him go now."

Danny released the black man, who smiled at him and shook his hand.

"You move fast for a big guy," said the black man.

"Thanks," said Danny. "You cuss good for a cop."

"Shit, I heard worse than that," said the black cop.

Danny's antiaggression training was in its second day. The course was taught out of Wayne State University in conjunction with the city and the police department. Danny hated doing the course, but if he hoped to get a detective's shield he had to erase the numerous cases of abuse on his record.

"How'd I do, Felton?" asked Danny.

"Fine," said Felton Mills, a thin white cop who ran the program. "Sit back down over there."

Danny went to sit with the other five men and two women in the class. He knew most of them, hotheads all. One, a black cop named Leary, had even been accused of murder, but it was never proven. That incident had cost him three months' salary, his wife, and any hope of ever being a high-ranking officer. All of the attendees looked sad and angry. In the age of political correctness, a cop who used force was always opening himself up for possible suspension, or worse, jail.

Danny knew how they felt. In the field, when things got hot, he saw red, and the next thing he knew, he'd be beating some guy over the head. It was such a cliché, Irish hothead, but he'd inherited it from his father, who had worked back in the day when you'd get suspended if you didn't kick some ass every day.

"Of course if that had been a real confrontation, you wouldn't have gotten to me that easily," said the black cop who'd just done the demonstration with Danny.

Danny turned back to the man. "If that had been a real situation, no one could call me off you, Larry."

"Shoot, I woulda tossed your ass a country mile," said Larry. He laughed with derision.

"I don't think so," said Danny, continuing to his seat. "Your skinny little legs would have broken under the weight."

The others in the class laughed loudly. Danny took his seat and was surprised to see Larry coming at him.

"You tryin' to embarrass me?" said Larry.

Suddenly, the officers stopped laughing. The room was quiet.

"What?" said Danny.

"This class is serious," said Larry. "You're here because it's easy beating up on niggas from behind a badge, but try one who ain't afraid of your ass."

"You need to shut up," said Danny.

"No, I don't," said Larry. "Tryin' to embarrass me up in here. I know all about you, Danny Two Gun," he said the name with contempt. "Grew up in the 'hood, and so you think you black, but you ain't. You a damned fool."

Danny shot up out of the chair, knocking it over. He took a step toward Larry, only to be stopped by Felton.

"Anger, Officer Cavanaugh, is more than what you face in the field. It's what's in you each day of the year. If you don't learn to control and channel your anger in all phases of life, you'll never be an effective police officer." Then, to Larry, he said: "Good work, Officer Saunders."

It took Danny a second to realize what had just happened. Larry had provoked him as part of a test. Felton wanted to see if he could control his temper if the insults seemed to come from a real situation. He had failed. Danny went back to his seat, feeling embarrassed. Larry smiled and placed a hand on his shoulder.

"Don't feel bad, man," he said. "Everybody fails that test. I did."

The rest of the class moved quickly for Danny. He left the building at nine, and walked back to his car. From there he drove home to his house on Forrer on Detroit's northwest side. It was a nice little neighborhood that was home to many police officers. He pulled his old Mustang into the driveway and went inside.

The house was modest and clean. The furniture was cheap, but tasteful. Pictures of his father and family hung on the walls. A patrolman's hat sat on a small lamp on an end table. Danny never thought that he'd ever actually own a house. It wasn't his style, and after his divorce, he was tapped out. Property values in the city were rising, thanks to the mayor's new economic plan and the prospect of casino gambling. Thank God for the credit union, he thought.

" 'Bout time," said a woman's voice from another room.

Danny walked into the kitchen, where his partner, Vinny, was warming up a plate of food in the microwave.

"I almost went to sleep on your ass," she said.

"I just would have woke you up," said Danny. He went to her and kissed her lightly on the forehead.

Venice hit a button on the microwave, and the machine hummed to life.

Venice Shaw was what people used to call a "handsome" woman. She was not a classic beauty but possessed enough good looks to turn a head or two. She was tall, about five nine, and had dark hair done in tiny dreadlocks. She was a bit of a tomboy, and carried herself without much grace. But she had a fabulous body. A workout fanatic, she lifted weights and ran three miles a day. Even in a uniform, you could see her attributes, and now, dressed in a big shirt and nothing else, Danny could see it. She was beautiful. More important, he had finally found a woman who understood the job, because she was part of it.

The department frowned upon partners dating. It wasn't a secret that they were lovers, but they didn't publicize it. Aside from being a good lover and a friend, Venice was a hell of a cop. On the job, she was all business, and he'd go through any door, knowing she had his back.

"That my dinner, Vinny?" asked Danny.

"Yeah," said Vinny.

"Did you eat without me?"

"I skipped dinner. I'm not feeling too well," she said.

"You sick? Maybe we should see a doctor about that."

"No, I'm okay. Just been running too hard, that's all. So, how was it, the class?"

"Painful, but I'm gonna stick it out. I gotta make it work this time."

Vinny reached across the table and took his hand. "I don't want you to put your whole life on some stupid-ass class," she said. "You're a good cop. You just need to learn when to pull back."

"You're just saying that 'cause you want me to have sex with you," said Danny.

"I don't need to be nice to get into your pants," she said. "You're easy." Vinny stood and opened her shirt a little. Her breasts were small, but perfect. Danny could feel his pants tighten. He reached out and pulled her to him. Vinny straddled him. Kissed his neck. Danny was always amazed by her. At work, Vinny was a hard-ass cop who cursed, drank, and would shoot a perp before he could sneeze. At home she was a soft, loving woman who just wanted peace and calmness. He envied her strength and control. He dragged the street home with him every night. Somehow, Vinny commanded the dirt to stay out of her private life.

Vinny took off Danny's shirt as the microwave bell sounded. She got up and took out the plate, bringing it back to Danny. She took off her shirt, standing before him naked.

"What are you doing?" asked Danny

Vinny didn't say anything. She put the food down on the table, and then pulled down Danny's pants. Soon, he was inside her, and they were making love. The chair creaked as their rhythm moved it. Vinny then took the plate and began to spoon food into Danny's mouth.

"Which one is better?" she asked into his ear.

"More food," he said. She hit him playfully.

The phone rang, and Danny's head turned. Vinny missed with the spoon and the mashed potatoes smeared on his cheek. She licked it off. The phone rang again and he heard the machine pick it up. The voice of the caller was lost in the moans of the couple as Danny continued to make love and eat his dinner.

Vinny's back straightened, and she gripped Danny's shoulders tightly. Soon after, Danny was yelling, and holding Vinny close to him, kissing her all over.

Later, they sat and watched TV together. Vinny was in a robe, reading a criminal procedure book. Danny watched a rerun of *Cheers*.

"You really into that shit, huh?"

"I want to be a lawyer one day," said Vinny. "Can't run the street forever."

"I lose more friends to law school," said Danny.

"Speaking of Marshall, I heard on the news that he has a suspect in the Douglas assassination."

"Who?" said Danny, suddenly uninterested in TV.

"Mbutu. He stood in front of the Federal Building and all but confessed to it."

"No shit," said Danny. "That fuckin' Mbutu ain't nothing but trouble, anyway. Still pushin' that tired-ass, black power shit, gettin' all them poor people excited, then taking their money *and* their hope. I hope Marsh hangs his black ass."

Vinny laughed.

"What?" asked Danny.

"You sound just like my Uncle Charles."

"I come by it naturally, woman. Paid my dues in the 'hood, you know."

"You won't let me forget."

The difference in their races had never been a problem for them. Vinny sort of looked at Danny as a black man who didn't have black skin. And that's how he handled himself. Some black officers didn't like it. They thought that Danny was mocking them.

Blacks were funny about race. It was a burden, but also a prize. The manner, the cadence of voice, the undefinable quality of black brotherhood, was a treasure not to be shared by those who didn't carry the burden of it as well.

Danny ignored those who disliked him for what he was. His history was all he had, and it just happened to be in an all-black neighborhood. It was his birthright, and he was not about to disown it.

Danny noticed the answering machine light flashing. "Let's see who called during my dinner," he said, smiling at Vinny. He walked over to it and pushed the button.

"Hello . . . ," said a man's voice.

Marshall, Danny thought. Probably calling him to talk about the case.

". . . bet you never thought you'd hear my voice again. It's Moses Jackson."

"I'll be fucked," said Danny. "Vinny! Come here." Danny stopped the message.

Vinny got up and walked across the room. "What? Something wrong?"

"Remember I told you Marshall had a twin brother, a lowlife?"

"Yeah," said Vinny. "I always found that hard to believe, as straight as Marshall is."

"Well, this is him on the machine."

Danny hit the button on the machine again.

"Hello, bet you never thought you'd hear my voice again. It's Moses Jackson. Marshall's long-lost twin brother. You're probably wondering why I'm calling you. Well, my brother won't return my calls. I had to call in a few favors, but I got your number from some nice men here at the county jail. Anyway, Marshall is too large for his poor relations these days. I've been trying to talk to him, and let him know that I have the key to that case he's prosecuting. I will only tell it to him. I know you and him are tight and all—"

In the background a voice said, "Time's up."

To the voice Moses said, "All right, dammit. I'm almost done." Then into the phone: "Tell Marshall that if he wants to solve this case, to come and get me. Get me out of this fuckin' jail. He can call me here."

The message ended.

Danny looked at Vinny, then walked by her.

"Do you think he's for real?"

"I don't know," said Danny. "But I'll find out."

Danny picked up the phone and called the county jail. Moses was bad news. Danny remembered how Moses had teased him and fought with him when they were younger. Moses had always been jealous of his friendship with Marshall. He'd run across his crew a few times, but he'd never caught the man himself. But apparently, someone else had and put him in the joint. Good, Danny thought to himself. That's where he belonged.

He remembered that Moses was a very smart man whose only purpose in life seemed to be to do wrong. It was funny how memories distilled themselves into neat little explanations of character and event. When he thought of Marshall he thought of friendship and good times; when he thought of Moses, he felt resentment, anger, and trouble.

"This is Officer Danny Cavanaugh," Danny said into the receiver. "I need to talk to a prisoner . . ."

Moses Jackson walked into the conference room in leg irons. He had a smile on his face. Danny was sitting at a small wooden table, waiting for him. Danny looked angry as he watched the ghost from his past come closer. He could see Marshall's face in his fraternal twin's. It was creepy, yet fascinating.

"Excuse me if I don't shake hands," said Moses.

"Right where I knew you'd always be," said Danny. "I only wish I coulda been the one to take your monkey ass down."

Moses sat on a creaky wooden chair. "Way I hear it on the street, you'd rather kill a nigga than take him in."

"Depends on the nigga," said Danny. "I'd give you a fifty-fifty chance of making it to prison."

Moses laughed, and Danny felt as though he were a kid again and Moses was about to lash out and strike him.

"Been a long time, little Danny," said Moses.

"Not so little anymore."

"I know. Big bad-ass marine and shit. I guess I'd have a rough time kicking your ass now, huh?"

"You wouldn't even come close."

"Damn. You still sound just like a brother. All them years in the 'hood just won't fall off your ass, huh? So, you still fucking black women, or did you grow up and come to your senses?"

Danny started to get up, then kept still. His hands shook a little. He remembered his classes. He waited and let the heat subside.

"You'd better watch your mouth. People get hurt in jail easy."

Moses laughed again. "So, how's my brother?"

"Cut the shit, muthafucka. I'm only here to find out if you're telling the truth, then I'm out."

"Damn, you sound all mad. You still got a short fuse on you, huh?"

"You ain't never gonna change, are you?" said Danny. "You still try to play everybody you come into contact with. Still trying to put one over on people, even if it don't make a difference if you do. Well, you know what, you can just cancel all that noise with me. I've heard it before."

"You don't know me anymore," said Moses. "So, don't presume shit about what I do." Moses was angry now, and that made Danny happy.

"Who's got the short fuse now?" Danny asked. Then he laughed at him. "So, go on, spill it, then you can go back to your cell, put a cork in your asshole, and go to sleep."

Moses was pissed off again, but he tried to cover. "All right," said Moses. "My brother has the wrong man. Mbutu didn't kill nobody."

"What proof do you have?"

"If I told you that, I'd never get out of here, now would I? No, I'll only talk to my brother, but I will tell you this. I know they won't find a slug in the body—just pieces."

Danny searched Moses' face. After years of training, he could tell most of the time when a scumbag like this was lying. He looked deep into the man across from him, and saw only calmness and determination, the foundation of truth. And if it was indeed the truth, he had an obligation as Marshall's friend to tell him. It was always difficult to cut a deal with a person like Moses. Trading a little bad for a lot of good was ultimately pleasing, but while you were in the middle of it, you felt like dirt.

"Okay," said Danny. "I'll bring Marshall the message, but if this is some kind of bullshit, you'll be sorry you ever laid eyes on me."

"I can live with that," said Moses as he got up.

"Livin' with it won't be the problem," said Danny. Then he walked out, leaving Moses behind him.

16

Faceless Men

Marshall entered the office and immediately knew something was wrong. The office was his second home. And like a home, he knew when a picture was askew, a pillow in the wrong place, or when someone had been sleeping in his bed. The office was quieter than normal, static, as if everyone was under surveillance.

Jessica walked up to Marshall. She was dressed in a little business suit and heels. Her cotton blouse was opened to her cleavage, and she smiled flirtatiously as usual.

"Mr. Williams wants to see you," she said.

"I thought he was out," said Marshall.

"He was. He got in late last night. He's in with some men." Then she leaned into him and said: "I think they're from the CIA."

"CIA?" Marshall whispered to no one in particular. That explained the strangeness in the office. No one liked it when they came around. The FBI guys were bad enough with their boxy suits, and stoic manner, but the CIA was worse. They didn't act superior, they acted omnipotent, like you had to do whatever they wanted, or they would tell you who shot Kennedy, then execute you.

Marshall called them Faceless Men, people who were so bland and imperturbable that you felt that even their faces might not be real.

"Thanks, Jessica," said Marshall, and walked to Nate's office.

Marshall entered to find Nate talking with the two operatives. One was a pale, thin man, with very black hair. The other was tall and muscular, and had one of those five o'clock shadows that never went away.

"Nate, you wanted to see me?" said Marshall.

"Yes," said Nate, who, unlike everyone else, looked very comfortable around the two men. "These are Agents Van Ness and Easter from Langley."

"Hiya doin'?" said Van Ness. He was the pale man. He grabbed Marshall's hand and pumped it. "Art Van Ness."

Marshall was shocked at the move. He almost took a step back. CIA agents were never so openly emotional. Easter was big, silent, and expressionless. He was the normal Faceless Man.

"They're going to be following the Douglas assassination," said Williams. "Toby and I have sanctioned their involvement."

"We're coordinating with Agent Sommers and her people," said Van Ness. "We'll confer with you from time to time, if you don't mind."

"Why is the CIA interested in this?" asked Marshall. He knew why but wanted to see what the agents would say about their proposed involvement.

"The agency, of course, is interested in the national security implications of this," said Van Ness. "So, if you have any trouble with anyone, we'll have them killed." Van Ness laughed. Nate joined him. Easter snorted quietly.

A sense of humor? thought Marshall. He didn't know if he should feel better about Van Ness's humanity, or be terrified by it. What was he covering behind that good ol' boy act? Marshall decided to find out.

"National security?" said Marshall. "So, are you working with the NSA?" asked Marshall.

Van Ness bristled a little. To a CIA agent, the National Security Agency was at most a PR department with a small, specific purpose. The CIA was generally interested in everything, and they didn't like it when someone assumed they had any limitation.

Van Ness's eyebrows fell over his blue eyes at Marshall's statement. Then they rose swiftly, covering his emotion. It happened in the time it took you to blink twice.

"Nope, we're flying solo," said Van Ness, smiling. "The NSA's duties cover a broader range of security issues. We're concerned about the domestic implications of this."

"I see," said Marshall. Van Ness's answer was perfect fed-speak. Compliment the other lesser agency, then reassert your authority. "Well, I'll help in any way I can," said Marshall. "I can give you my files if you—"

"We have them already," said Van Ness. Easter had what should have been a smile on his face. On him, it was a slightly upturned line.

"I gave the files to them," said Nate Williams. "I wanted to save time."

Now Marshall bristled. What would possess Nate to commit this kind of betrayal?

"Fine," said Marshall. "I'm checking the ballistics report today. Or do you gentlemen already have that data too?" He saw Nate frown at his sarcasm.

"Hell, I wouldn't be surprised," said Van Ness, laughing. "No, I'm kidding, we'd like to see it as soon as you get it."

"Okay," said Marshall. "Nate, after we get the ballistics report, I'll be back to you for a decision to indict."

"We need it fast," said Nate. "We can't hold the suspect much longer. So far he hasn't objected. It's as if he wants to stay in lockup, but sooner or later we'll need to shit or get off the pot."

"Noted," said Marshall. "Fellas, I guess I'll be talking to you down the road."

"Absolutely," said Van Ness. "It was nice to have met you."

Marshall took this to mean that the meeting was over, even though he didn't say he was leaving. Nate gave Marshall his "I've got private things to talk about" look. Marshall didn't like to be dismissed, and he certainly didn't like this happy-ass CIA agent, either.

He left Nate's office and walked quickly into his own office to find Serrus Kranet and Bob Ryder waiting. Roberta Shebbel and Walter Anderson sat in a corner silently. Roberta scribbled on a large legal pad. Ryder was looking at his watch.

"Late," said Ryder. "Not like you."

"I was dragged into a meeting with Nate and some CIA agents."

"My God," said Serrus.

"What do they want?" asked Roberta.

"To meddle and steal glory like always," said Walter.

"This is a shock," said Ryder. "I wonder if Toby knows about this. I should call her—"

"She knows," said Marshall. "Nate told me."

"Then why wouldn't she tell me?" said Ryder. He looked like a hurt child.

"Look, there's nothing we can do about it," said Marshall. "Let's get to work and let the CIA chase their shadows. So, Serrus, whatcha got for me?"

"Well, as you know, the rifling of a gun is distinctive and individual to a weapon, and as an identification system is better than fingerprints," said Serrus.

"Our case is filled with circumstantial evidence," said Marshall. "We might be able to put Mbutu at the murder scene, and lord knows he has motive. But the bullets and the gun will give us the hard evidence we need to lock down this case."

"Unfortunately it will not be that simple," said Serrus.

"Why isn't it simple?" asked Ryder. "I thought the gun matched the caliber of slug and—"

"But as you know, we've been having trouble with the bullets that killed Douglas. They fragmented, and as such, we cannot perfectly match them to Mr. Mbutu's weapon by the rifling marks on them."

"Right, but how accurate can we get?" asked Marshall.

"Even when reassembled, the fragmented bullets that killed Douglas can be matched only with a fifty-five percent certainty," said Serrus.

"Shit, is that all?" said Ryder.

Marshall smiled a little. Ryder didn't seem like the type to curse. He sounded like a ticked-off kid.

"What about the other bullet, the one in the stage?" asked Marshall.

"I have good news on that. It's not as bad as we first thought. That one matches Mr. Mbutu's gun. It's damaged, but the match is closer. I'd say eighty percent. It will give a defense counsel, excuse the pun, ammunition, but it'll hold up."

"That's something," said Marshall. "We got our foot in the door then. If we can prove that Mbutu shot any of the slugs found, then the others can be linked to him, fragmented or not."

"The only good slug is imbedded in the second victim," said Serrus. "It's lodged next to his spinal column. If we go in, he'll in all likelihood end up paralyzed."

Marshall looked at Roberta, who was about to burst from the need to speak. "You want to say something, Roberta?"

"Yes," she said a little too loudly. "Notwithstanding the hair we found, the ballistics are the heart of our case, as you said. Juries normally hold on to scientific evidence like the gospel. The bullet in the stage should hang him. The defense will try to keep it out, but they'll fail, then they'll try to discredit it. That's where you come in, Mr. Kranet. If you hold up, so does our case.''

"Yes, I really need that pressure," Serrus said, laughing.

"But why did the Douglas bullets fragment, and not the one in Judge Miller, and the stage?'' asked Walter.

"That's a good and troubling question," said Marshall. "Doctor?"

"Well, bullet fragmentation can arise from many sources, speed, angle, impact. There are a hundred reasons.''

"A hundred anything sounds like reasonable doubt to me," Bob Ryder said. "We have to do better than that."

"So, as to Douglas," said Marshall, "the defense can't prove that the bullets didn't come from Mbutu's rifle, but unfortunately, the government has the burden of proof.''

"Which means there's a good chance that we are going to get fucked on national TV," said Ryder.

"Calm down," said Marshall. Ryder was unusually upset. He seemed pissed off that Toby called in the Faceless Men without telling him. "Will the variation on the bullet that landed in the stage cause us a problem in court?'' asked Marshall.

"From my experience, no," said Serrus. "The defense will attack it, but the results should be good evidence.''

"Then we got him," said Ryder.

"It would seem," said Marshall. "But the real question is why would Mbutu come here and surrender the murder weapon like this?''

"He's arrogant," said Ryder. "All of the other evidence points to him. We can find people who put him at the commencement, and he fits the general description of the men in the tape. I say let's arrest him for the murder right now.''

"It seems like a solid case," added Walter.

"But we don't have any of his blood and hair samples to match the one we found in the crawl space," said Marshall. "If Mbutu's hair doesn't match, we will have started the case for nothing.''

"And Mbutu won't give us the samples unless we indict him," said Ryder.

"Most cases are built on circumstantial evidence," said Roberta. "We've already got more than most cases I've been on.''

"And if it gets out that we had this much and didn't indict," said Walter, "everyone will think we're hiding something.''

"Yes," said Marshall. "And that heat would be coming not only from the people and the media, but from Washington as well."

Marshall thought a moment. He knew that as a prosecutor the power to decide who was to be prosecuted was an awesome one. Once the scrutiny of the government was upon you, there was a taint that went with it that even the constitutional presumption of innocence could not countermand. But his gut told him that Mbutu was dirty.

"Okay," said Marshall. "I'm going to Nate and Toby with a recommendation to indict Mbutu for the murder."

Marshall rose early the next day. Mbutu's picture was once again on the front page of both Detroit papers. His image had even pushed down a story out of D.C. about lobbyists picketing the Supreme Court because of inaction on important issues. Douglas's death had completely shut down the court.

Marshall quickly left his house for the office. Toby was flying into town for a news conference, and he didn't want to be late. He also didn't want to talk with Chemin. A confrontation would have him screwed up the whole morning.

On the drive to work, the cold January morning was fierce. The wind whipped snowbanks across the pavement as he drove on the Lodge freeway into downtown.

The lobby of the Federal Building was a madhouse as Toby, Nate Williams, Marshall, and Bob Ryder stood at a podium.

Marshall was nervous. Media work was not his thing. Ryder smiled. This was what his boss wanted, and he was happy to give it to her.

"At nine-thirty last night, we arrested Daishaya Ali Mbutu, also known as Deion Wilson, for the murder of Farrel Douglas, and the attempted murder of Wendel Miller. Many of you saw Mr. Mbutu incriminate himself right outside this very building. He turned over an automatic rifle which we will prove is the murder weapon."

The questions came flying at Toby.

"Do you know the identity of the man who was shot the day of the assassination?" asked a CNN reporter.

"I will answer that," said Toby.

Marshall looked shocked. As far as he knew, the man remained a mystery. He glanced as Nate, who waited calmly for Toby to speak.

"The man's name is Anthony Collier. He was born in Florida and is a known subversive."

"What was his connection to the killing?"

"I can't answer that question," said Toby. "That's all we can say for now." She pointed to another journalist and went on.

Toby answered the rest of the questions with finesse and political savvy, not giving up too much, and always couching her answers as though she was shielding some greater truth. In the end, the press didn't get much more than she had already told them.

Marshall followed Toby and Nate Williams back upstairs. The usual calmness of the courthouse was gone. The reception area was filled with pure energy. The press, staffers, security, and civilians lined the room, talking. If he had any doubt that this case was different, it was gone. Only a truly singular event could turn the normally staid federal building into a den of chatter. They moved to an elevator bank. Toby pushed the elevator button and waited for the car.

"Fucking newspapers," said Toby. "We should repeal the goddamned First Amendment."

Nate Williams laughed. "Then who would print the tabloids, Toby?"

"Okay, Mr. Jackson," said Toby. "The answer to the question you're not asking me is: we just found out about the mystery man a few days ago. The CIA got the lowdown on him. Someone, probably your Mr. Mbutu and company, worked hard to erase all traces of Mr. Collier. But he had a juvenile record in Florida that was never expunged. That's how we got him."

"Can we link him to Mbutu?"

"You tell me," said Toby. "That's your job. We'll get this guy's entire life. You find the connection."

"So, why wasn't I told?" asked Marshall. He didn't try to hide the upset nature of his voice.

"Everyone is all over this case," said Toby. "There have been leaks, and I wanted to be the one to give out the facts."

"Okay," said Marshall. "How about telling me why the CIA is all over my investigation."

There was silence at this statement. Nate looked at Marshall with mild anger. He didn't believe it was ever proper to question authority.

"It's quite normal procedure," said Toby. "So, what's your problem?"

"I'm concerned that the defense could use it to their advantage," said Marshall. "They might say the CIA is here because there's more to the case than meets the eye."

"A good point," said Toby. "I'll tell them to keep a low profile. Right now, we need to think about the defense team. I have no idea who's gonna catch this one."

"Mbutu hates lawyers," said Marshall, "but I know all the national sharks will want this case."

"It'll be Gerald Price out of Chicago," said Ryder. "They served time together in '69."

"Price is a Republican now," said Marshall. "Mbutu thinks he's a sellout."

"I put my money on Cochran," said Williams. "He's the best trial lawyer right now."

"Jesus, I hope not," said Toby. "If he takes the case, I might have to do it myself."

Marshall winced a little at this statement. Would Toby take the case from him out of fear? He didn't think so, but her quick remark caught him off guard. Suddenly, there was a commotion behind them. Marshall turned to see Danny pushing his way past an FBI man, flashing his DPD badge.

"Let that man through," said Marshall. The FBI men moved, and Danny walked over to Marshall. Danny looked troubled and frustrated.

"What's up?" asked Marshall.

Nate Williams tapped Marshall on the shoulder and pointed up, as if to say meet us upstairs. Then he, Toby, and the others got on the elevator and went up.

"I have a message from your brother, Moses," said Danny.

Marshall frowned at the name. It seemed no matter how far he got, he could never get away from Moses. "What did he want?—look, come on upstairs with me."

Danny and Marshall got on an elevator and went upstairs. As soon as Marshall was off the elevator, he was pulled into a meeting with Toby.

"Go into my office and wait for me," Marshall said to Danny.

"Damn, how do they keep this place so clean?" asked Danny, looking around. "Makes me nervous." He went into Marshall's office and waited.

Marshall walked into Nate's office. Toby was intense and brilliant in her assessment of the situation. Marshall could see why the president had appointed her. She laid out all of the pitfalls of the case and how they should proceed. They would raid Mbutu's Brotherhood headquarters, and they would bring out everything in his FBI files. They would counter the expected defense to paint Mbutu as a black hero by painting him as a fallen militant, desperate for attention and driven to extremes.

They took a break after an hour. Toby was calling the president to give him an update. Marshall left the meeting and headed back to his office. He felt drained by Toby's passion and assessment of their case. He expected to find an empty room, but Danny was still there, waiting.

"Damn, you lawyers talk a lot," said Danny.

"I don't have a lot of time, man," said Marshall. "Why did my brother call you?"

"He's in jail."

"I know he doesn't expect me to help him," Marshall said.

"I think he does, but he's dealing. He says that he has evidence in your case."

"I have a suspect, a murder weapon, and the goddamned attorney general. What the fuck do I need his ass for?"

Marshall was suddenly angry at the third-party request. All his life he'd suffered Moses. Each time he threw him in the ocean of his forgettable past, he rose like some science fiction monster, hell-bent on destruction.

"Well, I told him all that," said Danny. "And I don't know if he's lying, but he says Mbutu didn't do it, and he can prove it."

"How? How can some criminal in a state prison help me in a federal case?" Marshall made an effort to calm himself, but it still wasn't working. Even the rarefied domain of the federal government was not enough to keep his brother out of his life.

"He told me something," said Danny. "He said you wouldn't find a slug in the body—just pieces of it."

"What?" said Marshall. He took a few steps. It must be some kind of a leak, he thought to himself.

"Is it true?" asked Danny.

"Look, I can't—" Marshall saw the seriousness in Danny's eyes. He guessed that talking to Moses had affected him too. He couldn't lie to him. Danny would know. "Yes, the bullets fragmented in a way that no one can explain, but only in Douglas's body."

"Then he's got something," said Danny.

"I don't know," said Marshall. "But I got a man facing lethal injection, and the attorney general across the hall talking to the president. I guess I should find out.''

Marshall walked Danny back downstairs and out of the building. They were silent in the elevator, but he knew they were both thinking about Moses. Like a specter from the past, he was suddenly back in their lives, and he knew that no good would come of it.

17

Witness

Marshall was driving toward the office the next day. The morning was beautiful, pale blue skies and radiant sun. The snowfall that they'd been expecting hadn't come. It was a cold day, but a dry one. He'd take that in Michigan anytime.

Marshall was already putting together the case, formulating an outline for how to proceed. He needed a basic foundation before he could be specifically effective. He knew that he'd attack with the film of the death first, to imbed that in the jury's mind, then he'd go straight for something personal about Mbutu himself, tying him to the atrocity they'd just seen.

In the back of his mind, though, he worried about seeing his brother later in the day, and he kept hearing the too-jovial voice of CIA Agent Van Ness. He didn't know how he would feel seeing Moses again. He just hoped that he could do it and maintain a professional demeanor. There was so much bad blood that he couldn't guarantee he wouldn't try to strangle him.

Mbutu was refusing to allow a blood and hair sample to be taken. The fact that Mbutu had no lawyer would stop a judge from ordering him to do it. Any such order without benefit of counsel would surely be reversible error. Marshall knew the order would be granted, but it would have to come after a lawyer was appointed. Only in a case like this would a counsel be appointed this late. Mbutu was seeing many local and national lawyers. Marshall had heard that it was literally a waiting room of them at the lockup. Although there was not a lot of money in the case, it had a value that could not be counted. Fame, notoriety, and media access were the real treasures of defending Mbutu. In the age of Court TV, book deals, and movie rights, the case was a potential gold mine.

No judge had been assigned yet. Apparently, there was a lot of wrangling behind the scenes to get the case. The rotation had sent the case to Judge Gerren Dutton, the newest judge on the bench. He was too green for a case of this magnitude, so a reassignment was in order. In the interim, his old friend Judge Langworthy had the case.

Marshall walked into his office to find Stephen Bradbury sitting in his chair smoking a long cigar.

"There's no smoking in this building. You're fired," Marshall said.

"You're almost right," said Bradbury, shoving a cigar into Marshall's hand. "I'm going to be nominated."

"For what?" asked Marshall, then his eyes widened. "Good God, for the Supreme Court?"

"Yes." Bradbury smiled. "The rumor was true. I got a call from both our senators last night, then the president. The president is going to announce it as soon as he feels the time is right. He'll float my name around and test the waters, you know the drill. But not too long. The Court wants to get moving."

Marshall hugged his old friend. This was every lawyer's dream, and now it had come true for Bradbury.

"It couldn't happen to a better man," said Marshall. "I don't really know what to say."

"Don't say anything, just enjoy that ten-dollar cigar and bring your pretty wife to my party after the announcement."

"I will," said Marshall. The mention of his wife sent troubling thoughts of Chemin through his head.

"Look, I gotta go. Word is getting around, and I'll have to do some damage control with my peers."

"Yes, and congratulations again."

Bradbury walked out of the office; no, he literally *floated* out, Marshall thought. It was surreal. He was going to be the friend of a Supreme Court justice. It didn't seem possible that someone like him was now so close to greatness.

His phone rang. He wondered if it could be Chemin. She didn't call him at work anymore, but he'd sneaked out of the house like a thief, and maybe she was pissed off. He picked up the receiver.

"Hello," he said.

"Marshall," said a woman's voice.

"Who is this?"

"Oh, it's me, Jessica."

"Jessica, why are you calling me in my office? You can come in if you want."

"I work for the FBI side now," she said. "It's Agent Sommers calling."

Marshall remembered that Jessica had made some sort of transfer to the FBI side of the task force.

"Right," said Marshall. "I'll take it."

"Hold on," said Jessica. Then she said. "See you later."

A moment, then Sommers picked up the line. "Hello, Marshall," she said.

"What's up?"

"The fuckin' CIA," said Sommers. She laughed a little.

"I know. I met them too. Listen, don't let them get to you. Just do your job."

"I am. I'm calling to tell you that I think I have two eyewitnesses for you on the Douglas case."

"How can you say something like that so casually?" Marshall said. "That's great news."

"Well, they're shaky, but I think they may have seen something useful."

"I'll be right over," said Marshall. "Hold the ID until I get there."

Marshall stood in the dark room as the witness watched Mbutu and several other men walk in. The witnesses were a sixtyish black man named John Johnson and his wife Marie. She held her husband's arm like a high school sweetheart.

The lineup had six men in it. All of them were Mbutu's age and height. Two of them even had dreadlocks. Marshall was not taking any chances that the defense would call the lineup unfair.

Ryder and the rest of the team stood in the back, trying not to look like the crowd they were.

Clarence Daniels, a public defender, stood behind Marshall, watching for signs of abuse. He'd been assigned as interim counsel in the case by Langworthy. Mbutu still had no attorney, and that was beginning to bother everyone.

Mr. Johnson had attended the commencement at Wayne State University to watch his grandson become a lawyer. He and his wife had gone out to the bathroom when the commotion began. In the confusion, Mr. Johnson had seen a man come out of the door leading to the upper part of the building.

Mr. Johnson had already looked at pictures of Anthony Collier. He acknowledged Collier was not the man he'd seen.

"Take your time, Mr. Johnson," said Sommers.

Johnson looked the men over for about a minute, shaking his head. Then, finally: "No, I don't see him," he said.

"Are you sure?" asked Marshall. "Look again."

"Don't have to," said Mr. Johnson. "The man I saw was shorter, and had a really big nose. He was black, but we don't all look alike."

"Mr. Johnson," said Ryder. "Maybe you need more time."

"The man is sure," said Daniels. He made notes on a small pad. "Don't harass him."

Sommers released the lineup participants. They filed out of the room. Mbutu stared at the two-way mirror as if he could see through it. He smiled a little.

"Shit," said Sommers.

"That's the word for it," said Daniels in that smug, condescending way that only a defense lawyer can.

Daniels said good-bye and started to leave to see Mbutu. Presumably to tell him the good news that he could not be placed at the scene of the crime by these people. Then suddenly, he stopped and turned to Marshall.

"Put some agents on these two," said Daniels, referring to the Johnsons.

"What for?" asked Sommers.

"Because if they were government witnesses you would."

Sommers looked at Marshall.

"Do it, Chris," said Marshall. Daniels was just a makeshift counsel, but he was smart. Any good lawyer would protect a witness who was useful to his client. Daniels smiled a little, pleased with himself.

"We don't need a cop in our home," said Johnson.

"I'd feel better," said Marie.

"The agents won't be in your house, Mr. Johnson," said Sommers. "They'll maintain surveillance from outside."

"Well, if you send them, make sure they're white," said Marie Johnson.

"Why does that matter?" asked Daniels.

"To let people in the neighborhood know," said Marshall. "Any white man watching a house in her neighborhood has to be a cop."

"Right," said Marie.

"Oh, you fuss too much," said Mr. Johnson. They walked out arguing.

"They remind me of my own folks," said Sommers. "So, one for their side, huh?" Sommers patted Marshall on the back and walked out.

"Well, that was a setback," said Marshall to his team.

"But we still have the gun," said Ryder.

"And we'll get a DNA test as soon as he gets counsel," said Roberta.

"You guys trying to cheer me up?" asked Marshall.

"We're trying to cheer ourselves up," said Walter. "That sweet old man will be a great witness."

They all filed out of the little room. Marshall walked along, oblivious to the chatter of this team. He stared at his watch, noting that he was only an hour away from a reunion with his brother.

18

Twinning

Marshall walked through the long corridor at Wayne County Prison as if he were going to an execution. Danny walked at his side, humming a tune, oblivious to the dolor in the air. It had been a long time since Marshall had visited the state's county jail. After he became a fed, he no longer had a reason to go to state institutions. But that's where his brother was. He'd forgotten the feeling, the hopelessness, the *heaviness*, of the place. He remembered being locked up in the federal holding pen. That was a holiday compared to county.

Marshall walked into the meeting room and saw Moses sitting in a chair smoking a cigarette. He seemed calm, almost happy. Then Marshall grew angry. All the pain and grief his brother had inflicted on him and the family came back to him. He saw his father smiling and filled with life, then cold and dead in a casket. Suddenly, he wanted to grab Moses, beat the information out of him, then go have a drink to celebrate.

"Smug muthafucka, ain't he?" said Danny.

"Always was," said Marshall. "You wait here."

Danny took a seat by the door, and Marshall walked over to his brother. Even though they were fraternal twins, you could see many similarities in them. The curve of the jaw and the shape of the nose were the same. It was their eyes that really set them apart. Marshall's were wide and alert. The kind that looked into you with interest and intensity. Moses' eyes seemed to sit higher, and held two flat brown spheres. They might have been regarded as handsome, but they were narrow, fierce-looking ports that cradled danger and insincerity. He could make them anything he wanted, from the hurt look of a child, to the malevolence of a killer.

Marshall looked at his brother with regret and anger. Moses' eyes held nothing.

Moses stood and held out his arm, as if to hug his brother. The shackles on his arms sang a sad song as he did.

"You can cut that shit right now," said Marshall, stopping in front of his brother.

Now Moses' eyes sprang to life. It was the hurt look of a sibling. "Damn, family ain't what it used to be, huh?" said Moses. He sat down. Marshall sat across from him. "Long time. Long, long time."

"I understand you have information on my case." Marshall tried to sound as businesslike as he could.

Moses just ignored him. "I was telling the guard how we used to steal apples from our neighbor's yard. How I would climb and you would catch and bag. You'd call that accessory during the crime or something, right?" Now his eyes were playful, the long-lost brother.

This was classic Moses, Marshall thought. He was on the make already, trying to put him at ease, with familiar connections to fond memories. Hey, we're related, and we both used to be criminals, was what Moses had really just said. For the first time, Marshall thought that maybe he really did have something useful. Moses never tried to con you unless it was serious.

"The one thing I used to like about you was that you didn't talk a lot of shit," said Marshall. "I can see that's changed."

Moses looked shocked. "So, you're all business, huh? I can dig it." He smiled, his eyes now held the look of an amused old friend.

"I'm a little busy these days, in case you ever read a newspaper."

"I know." Moses snorted a little. "Bad-ass fed, looking to avenge the murder of that Uncle Tom. I wish I could have shot him myself."

"How can you have a political opinion about him?" asked Marshall. "You're a criminal. Liberal or conservative, he would have spit on you."

"The same go for you? You hate me because I chose a different lifestyle?"

"Crime isn't a lifestyle. It's a pathology, a sickness. But you never could see that. You aren't normal in the head."

"Normal like your boy over there?" Moses pointed to Danny. "Now, he's sick. I hear about him all the time, beating up brothers, bustin' heads.''

''Danny's not on trial here. You're wearing the jumpsuit and chains, in case you haven't noticed.'' Moses looked pissed off at this statement, and Marshall felt good about that.

''I can't believe you still runnin' with that wigger. I can't believe you'd pick some white man over your own damned brother, your *twin* brother.''

''He's more of a brother than you ever were. In both senses of the word.'' He had played into his brother's hand. Moses wanted to get him angry, and yet he seemed to still be hurt that he'd picked Danny over him. It was sometimes hard to tell when Moses was conning and when he was truly being human. ''Now, tell me what you know about my case, or I'm going.''

''Okay,'' Moses said. He leaned back farther in the cheap iron chair. ''A few days before that Uncle Tom Douglas caught them bullets, one of my men, a brother named Carlos, got a job from some dude. The client wanted us to cop a ride for him, then dispose of it. Simple enough. My man Carlos did the job, only after it was over, this client burned him. Shot him hit man style. One behind the ear, one in the heart. Only the hitter didn't know we checked up on him while he was in town.''

''So what?'' asked Marshall. The story was intriguing, but so far, it had no connection to the case.

''So, I know his name,'' said Moses. ''He was staying in a little motel on the east side. We went looking for his ass, but he was gone, left in the middle of the night. Then the motel manager told us an interesting story.'' Moses leaned back in his chair, enjoying the captive audience he had. ''Some guy is in his room with a woman fucking her and something falls on his head. The man finds what hit him and it's a *bullet*, a long, black bullet.''

''Keep going,'' said Marshall.

''Well, it fell through a hole in the floor of that cheap-ass motel and hit that man in the head. I paid the manager five bucks for it.''

''Do you still have it?''

''Naw, that thing was so strange-looking that we just had to see what it was all about, so we fired it from a rifle, and I'll be damned if that muthafucka didn't *explode* when it hit the wall. No slug, just fragments.''

''So what's his name, this client?'' Marshall put everything he had into hiding his excitement, but he knew he had probably failed.

''Not gonna be that easy,'' said Moses. ''I want out of this fuckin' place. I want to go to a federal jail, and I want help getting rid of this bullshit I'm in.''

"That's a lot to ask for just a name,'' said Marshall. He tried to hide his excitement. If he let Moses know he needed him, the ante would keep going up. "At least give me a description.''

"No. I got the name, but it's gonna cost you.''

Marshall thought a moment. Moses' deal was the least of his worries. If this client was an arms dealer then he supplied the killer with the special ammunition, or maybe he was the triggerman himself. "I'll think about it,'' said Marshall.

"*Think*? What the fuck does that mean?''

"I'm going to sit down somewhere and decide if this, if you, are worth my time.'' He wanted to stay cool, make his brother sweat a little. He would wait and see what this information was worth.

"You wait too long, and the deal's off,'' said Moses.

"That's your choice. This might take some time.''

"Shit, I got time,'' said Moses. "My social calendar is completely clear right now.''

Marshall got up. Moses stood and extended his hand. Marshall turned from him.

"No handshake, no deal,'' said Moses.

Marshall turned back to his brother. Moses smiled like the devil. This cheerful demeanor made Marshall sick, but he didn't let it show. He always was a smart bastard. And he wasted it on worthlessness. Marshall took his hand and was surprised when Moses grabbed him and hugged him. Marshall could hear Danny jump up behind them.

"You still my brother,'' Moses said as he kept up the bear hug.

"It's cool,'' Marshall said to Danny, who was several steps to the men by now. Marshall pushed his brother away. "You fuck me, and I swear, I'll make sure you never get out of prison.''

Marshall walked away. He decided to keep this to himself for now. No need getting Toby, Williams, and the damned president all excited right now. From behind him he heard:

"Tell Mama I said hi.''

Marshall and Danny left the prison and headed outside. Danny was unusually quiet as they walked along. Danny was the kind of man who never had a thought that was unstated, especially when it might be controversial. He was brewing inside about what he'd just seen.

"You're not going to say anything about my brother?" asked Marshall as they stepped outside.

"I don't trust him," Danny said with a quiet seriousness that Marshall had rarely heard in his voice.

"You okay, man?" asked Marshall.

"Yeah . . . it's just that seeing him again reminded me of being little, and then I thought about all the shit I used to take from him and all the other kids our age, you know."

"I do know. I had a lot of bad thoughts bouncing around in my head when I saw him too. Seems like we all grew up too fast, like we were all in a goddamned hurry to get to the future so we could get here and regret our past."

"So, whatcha gonna do?" asked Danny. "I mean, if he's telling the truth . . ."

"It could help me, but I'm not going to let him hustle me the way he does everyone else. And no matter what I do, I am not going to let my brother out of prison."

Marshall went back to his office, carrying the burden of the case and seeing Moses again. Toby had flown out of town, taking the pressure and power of Washington, D.C., with her. He conferred briefly with Bob Ryder then decided to work on the arraignment a little more.

Mbutu had not named an attorney yet, and Marshall could not believe that he'd try to represent himself in a case like this.

The arraignment would be a simple matter. No magistrate would let Mbutu out on bail.

So, why was he worried? he asked himself. Marshall had a feeling of dread in the pit of his stomach that he couldn't shake. Perhaps it was nerves, or the terrible thoughts his brother brought him.

Marshall pushed himself away from his desk and popped a CD into his player. He made sure to keep the sound low. Soon, the smooth tenor of Maxwell wafted over the room. He was feeling better already.

He worked for a while, putting together a preliminary outline of his case. It was good to see it in black and white. The nature of the process was comforting to him. But it wouldn't be right until Mbutu named a counsel. A legal adversary would complete the picture of what was to come.

Suddenly, there was a knock at the door.

"Come in," Marshall said loudly.

Jessica Cole walked in, looking surprised. She was smiling and her dark eyes seemed to shine as she came closer. Marshall suddenly felt uncomfortable noticing how pretty she was. He remembered that she had some kind of crush on him.

"I thought I was the only one here," she said.

"As late as it is, you should be. I need to get going soon myself."

"I'm sorry about that weird call. I'm helping the FBI on your case, trying to get more experience, you know."

Before Marshall could say anything else, Jessica was sitting down across from him. She was wearing a midlength skirt, and it rose up to her thighs as she sat. Her legs were pretty and completely unblemished. Marshall visibly blushed. He and Chemin were on some very rocky road, but he was still married, and in legal terms this was at least the appearance of impropriety.

"I'm sorry for staring at you all the time," she said.

"Really?" Marshall was amused. "I hadn't noticed."

"You're sweet to lie. I can see the look in your eyes when I do it. I guess I'm not really good at hiding how I feel about you."

"And how is that?" Marshall asked against his better judgment. Part of him wanted to get out of the coming conversation, but most of him was flattered and wanted to hear more. It had been a while since a woman had shown any interest in him.

"Well, you know, I like you, I mean it's more than that, not love or anything but . . ." Jessica stopped suddenly. She looked terrified and blushed so hard that she partially covered her face. "I should go." She sprang up.

"Don't feel bad," Marshall said. "I know how it is. Look, you know I'm married and—"

"I don't care."

"Excuse me?"

"I said, I don't care, Marshall."

Marshall was shocked at hearing those words. Most women he knew cared a great deal. They were not given to screwing around with what was not theirs. But Jessica was apparently different. He didn't think she was immoral, but his commitment and all of its religious and societal implications apparently did not impress her. *"I don't care."* It sounded like a mandate, a rule of law, the way she said it.

"Jess, you don't know what you're saying, do you?" said Marshall.

He didn't know if she did, and more troubling was why he wanted an answer to that question. But it was too late, he'd said it.

"Yes, I do. I've been thinking about this a lot." Jessica sat back down. "I've had these feelings, and I can't stop them. And I notice how sad you are these days."

"I'm not sad. Just busy," Marshall lied.

"You stay at work later and later, and come in earlier and earlier. So, you can't be happy at home, you know. And you used to send flowers to her all the time, and now you don't. And that picture." She pointed to a picture of Chemin on a credenza behind him. "It used to be right on your desk next to the phone. Now it's behind you, where you don't have to look at it all the time."

"I should hire you as my investigator," said Marshall, feeling a little embarrassed. "All true. I'm having some problems, but it's all in the normal course of marriage. I love Chemin, and we'll get past this."

Marshall noticed how she looked at him now. It was a beautifully hungry and lustful look, the kind that men dream about seeing.

"It's really nice of you to like me," he said. "But nothing's gonna happen between us."

Jessica stood up, and Marshall thought she would say something sad, then leave, but instead she walked over to him. He caught the scent of her perfume. She moved her body close to him and stared at him unwaveringly.

"I'm taking this course in college. It's about how to be aggressive in business. My professor says that to get what you want, you have to do the things that most people won't do. You have to jump over the bullshit manners of life."

She took his hand and placed it on her breast. Marshall was breathing hard and did not fight it.

What the hell am I doing? he heard himself say inside his head even as he caressed the young girl. He'd always thought of Jessica as a little secretary who was probably lucky to have the job she had, but apparently she possessed a fierce intellect and a strong will. It was surprising, and exciting.

"I'll be here for you if you need me," said Jessica. "I want you to know that."

Marshall pulled his hand away gently. "I shouldn't have done that. I'm sorry."

"Don't be. I made you do it."

"You should go now," Marshall said, and he knew it didn't sound convincing. He breathed easier when she stepped away. Then she stopped and turned back to him.

"She must be crazy," she said. And then, she walked out.

Marshall looked after her. He became aware that his heart was beating faster. What had just happened was wrong in a thousand different ways. No matter how bad his relationship with Chemin was, he could not do the thing he now had in his mind.

He sighed heavily. Then he moved to his credenza, took the picture of Chemin, and put it back on his desk.

Marshall entered his house that night to find Chemin curled up on the sofa, watching TV. She looked beautiful as the light from the TV flickered on her face. Her Hallogent handcart sat next to the sofa and a table littered with papers. She'd been working, compiling the never-ending data for her company.

He moved closer, not wanting to start a conversation but needing to say something to her to purge the feeling he had in his heart. She was his wife, he thought, and another woman had made advances toward him. In better times, he would have told her, and they would have had a good laugh. But now it would start an in-house riot, and he didn't need that. The arraignment was coming, and he needed his head clear. Still, he wanted to engage her, to remind himself that his commitment, though fractured, was still viable.

"I don't care," he heard Jessica say in his head as he moved closer to his wife. She glanced at him and said nothing. She looked back to the TV. He sat next to her, unsure of what to say.

"What are you watching?" he asked. It was a stupid question, and as such gave away his awkwardness and apprehension. With all the trouble in his life and marriage, that was the best he could do. He wished in an instant that he could take it back and say something profound, loving, and healing.

Chemin turned, and looked at him with mild annoyance. "I'd almost forgotten that I live here with you," she said. "There's a certain solace to singleness that just came back to me recently. It's not so bad, when you think about it."

Marshall was silent. Once again, her wit was cutting and pinpoint accurate. Marshall suddenly felt silly. He was into his case and had again let his life float away. Chemin was moving further from him, and he was powerless to stop it.

"I do still live here, Chemin," said Marshall defiantly, as if he needed to convince her.

"You know what I did at work today?" she said. "I got on this computer we call The Eye. We call it that because it has one of the biggest databases in the world. I looked up *marriage, counseling, divorce, separation,* everything related to our situation. And you know what? We're not even close to being unique. Relationships are failing all over the world, Marshall. Our think tank guys at Hallogent say it's because crumbling morals and sexual promiscuity have led to a devaluation of commitment. We see commitment as death now. So, I guess we're part of a revolution. A revolution of selfish losers who are doomed to ruin good relationships then live our lives alone. Then I thought, It's not me. I'm not the one who gave up on us. You did. So, as our fading marriage adds to this pathetic statistic, you remember that, you remember that it's not me who put us there."

He felt as if he'd been hit by a car. In a way he had. She had summed up their problem and juxtaposed it against the decline of modern civilization. And the worst part of it was that it was true, all of it.

He left her and walked away, content to lick the wounds inflicted by the Chemin Express. He wished she would say something to reengage him, an apology, but she didn't. His inability to move forward in their relationship was a personal nightmare, but the heaviness of the silence behind him was just as awful.

He turned against his better judgment and took another look at her. She shifted her feet beneath her on the sofa and had a curious half-smile on her face. Marshall moved up the stairs to their room. He decided to go to sleep early. Suddenly, he wanted only to rest, to be strong and focused for the fight tomorrow.

19

Legend

Marshall and his team sat together, waiting for Mbutu's counsel to arrive. Mbutu sat alone on the other side of the room. The courtroom of Magistrate Paul Kapinski was packed for the arraignment.

Normally, Mbutu would have been arraigned quickly and unceremoniously, but Mbutu had put off the court date in order to get counsel, or so he kept saying. He really wanted an audience, a media one. Neither Nate Williams nor Toby had even tried to fight the trial being televised. It would seem like a cheat to the public, and it deprived the government of the chance to put on its best face.

"Whoever his lawyer is needs to learn to be punctual," said Marshall. He shifted in his seat, looking at the door.

"Mr. Jackson?" said the magistrate. "Do you know what the delay is?"

"We don't even know who opposing counsel is," said Marshall.

"All questions will be answered in due time," said Mbutu. His followers in the gallery applauded loudly.

"No statements or speeches, Mr. Mbutu," said Kapinski, a fortyish man with, of all things, a ponytail.

Normally, in a case of this magnitude, the trial judge would pull rank and do the arraignment himself. But the judges on the district bench were fighting over the case, or so Marshall had heard. They all wanted it, and so the normal procedure was being followed.

Ten minutes later, the courtroom doors opened, and in walked a black man dressed in a suit with a sash made of kente cloth. He was about sixty or so and had salt-and-pepper hair. He walked regally, as if entering a king's chamber.

"Jesus," said Marshall. "I don't believe it."

"I thought he was retired," said Ryder.

"Apparently not," said Walter.

"Muhammad Rashad, for the defendant," said the tall man. "Excuse my tardiness, but I had to come from New York, and I only got the assignment last night."

"Apology accepted, Mr. Rashad," said Kapinski. The magistrate seemed to be just as in awe as everyone on the prosecution team.

Marshall was now greatly worried. Muhammad Rashad was a legend in civil rights circles. He was a former Black Panther who graduated from Harvard with a perfect grade point average. He was a certified genius who had several degrees. Rashad had marched with Dr. King, was an advisor to Malcolm X, and had uncovered a promotion conspiracy against black servicemen at Fort Bragg that resulted in a general being court-martialed.

Rashad had been the toast of the legal profession for a while. He'd authored several books on criminal procedure, including *Defense of Life,* which was required reading in every law school. Marshall had waited in line for an hour to get a signed copy. He was sure that Kapinski and all the other lawyers had read it as well.

Rashad's life had seemed charmed until his wife and daughter died in a car accident. Rashad flew into a clinical depression and alcohol abuse. He came out of it three years later but had no more taste for litigation. He retired to lecturing, writing books, and living in semiobscurity. But now, here he was, taking his place as Marshall's opposition.

Rashad hugged Mbutu tightly, and for the first time, Marshall noticed that there was another person at the table. She was a striking woman with jet black hair. She was about thirty or so, and wore a skirt so short that it was probably not appropriate for court.

"Leslie Reed, also for the defendant," said the woman. The magistrate acknowledged her. Leslie shook hands with Mbutu, and they all sat down.

"Hubba hubba," said Ryder.

"You can say that again," said Walter.

"You both need to pull your brains out of your pants," said Roberta. "Leslie Reed is as smart, mean, and nasty as they come."

"What do you know about her?" asked Marshall.

"She's a very good trial lawyer, with a string of wins going back several years. I met her at a conference for women lawyers last year," said Roberta. "Millionaire lawyers, federal judges, but *she* was the keynote speaker. And she's only thirty-six."

"Well, we have our little dream defense team, don't we?" said Marshall. He nodded to Rashad and Leslie, who both suddenly looked larger than life.

The magistrate asked them if they were ready, and both sides acknowledged. Suddenly, Marshall felt a surge of adrenaline, his stomach tightened and his mind became alert. He always got this way when it was time to litigate. It was a predator's game, and his natural instincts always got him ready for a fight.

Kapinski read the case into the record, then asked Mbutu how he pled.

"Not guilty, Your Honor," said Mbutu. His supporters, members of the Brotherhood, clapped, despite Kapinski's warning.

"Bail?" asked Kapinski.

"None," said Marshall. "This man murdered a justice of the Supreme Court. I don't think there's anything left to say."

"Just this, Your Honor," said Rashad. "My client surrendered voluntarily, saving the government precious resources and time. He has not hidden from justice but has come to confront it head on."

"So, what is your request for bail?" asked Kapinski.

"None, Your Honor," said Rashad, "but my client would like a special arrangement made so that he can take an active part in his defense. He'd like the power to question certain government witnesses from the FBI and CIA, as well as do part of the opening and closing arguments."

"I am just the magistrate, Mr. Rashad. I can't—"

"We will oppose," said Marshall. "Allowing this power will let the defendant testify while still using the Fifth Amendment to block the government's cross-examination."

"He makes a good point, Mr. Rashad," said Kapinski.

"There's no danger," said Rashad. "My client is just trying to protect himself."

"I'm sorry," said Kapinski, "but I can't grant your request. No bail, and defendant will be held—"

"Then we have one other request," said Rashad. "Will you allow my client to reside in the government's special prison quarters? This case is of a magnitude that warrants it."

Marshall was suddenly aware that they all had been played. The government's special quarters were really nothing more than a nice, guarded hotel room. Rashad was a cagey lawyer. Come in late and shock everyone, ask for the sun, then get the moon. Retirement had not deprived him of his edge.

"The government opposes," said Marshall, but he already knew that he'd lose on this point. Rashad had put the issue in the air, and Kapinski was relishing his role as de facto trial judge.

"Noted," said Kapinski. "I'll make that recommendation to the judge once this case is assigned. This matter is closed. Defendant is remanded to custody."

Marshall was upset. He'd clearly been outsmarted, and the TV cameras had captured it all. He was sure that some panel of legal experts would note this, then say how he should have seen it coming and should have worn a better tie.

"Toby will want to talk to us about this turn of events," said Ryder.

"I know," said Marshall. Rashad was serious business. And judging from the TV reporters who swirled around him, he was serious news as well.

Just then, Rashad and Leslie walked over to Marshall. "We should confer, Counselor," said Rashad.

"Gladly," said Marshall.

Danny and Vinny pulled up to the Big Boy restaurant on Jefferson Avenue just north of Belle Isle. It was a beautiful winter day, and the Detroit River sparkled in the distance.

They had the day off, and Danny was in good spirits. The information that he'd gotten from the party store robbers had helped the drug force close down a major dealer on the west side. He had gotten partial credit for the bust. Danny also had passed the first level of his antiaggression course, an event that had not gone unnoticed by his superiors. He could see that gold shield becoming his. He already knew that he'd ask for his father's old number. Keep the tradition alive.

They sat at a table in the back. The waitress came over, and Danny ordered for them both.

"Who's gonna eat all that food?" asked Vinny.

"I am," said Danny.

"If you get fat, I'm dumping you," said Vinny.

"What?" said Danny. "You'd kick me to the curb over something like that?"

"Shit, men do it all the time. Get fat, get lost."

"Not me."

"Oh, so if I turned into one of them fat, three-hundred-pound, sittin'-up-on-Jerry-Springer-trailer-trash women, you'd still want me."

"Yeah," said Danny. "I'd get someone else to sleep with you, but you'd still be my girl." Danny laughed, and Vinny tossed a napkin at his face.

Suddenly, there was a commotion behind Danny. He turned and saw two black men at the cash register. One was muscular and held a shotgun. The other was thin and brandished a revolver. The shotgun was pointed at the head of a very frightened manager.

"Give it up!" yelled the man with the shotgun. The manager opened a register and stuffed money into a bag.

People screamed and ducked under their tables. Several people ran for the bathrooms, and waitresses dropped plates of food that landed with loud crashes.

Danny looked at Vinny, who was already reaching for her service revolver. Danny nodded to her, then placed his hands on both his guns.

Still feeling the rush of adrenaline from court, Marshall sat across from Rashad and Leslie Reed. Bob Ryder and the rest of the team were with him in the conference room.

Mbutu had been taken back to prison and was probably laughing at him on his way. Rashad had scored a minor victory, but it was nonetheless the first blow in the battle. Marshall could not help but be a little bit in awe of the man. It was like a baseball player meeting Hank Aaron or a priest meeting the pope. Rashad was legal royalty, and he carried himself as such. He casually walked into the room with Leslie Reed a step behind; he laughed and talked as if he were at a party instead of an assassination trial.

Marshall tried to match Rashad's calmness, but he knew he could not. He was still young in terms of experience, and he was pumped for the fight of his career.

"You could have just asked me to put Mbutu in special quarters."

"I would have, ten years ago, but these days you young lawyers litigate by resistance. You oppose everything. The art of knowing when to compromise has been lost.''

''I won't argue,'' said Marshall. ''I'm authorized to take a plea from you. I can give you some time to familiarize yourself with the evidence in the case if you like.''

''No need for that,'' said Leslie Reed. ''We won't be accepting a plea.'' She had what was almost a scowl on her face. Most lawyers had a negotiation expression, a hard-ass look to let everyone know that they meant business. It was commonplace, but somehow Marshall thought that this was more than a game face. Her dislike for him seemed genuine.

''Okay, then I guess we proceed to the next phase,'' said Marshall.

''We've seen your evidence,'' said Rashad. ''The whole case hinges on ballistics, and we can punch holes in that big enough to drive a car through.''

''We have DNA,'' said Marshall. ''You can't punch a hole in that.''

''We'll see,'' said Leslie. ''We'll see.''

''Your confidence is noted for the record,'' said Marshall. ''We'll need a blood and hair sample from your client ASAP.''

''We oppose that,'' said Leslie.

''Why?'' asked Marshall. ''If it doesn't match, your boy is off the hook.''

''We oppose because the scientific procedures used to match blood and hair are controlled by you and we cannot guarantee a fair result,'' said Rashad.

''Fine,'' said Marshall. ''I'm sure the trial judge will disagree with that great logic.''

''And what judge has the government selected?'' asked Rashad.

''It's random,'' said Marshall. ''You know that.''

Leslie Reed snorted a laugh.

''I'm sure the chief judge will want the case,'' said Rashad. ''That will suit us just fine.''

''So, what is it that your client wants?'' asked Marshall.

''Nothing,'' said Rashad. ''He wants his day in court. He wants to show this country that it is sick and needs to heal itself.''

''Jesus,'' Bob Ryder said from behind them.

''You can come and sit at the table with the grown-ups if you want, Mr. Ryder,'' said Leslie. She had a smile on her face that was positively evil.

''No, thanks,'' said Ryder, obviously a little upset. ''I'm fine back here watching you two tread water.''

Marshall loved the big-ball posturing attendant to litigation. It was always so much fun to watch lawyers try to win cases with psychological intimidation and words. It never worked, but he guessed that it was a way for them to fight the frustration brought upon by the slow process of justice.

"If we are through taking potshots at each other, we can agree on a trial timetable to present the judge."

"We want to go to trial as soon as possible," said Rashad.

"Sometime within the next six months?" asked Marshall. "That's fast, but doable."

"No, we mean within the next six weeks," said Leslie.

"What?" Marshall heard Roberta say softly from behind him.

"We can't do that," said Marshall.

"Isn't Ms. Newhall the one who decides that?" asked Rashad. Leslie grinned at the mild insult to Marshall's authority.

"I'll inform her, of course," said Marshall, "but I can safely say she'll oppose it. This case is much too complex to be rushed."

"Then I guess we'll find out just how 'speedy' a constitutional speedy trial can be," said Rashad.

"Will you stipulate to the taking of Mbutu's blood and hair sample?"

"I can't agree," said Rashad. "Surely you understand that a stipulation to something so crucial puts me in the statute."

He was right. A blood match would be a very persuasive piece of evidence, and a lawyer had a duty to try to keep it from getting into evidence.

"I'll see what my boss thinks," said Marshall. To his team, he said, "Let's go."

Marshall was happy. He'd gotten something out of the legend but had not really given up anything. Rashad's suspicion of the government was working against him. He would have to remember that during the trial.

"By the way, Counselor," said Rashad. "You should know now that we plan to throw out all statements made by Mr. Mbutu on camera and to you as well as all of your ballistic evidence."

"I welcome the challenge," said Marshall. "You might get the statements suppressed, but the ballistic evidence is sound." Marshall stood up and started to walk away. From behind him, he heard:

"Perhaps, but it only makes sense if my client fired those bullets," said Rashad.

Marshall turned to face the man, staring into him as if to make sure he had just heard him right.

"That's right," said Leslie. "Our defense will be that another shooter killed Farrel Douglas."

Danny now had both guns in hand. He watched the robbers with intensity.

"When they leave, we follow and call it in," said Vinny.

Danny wasn't listening. He was raising the .45 above the table.

"Don't," said Vinny. "There are too many people in here."

"Take it off, bitch!" Danny heard the muscular man say. Danny focused his attention on the man. They had the money from the register, and now they were robbing individual people. The muscular man had his gun on a heavyset woman and demanded her watch. The woman screamed and struggled to get it off. The thin robber kept his gun out in front of him on the crowd.

"Follow me," said Danny. Before Vinny could say a word, Danny was standing, both guns out in front.

"Police!" he yelled. "Drop your weapons!"

The muscular man turned. Danny's .9mm fired, catching the man in the throat. The man's shotgun fired into the floor. He let go of the heavyset woman. She fell back into her chair, unharmed. Danny hit the muscular man with the .45 in the chest, sending him flying backward.

The thin man turned toward Danny, when Vinny fired from behind him. Her shot caught the man in the side. The thin man's revolver fired, then he fell. His gun flew out of his hand and skittered across the floor.

Danny heard Vinny yell. He turned and saw her fall back into a wall, holding her abdomen. She was hit. Danny ran over to Vinny. Customers were running out of the restaurant, falling over each other, screaming.

"Dammit, I'm okay," she said. "Get him." She pointed to the thin robber. "Before he gets to that gun."

Danny walked over to the injured robber. The muscular man was dead, lying in a pool of blood. The thin man bled from his wound, but he was alive. His gun was well out of reach.

Danny's head throbbed. His heart raced, and all he could see was the man who had shot his Vinny. Danny stood over the man, holding both guns. He breathed hard, his eyes were narrow slits of rage.

"Okay, okay," said the thin robber. "Don't shoot, man! I ain't got no gun." He moved away from Danny, pushing himself away. He left a thick trail of blood on the floor.

"Shoot his ass!" a man yelled from outside the restaurant. A crowd had gathered at the window, watching the aftermath.

Inside, Danny followed the injured man, holding both guns on him.

"Danny!" Vinny yelled from behind him. "Don't!"

"Yeah, Danny, don't do it, man," said the robber wincing in pain. "Come on man, you can't shoot me."

Danny stopped suddenly, and the robber sighed in relief. Danny put his guns on a table, then grabbed the man, lifting him from the floor. Behind him, Vinny yelled something that he couldn't understand. His ears were filled with white noise, surrounded by his rage.

He hit the robber hard in the face. He heard a bone snap, and felt a hot flash of pain in his hand. The robber screamed something, but Danny kept hitting him, again and again. Blood flew, landing in sprinkles on Danny's angry face. The robber pleaded for his life, but the assault continued as Danny heard Vinny yelling behind him, and the muted cheers from beyond the restaurant's doors.

20

························

Langworthy

Chief District Judge Clark Langworthy was not in a good mood. His face furrowed at the lawyers' every word. His eyes darted from one face to the next, as if he was accusing everyone of something.

Langworthy was one of the last members of the old judicial guard. He was one of the few judges his age who had not retired. All of his friends were going out to pasture, but Langworthy was sturdy and looked like he would live forever.

Langworthy had fought in Korea, but had opposed Vietnam. He had become a civil rights lawyer in the 1960s and 1970s. He was a lifelong liberal who'd backed every Democrat from Clinton all the way back to Harry Truman.

He was also a smart judge and leader of the district court. He could be salty and profane, but he knew the law as well as anyone. Langworthy also hated Farrel Douglas with a passion. He had referred to Douglas in print as "a traitor to democracy."

Langworthy had assigned the case to himself, and no one was surprised. A case of this size and significance could not go to some junior jurist looking to make a reputation for himself.

Marshall had mixed feelings. While no judge worth anything would sway a case like this, Langworthy was clearly out of the Oliver Stone school. He had lit up like Christmas when he heard Rashad's conspiracy theory. Marshall also remembered that this man had thrown him into jail not too long ago in the Quince case and then had given unfavorable jury instructions, which probably caused him to lose.

Rashad was planning a war, and he was taking no prisoners. To engage the conspiracy theory was to invite chaos. Marshall had been on the phone for an hour with Toby and Nate Williams, talking about Rashad's intention to promote a second-shooter scenario.

Nate thought it was an insane, desperate attempt to find a defense. But Toby was worried. She felt that our society was always ready to believe a conspiracy. Off the record, she herself had doubts about major assassinations. So, Toby told Marshall to investigate the theory himself, so that the government could disprove it with hard evidence.

"Why are you here wasting my time with this?" asked Judge Langworthy. "The government's motion goes to the heart of this matter, Muhammad."

They were in Langworthy's chambers in the Federal Building. The Detroit River sparkled outside a window. Marshall and Roberta faced off with Rashad and Leslie. Roberta was glad to have finally been given the call. And she had been ready, masterfully putting the motion package through and getting all of the motions granted, except Mbutu's statements and the hair and blood samples, which were now in debate. Langworthy wanted a stipulation, but Rashad was fighting until the end. The room was thick with attitude and tension. Here in the preliminary rounds of justice, every punch was a potential knockout blow.

"None of what Mbutu said to us or on camera was coerced," said Marshall. "He spoke freely, and arrogantly, I might add."

"But the statements don't amount to a confession," said Rashad. "They are prejudicial and add nothing to the government's case."

"Muhammad has a point, don't you think?" said Langworthy. "Why are you planning to introduce the statements?"

"They go to motive," said Marshall. "He didn't like Farrel Douglas's politics." Marshall tried not to show his displeasure at Langworthy's use of Rashad's first name. The two men knew each other but not well enough to get Langworthy to recuse himself from the case. Their chumminess was already pissing him off.

"That specific statement was not made," said Leslie. "And you can't extrapolate it from anything he said."

"Your Honor," said Rashad. "My client was asked repeatedly if he killed Douglas. He didn't answer, as was his right, but to a jury, that might look like guilt. In court, my client never has to take the stand. Allowing this evidence is tantamount to violating his Fifth Amendment privilege.''

Marshall was about to say something, but Langworthy cut him off. He turned in his leather chair for a moment, looking at the ceiling. He seemed to enjoy his power over those in the room, but all judges did. It was a perk of the profession.

''I'm excluding the statements,'' said Langworthy.

''Your Honor—'' said Marshall.

''Here's why, Mr. Jackson. I worry that the statements, even though made out of custody, are more harmful than valuable as evidence. I also worry that many prospective jurors will have already seen the tape or have read about it in the newspapers. I cannot wipe away that prejudice, but I sure as hell can stop it from being reinforced in this case.''

Marshall was silent. Langworthy was a bastard, but he knew his stuff. The decision was right, under the circumstances. A judge's duty was to insure fairness as much as possible. Mbutu was already under a national microscope, which tore away at the presumption of innocence. Langworthy was just leveling the playing field.

''Okay, Your Honor,'' said Marshall, ''but we would like the record to show our strenuous objection.''

''It will,'' said Langworthy. He was ever so slightly annoyed by Marshall's request.

''Now, as to the DNA tests,'' said Rashad. ''We can't be sure of the government's procedures. I can't have my client's DNA analyzed by those who clearly have an interest in the test coming up positive.''

''The government represents the people,'' said Marshall. ''The defendant is one of those people and—''

''Please, not that old speech,'' said Leslie Reed. ''We need a chance to conduct our own test.''

''The sample isn't large enough, Your Honor,'' said Roberta. ''We've only got one shot here.''

''And given that fact, I think the government should conduct the test,'' said Marshall.

''Perhaps the defense will want to have an observer there,'' said Langworthy.

Rashad was about to respond, when Leslie blurted out: ''I think we need to have a hearing on the matter.''

Langworthy leaned back in his chair. ''Oh, is that what you think, Ms. Reed?''

"Your Honor, she didn't mean anything by that," said Rashad.

But it was too late. Langworthy was primed for a reaming, and he was not about to be stopped.

"Okay, Ms. Reed, here's your hearing: your motion has merit, but you cannot deny that a test will prove that the defendant was either there or not. The government presents a ton of case law showing that in every matter like this, the court rules in their favor and is upheld on appeal. You lose the motion, embarrass yourself, and incur my temporary, but considerable, contempt."

"We are not going to oppose," said Rashad.

"Good," said Langworthy. "Intimidating judges may work in New York, Ms. Reed, but in Detroit, we bite."

They left the judge's chambers as Langworthy lit up a cigar. In the hallway, Rashad was about to go when Marshall cut him off.

"Will you stipulate to DNA now?" asked Marshall. "It would make things easier and maybe score you some points with the judge."

"No," said Rashad. "Do your test. We'll be watching."

Rashad and Leslie walked off. Leslie was clearly pissed off and almost stomped to the elevator.

"He really tore her a new one," Roberta said as she laughed.

"Yes, but did you see how he suggested that they oversee our test? He didn't even allow them to make the suggestion. He gave it to them."

"I guess he did," said Roberta.

"He wants to make it look like he's being evenhanded. Yell at Leslie, then give them the right to look over our shoulder."

"Man, he's smooth," said Roberta.

"He should be, he's been at it most of his life."

Marshall walked back to his office, knowing that the blood and hair test would put Mbutu closer to a conviction, but not knowing what the unpredictable judge might do next.

21

Irish Eyes

Marshall returned home, feeling tired and frustrated. He pulled up to his house and noticed Danny's car parked at the curb. He must be inside the house, Marshall thought to himself. When he pulled in his driveway he noticed that Danny was inside the car. Marshall got out of his car and walked over to Danny. He was asleep in the vehicle, and he had a bandage on his hand.

Marshall knocked on the window, and Danny awoke with a start. He rubbed his head and opened the door. Marshall could smell the alcohol as the door opened. Danny had been drinking. But what would possess him to get drunk and sleep it off in front of his house?

"I'm fucked up, man," Danny said.

"Tell me something I don't know," said Marshall.

"It's Vinny, she—" Danny slipped and fell as he got out of the car.

"Damn. I got you."

Marshall helped Danny up, and then they walked toward the house. Marshall saw that the bandage on his hand was actually a cast.

"What the hell happened to you?"

"Vinny got shot and I got suspended," said Danny. He lost his footing again, and Marshall caught him, holding him up.

"Vinny was shot?!" Marshall almost yelled.

"Yes, but she's okay," said Danny.

"Where is she, can I see her?" Marshall had completely forgotten Danny's other news.

"She's in the hospital. I just left there. She's fine, really."

Marshall calmed himself. He sometimes worried about his friend getting shot on duty. It had never occurred to him that it would be Vinny who caught one.

Marshall took Danny inside and sat him at the kitchen table. He started to make coffee. Danny sat silently, staring at the wall.

"Okay. Vinny caught one and you got suspended because—"

"I kinda beat up the perp who shot her."

" 'Kinda beat up'? So, how badly did you kinda beat him up?"

"Intensive care."

"Shit," said Marshall.

"He'll live. But Vinny's really pissed at me."

Marshall heard a noise behind him. He turned to see Chemin in the doorway. She wore a shirt and clearly had on nothing underneath.

"Hey, Danny," she said.

"Hi," Danny managed to say.

"Vinny got shot," Marshall said.

"Oh God," said Chemin. "Is she okay?" She looked past Marshall at Danny.

"Yeah, she's fine."

"Can I see her? Where is she?"

"Mount Carmel," said Danny.

"Danny, I'm so sorry," said Chemin. "I'm gonna go call her right now."

Chemin turned and walked back upstairs.

"I'm fine too," Marshall called after her. "I'm alive and everything." She ignored him as she disappeared upstairs.

"Damn," said Danny. "It's colder than a muthafucka up in here."

"Yeah," said Marshall. "That's how it is these days. Look, we'll see Vinny tomorrow, but right now, you need to do something about your situation. I know a lawyer who can help. The first thing to do is get you back on the job."

"Fat chance," said Danny. "The city's been hit with some big-ass lawsuits in the last year. They won't even talk to me. I'm gonna get fucked up behind this."

"Not if I can help it," said Marshall. "You stay here tonight. Tomorrow, we go see my friend, and get this show on the road."

"Okay, that sounds cool," said Danny. "I don't want to be home right now. I'd go to the hospital, but Vinny kicked me out already."

Marshall stood and hugged his friend, and for a second they were kids again, fresh from another narrow escape from some neighborhood toughs, then they were soldiers on a night patrol in Europe. He hoped that this latest crisis would be resolved and become just another good story to tell over beers in some smoky club.

Danny walked off to the guest room. Marshall felt sad for Danny. He didn't love many things, but he was sure Danny loved Vinny. He didn't blame him for losing his cool.

Marshall looked up the stairs, knowing that Chemin was probably still awake. He sighed heavily and walked into his office.

Marshall awoke early the next day and took Danny to see Victor Connerly, a lawyer who specialized in defense. Danny seemed in a trance as they both slipped out of the house while Chemin slept. They rode in silence on the Lodge freeway in rush-hour traffic into Detroit's bustling downtown. Marshall had lent Danny a change of clothes, and his body strained against the too-small shirt he wore.

Victor Connerly was a fat man, about three hundred pounds or so. He'd been a pro lineman back in the 1980s and had parlayed the ex-jock thing into a thriving practice. Connerly owed Marshall more than a few favors, not the least of which was helping Connerly's son, Burt, get a felony assault charge reduced to a misdemeanor and community service. Connerly agreed to take the case for practically nothing. Danny seemed a little happier.

Marshall went to see Vinny at Mount Carmel Hospital. She was fine, although being laid up didn't seem to sit well with her.

When Marshall got back to the office he was greeted by Bob Ryder, Roberta, and Walter. They had a look of doom on their faces.

"What's going on?" asked Marshall.

"We tried to call you," said Ryder.

"My phone was off," said Marshall. I didn't want to be—"

"They're dead," said Ryder. "The Johnsons. They were both killed."

Marshall was stunned into silence. He walked slowly to a chair and sat down. He barely heard Ryder as he told him how someone had broken the security of the FBI men assigned to watch the Johnsons, and murdered them, and how the report was that it was unrelated to the Douglas case.

"We need to get to the crime scene," said Ryder.

"Right," said Marshall. "Where's Sommers?"

"She's already there."

"Good. She'll keep the local cops from walking all over our jurisdiction. Okay," said Marshall. "Let's go. Just you and me, Bob, everyone else keep working, and think about if this hurts us. We'll call Nate and Toby on the way."

"This is fucked," said Walter.

"That's a great attitude," said Roberta.

"Don't you start with me, Roberta."

"I am surely going to start with you, Walter. All you do is complain. We don't need to hear your negative comments anymore."

"Then don't listen."

"Try to be positive for once, will you," said Roberta.

"Don't talk to me like that," said Walter. "You're only the boss in your dreams."

"Please," said Marshall. "We can't fall apart now."

Roberta and Walter apologized to each other and walked off. Marshall got up and headed toward the door. Ryder followed, obviously still stunned.

"You okay?" asked Marshall.

"No, no, I'm not," said Ryder. "But I will be."

Marshall headed out with Ryder, already knowing that this would give ammunition to Rashad. He would say these witnesses were killed so they could not exculpate Mbutu. The judge would never let that kind of insinuation in the case, but it would only help keep Langworthy on their side.

Mbutu's conspiracy theory was silly, he thought. Still he had a nagging desire to protect himself. He decided then and there to call the county prosecutor and get the protocol for having his brother transferred into federal custody.

22

No Tales

The Johnsons' small, two-story house on Detroit's near west side swarmed with police and media. Marshall and Ryder were taken in the back way so the reporters would not know that they were involved.

The media had been informed that there was a double homicide. But Marshall was sure they'd seen the unmistakable cars and nondescript suits of the FBI. They would know something was afoot. The Johnsons' importance to the Douglas case would come out sooner or later, but for now, it was Marshall's opinion that those bastards didn't need to know.

Nate Williams and Toby had been informed. Toby had cursed like a sailor. Marshall had never heard the word *fuck* so many times. Nate Williams had vowed that FBI heads would roll. Then, ever the pro, Toby assessed the damage to the case, informed Marshall how to head it off, then hung up. Bob Ryder had been so nervous that he could barely drive the car.

Marshall entered the house on Ardmore Street and felt a sense of déjà vu. When he started his career, he'd done some public defender work and had been to many murder scenes. He'd never forgotten the impact of that first time. He was sick and barely held on to his breakfast. Since then, he'd become a fed, a much more savory occupation. But now he was back in the muck, and it was just as disturbing as he remembered.

The crime scene was an unsettling, bloody mess. The air of murder was thick and the chatter in the room subdued, as if out of respect for the dead. In the middle of the living room, two bodies lay together, surrounded by people. Marshall stood over the corpses as the FBI and local forensic men argued over procedure and jurisdiction.

The Johnsons had been viciously attacked and killed while watching TV. The TV still flickered in the background; an infomercial announced the benefits of fast weight loss.

The couple had been beaten with a heavy object, then stabbed and cut with a knife. Mrs. Johnson's head was gone, and so far they had not found it.

Most of the homicides in Detroit were garden variety. Someone was on drugs, domestic abuse, a robbery gone bad and someone was killed. But this, this had the earmarks of some sort of psychotic murder. And before Sommers said it, Marshall was already thinking the words she said to him.

"Looks like some sick fuck," Sommers whispered to Marshall. "See how the bodies are placed?"

"What do you mean?" asked Marshall.

"Sixty-nine," said Sommers. "Head to toe. Sex act."

Sure enough, the Johnsons had been placed head to foot. (Stump to foot, Marshall thought, then chastised himself for thinking it.) "I see," said Marshall.

"Jesus Christ," said Ryder.

"Is there another murder to match this one to?" asked Marshall.

"Not so far," said Sommers. "We checked locally, regionally, and nationally. This looks like a premiere sicko."

"Then are we checking for relatives and any current trouble they might have been having with neighborhood thugs?" asked Marshall.

"We're coordinating with Detroit local," said Sommers. "They're being assholes, but they're going to do it."

"Tell them they have to do it," said Ryder. "I hate when these local jerks fuck with us like this."

"We've got our behavioralist coming in on this," said Sommers. "But it looks like a local matter."

"Yes," said Marshall. "What else do we have?"

"Well, we got the headless corpse, the sexual statement in death, and some messages written in blood."

Marshall followed Sommers into a downstairs bathroom. On a wall was written something in a bloody scribble.

"What the hell does that mean?" asked Ryder.

"That's the question," said Sommers. "Come on, let's see the rest of it."

Sommers walked into the dining room. A newspaper had been opened to the obituary section, and put next to a page of comics from that same paper. In the kitchen, there was another cryptic bloody scribble on a wall.

Marshall grunted something, then walked out of the room. He went back into the living room.

"The blood in the bathroom looks older," said Marshall, "like he did that one first."

"Good one, Counselor," said Sommers. "Didn't notice that myself."

"An afterthought?" asked Ryder.

"Something like that," said Marshall.

Marshall, Sommers, and Ryder watched as the bodies were placed into plastic bags.

"Our men were outside all night," said Sommers. "They didn't see anyone go in or out."

"Then how did this happen?" Marshall was angry and didn't care who knew it.

"It was a low-priority assignment," said Sommers, clearly not liking Marshall's tone. "Two witnesses who were not testifying against a mob chieftain or a gang member. Jesus, it was routine. They had their guard down because it wasn't supposed to be up."

She had a point. Baby-sitting the Johnsons was not a serious matter. The agents has simply been told to watch the house and not interfere with their lives.

"They're downtown making out reports," Sommers continued. "They're good men, but this will hurt their careers."

"We need to get each and every detail," said Ryder. "I want every minute thing that happened last night—"

Marshall suddenly walked out of the room and went back into the bathroom, then he ran upstairs, and came back down and looked at the bathroom again.

"Something wrong?" asked Sommers.

"Maybe," said Marshall. "When Rashad hears about this, I'm sure he'll use this to further his bullshit conspiracy theory. We have to keep a presence so that he can't use information from the investigation against us. Go to the local cops and tell them that this case is ours for the foreseeable future."

"Gotcha," said Sommers. She walked off and proceeded to stick it to the local police detectives.

"Okay," said Ryder. "That was good, but what's really bothering you?"

"This crime scene is too good," said Marshall. "Too good."

"Good?" asked Ryder. "Did you mean to use that word?"

"No, I mean, yes I did," said Marshall. "I took the behavioralist course at Quantico."

"We all did," said Ryder.

"Well, this crime scene doesn't fit the general pattern of a psychopath, but it seems like a forced attempt to do so, like the killer wanted us to think that he's crazy."

"What do you mean?" asked Ryder. "Of course he's crazy. Only a nut would do something like this."

"Sure," said Marshall. "But a real nut doesn't *think he's crazy*. Run with me here. The scene is too neat, a psycho has fits of rage, and makes a mess of things. Second, the victims were made unconscious before they were killed. Although not unheard of, most killers would rather have live victims, as their suffering is what he wants to witness."

"Because he's probably dreamed or fantasized about it," added Ryder. "I remember that from the FBI course."

"And these writings in blood are just a little too creepy and weird and they don't really say anything."

"Jesus, Marshall, do you know what you're saying here? You're agreeing with a potential defense."

"No, I'm not," said Marshall. "I'm just making sure we don't hand more evidence over to Rashad. He'll say what I just said, but we have to understand it before we can defeat it."

"True," said Ryder.

Marshall had covered well. What he was really thinking was that the killer was trying too damned hard to make everyone think he was crazy. Killing is a psychopath's *obsession*. People who work to make it look as if a nut has done it have killing as their *occupation*. One thing he did know was that the Johnsons would never testify in the case now. And Rashad's assertion that Mbutu was not the man going up those stairs would never get in.

Marshall looked back at the crime scene with a sense of dread. If he was right, then that meant a real-life conspiracy.

"I found it!" said a man wearing the forensic tech jacket.

Marshall turned to see an FBI forensic tech rise from the fireplace.

"It was stuck in the shaft of the chimney," said the tech.

He stepped back, and turned to the crowd. In his hands, he cradled the sooty head of the late Mrs. Johnson. Groans and gasps sounded in the room. These were people used to seeing death, but the killing of the elderly couple had left them all stunned.

"Bag it separately," said Marshall. "Good work."

Marshall turned to say something to Ryder, when his eye caught something that upset him. He glanced out of the front door and saw Sommers talking excitedly to a Detroit police detective. But that was not what caused him anxiety. It was the sight of CIA Agents Van Ness and Easter sitting in a sedan and quietly driving from the scene.

23

Spoon's Window

Moses sat in a corner of the gym in county jail while the other inmates worked out. He sat with his back against a wall, and the metaphor was not lost upon him. He was in trouble. Marshall had not gone for the bait and had left him in county jail to rot. And to make matters worse, the word was out that someone had put a hit on him.

Dake and Nita's betrayal was only half over. They had him in jail, but now they had to kill him before he got out of prison. Only that way could they fully consolidate their power in the crew.

Moses had pled not guilty to the burglary, assault, and attempted murder charges. He stood in court before the same judge who had sent him to prison four years earlier. He could almost hear the judge and lawyers laughing at him. He'd been caught with the goods and the gun. His attorney, Ted Walker, had represented him at the hearing but had resigned by letter soon thereafter. Moses had been so angry that he'd hurt his hand slamming it into a wall. Walker had been bought, which was not hard to do. He was fucked on the case now, but what worried him more right now was the beefy white man staring at him from the opposite corner of the gym.

The man had been watching him for about ten minutes. He looked like a hitter, thought Moses. He was hard and tough and had that air about him that said that he had given up on every moral principle of normal life. He was heavily tattooed and had scars over his arms and face. It was a grotesque sight seeing the colorful designs over the raised scar tissue.

Moses decided to test the man. He moved away from the corner and walked toward the door. The man didn't move. But when he did leave, the man walked out behind him a second later.

In the hallway, the guard was gone, a sure sign of a hit. When you took someone out you had to pay the guard off, so you didn't compound your own situation. Moses didn't have much time. He had to take the hitter out and not get tagged with the blame. If he was caught assaulting the man, he'd never get out of prison.

Moses pulled out the thin metal bar he'd been hiding in his pants. It was iron, dense, and portable. He'd paid a lot for the item, but it was worth every dollar, favor, and packet of drugs he'd paid for it.

Moses turned suddenly and moved back to the door of the gym. The hitter was coming out, a screwdriver in his hand. Moses swung the metal bar, striking the hitter squarely on the temple, tearing a gash in his head. The hitter dropped his shank and fell to his knees. Moses swung the bar again, breaking the man's jaw, and spraying blood on the doorway. The hitter fell back inside the gym, blood pouring from his face.

Moses ran as quickly as he could back to his cell. He wiped the bar clean of his prints and tossed it in another inmate's cell. Soon, the wing was put on lockdown. The would-be hitter was taken to the hospital, and the inmates in the cell where Moses had thrown the metal bar were taken away for questioning.

Later, Moses sat in silence in his cell. His cell mate, a young Latino boy called Turgo, read a book and coughed loudly from a cold he'd acquired.

This was just the first attack, Moses thought. They'd come after him in numbers the next time. He'd have to have a gun to fight them off, and even the best ounce of home-grown couldn't buy that in jail. He could seek help from some of the gangs inside, but the price was too high, and it was not money or cigarettes he was talking about. He was not about to punk himself, have sex with another inmate for protection, but the alternative was surely death.

Moses was brought in for questioning on the assault. He was taken into the chief of security's office. He sat outside with about ten other men. Guards stood over them, watching. Moses recognized some of the men as being associated with prison gangs. These men were probably habitual offenders who had been institutionalized to their bones. They embraced the social order of prison. Not many things scared him, but these men did.

Moses was taken into the office. He sat in the room with the chief, Harry Witherspoon, a burly man everyone called Spoon.

Moses sat on an old wooden chair. Even though Spoon's office had nice, comfortable furniture, cons were made to sit on the hard chair as a reminder of their lack of worth. Against a wall, Moses could see outside through a window. A commercial truck was unloading supplies.

Spoon's window had just been put in the wall. It was made of glass, but it also had a grate on it. It should have had the thick, bulletproof glass used in prisons, but the security glass was on order and had not come in yet.

It was unusual for a prison office to have a window in it. Paranoid penal officers never wanted there to be any way for anyone to get out other than through the main entrance. But the county lockup was not a maximum security prison, and Spoon was terribly claustrophobic. He insisted that the window be installed to keep himself from going stir-crazy.

Out of the window, Moses could see the street. The county lockup was downtown right near a commercial district.

"The man who was beaten was in a gang," said Spoon. "A rival gang has been blamed for the attack. If you know anything, you'd better tell me now."

"I told you all I know," said Moses. "Just take me back to my cell."

"You're not going back," said Spoon.

Moses was shocked for a moment. Spoon's demeanor was hard and unemotional, as though he meant that Moses was never going to see the light of day again. Then Spoon added: "The feds are taking you. That's why we did this tonight. Normally, we'd wait for morning, after tempers cooled. But they want to take you right now."

Moses breathed easier. His brother had finally come through, he thought. "Okay, I'm ready to go."

"Why do the feds want your lousy ass?" asked Spoon.

"I got connections," said Moses.

"Don't you get cute with me, you fuck. I know you were involved in that beating, and after the feds are done with you, I'll prove it—"

A shot went off. A second later, the door burst open as a guard struggled with an inmate over a riot gun. Outside the office, all of the cons who were gathered fought in a free-for-all with guards and one another. Spoon had made the mistake of mixing the gangs, and a fight was the result.

Moses hit the floor as the riot gun discharged again, hitting Spoon and shattering the window in the office. Spoon fell to the floor. The guard and the con struggled on, falling to the floor, rolling over each other.

Moses looked at the window. There was still a grate on it, but he would never have another chance like this. More guards would all be coming in just a few seconds, and the entire place would be on lockdown. Right now, no one noticed him in the commotion.

Moses jumped up and threw himself into the window with all his strength. The grate gave way, and Moses fell onto outside pavement. His body was racked with pain as he hit the ground. He fought it off and moved toward the supply truck.

Moses heard another shot, and an alarm sounded as he pulled at the truck's rear door. It opened partially, and he squeezed himself through.

Moses sat inside the dark truck for what seemed an eternity before it pulled off. He could feel boxes on his back. He couldn't go far; they'd miss him and know he'd run. So as soon as the truck stopped, Moses climbed out and ran off. He was on Gratiot, not far from the jail. He wouldn't last long wearing the bright jail uniform, so he crossed the big street and headed for a residential area. He jumped a fence and went into a backyard of a house and just sat for a moment.

He needed wheels to get away from this area. On foot, he was doomed. He went to the front of the house and looked around. The street was dark and deserted. In the distance, he could see the Renaissance Center towering above the rundown little houses in the area like the Emerald City of Oz.

Moses saw a car roll down the street. It stopped several houses away. A man got out of the car. He was carrying two white bags that probably had takeout in them.

Moses didn't hesitate. He ran as fast as he could and jumped on the man.

''Shit!'' the man yelled. He fought, lashing out with a hand that caught Moses in the chest. Moses hit the man hard and grabbed for the keys that had fallen on the sidewalk.

Moses took the keys and got into the car and drove away. He could hear the man behind him cursing loudly.

Moses drove eastward. He had many friends in that part of town. He'd have to move fast before the news of his escape hit every ear in town.

He wondered how his brother's face would look when he learned that he had helped him escape. He had a lot of work to do. He'd have to ditch the car soon, or even maybe torch it, then get some decent clothes. Then he'd leave town—right after he killed Dake and Nita.

24

Flight

Marshall and Danny sat in the back of Vinny's hospital room as Vinny's family members crowded around her. Marshall had only spent a little time talking to Vinny. It was all he could manage with so many people there. He wasn't upset, though. He had other matters on his mind.

Rashad had learned about the death of the Johnsons and leaked a story to the press. In both Detroit newspapers a story about the murders appeared, questioning whether a conspiracy theory was possible. It wasn't a public support of Rashad's defense, but it was damaging to the government's case.

There was a big crowd at Vinny's bed. Only a cop was allowed to have so many visitors at one time. Vinny was the ninth of ten children, and it seemed like all of them were in the room, or out in the hallway, waiting to see her. The little room was filled with flowers and gifts from cops and family. Vinny seemed in pretty good spirits.

The Shaw family was a close-knit group. Mom and Dad were both retired teachers, and the other siblings were all law-abiding-go-to-church-every-Sunday kind of people. They brought light, laughter, food, and gifts for Vinny. They also brought disdain for Danny. At times, Marshall forgot that Danny wasn't black, but the nasty looks from Vinny's people certainly reminded him. They couldn't see that Danny was the same as all of them.

Marshall had been tap dancing all day, trying to explain to Rashad (and indirectly to Judge Langworthy) that the Johnsons' deaths were not part of some plan to lock up Mbutu. Rashad had almost cheered when he heard the news. This was all the proof he needed. Marshall's challenge would be to keep him from using the Johnsons to influence the jury. Somehow, he knew that Langworthy would allow it to sneak into evidence in some supposedly innocent form.

After meeting with Rashad, Marshall thought long and hard about his brother. Moses' words echoed in his head over and over. So, that morning, he'd requested that his brother be transferred to the federal jail. It wouldn't hurt to have him safe, just in case he did have something.

The Johnson crime scene lingered in his memory. He kept seeing the cryptic words in blood, and Mrs. Johnson's head being pulled from the chimney. Sommers still had nothing on the case. The pattern matched nothing they had, and no other similar killings had occurred since.

Marshall's gut told him it was a fake, and if he was right, he might yet need Moses' information not just for the case but also to save his career.

"I hate this shit," Danny whispered. "See that fat one there, that's Vinny's sister, Renitta. One time, she did one of them things they do for drug addicts, to stop her from seeing me."

"An intervention?" asked Marshall.

"Yeah, that's it," said Danny. "The whole family held her hostage for an hour, tellin' Vinny how she shouldn't see me."

"That's serious, man."

"Fuckin' right, it was. But Vinny, she came home, and told me about it, and we laughed like hell. But I was pissed about it, you know, inside. That Renitta is an evil-ass bitch."

Renitta heard Danny's voice and shot him a mean look.

"Did you say something to me?" asked Renitta. She was a hefty woman, one of those who was big and proud of it.

"I was talkin' to my man here," said Danny. "Not you."

"Uh-huh," said Renitta. "Tell him about how you almost got my baby sister killed trying to be Dirty Harry."

"I know all about it," said Marshall.

Renitta gave Marshall a nasty look, then waddled back to Vinny, who was stuffing her face with a rib bone.

"Let's get out of here," said Danny.

Marshall and Danny stepped outside, then walked away from the overflow crowd waiting to see Vinny. A couple of the men gave Danny cold looks as he and Marshall walked by.

"You know as bad as my career is, I'm more upset about the way these muthafuckas are looking at me right now."

"Forget about them. Vinny is all right, and you need to get your damned career back on track."

"I got a hearing coming up," said Danny. "That lawyer you got me, Connerly, that guy is good, man."

"I told you."

"He got my pay reinstated, and he intimidated the shit out of the IAD."

"IAD? What the fuck are they in this for?"

"Routine. Besides I got a bad rep, remember? They're always sniffing around, looking to jam you up, you know."

"So, the police investigation board can't condone what you did to that robber, but they can give you a slap on the wrist."

"That's what I'm hoping for," said Danny. "So, I'm cool for now, but you, man, how the fuck did your witnesses get waxed by a serial killer?"

"I don't think they were," said Marshall. "The media has been all over it saying that, but they don't know what I know. That crime scene wasn't . . . evil, you know."

"Yeah, I do know," said Danny. "There's a sick, nasty-ass humanity that you see at a killing."

"Right, and it wasn't there. That crime scene was damned near clinical, too planned and set up."

"If it was, then you got some big-ass trouble, my brotha. I remember a couple of years back, some dirty cops were mixed up with this drug gang called the Union."

"I remember that. A lot of people went to jail."

"It came back to bite everyone in the ass. And all the clean guys who were looking the wrong way got caught up in the shit. You need to watch your back because if your house is dirty, you might be next."

Marshall sat in silence for a moment, the gravity of Danny's words upon him. Danny was a lot of things and certainly no one to be giving advice these days, but he did know crime. In that area, he was an expert.

Marshall and Danny decided to go out and get something to eat. Vinny's people had brought a lot of food, but Danny didn't dare ask for any. They were walking out of the lobby when Marshall's cell phone rang. He fumbled to take it out of his pocket.

"Marshall," he said.

"This is Sommers. I kinda got a situation."

"Shoot."

"You know you could have told me what you were doing with your fucking brother," said Sommers. "Maybe if you had, he wouldn't have escaped tonight."

Marshall almost dropped the phone. He wanted to ask her to repeat what she had just said, but he had heard her right. Moses had gotten away in transport.

"How—where are you?"

"I'm at county. A little riot broke out and in the commotion your brother escaped before the agents could do the transfer."

"I'll meet you there," said Marshall. He hung up. Sommers was obviously pissed. He hadn't told her about his brother because he was growing distrustful. But she was right, if he had let her do the transfer, she would have gone herself, and Moses would probably be in jail instead of out on the street, probably on his way out of the state. And the worst thing was, he still had the information Marshall sought.

"I gotta go, Danny. I had Moses transferred, but he escaped."

"Damn, that sneaky bastard," said Danny. "Okay, I can get some guys on the street and—"

"Danny, you're not a cop right now. You just get some food and go back to Vinny. I'll call you."

Danny stood for a moment as the statement settled upon him. He was not a cop, and that fact had just slammed home.

Marshall took off running toward his car. The night was cold and a light snow was falling. He could feel the adrenaline pumping through his body already. He was angry, excited, and just a little scared.

"Watch your back," he heard Danny yell behind him.

Marshall stood next to Agent Sommers as Spoon talked to an FBI agent from a stretcher. He had been hit by the spray of the riot gun, but he was okay. By the time the riot had been contained, Moses was gone.

Sommers was pissed and had barely looked at Marshall when he arrived.

"I'm sorry I didn't tell you," said Marshall. "This thing with my brother wasn't something that you were supposed to be concerned with. I'll tell your superiors that it was not related to our case."

"They won't care. Not calling me in was a matter of trust, or more to the point, a lack of it. It hurts me no matter what you say."

"I know you're pissed, but we have got to find him. He's got a lot of friends out here in the street."

"I'll find him," said Sommers, "but I can't guarantee that he'll be in one piece after we do."

"None of that shit," said Marshall. "I need him alive. We are not in the revenge business, Agent, we're in the justice business."

Sommers didn't say anything. She walked off and talked to some of her men. Marshall hated to be so nasty with her. It was really Moses that he was angry with. The little bastard had gotten away and put Marshall in deep shit once again. He realized in that instant that relatives are either a lifelong blessing or a lifelong curse. Moses was certainly the latter.

He was worried. He had only moved to transfer Moses because of his suspicions about the Johnsons.

"If your house is dirty, you might be next," he heard Danny's voice say.

Marshall's mind was racing with the possibility of a conspiracy. He could no longer deny it: recent events made it easier for him to win the case. The Johnsons can testify that Mbutu was not the man, and suddenly they're dead in a manner that arouses suspicion.

The trial would be starting soon, and he'd be totally immersed in litigation and media coverage. Going to trial was like submerging yourself in water. The process enveloped you, and the way you had to focus your attention was much like holding your breath.

Suddenly, he was scared. If there were shadowy forces at work then they were inside the government itself. He was not afraid for himself but for the innocents he knew. Ruthless people didn't care about guilt; anyone in the path of their goal was expendable. He thought about Chemin and Danny. If anything happened to them because he was underwater during litigation, he knew that he'd never be able to live with himself.

He was going to have to be more than a prosecutor now. He had to be a cop, a soldier, and a detective as well. Trouble was coming, and it felt like staring into a train's light in a dark tunnel.

Marshall watched as they put Spoon into the ambulance. He wondered where his brother was and how they would find him in his natural habitat, the violent and dangerous underbelly of the city.

Part 2

CRIMINAL JUSTICE

25

······························

Trust

Marshall listened quietly as Sommers raged on in his office. He was cool. He sat and let her go. If his marital difficulties with Chemin had taught him anything, it was to say nothing to a woman when you were clearly wrong.

Marshall watched as Sommers paced before him. It would have seemed belittling if it weren't for the fact that she was more mad at herself than she was at him. This had clearly jeopardized something for her within the FBI that had nothing to do with him or the Douglas case.

The FBI was a tough, very bureaucratic, by-the-book agency. Agents were selected from the choicest groups of law enforcement candidates. Many of the cops he knew had tried to get in but had failed. Even Danny had flirted with the idea, but he didn't have a college degree, which was a prerequisite. The agency prided itself on its elitism, so slipups were not common, but when they did occur, heads usually rolled.

Moses' escape had made the local news, and had even popped up on CNN. Pictures of him were in every newspaper and flashed on each newscast. If Marshall knew his brother, he would change his look, lay low until the heat was off, then blow town as fast as he could.

"Your statement on the transfer says your brother was wanted for questioning," said Sommers. "What was it about? Or is that a secret too?"

"It was about an ATF case," said Marshall. "I needed information on a gunrunner named Quince that I prosecuted but failed to convict.'' Marshall answered quickly so Sommers would not get suspicious. It was only partially true, but it would do for now, he thought. ''I'm closing out the case and giving it to another lawyer, I just wanted to be thorough. Look, the Douglas case has us all at our wit's end. I just lost track of my priorities for a moment.''

''My boss is thinking of pulling me off of the Douglas investigation,'' said Sommers. She was calming down now, her voice taking on a more moderate tone. ''He thinks that obviously I didn't inspire confidence in you, so you left me out of the loop.''

''It wasn't that big of a deal. I don't even know if my brother had anything I could use.''

''So, why did you have him transferred?''

Marshall thought carefully about his answer. He couldn't tell Sommers the truth, but the lie had to have the ring of truth.

''I was covering my ass,'' Marshall said. ''You know how it is. If I didn't follow up—''

''I know, I know,'' said Sommers. ''It comes back to bite you in the ass.'' She calmed down a little more, then: ''So, I got a call from that Van Ness asshole from the CIA.''

''What did he want?'' Marshall said.

''He wanted to be filled in on all this. He wouldn't say why.''

''Why didn't he call me?'' Marshall asked.

''I couldn't tell you.'' Sommers grew silent for a moment, taking on a concerned look, one that suggested that something bigger was on her mind. ''He bothers me,'' she said. ''I just don't know why all of a sudden these guys are all over the place.''

''I'd like to know the answer to that myself,'' said Marshall.

''Damn! I don't need this right now. I'm up for a promotion. Do you know how hard it is being a woman in this job?''

''I don't want to compare hardships, but I am black, in case you haven't noticed,'' said Marshall.

''Yes, but at least you're a man—forget it. I'm sorry. I don't mean to sound like a whiny feminist. This is the profession I've chosen. This is how the game is played. I'll take my lumps whatever they are. I'm just gonna have to do some dancing.''

''I'll be dancing for Nate and Toby today myself,'' said Marshall. ''They don't want the case to go into meltdown over something stupid.

They've been on the phone all day, spinning the escape away from our case. Look, if it means anything to you, I'm sorry.''

''Well, the Bureau will find your brother. But in the meantime, please keep me informed.''

They made more small talk about the case, then Sommers left. Marshall felt a little sorry for her. She was right. Even though he was black, it was a man's world. Sommers probably had to be twice as good to have gotten as far as she had.

He often wondered why women joined law enforcement. Sommers was a bright, attractive women and probably could have been successful in many other professions. Why carry a gun and chase scum for a living?

He chastised himself at the sexist thought. She became a cop for the same reasons men did. Most cops were psychologically much like the men they chased, except they had a stronger moral compass. So if this was true, then Sommers had many criminallike tendencies in her character. He didn't see them, though, not the way you saw them in male cops like Danny. Danny was clearly the other side of the psychological coin.

Marshall worked for an hour, then went to see Nate and Toby. He told them the story, leaving out his suspicions about the CIA and the death of the Johnsons.

Toby was on the speakerphone from Washington. She was upset but seemed more worried about the media making her look bad. She had just been the subject of a *New York Times* article touting her as a presidential candidate. She never brought up the fact that Marshall had a career-criminal brother. For that he was grateful. Nate assured her that the press would get nothing concerning the escape that would embarrass her.

These moments always fascinated Marshall. Power was awesome when you were so close to it. Most people lived their lives believing that there is some Great Authority out there that protected fairness and assured justice. In reality, it was not true. People made the laws and executed them. People printed the newspapers and swayed public opinion. And these people, these men and women, were just as fallible, weak, stupid, and susceptible to pressure as any of us. The only Great Authority of life was money, power, and the inborn instinct for self-preservation.

This made Marshall more worried than Nate or Toby. If anyone found out that his brother had information on the Douglas case, he was through in the department. Toby would have his ass for not telling her, and Langworthy would disbar him for nondisclosure. They would have to. Someone would have to pay so that the myth of the Great Authority would be served.

"So, when do we get the results of the DNA tests?" asked Toby.

"Maybe today," said Marshall. "Mbutu wanted the doctor limited to DNA testing only. We agreed, of course."

"If that test is negative for him, we'll all look like fools," said Toby.

"It won't be," said Nate. "Everything I know tells me it was him up there."

"I agree with Nate," said Marshall.

"And if it is positive," said Toby, "then we quickly go in for the kill."

"You should know, Toby, that Rashad wants to speed the trial up," said Marshall.

"Why? We're already on a fast track," said Nate Williams.

"Yes," said Marshall. "But it seems that they want to go even faster. He wants to go in a month."

"What's that bastard up to?" Toby asked aloud. "He's making every wrong move in this case."

"Maybe Rashad's lost it," said Nate. "After all he's been through in the past years, losing a child, mental breakdown, it's conceivable he's not the man he used to be."

"I don't think so," said Toby. "I saw that man on a special segment of *Nightline* last month. He was talking about criminal procedure. His analysis of the Constitution, its laws, and their application was the most brilliant, thought-provoking legal analysis I'd ever heard. I don't believe for one minute that he's lost his faculties. He just wants us to think he has."

"I've decided not to take him up on his offer," said Marshall. "It gives him too much control over what we do and when we do it. Langworthy will only go that fast if the government agrees."

There was silence on the phone line for a moment. Faintly, Marshall could hear the soft crackle of the phone's connection.

"Agree to the motion," said Toby.

"Excuse me?" said Marshall.

"Stipulate with Rashad to speed things up. I think he's trying to use the media to his advantage. Think about it. Normally, it's the defense that drags a case along, trying to let memories lapse, evidence get stale. Rashad has already tipped his hand: conspiracy. What better way to bolster this theory than by yelling to the world that his case is so strong that he's ready to go now."

"Are you sure, Toby?" asked Nate. It was rare for him to question her, and he looked concerned about it.

"With all due respect—" began Marshall.

"You know, I hate that term," said Toby, cutting him off. " 'With all due respect.' What it really means is: I think you're full of shit. Don't 'duly respect me' Marshall, just do it, and get your team on its toes, because when I go to trial, I mean business."

Marshall glanced at Nate to see if there were any signs of support in his eyes.

Nate was silent, which meant he was agreeing with her, or had been steamrolled. Either way, Marshall was fighting a losing battle.

"Yes, ma'am," said Marshall. "I'll let Rashad know today."

"Prepare a stipulation and have it ready," said Toby. "If he backs off, then we leak it to the public. If he signs it, we go to trial ASAP."

"Looks like we got a live one," said Nate. He smiled, but Marshall could still see the concern in his eyes.

"Yes, let's see what he's made of," said Toby, finishing the thought.

They were quite a pair, Marshall thought. They seemed of the same mind at times. When they were together, he noticed that their body language complemented each other. Toby leaned toward him, and vice versa. It was as if they were married, or joined in some other way beyond a professional relationship.

Nate and Toby had known each other for many years and were both happily married to their respective spouses. So Marshall didn't think they were involved sexually. Still, there was something between them, these two, something deep, mysterious, and just a little disturbing.

This was Marshall's last chance to stop this foolhardy move, but looking at Nate's complete compliance at this moment told him that he'd be running into a brick wall.

For a second, he considered telling them everything that he suspected, that the Johnson double murder was a setup, his brother knew valuable information, and the CIA was creeping around like ghosts. It seemed as if someone was trying hard to make sure that he didn't lose this already very winnable case. But he let the thought go. This case was a career-maker, and even though he considered himself a maverick, he was no fool. There are some things that a lawyer doesn't do, and pulling the attorney general into a crazy conspiracy theory was probably number one on the list.

"I'm on it," Marshall said.

He left Nate's office and went back to his own. On his desk were two messages from Chemin. She'd called from her office at Hallogent and wanted him to call back. The last one was marked URGENT. He picked up the messages and looked at them with a sense of doom. What did she want? Lately, she never called him at the office. He feared the very worst.

He picked up the phone, then put it back down. He was afraid, scared of what she wanted. A divorce? More therapy? He didn't need that trouble in his life right now. It was far from courageous, but he'd wait and talk with her later after he got back home.

Marshall decided instead to call Danny. Danny's case was going well, so far. The man he'd beaten pled guilty to the robbery and assault charge, but he was suing the city. He knew he was screwed on the robbery charge and wanted only to get the money in the police misconduct case.

If the city could get rid of the case, then Danny could be in the clear. The city didn't like to fry cops, but they hated to write large checks to plaintiffs.

Danny was in pretty good spirits when he picked up the phone. "Hey man," he said to Marshall. "You're in the paper every day."

"Don't remind me," said Marshall. "That escape cost me."

"Don't panic. Moses is like a fuckin' bad penny. He'll turn up again, and when he does, somebody will put him down for good. Just wish it could be me."

"I just called to see how you were doing," said Marshall.

"Okay," said Danny. "Hangin' in there, you know."

"Just lay low and let the lawyers handle your suspension. You take care of Vinny. I'm sure she needs you right now."

"Shit, she's damned near back on her feet already. That's one tough woman I got."

"I know that."

"I just gotta get me something to do. The time off was good at first, but this sitting on my ass is killing me."

There was a hanging silence on the line, and Marshall knew what Danny was thinking even before the words came out.

"You and Chemin any better?" asked Danny.

"No. I've been too busy to even think about it."

"Yeah, well you hang in there too. Man, we're a fucked-up pair, ain't we? We could swap lives and it wouldn't make a damned bit of difference." Danny laughed and Marshall had to join in.

"Look, call me as soon as something happens in your case, okay," said Marshall."

"You got it, brotha. Peace."

"Bye."

Marshall hung up the phone, then walked over to the conference room, where he knew Mbutu and Rashad would be waiting. He stopped at the door to the conference room for a moment. Toby was eager to call the bluff she'd attributed to Rashad, but he was a little apprehensive about going to trial so soon. These things were delicate matters never to be taken lightly.

Now he knew why lower level lawyers got high-profile cases. Their bosses were political players, who put their subordinates' careers on the line while maintaining the appearance of being in charge. It was a no-lose situation for Toby. If he won, then she'd be the brilliant, avenging attorney general who brought a murderer to justice. If he lost, then she'd be the righteous attorney general whose trusted soldier had failed her. But it was a bad deal that young lawyers kept taking because they had to, because it was their job, and basically lawyering was a shitty occupation and everyone wanted to break out of the pack.

Rashad and Mbutu sat next to each other in the conference room. Marshall had purposely not called in the team. That would signal that something major was up, and he didn't want Rashad to know that this meeting was serious.

"This can be quick," said Rashad. "Do you accept our terms to go to trial next month?"

"No," said Marshall. He was disobeying Toby's orders, but he wanted to see if he could get anything out of them.

"I knew it," said Mbutu. "Let's go."

They were about to get up when Marshall said: "However, if you add two weeks, I can do it." Marshall was shooting from the hip now. Two weeks would be a concession that he could sell to Toby and he could live with himself. The extra fourteen days would be a welcome cushion in case anything went wrong. Also, if for any reason Langworthy extended their timetable, he would have that much more time.

"Why?" asked Rashad. "We're talking a capital murder case, why do a few extra days make a difference?"

"Because it does," said Marshall. "So, either take the offer, trial in six weeks, or we'll let the judge decide."

"No," said Mbutu. "I need the time—"

Rashad cut off his statement with a hand. He took Mbutu aside. Mbutu coughed hard, and it sounded bad, as if he were coming down with something. Marshall covered his face. He didn't want to get sick while working on the case.

"Okay," said Rashad, walking back to Marshall. "We agree to your schedule."

Marshall shook hands with Rashad, then left. He immediately called Toby and Nate and told them the news. Toby was upset about the haggling, but she was ready to go to the press and say that the government was going for swift justice.

Bob Ryder and the litigation team were upset at the news. The fast-track schedule would have had them in court in midspring. That was moving fast as it was, but six weeks felt as if they were being fed to the lions. They argued and cursed, but in the end, they accepted it just like Marshall had. They were all young lawyers too and knew the drill.

Marshall went back into his office and rested. He just wanted to get the trial over with now, to put it past him. Suddenly, he wanted swift justice too, to put Mbutu away, and save his failing marriage.

He glanced at the picture of Chemin on his desk. They were moving even further apart with the trial coming on. They even came home at different times so as not to run into each other. They were in separate worlds and seemed to be content there. It was easy to see their marriage was going to end, and for the life of him, he couldn't think of how to stop it.

Of course he could give up the case, he thought. He could go to Toby and resign and let someone else take over his duties as hero/fall guy. Then he could go back to figuring out how he could get over his fear of extending his lineage with the woman he loved. But he could never do that. This job had become his salvation. The lessons of the ghetto were always with him. What would he do if he let his career go? What if it didn't work out with Chemin? He'd be alone *and* stuck in a dead-end job. No, he'd have to stick it out, find a way to save his marriage and win the day in court.

There was a loud knock at his door. He heard voices on the outside.

"Come on in," he said.

The door opened and there stood his litigation team huddled around a messenger. The messenger was a kid and looked like a frightened animal surrounded by hungry wolves.

In the hands of the startled young messenger was an envelope that had to contain the results of Mbutu's DNA test. In the envelope was the future of their case. If the hair they found in the crawl space didn't match Mbutu, then they would have to release him, and he'd be left with nothing. Everyone involved in the case would run away from the failure, and his career would be ruined.

Marshall signed for the package and sent the messenger away. His hands shook a little as he tore open the envelope and read the top sheet of the report. He smiled, and for the first time in a long time, excitement filled his heart.

"We got him," he said.

26

Served Cold

Moses was almost ready. He'd been working, planning, and waiting patiently since his escape from prison. He sat on the dirty old sofa in the dank basement of the drug house on the city's east side. The walls were brown but seemed to have been a different color at some point. The ceiling was cracked and there were holes in the concrete floor. The only light was from an old lamp in the corner. A brand-new bulb was screwed into its socket, almost mocking everything else in the room. Sunlight glowed behind the dirty windows at the top of the walls.

The house was a low-level drug den run by a man they called Half and Half. He'd gotten the name because he was part black, white, Asian, and Native American. Everyone called him Half. Moses couldn't remember what his real name was. Half was Moses' emergency friend. Not even his old crew knew about the relationship. Moses had saved Half's life by getting him off the hook with some dirty cops who were squeezing him for payoffs. That favor was now due.

After Moses escaped, he ditched the car he'd stolen and slept with some homeless men under a freeway overpass. The next morning, he'd come to Half's house. Moses went in, but only after he made sure no one saw him enter. Half had given Moses clothes and food and kept him in the basement. All the time, Moses waited patiently.

He'd been with Half a few days now, and he knew that everyone would think that he was gone. Dake and Nita would think it, and they were probably out of hiding as a result. That's what he wanted. He wanted them to be cool and casual, just to go about their lives. Today, he was going to start his plan.

Half stepped slowly down the stairs into the dim basement. He was dressed in baggy jeans and a T-shirt that was stained with white powder from making drugs in his kitchen.

Half was a good-looking man of about thirty or so. And even though he was multiracial, the black part of him seemed dominant, from his tan skin and broad nose, to his dark curly hair. He looked in good health, and Moses was glad to know that after all these years, Half hadn't succumbed to using his own product.

"He's here," said Half. His voice was thin and scratchy. He had a habit of grabbing his crotch, a mannerism that Moses had seen many times but didn't know where it came from.

"Tell him you need a gat, preferably a Glock and a pump-action shotgun and ammo," said Moses.

"The muthafucka is nervous, you know. Said he just got out of the joint, and he thinks the man is watching him. He checked me for a wire and kept asking me why I wanted the guns, that I wasn't no known shooter." Half grabbed his crotch.

"Tell him to go fuck himself if he doesn't want to do business with you. Tell him you'll go to Benny Milton or that Kirkland nigga from the west side."

"I don't know about this shit, Mo'," said Half, grabbing himself again. "This ain't my thing, you know. Guns and shit. You out the joint, nigga, why don't you just go?"

"Oh, so you just gonna punk out on me now?" said Moses. "If it wasn't for me, your ass would be in a hole over on Six Mile, muthafucka."

"Come on man, I—"

"Come on, my dick! I didn't have to do what I did. I did it because I'm a cool muthafucka. I don't like to see a good man get jammed for nothing. And when I need you, you gonna give me this bitch-ass shit."

Half was scared, and that's what Moses wanted. Half was just a wannabe gangster. He liked the money, the power, and the women, but he wasn't tough or particularly smart. A little intimidation went a long way with a man like that.

"Look, I'm gonna help you, nigga," said Half. "You don't have to get all upset."

"Then don't question my shit," said Moses. "Now go and tell him what you need and don't forget the silencer. I'll need it."

Half left and Moses followed him partway up the stairs. He wanted to make sure that he didn't fuck up the deal. Moses peeked through the old wooden door into the kitchen as Half talked with Lewis Quince.

Quince was indeed nervous as they talked. His eyes darted around as Half's workers used several microwaves to make the drugs. A little black girl of about seven or so sat in a chair looking out the window watching the backyard. Half was bringing them in young, he thought. Then again, kids were reliable.

Moses had forgotten how imposing Quince was. He had a face that could only be described as severe. He was much taller than Half and looked down on him with a scowl. Quince didn't seem happy about the pending transaction.

Quince was also a mean bastard. He'd killed several people that Moses knew of but had never been prosecuted for them. One kid Quince had locked in an old refrigerator and suffocated. He'd also shot an ATF officer and gotten caught, but somehow he'd beaten the rap. He hoped Half didn't piss Quince off, or he'd have to intervene and risk exposing himself.

"What did you go downstairs for?" asked Quince.

"I had, uh, some shit to do," said Half unconvincingly.

"You know what? I think you working for the boys."

"I told you, I don't work for the cops. Look, if you don't want to sell me the shit, then I'll just—" Half looked confused for a second. He grabbed himself nervously.

Moses cursed silently as he realized that Half had forgotten the names he'd given him.

"Just what?" said Quince.

"I'm gonna go to Benny or that Kirkland nigga from the other side of town," said Half, remembering what Moses said.

"Shit, they can't deliver. Benny caught a drug case, and Kirk, that muthafucka sells them cheap Mexican guns. You'll blow your god-damned hands off trying to shoot one of them things."

"I'll take my chances," said Half. "Go on, bounce."

Quince made an annoyed noise, then turned and walked out the door. Half turned to Moses and shrugged. Moses was about to call Half over, when Quince came back in holding a shotgun. One of the drug workers screamed and knocked over a tray of crack. Another ran out of the room.

Half threw up his hands and began to back up. The little black girl who watched the backyard didn't even flinch. She looked at Quince, then went back to her job. To Moses, that was the scariest thing he saw. The kid was gone, lost to this world.

Quince stood with the gun trained on Half and the others, staring at them. For a second, Moses thought Quince was going to shoot everyone in the room, cut his losses because he thought he was being set up. Then he smiled a little and lowered the weapon.

"When your pants dry, you can check out this one first," said Quince. Then he tossed the shotgun to Half, who caught, then almost dropped the weapon. "It's not loaded."

"What about the Glock?" said Half.

"All I got is forties, but they burn." Quince took a black gun from under his shirt and put it on the table. "These pieces are clean and untraceable. I'll take two thousand for the whole set with ammo."

"What about the silencer?" asked Half.

"I got it, but it's hard to silence a Glock. It'll work, but you got maybe three, four rounds before it's barking again."

"Cool," said Half. "Five hundred for all of it."

Moses was pleased. Half had remembered to haggle. Never let anyone sell you something for the first price. He knew the guns were probably stolen, and Quince was making all gravy on the deal. But Quince's best quality was that his pieces were clean. You use one and get busted, you won't be looking at a fucking double murder. So the price was partially justified.

"Look," said Quince. "I'm hot after the fed bust. I got expenses, people to pay. I'm not about negotiating. Two thousand."

"Seven hundred, or get the fuck out," said Half. He grabbed himself again, this time with confidence.

Quince looked hard at Half. Moses could tell that he suspected something, but he didn't know what. Moses knew Quince would take the deal. He had no choice. He was fresh out of the joint and needed to make deals to get back in.

"All right," said Quince. "But don't ever get in a jam and need me in the future."

Half paid Quince and Quince walked out. Half waited until he was sure Quince was gone, then he brought the weapons to Moses in the basement.

"You did good," said Moses. "Two thousand, that muthafucka was trippin'."

"I was going to kick his ass," said Half. "Pulling a damned gun on me."

Moses gleefully loaded the Glock and the shotgun. He practiced whipping them out. The silencer fit, but it wasn't perfect.

"This silencer is cheap, but it'll have to do," said Moses.

"So, what's this all about, man?" asked Half.

"Less you know, the better," said Moses. "Read about the shit in the papers." He whipped out the shotgun and cocked it. He saw Dake's and Nita's faces in the darkness.

Outside, Quince was walking back to the alley behind the house. Half may have been a lot of things, but he wasn't no shooter. And he was acting crazy, like he was hiding something. Quince suspected cops, but when he came in with the gun, that would have been the end of that game. Still, he had to know what was up. If he went down again, he might not get a sympathetic judge like the last one. Thank God for that old bastard, he thought.

Quince sneaked around the back of the house. A guard, a kid of about thirteen, kept watch. Quince thought about taking him out, but it wasn't worth killing a kid just to see what Half was up to. Soon, the kid walked out to watch the front.

The little girl sat in a window watching the backyard, so Quince circled around to the side and crossed to one of the basement windows. They were small and covered with dirt and debris.

Quince knelt by one and tried to get a look in. He wanted to see what Half had going on in that basement. He would have only a few minutes before the little kid circled back.

Quince peered inside the window. He squinted to see and tried not to make any noise. He saw Half talking to a man who he couldn't see very well. Then suddenly, the man turned. Quince smiled as he saw the face of his old friend and good customer, Moses Jackson.

27

....

The Bargain

Once again, Marshall was in his office late. Chemin had called again, and he had put her off, still afraid of what she might have to say.

It was dark outside, and the team had disbanded long ago. He was happy about the results of the DNA test. They had a solid case now. The test put Mbutu in the killer's crawl space, and no conspiracy theory could refute that fact.

Their only problem was that they had used the PCR, or polymerase chain reaction test. This was the test used when the sample was small. They only had the one hair. PCR was only accurate to one in a hundred. The restriction fragment length polymorphism, or RFLP test, was accurate to within one in a billion. He would have preferred to use that test of course, but they had to go with the less accurate test because of the size of the sample.

PCR had been successfully challenged in the courts, so Rashad would try to suppress. Roberta was already working on a response to the inevitable motion. It would be a fight, but one that he would ultimately win.

He'd spent the last few hours looking at the tape of the assassination. He'd watched Farrel Douglas's head explode over twenty times. It was horrifying, and something else—it was familiar. He didn't know how else to put it. He'd seen the murder before, and he couldn't for the life of him tell where. He watched it again. Douglas stood at the podium, looking handsome and proud, then he grabbed his chest, a second later, his head exploded in blood and tissue.

"Damn," Marshall said to himself. "What is it?"

The way the shots came, the way Douglas grabbed himself. It was like some recurring dream, ghostly, frightening, and familiar. Death was something that you never forgot when you saw it live, and somewhere in that anguished part of his memory, a bell was ringing, calling to him to remember.

He heard a light tapping on his door. His first thought was that it was Bradbury, but when the door opened, it was Jessica, peeking around the door and smiling.

"Hey," she said.

"I was just leaving," said Marshall.

"Me too," said Jessica. She was in another tiny little skirt and a white cotton blouse. Marshall lingered on her a little too long. "I had some stuff here I was taking to my new office. And what should I see, old Marshall burning the midnight oil again."

"I'll walk you to the garage," he said. He got up and grabbed for his briefcase. He was suddenly nervous and wanted to leave before she could start talking to him.

He threw some papers into his briefcase, then looked up to see Jessica walking toward him with an unmistakable look of lust on her face. He was transfixed for a second. Was it his mind playing a trick, or was she really doing what he saw?

"Jessica, what are you doing—"

"You can leave if you don't want me," she said.

She moved across the room, coming toward him. Marshall again had the feeling that it wasn't real, that his mind had warped on him. But it was real, and she was almost to him now.

"Jessica, I can't do this," he said.

"I know you don't want to. One of the many reasons I want you so much."

She pushed herself against him. Marshall stood still. He wanted to speak, to move, but he didn't. All he could think of was making love to the young woman. It had been months since he and Chemin had been together. Months without the heat he was feeling right now. Because of that, in that way that only men have, he felt that he *deserved* to have her if he wanted.

He was suddenly aware of his erection pushing against his zipper with urgency. She embraced him, pulling his face to hers. Her tongue went into his mouth, and he kissed her back urgently.

His reason was gone. He was so involved in his work, and dodging the wreck that was his marriage, that he'd forgotten that he was human and in need of human companionship. Now, the fact that Jessica wanted him was exciting, vital, and right.

She pulled his head away and dropped to her knees. She quickly unzipped his pants, and slipped him inside her mouth. The rush of heat took his breath away. He threw his head back, and grabbed her hair. It was good beyond all reason, and that single thought echoed in his brain, pushing back all other logic.

Jessica got to her feet and kissed him hard. She pulled up her skirt, and he grabbed her ass. Marshall picked her up and sat her on his desk, moving between her legs. He kissed her, his mouth moving to her chest where he was surprised to find that she wore no bra.

Jessica moaned loudly as he took her breast into his mouth. She fell back on the desk, knocking over the picture of Chemin. Marshall noticed the picture as it fell. He looked at it, then tried to look away but couldn't. Chemin was in his head now, and all of their history poured from his memory. He saw himself courting her, marrying her, then making love to her. All the dark, wonderfully secret things they'd said to each other surfaced inside his mind.

"God," he whispered. "No."

He pulled away from Jessica, and put himself back into his pants. She grabbed at him, but he kept her away. She looked hurt like a child, her eyes filled with passion and need.

"What?" she asked. "Did I do something?" She was breathing hard. "Did I do something wrong?"

"I can't," Marshall said. "I'm sorry. I shouldn't have done this."

Jessica took a step away from him. "Marshall, I need you," she said. "Please, don't leave me like this."

"No," he said with conviction, more for himself than her.

Jessica suddenly turned, embarrassed. For a moment, they just stood across from each other, silent. Marshall prayed that she wouldn't come after him again. He didn't know if he could resist a second time. Then Jessica moved to the door. Marshall stopped her before she could leave.

"Don't you run out on me," he said. "We should talk about this."

"Why? You don't want me." She was getting misty.

"Yes, I do," said Marshall. "I do, but . . . my marriage is weak right now, hell, it's probably over, but I can't walk away from it—even for someone like you.'' Marshall was close to her. He wanted to touch her, but he didn't trust himself.

"I don't really want to take something that's not mine,'' said Jessica. "I just—I just thought you wanted to be taken."

"Maybe I did. I'm sorry.''

Jessica wiped her eyes. "So, what am I supposed to do with my feelings, Marshall?''

"Give them to someone who can be with you,'' he said.

She looked up at him, and he was struck by her beauty. For a second, he wanted her again, but he knew the moment was lost now, his reason, his sanity was back.

"Good-bye, Marshall,'' said Jessica. Then she looked away, and walked out the door. Suddenly, she stopped. She took a step back into the room. Marshall thought that she was going to come at him again, then his heart nearly leapt from his body as Chemin walked through the door.

He was beyond shock. This was hell, he thought. Any moment the Devil would rise from the floor on a fiery mound, and proclaim ownership of his immortal soul. He wanted to disappear, shrink to the size of an atom and fly away. It was a foolish thought, but only embracing the impossible allowed him to react to the situation he was now in.

Jessica fixed her clothes nervously. Marshall's brain quickly processed what his wife was seeing. Her husband and an attractive young girl half undressed in his office late at night. He suddenly thought of the phone calls he had not returned and the fact that the guards all knew Chemin and had probably let her in.

"Chemin—'' he said. "Look, nothing happened—''

Chemin took a step toward Jessica, raising her fist. Jessica didn't move, staring right into Chemin's face. This shocked Marshall and seemed to surprise Chemin, who nonetheless seemed ready to bash the young girl's head in. And Jessica was ready to take the hit, ready to pay for what she had done.

Chemin stopped and lowered her arm. She raised her finger to the young girl, her hand shaking with rage.

"Get your lucky ass out,'' she said.

Jessica moved around Chemin, and walked out of the room almost defiantly. She was a surprising woman, he thought, foolish, but strong. Suddenly, Jessica stopped in the doorway, and Marshall thought she would turn and say something that would cause Chemin to pounce on her. He saw himself pulling them apart, handfuls of hair being ripped from the other's head. But Jessica didn't say a word. She kept walking, her heels clicking on the floor and trailing off like plaintive tapping.

Chemin turned her attention to Marshall. He fixed his clothes, tucked in his shirt, and straightened his tie, as if this would purge his sin. For a moment she just looked at him, stared at him as if she could slay him with her glare.

"Was it good?" she asked. Her face was contorted, and her eyes had a sad, hurt look that he'd never seen and hoped never to see again.

"Chemin, I got weak, but we didn't do anything," he said. He heard his own voice, and even to him, it sounded pathetic.

"Answer me, you motherfucker. *Was it good?*"

"Don't swear at me."

"Don't swear?" she said incredulously. "How about I go out and fuck some guy in *my* office. Is that permissible in a marriage?"

"What damned marriage, Chemin?" he snapped. He regretted the words as soon as he had said them, but it was too late to take them back. He'd opened the box.

"So, I see. You were justified, you had needs. My wife doesn't understand me," she said in a whiny voice. "People work out their problems, Marshall. They don't go and screw the secretary when things get tough!"

"We—nothing happened. Look, Chemin—"

"Please don't say my name," she said. "I don't like the way it sounds out of your mouth right now."

"I can't win this. So, go on, curse me, do whatever you want. I don't care anymore." He walked back to his desk and turned his back on her.

"Always the attorney, aren't you? Give up and plea-bargain the unwinnable case. What do you want, five to ten years of yelling with time off for good behavior? Well, fuck that. I saw you, and I demand to know what happened. *Was she good, dammit!*" It was classic Chemin, attacking with humor to make it sting all the more.

"I'm not having this conversation with you. Nothing happened."

Chemin laughed. "You are so transparent. You can't say you didn't have sex with her, can you? So, what did you do, Marshall? How far did it go before I came in?"

"Can we just talk about our problem? How about us?—"

"Did you suck her titties?"

"Aw, Jesus."

"Did you lick her? Did she go down on you? How much of nothing happened, you sorry bastard?"

"Okay, fine, you want to be nasty, then yes, I wanted to fuck her," said Marshall. "Like any man I thought that some gratuitous sex would make me feel better, that if I just went through something human, I could forget that I've failed with you. But it didn't work. I couldn't do it because I'm stuck with feeling that our relationship is the center of my fucking life, that I need you, and I can't let that go."

There was silence for a moment. Chemin looked at him and her eyes seemed twice as big as they were, as if she were looking right into him, searching for something. Then she dropped her coat to the floor. She was dressed in a navy business suit. She took off her jacket, kicked off her shoes, and started to unbutton her blouse.

"What are you doing?" asked Marshall.

"I want you to fuck me," she said.

"What? What the hell—"

"You say you didn't screw that girl, you say I mean so much to you. Then fine. I want you to fuck me and give me a baby, right now."

Her blouse was open, and she took it off. He tried not to notice her breasts, but it was impossible. Once again she had managed to subdue his mind with her moxie.

"Don't do this, Chemin, this is crazy."

"No, it's justice. You owe this to me. The one thing I want most in the world, you don't want to give me. You betrayed me tonight with that woman. If you want to make it right, then pull off your pants and let's get down to business."

She started on her skirt. Marshall went to her and stopped her. He didn't know how to feel. He was angry at her actions, and yet there was a perverse logic to it.

"Chemin, this is not going to happen," he said.

"If you had sex with that girl, I'd appreciate it if you washed off your dick before you fuck me."

"I'm not going to—" He couldn't even say the word. It was a vulgar enough term, but Chemin's actions and intent had made it sound downright evil.

She looked up at him. Her eyes were filling with tears. Her hand trembled inside of his. He was reminded of the first time he saw her, and how there was a power about her, an energy, that took his breath away. It was still there, he thought, after all their time together and their awful recent troubles, she was still exceptional.

"This is what it means to be a woman," she said. "Like you're naked and begging for the world to have mercy on you. All I want is to be beautiful, and have my man appreciate me, but it always comes down to taking shit, settling for shit, or watching your shit slip away. Well, this is where it stops for me, Marshall. I think far too much of myself to live this way. I'm too good a woman to take this from you. So either you fuck me, or you can't have me anymore."

Marshall released her. He stood there, not knowing what to do. Her intellect was awesome, and he thought at that moment that she would have made a great lawyer. She'd used his indiscretion to bargain for life itself, and in the process, she'd humiliated him and reduced the act of sex, his manhood, to a mere commodity.

If he did what she wanted, then he'd be her prisoner for the rest of his life. If he didn't, he'd lose her and gain admission to the Club of Losers who could not handle the simple act of love. He stood on the crossroads of his own life and looked in both directions. This was the moment he'd dreaded since they'd started to have trouble. He'd thought many times of what he would give to save his marriage. And after all of this turmoil, he still did not know the answer.

"No," he said. "I can't."

"That's what I thought," she said.

Chemin laughed bitterly as she dressed. She walked past him to the door. Without looking back, she said: "Call your lawyer." Then, she walked out of his life.

28

Shadow Government

There is no federal government. The United States is just that, a group of sovereign states joined by common cause. In a sense, the federal government is the glue that holds them together. It is like a shadow, a thing that is constant, but seldom noticed.

These thoughts always filled Marshall's head when he argued a case. He needed to keep the jurisdiction in perspective. The federal government was a heightened authority of each state it sat in. Its power was awesome, and he needed to know that it was always with him.

Marshall rose to argue Rashad's motion to suppress the DNA evidence. The courtroom was clear of media and any gallery. Langworthy didn't feel that this matter should be open to the public and run the risk of tainting potential jurors. So only the lawyers were allowed in this day. Marshall and his team crowded one another at a table. He didn't want to have Roberta and Walter sit behind him as they had on previous occasions. They were in trial mode now, and the team had to be seen as one. Rashad and Leslie sat on the other side of the courtroom, looking calm and sure of themselves. Mbutu didn't look so good. He was flushed, and his eyes were pink, as if irritated. He was sick, but Marshall didn't know from what.

Marshall struggled to keep his mind on the case as they waited. Chemin had not been in the house for two days, and he didn't know where she was. He'd called everyone she knew. He was sure her friends were lying to him, but he couldn't be a hundred percent certain. She hadn't even come into work. This was how lawyers had nervous breakdowns, he thought. When your life and emotions are pulled apart in different directions, something has to snap.

"Look alive," said Ryder. "The judge is coming in."

Marshall nodded to Bob Ryder, who seemed to be very concerned about him. Roberta and Walter had both separately asked him if he was okay. He'd given positive responses, but he was sure that the look on his face betrayed the statements.

Langworthy entered the court carrying books and papers. He sat down and began to shuffle them, looking for something.

Rashad's argument was that the PCR test was not accurate enough to be admissible. That one in a hundred was prejudicial but not probative of any salient fact in the case. Rashad had cited the cases from California that had successfully challenged PCR testing.

"I've read the motion and response," said Langworthy. "I don't think I need to hear any argument."

"I would like to say something," said Rashad.

Langworthy looked upset at this statement. "Very well," he said. "Proceed."

"Although the cases are not on point for exclusion, we feel that the time has come to invalidate PCR as admissible evidence. The sample was small, one single hair, Your Honor. And the chance that the test is wrong is one in a hundred. That isn't sufficient to risk the life of a man."

Langworthy looked at Marshall.

"Mr. Rashad is asking the court to take an unprecedented action," said Marshall. "While PCR is not as accurate as the RFLP test, it is nonetheless accepted as a definitive analysis. The defendant doesn't cite any cases because none are on point for his request. There is precedent to challenge the test, but there is nothing that says it should be invalidated."

Marshall sat down. Langworthy started his decision when Roberta tapped Marshall on the shoulder.

"The prejudice," she said.

"What?" said Marshall.

"Prejudice," said Roberta. "In their motion. The balance of probity versus prejudice is his basic argument."

"Your Honor," said Marshall. "Please excuse me, but I'd like one of my team to add to the government's response." Marshall had blown it.

He was not prepared to finish the matter and hoped Roberta would bail him out.

"Okay," said Langworthy. "But next time, please be more organized, Counselor."

"Sorry, Your Honor," said Marshall.

Roberta was shocked and obviously afraid. Marshall smiled to reassure her and urged her on. She got up and went to the podium. She was not a good public speaker, but evidence was her strong suit. She cleared her throat and gripped the side of the podium so hard that Marshall could see her knuckles whiten.

"Very simply, Your Honor," she began, "we'd like to note that in addition to the arguments already heard, any prejudice to the defendant brought by the PCR test is minimal and doesn't begin to outweigh the probative value of the evidence. The test is highly regarded and has been accepted in thousands of cases throughout the country. It has been used to convict, as well as exonerate, defendants in criminal cases. In short, it is a standard that has been tested and proven vital to the process of justice."

"The RFLP test is accurate to one in a billion, Your Honor," said Leslie Reed, coming to the podium. "This PCR business is only one in a hundred. That leaves too much opportunity for chance, error, and mistake. The test of prejudice versus probity is more than a catch phrase. It is the essence of the evidence rules, the unstated test for all evidence. So, it's vital that we understand what we're talking about here. A one in a hundred chance of a mistake. That's roughly the odds of a car accident, or bumping into an old friend. Would any of us stake our lives on those odds? I don't think so. The nature of evidentiary prejudice is that there is no balancing factor of fairness to the evidence in question. You balance this limited test against the power of the term DNA, science with a capital *S,* and a jury cannot help but be prejudiced by the comparison. We are not asking the court to part the Red Sea. We are merely requesting that Your Honor place a higher worth on the sanctity of a man's life than on this dubious and soon to be outdated analysis. I invite the court to read Slough, Trautman and McCormick's analysis of this theory. For this reason, we ask that Your Honor invalidate the test and exclude the evidence, or at the very least grant us a special hearing on the matter to determine this issue."

Marshall saw that Roberta seemed dazed. She was good when she had research, but weak when it came to thinking on her feet. Finally, Marshall saw the value of Leslie Reed. She was a legal theorist, a lawyer who challenged the essence of the rules with simple logic and reason, which were the building blocks of all law. He was impressed and noticed the broad smile on Rashad's face. If the judge was sufficiently impressed by her theoretical argument, he might just be attracted to the idea of creating law, giving the defendant an instant issue on appeal and making the fight over the DNA test a small trial-within-a-trial. He had to counter her argument with one that was just as attractive to the judge.

Marshall rose and went to rescue Roberta. "Ms. Reed's point is well taken," said Marshall, "but contained within it is its fatal weakness. If PCR is so shaky, as she says, then isn't that reasonable doubt itself? Can't she sway a jury with the failings of the test, and doesn't the defendant win in that fashion? If PCR is not good enough, then a jury will see that, and their client will go free. And I remind Your Honor that rule 403 also empowers a judge to protect against prejudice by giving a limiting instruction on the evidence in question."

"I've heard enough," said Langworthy.

The lawyers sat down. Roberta whispered a "thank you" to Marshall, who returned the favor.

"We're all very clever here today," said Langworthy. "But the law is clear on this. PCR is valid and was the only method available to the government. I will neither invalidate its use, nor will I diminish its worth in the criminal justice system. The defense will get the chance to challenge the process, and I will keep in mind that an instruction to the jury might suffice as protection for the defendant, if in fact any protection is warranted. The DNA test results will be admitted."

Langworthy gaveled and left the courtroom. The bailiffs came for Mbutu, and he went into another fit of violent coughing. Rashad seemed concerned and helped Mbutu out of the courtroom.

"Is he okay?" asked Walter to no one in particular.

"He's got some kind of bug," said Marshall. "Prison is not the most sanitary place on earth."

"What the fuck was that just now?" asked Ryder. "That was sloppy."

"I apologize," said Marshall. "I forgot the rest of the argument. But it was clear that the judge was going to rule in our favor."

"You know that's never clear," said Ryder. "If Roberta hadn't interceded, the judge had an open door to rule against us or at the very least give them a hearing that would embarrass us."

"Marshall saved the motion," said Roberta. "And it's our job to watch his back."

"Come on guys," said Walter. "We don't need to do this."

"He's right," said Marshall. "Bob is right. I blew it and it's inexcusable. We can't take chances on a liberal judge like Langworthy." Marshall paused a moment to make sure they were all listening to him. "I think you all have a right to know this. I'm having some trouble at home. My marriage is—well, it's probably over."

The others all reacted as he knew they would, with sorrow and compassion. Bob Ryder seemed particularly embarrassed by the confession.

"So I want you to know that I appreciate your help today, but from now on, I'll be at full strength. The pressures of the case just derailed me for a moment."

"We can all understand," said Ryder. "Jesus man, I didn't know."

"It's okay," said Marshall. "It's no excuse for what happened here today. Let's go. We've got jury selection coming soon, and we'll all need to be on our game for that. They've hired a jury consultant, April Kelly out of Chicago."

"Damn," said Ryder. "How can they afford her?"

"They can't," said Marshall. "She was one of Rashad's law students when he was teaching. Besides, this is a national case. She's advertising."

They filed out of the courtroom and went back to their offices. Marshall tried to feel a little better about his situation as he sent everyone on their assignments.

He returned to his office to find a note on his door that read: BRADBURY ON C-SPAN. He turned on the TV and watched as Bradbury testified before the Senate. They asked all kinds of embarrassing and silly questions, trying to find which way he might vote on the issues.

A senator from Georgia grilled him about a trade bill and how it might hamper American companies from becoming global. But Bradbury was a rock and didn't break. He answered the question, but didn't really give up an idea of how he might vote. He was going to make it, Marshall thought. The sonofabitch was going to the highest court in the land.

Marshall soon grew tired of the questioning and turned on his VCR and popped in the tape of the assassination and watched it again. What was it about the way Douglas was hit that was so familiar? He watched it again and again, going over the exact moment of impact.

He loosened his tie and tried to relax. He noticed a stack of phone messages on his desk. He rifled through them, but there was not one from Chemin. He was hoping that she would tell him where she was and that she'd calmed down from her anger. But there was nothing. There were five messages from Danny, though. The first of which said "Read the paper."

Marshall had been so busy that he had not even looked at the day's paper. He took it out and opened it up. There on the front page was a picture of Danny under a caption: COP UNDER FIRE FOR BEATING.

Marshall sat across from Danny at a little café in Trapper's Alley. The place was crowded as usual.

Danny looked like his life was over. Maybe it was. The man he had beaten had filed a ten-million-dollar suit against the city. The city had responded by cutting off Danny's pay and hanging him out to dry in the press.

The terrible thing was that Danny didn't understand why it was happening. The lawyers were using race to ignite the fear of the politicians of the mostly black city government. And Danny, despite what he thought and believed in his heart, was a white man.

"I don't believe this shit," said Danny.

"It happens all the time," said Marshall. "They're using you to make a point."

"Damn, I wouldn't care if he was white. I woulda done the same thing."

"Danny, you are not a black man to the rest of the world. To me you are, but I don't count. I don't run the city and make my living serving a black constituency."

"I can prove it. I can prove I'm not prejudiced. I'll get on the witness stand and I'll tell them where I'm from, what I've done my whole life."

"That'll just make it worse," said Marshall. "The lawyers will just say you're mocking black people, trying to save your ass by assimilation. Look, this is some serious shit. These people will come at you with everything they have."

"I know. But do you think people will believe it? Will they believe I'm a racist?"

Marshall's heart was breaking for his friend. Danny was a white man who had been raised as a black one. In the process, he'd gained a love of a people and the power of their culture, but he'd lost something too. He didn't know just who he was. He was looking for some validation from his friend, and Marshall just couldn't bring himself to lie to him.

"Yes, Danny, people might believe it. And not just because they don't know you, but because race is a weapon. Race clouds people's minds, and while they're angry about it, someone can steal the world from you.''

Danny looked like a lost kid for a moment. He hung his head as if ashamed, and fiddled with his hands like he didn't know what to do with them.

''Vinny has to go back to work,'' he said. ''And they took back my pay again.''

''I'm sorry, man.''

''And the goddamned reporters are all over my place.''

''Look, you can come and stay with me,'' said Marshall. ''I've got plenty of room.''

''No offense,'' said Danny, laughing a little. ''But I don't want to get into the middle of another war.''

''Chemin is—'' Marshall's voiced trailed off. He didn't want to tell him Chemin was gone. Feebly he thought that if he didn't say it, it wouldn't be true. ''I don't know where she is. She left me.''

Danny was shocked for only a second or two. Marshall could tell that Danny had seen this coming but was too nice to have ever said anything about it.

''Dang,'' said Danny. ''I'm sorry, man. Boy, what a pair we are, huh? Dumb and fuckin' dumber.''

''She came to my office and caught me with a coworker.''

''She busted you fucking someone?'' Danny's eyes were wide. ''Damn, I didn't think you had that in you.''

''I don't. Nothing happened, but we did get into the clinches a little.''

''What kind of clinches. What happened?''

''I don't want to talk about it.''

''Come on, man, you know the rule.''

The rule Danny was referring to was the one that says a friend never hides anything from another friend. Danny had shared many embarrassing things with Marshall. It hurt but made the other friend feel important. Not even in his current pain could he deprive Danny of that.

''We kissed,'' said Marshall. ''And then she kinda went down on me.''

''Holy shit!'' Danny almost yelled.

''We didn't finish or anything, but that was bad enough.''

''Chemin walked in on you with your dick in some girl's mouth?''

''She never saw that. I somehow managed to say no to her, but she did catch us fixing our clothes back.''

"Was there a fight?" asked Danny. He'd forgotten about his own troubles and wanted to know how his friend had fallen from grace.

"There was no fight, but it was bad. Chemin demanded that I give her a baby or she'd leave me."

Danny just rubbed his head and mumbled "Oh Lordy" over and over.

"Well, of course I couldn't do it under those circumstances, so she walked out."

"I told you when you married her, she was a piece of work."

"You have no idea," said Marshall.

"So, where is she?" asked Danny. "I hope nothing's happened to her. There's some crazy-ass people in Detroit."

"I don't know. I've called her friends, but they say they don't know. I know they're lying, which makes me know she's okay."

"So, you think she's gonna divorce you?" Danny suddenly sounded sad for his friend.

"At least. But if I can just talk to her, I know I can get her to reconsider."

"Do you want to?" asked Danny.

"What?"

"Maybe you should let it happen. You haven't been happy for a long time, man. Maybe this shit just ain't in the cards for y'all, you know what I'm sayin'? A muthafucka can't live his life worried about his woman all the time."

"I know," said Marshall. "I know. It's been a struggle. A relationship is supposed to make life easier, not harder."

"Look, man, I can't make that decision for you, but I will take you up on your offer, and I'll see if I can find her and make sure she's all right."

"That would be good," said Marshall. "Just don't let her know you're doing it. That'll only make matters worse."

"I'll be cool about it."

Marshall gave Danny the key to his house. "Take this, go in, have a beer, and I'll be back later. I have to go now. There's a little murder trial I have to attend to."

The two men hugged. Marshall walked to the People Mover, a local transit train that made a circuit of downtown Detroit on a raised tram. He waited at the station in Trapper's. Out of the window, he could see the streets of Greektown teeming with people. The smell of food filled the air.

The train arrived and he heard the automated voice announce its destination. He got on the train and sat down. The train rolled off, moving out of Trapper's back toward the other side of downtown.

He tried to think about anything but the case, trying to keep his mind occupied. A placard advertising a tribute to several actors stared down at him from the top of the car. THE KENNEDY CENTER HONORS the ad boasted.

''Jesus,'' Marshall said out loud. Several people looked at him with surprise. One woman moved ever so slightly away from him. Danny was right about the city being full of crazies, and he had just acted like one.

He got off at the financial center and hurried back to the office. He went through the material he'd gotten from Toby on American assassinations. He put in a tape and watched it, then he put in the tape of Douglas's murder on another monitor. It was a match. The familiarity of the killing had come from history. It was the Zapruder film that he had thought of. Douglas was shot in the torso and head in the exact same manner as President John F. Kennedy.

29

Criminal Lawyer

Moses sat in Half's old Plymouth Duster on Wyoming and watched his ex-lawyer, Ted Walker, buy his dinner. Walker was at the take-out window of Greene's Hamburgers on the corner. The smell of food made Moses' stomach growl. He'd been following Walker all day and had not stopped to eat. It was okay. He needed all the edge he could get for this job. He wasn't afraid of dealing with Walker. He had certainly taken out men before, but what he had planned for Walker was really not his sort of thing.

Walker got his burgers in a white bag that was already staining from the food inside. He got into his car, a red Seville STS. At the wheel was a black man who could have only been a bodyguard. Even though he was sitting, Moses could see that the man was pretty large.

Ted was smart, Moses thought. He knew an enemy was at large, and even though any smart man would have jumped town, Walker was not taking any chances. The driver pulled off with Walker. Moses waited a minute, then drove off behind them, cutting through the restaurant's parking lot.

He followed Walker as he drove down Six Mile, deeper into the west side. It was late afternoon and would be dark soon. That was good, thought Moses. He'd need cover of darkness to finish his job.

Walker slowed at the Southfield Freeway entrance, and for a second

Moses thought that he wasn't going home. But Walker continued west into ritzy Rosedale Park.

Walker's car turned down a beautiful block in the neighborhood. Nice houses, green lawns, and fancy mailboxes adorned each residence. Walker and his bodyguard stopped at a white two-story house at the end of the block and went inside.

Moses parked his car on a side street and hoped it didn't attract too much attention. Many of the cars in the area were new, and his might stand out among them.

Moses caught a glimpse of his face in the rearview mirror. He was looking very different now. He'd shaved his head and cut off all his facial hair. He didn't like it, but it did make him look very different, younger and cleaner. He'd been out all day and didn't believe that anyone had recognized him.

Walker had been married but had gotten divorced two years ago. Moses hoped that he wasn't living with anyone. That would only make the job much more complicated. The bodyguard would be trouble enough.

Moses got out of the car and slowly made his way around to the back of the house.

Dake and Nita could not have betrayed him without the help of Walker. They needed to make sure that he didn't beat the rap, and buying off an asshole like Walker was as easy as showing him the money.

Moses went into Walker's backyard. He had a standard alarm on the place, one that he'd foolishly let Moses pick for him. It was easy for Moses to disable it

Moses looked inside a window. The bodyguard was armed and sat on a sofa while Walker ate and talked urgently on the phone.

Moses would only have one chance at this. He checked his gun, making sure the silencer was on it. Gunshots in this neighborhood would certainly arouse suspicion.

He went to the back door and disabled the lock on the doorknob. He turned the knob slowly by degrees, careful not to make any loud noise. It was a pretty big house, and Walker was in the front part of the home. He hoped they would not hear him so far away. It was ironic, Moses thought, that so many times he'd used his skill to break in to steal. This time he had no intention of taking anything.

The door opened. His heart was beating fast as he stepped inside. If he had been heard, the bodyguard would be waiting for him.

He entered the house into a rear pantry off the kitchen. No one was around.

Moses heard Walker's muffled voice on the phone in the living room. He removed his gun from his waistband and moved toward the front of the house. Soon, he could glimpse Walker. He was still on the phone, talking loudly to the person on the other end.

Moses panicked. The bodyguard was gone. Where was the bastard? Maybe he had heard him coming in and was sneaking up behind him. Moses nervously looked around but saw no one. Walker yelled something into the telephone then hung up and sat down.

Moses heard a toilet flush. The bodyguard was taking a leak, he thought. That made things perfect.

Moses stepped into the room as the bodyguard came out of the bathroom tugging on his zipper. He was a thickly muscled man whose suit fit him terribly.

Moses raised his gun, thinking absently that the man had to be at least three hundred pounds. The bodyguard caught sight of Moses. A look of terror spread over his face. He reached into his jacket, yelling something that Moses couldn't understand.

Moses fired, hitting him in the cheek. The silencer reduced the sound to a loud "pop." The wounded man grabbed his face, still trying to take out his gun. Moses' next shot caught him in the chest. The sound was louder now, clearly a muffled gunshot. The bodyguard fell to one knee. Moses shot him again in the chest, and the sound was even louder, though still muffled. The bodyguard collapsed on the floor face first.

Moses turned the gun toward Walker. The silencer had done its job, but it was probably shot now. He pulled it off the barrel. "Hey, Ted," he said.

Walker choked on the last bite of the burger he was eating, spitting it up on himself.

"You should watch that," said Moses. "Red meat's a killer."

"Moses," said Walker. Fear filled his eyes. "Whatever you're thinking, you're wrong, man."

"I don't have a lot of time to fuck with you. No games, no lies. Get up, and go into the kitchen."

Walker got up on wobbly legs and started to move. Moses raised his gun, and hit him hard on the head. Walker fell to the floor, yelling and grabbing at his head. Moses hit him again, and Walker went out, falling to one side.

Moses picked up the lawyer and dragged him into the kitchen. He pulled out a rope he'd gotten from Half and tied Walker to a wooden chair.

Moses finally noticed his surroundings. Walker had a house filled with expensive furniture and art. Ted was living pretty goddamned good, Moses thought. How many brothers had he helped railroad into prison to get all this shit? Walker was one of those criminal lawyers who had forgotten that he was supposed to be above the dirt he dealt in. He'd helped Moses launder money, taken drugs for payment, and had bribed at least one judge. The only problem with a crooked lawyer is that you never know when he'll turn on you.

Moses tied Walker's torso and legs to the chair, then tied his hands to the armrests at the wrist. Then he gagged him with a greasy kitchen towel. Now he had to wake him up. He hoped the bastard didn't have a concussion.

Moses heard a sound from behind him.

He turned and went back into the den. The man he had shot was on one knee and was pulling out a .45 in one hand. He was covered in blood and appeared very weak. The wound on his face was puffy and pinkish, a stream of blood ran down his jowl into his thick neck. His blue shirt had a large purple stain on it. He was breathing hard and blood bubbled through his thick lips.

Moses had to get him quick. If the dying man fired the gun, surely a neighbor in the well-heeled neighborhood would hear it. The silencer on his gun was off, and if he fired it, the sound would be just as loud.

"Damn," Moses said.

He quickly grabbed a knife from the kitchen. He went into the den and walked up to the man. Blood was everywhere. Moses easily took the gun from the dying man.

Moses stepped behind the man and buried the knife into his back. The bodyguard gagged and fell forward. Moses pushed the knife in hard with his foot until the man stopped struggling. He hated this. It was so much easier to shoot a man. This cutting and stabbing shit was for sick people.

Moses removed the knife and went back into the kitchen. He was surprised to find Walker awake. He struggled in the chair, tears streaming down his face.

Moses walked over to Walker and cut half through the baby finger on his right hand. Walker yelled, but the gag muffled it. Moses tied a rag around Walker's hand to stop the bleeding. Moses waited for him to calm down.

"Okay, now that we understand each other, let's talk. Did Dake and Nita pay you to leave me in jail?"

Walker shook his head. Moses laid the knife on the baby finger on his left hand. Walker nodded his head vigorously.

"Okay," said Moses. "And did you pay the guards to have that sick muthafucka try to kill me in jail?"

Walker nodded again. Moses cursed, then cut another finger on Walker's right hand. Walker screamed a high-pitched scream and almost rocked the chair over.

"You fuckin' piece of shit! You should know I don't kill easy." Moses waited for the man to settle again. This was so sick, he thought, but effective. "Now for the big one. Where are those two muthafuckas? I'm gonna remove this gag, and when I do, you talk nice and soft, or else."

Moses removed the gag, Walker heaved, sucking in air. He cried like a child.

"Go on, tell it, nigga."

Walker's eyes were filled with tears. "Please, please man, don't do this."

Moses raised the knife.

"Okay, okay. They . . . they're in a house in Warren."

"What street, fool? That's a big city." Walker's hand was dripping blood all over the floor. He had to get the lawyer to tell it all soon, or Walker would pass out.

"Chapel . . . Eight Mile . . ." His voice was filled with pain and terror.

"Figure no one would look for them in the suburbs," said Moses. "They always was smart those two. Where's the hustle now?"

"A warehouse in Detroit . . . Tybo's. Let me go . . . I can pay you," said Walker. "I got money hidden . . ."

"Where is it?" asked Moses.

"No!" Walker yelled, then grimaced in pain. "You let me go, then I'll tell."

"No," said Moses. "The money is in this house. A good thief knows that a man never keeps his stash too far away."

"No," said Walker. "It's at the airport." His bloody hand shook violently.

"Sorry. But you never were a good liar." Moses put the knife to his throat and cut it as Walker yelled.

Moses watched him die, then looked around the house. The phone rang and he let the machine pick it up. It was a girl named Terry who wanted to have a rendezvous with Walker.

"Too bad, Terry," said Moses. "Gotta find you some new dick." Moses laughed.

Moses checked all the usual places people hide money, closets, floorboards. Walker had a safe but was too smart to put anything there. Moses finally found the money in a freezer in his basement. A stupid place, thought Moses. There was about ten thousand in large bills. This money would help him, he thought.

He had to get to Dake and Nita soon. When they found out Walker was dead, they'd know who did it. They'd run and then he'd never catch them.

Moses went back upstairs and cleaned up the mess he'd made. He cleared out the freezer and put Walker inside. The bodyguard he hid in a room in the basement. It was cool and damp, and would keep the bodies for a while, he thought. It was quite a job and took him two hours.

Moses finally stepped out of the house into the cool of the night. Someone was cooking fried chicken, and it smelled good. His stomach growled again. He was sweating, tired, and now he was hungry. The money bulged inside a paper bag he'd found in the kitchen. He decided to go and get something to eat. He deserved it.

Moses got into his car and drove. He never saw Lewis Quince, who'd been following him all evening.

30

....

To Speak the Truth

Marshall had been prepared for a fight during the preliminary examination. The hearing to find probable cause was an intense first look at the weaponry of the enemy, but the matter had been calm and relaxed. Normally, Marshall would have been ecstatic that the defense had not bothered to put up a fight, but Rashad was too smart to make anything easy. He was focusing his efforts elsewhere.

Langworthy listened casually as Marshall showed the tape of the assassination and presented the DNA evidence. Even though the PCR test was vulnerable, it was still enough, along with the illegal gun and ballistics evidence, to keep Mbutu in jail on the charge. Rashad's light cross-examination of witnesses didn't do anything to change that notion. Langworthy then quickly ruled that the case should proceed.

Marshall had expected this. No way was Langworthy going to kick the case at this stage. Even a liberal judge was not that foolish.

Marshall's team had been shocked when he showed them the Zapruder film and compared it to the Douglas assassination tape. Their faces expressed something akin to terror as they realized the similarity. Walter had to leave to get some air. Ryder dismissed it as a coincidence, and Roberta noted that they didn't have to tell the defendant of the similarity as it was not relevant evidence. Marshall didn't know what it meant, but he felt better just sharing the secret with someone.

Marshall readied himself for a procedure much more important than the probable cause hearing. The crucial undertaking of jury selection had been rushed like everything else in the case. The jury pool was large. Normally, people tried to get out of jury duty, but everyone seemed to want in on this case.

April Kelly, Rashad's jury consultant, was a tall woman with brown hair and piercing blue eyes. She'd come into court and had never even looked at Marshall and his team. She only had eyes for the jury pool.

A jury consultant was essentially a paid observer of human nature. They assisted in picking a sympathetic jury for a party in a lawsuit. There were no formal requirements for this job. Many consultants, however, were trained psychologists or behavioralists of some kind. There were even several well-known "psychic consultants" who worked throughout the United States. Kelly was one of the best. She was a lawyer and had a psychology degree.

Kelly sat with Rashad, Leslie Reed, and Mbutu as the voir dire took place. The words *voir dire* mean literally "to speak the truth," as potential jurors are asked questions to see if they are fit for service.

Mbutu looked a little sickly and ashen. Marshall remembered that he'd had some ailment and also had recently gone on a hunger strike, like the old civil rights leaders. His organization was really going to extremes to recruit members and reestablish its power, Marshall thought.

Marshall kept in mind that in this capital case, each side had twenty peremptory challenges to jurors. He could excuse a potential juror for cause, such as bias or prejudice, but forfeited a challenge when he removed one without cause. The battlefield in jury selection was to get rid of an unsympathetic juror for cause without using a precious challenge. It was a somewhat silly game that was part skill and part intuition.

On the first day of selection, Marshall had used only six peremptory challenges. Rashad had used eight, but only four jurors had been chosen so far, and they were all white. Three men and one woman.

They needed a twelve-juror panel and six alternates. Marshall's biggest problem was finding a black juror who didn't have some prejudice against Farrel Douglas. There weren't a lot of black jurors in the pool, and if Marshall dumped them, Langworthy would put a stop to it. He was not going to let this case proceed with an all-white jury.

Kelly controlled the process for the defendant. She frowned, whispered, and chuckled as the jurors were questioned. The three jurors who looked good for Marshall had been dumped by Rashad at Kelly's direction. She was good, he thought, and as the pool thinned out, he wished he had a consultant of his own. But Toby frowned on such practices. Defense attorneys got to use the tricks of the trade, but the government had to make do with the occasional jury selection seminar and the truth.

In many cases, the jury pool was depleted to the point where the case had to make do with the losers who were left. Marshall didn't want to get into this situation. He needed quality people to understand the complexity of the case.

A black businesswoman took the stand. Marshall noticed that she wore only a wedding band and no other jewelry. A good sign of conservatism, he thought. She was about thirty-five and good-looking. She walked with a straight back, her head held high. This could mean a strong personality, the kind that influenced crowds.

"State your name," asked Marshall.

"Debra Gibson-Chandler," said the woman.

A hyphenate, thought Marshall. That could mean independence or some bias against men. Feminism was a desirable trait, but too much of anything made you a bad juror. Chemin had chosen to hyphenate, a fact that had always pissed him off just a little.

"What do you do for a living?"

"I'm an accountant for Dipolle and Meyers."

"Are you married or single?"

"Married eight years with three kids," she said with pride.

"Do you have any knowledge of this case, ma'am?"

"Of course I do." She looked a little annoyed at the question.

"Have you formulated any opinion about the case?"

"No."

"Did you know Justice Douglas?"

"Yes, I mean I knew of his work."

"Did you like Farrel Douglas?"

Debra took a second. She thought about the question, then:

"I didn't know him personally, but I assume you mean as a judge."

"Yes, that's what I mean," said Marshall.

"He seemed to be a good man, a smart one."

Marshall tried not to show the happiness he felt. Having a conservative black juror in a case like this would help him. The whites on the panel would tend to listen to her because of her race. Marshall asked a few more well-placed questions, which Debra answered with aplomb. Once you were sure you liked a juror, you had to ask defensive questions in anticipation of a challenge for cause.

"Thank you, Ms. Chandler. The government has no objection to this juror."

Kelly whispered to Rashad, who rose and approached Debra.

"Ms. Chandler, is it?"

"Yes."

"Would you classify yourself as a conservative?"

"Objection!" said Marshall.

"You know better, Mr. Rashad," said Langworthy.

"Sorry, Your Honor," said Rashad.

The question was not appropriate, but it had not been asked to get an answer. Kelly was watching Debra's expression, looking for a reaction she could read. Rashad immediately went back to Kelly, who whispered to him urgently.

"Ms. Chandler," said Rashad, "have you read about this case?"

"Yes, in the newspapers."

"Watched coverage on the news?"

"Some, but not much."

"Did you know Farrel Douglas wrote a book?"

"No."

"Are you surprised he'd written a book?"

"No. He was a judge, an intelligent man."

Rashad thought a moment. "You Honor, may this juror be excused a moment?" asked Rashad.

Langworthy asked Debra to leave. She did, looking a little confused.

"We move to dismiss this juror for cause," said Rashad.

"On what grounds?" asked Marshall.

"What is the cause?" asked Langworthy.

"Bias," said Rashad. "This juror obviously is a Douglas fan."

"I don't see that," said Marshall. "Does not hating a man make you a fan?"

"She has read about him, she characterized him as intelligent. She's obviously a supporter, and ready to convict anyone accused of killing him."

"Nonsense, Your Honor," said Marshall. "If the defense doesn't want Ms. Chandler, let them use a challenge, but this is the thinnest of arguments so far."

Marshall was calling them out. Rashad was getting low on challenges, and this was a black juror. If Langworthy gave this to him, he'd have to give Marshall something else down the road. With eight jurors left to pick, wasting a challenge on this potential juror would be foolish. Chandler wasn't clearly biased for either side.

"Sorry," said Langworthy. "I don't see any bias. You don't want her, use a challenge."

Rashad went back and talked with Kelly.

"We'll allow the juror," said Rashad.

Marshall was shocked. What was this latest game about? Clearly they felt threatened by Debra, and if that was the case, why not dump her? Kelly smiled at Marshall as he looked over.

They pressed on, person after person. Soon, Marshall's head was spinning from the monotony of asking the same questions. Voir dire wasn't really about finding bias. It was about finding *acceptable* bias. Everyone brought bias to a case. It was the nature of human beings to choose sides. What you didn't want was a juror with a bias rooted in prejudice or ignorance.

Late in the afternoon, after adding two more jurors to the panel, Langworthy started to look tired. They added another white woman and a white male. Marshall was down to six challenges, and Rashad had only four with half a jury picked.

"We'll call it a day," said Langworthy.

The session broke up. April Kelly looked smug as she shook hands with Rashad. Leslie Reed seemed cool toward April. Maybe she didn't like jury consultants, or maybe it was personal. The media had been making much of Reed's wardrobe, her colorful suits and short skirts. Perhaps she didn't like having another woman on the team.

Marshall and his team left. Ryder looked worried as they walked down the hallway.

"Something up, Bob?" asked Marshall.

"Yes, I think they're up to something," said Ryder.

"I don't know what it could be," said Marshall.

"They should have bounced that Chandler woman," said Roberta.

"Yeah, she was cool, but clearly a more conservative kind of person," said Walter.

"I felt that too," said Marshall. "But maybe this was their screwup. Ms. Chandler is a strong person, and she feels like a good choice for us."

Marshall and the team went back into the office. Agent Sommers was coming out of Nate Williams's office. She looked upset, and Marshall hoped that he was not in dutch with her again. He walked over to them and had the strange feeling that he'd done it before. He hated those feelings of déjà vu. They always led to something bad.

"What's up?" asked Marshall.

"We've had a tragedy," said Sommers. "Nothing involving our case, but you probably want to know."

Marshall's heart sped up. It was Chemin, he thought. Something had happened to her. But why would the FBI be interested in that?

"It's Jessica Cole," said Nate. "She's been killed."

31

Barbecue

Danny watched Chemin as she got in her car and drove away from the drugstore. He'd followed some simple leads and found out that she was staying with her friend, some woman named Rochelle Sheppard.

Chemin was living with the woman but had not been into work in a while. She'd called in sick for several days, and no one was the wiser. Danny supposed that Chemin just needed some rest. If he caught Vinny doing some guy, he'd need a mental health day too. Of course, the guy would need a coffin, he thought.

Danny tailed Chemin around the city, following her from the plaza on Livernois and Seven Mile. He tried to keep his mind on following her and from the wreck his life had become. The job he was doing for Marshall helped, but his head was still filled with images of the man he'd beaten and the damning headline in the newspapers.

Chemin headed north across Eight Mile Road into Southfield, a trendy suburb filled with affluent blacks. "Detroit North" was what the locals called Southfield these days. The sky was overcast, and a cold wind whipped across the city. It felt a little like Chicago, Danny thought absently.

His mind wandered back to his problem as he drove along. All he'd done was beat some scumbag who had it coming. Shit like that happened every day. The robber was a lifetime criminal asshole named Tyrell Stevens. He was a small-time thief and drug user who'd tried to graduate to the big time by bagging a goddamned restaurant. He needed his ass kicked for being stupid. Stevens was headed for an attempted murder case for the robbery and a possible life sentence. Why anyone would care about that waste of skin was beyond Danny's comprehension.

"Danny, you are not a black man . . ."

Marshall's words came back to him. His friend was right. Racial politics was a reality he could not escape. The city was mostly black and struggled financially. Even though it was at the start of an economic comeback, it was still a town that fought for its municipal dignity, a city that counted its homeless in order to keep its population above the magic one million number. In such a place, a white cop who beat a black man might as well put a bull's-eye on his forehead.

But if he was not a black man, then he didn't know what the hell he was. He was a Catholic, but so were many blacks in the city. His father was into their Irish heritage but didn't really press the point at home. And all of his older relatives had always stressed that they were *American* first.

He'd been steeped in the culture, seduced by the soul of blackness. He felt powerful, fearless, and righteous when he thought of himself. The concerns of the black community were his concerns, and the politics were his also. If some other white had beaten that robber, his first thought might have been that the cop was some kind of racist. Only because he was special did Danny think the rules did not apply to him.

When he looked in the mirror, the face on the other side didn't seem right. It didn't fit what was inside his head and his heart. Maybe he wasn't a black man, but he certainly wasn't just a white man either.

Vinny was taking the situation as well as she could. She was working again, so there wasn't a lot of time for her to berate him about what had happened. She had told him many times that if he didn't control his temper, he'd regret it. Women could be a pain in the ass for always being right about everything.

Chemin turned into a professional complex and quickly exited her car. Danny drove by and parked in a fast-food joint down the block near Eleven Mile.

He got out of his car and walked over to the building. The cold wind attacked him as he did. That first blast of cold air was always the worst when you got out of a warm car.

The building was a two-story complex that housed a lot of medical professionals. He hoped that Chemin was okay. Maybe the stress of seeing her husband with another woman had caused some sort of physical ailment.

He couldn't believe that Marshall had cheated. He knew that all men entertained these thoughts. Hell, he did all the time, but he never thought Marshall would cross the line. Although, he reasoned, if anyone had a right to get a piece of ass, it was Marshall. Chemin had cut him off so badly that no one would blame him.

Danny went into the lobby of the building and walked up to the security officer. There was a sign-in sheet on a counter. Danny moved to the guard, a skinny, bespectacled man. The man eyed Danny suspiciously and shifted in his seat. Danny didn't like this. The man was probably one of the police academy rejects who took this job in order to feel like a cop.

"Wha'sup?" Danny said.

"Can I help you?" asked the security guard. He had that hollow, pseudoauthoritative tone that all rent-a-cops use.

"Looking for a Dr. Kismazz," said Danny. He smiled.

"No doctor here by that name."

"Oh, really, I must have the wrong address." Danny checked the sign-in sheet.

"There's another complex across the street," said the guard. "Try that one."

"Right," said Danny. Then he walked away. Danny chuckled softly. "Kismazz" was an old neighborhood joke for "kiss my ass." He remembered how he and Marshall used to say it to other kids and laugh like hell. The guard had no idea that he'd been insulted, but it was funny to Danny just the same. He stopped by the tenants' roster on the way out and took a peek at the doctor that Chemin had signed in to see. Danny stopped on the name "Dr. Claudia Wellbourne—Psychoanalyst."

"A fuckin' shrink?" Danny said out loud. Had Chemin gone nuts?

"Is there some problem?" asked the guard. He stood up in his chair and put his hand on his side arm. Danny noticed this and had to suppress a laugh.

Danny left and got back into his car. He sat on the street and played the radio. He was in a mess, but what was going on with Marshall and his wife? Chemin was always high-strung, but he had no idea that she needed to see a shrink.

More important, why hadn't Marshall told him? They shared everything, but he'd withheld this for some reason. Danny was a little hurt, but maybe it was embarrassing. He decided that he would tell Marshall that he knew, but he wouldn't make a big deal out of it.

An hour later, Chemin came out of the office, got into her car, and drove away. Danny followed her back into the city.

He was surprised as Chemin went back to her own house and went inside. Danny parked down the block then sneaked back to the house. It was really cold outside, but when he did a job, he was thorough.

This was some weird shit, he thought. He was staying there temporarily, and spying on the real owner. He went to a window and looked inside. Chemin was not there. He thought for a second that she might be upstairs, when he heard a door slam shut.

Danny made his way around the back and saw Chemin by the barbecue pit. She had a pile of clothes on it. Chemin looked at the clothes for a second, her face showing a sadness that Danny had never seen. Then she sprayed lighter fluid on the clothes and set them on fire.

32

....

Clean Kill

Marshall stood over Jessica's lifeless body in the morgue. He felt sad, angry, and strangely guilty to see her half naked on the slab. She was naked from the waist up, and the fresh scar from the Y incision seemed to split her in two. Her face was cleaned up, but it was still a mess. Whoever killed her had beaten her about the head. Her right arm had been broken and bruised, probably trying to shield herself from the blows.

Marshall felt sick seeing her breasts sticking up, the same breasts that he'd caressed, that had pulsed with vital life not so long ago.

Jessica had been killed outside her apartment on the near east side. She'd been beaten with a heavy, blunt instrument, probably a lead pipe, said the coroner. She'd done a lot of bleeding and had probably lingered a while before going. Her purse was not found, and there was no evidence of sexual abuse. It looked to be a robbery, another casualty of the big city. The police forensic people had found nothing to link her to the killer, no hair, blood, or fiber. It was clean.

Marshall stood with Agent Sommers. The coroner, a dreary-looking woman named Dr. Waters, worked across the room on another body.

"So it was a garden-variety robbery?" asked Marshall.

"Looks that way," said Sommers. "The police are checking her out to see if she was involved in drugs or anything like that."

"She was a good person," said Marshall. "They're wasting their time." He had a note of anger in his voice.

"You okay?" asked Sommers. "Was she a close friend?"

"Yes. She had a crush on me."

"I see. Was it mutual?"

"No," said Marshall a little annoyed. "But I saw her every day, and I liked her."

"Well, I think we can go now," said Sommers. "We are going over her apartment to make sure she didn't have any confidential papers in her possession."

Sommers walked toward the door. Marshall couldn't take his eyes off the dead girl. He stared into her battered face and thought of her as she was, beautiful, confused, and in love with him. Suddenly, he saw the Johnsons lying on the floor, and the sooty head of Mrs. Johnson being taken from a fireplace. There was certainly a lot of death around him all of a sudden, he thought.

"What was Jessica working on for the FBI?" asked Marshall.

"What?" asked Sommers.

"Jessica, what was she doing for the FBI on the Douglas case?"

"She was just a secretary. And she was helping to coordinate our fact-finding."

"Then why would she have anything confidential in her possession?"

"She probably wouldn't," said Sommers, "but our good friends at the CIA suggested it as a precautionary measure. You know how they are."

"Yes, I know." Marshall was worried. Detroit was a place where people died like any other city, but why Jessica and why now? Why did the FBI search her home, and why did the CIA prompt it?

These were troubling questions, almost as troubling as the dead woman who lay before him. Marshall decided to do some looking of his own as he reached down and pulled the plastic cover up and over Jessica's tortured face.

Marshall went back to the office and told the team what had happened. They all reacted with grief and shock. Roberta was especially upset. She and Jessica had been casual friends. She excused herself and went into the ladies' room, where they assumed she had a good cry.

They all went back to work, but there was a pall over their effort for the rest of the day.

Marshall got home late that night. He found Danny in the den watching

TV with Vinny and drinking a beer. Vinny looked great. No one would not have ever thought she'd been shot recently. Since Danny had come to live with him, Vinny had sort of moved in too. It was a little crowded, but he appreciated the company.

Vinny read a book nestled under Danny's arm. They were hugged up on his sofa, looking very much in love. It was funny how Danny, who never had a life, now had love, and Marshall's life had fallen apart. Danny seemed quite happy even though he was out of a job and had almost beaten a man to death just days ago. They were quite a couple, he thought.

"Are you two kids having sex in my house?" asked Marshall.

"Already did that," said Danny.

Vinny elbowed him in the stomach. "Don't listen to him," she said. "We didn't do anything."

Marshall got comfortable on the sofa and drank a beer with Danny. He was still troubled by Jessica's death and wondered if he'd ever be the same.

"You don't look so good," said Vinny.

"He looks like shit," said Danny. "Just like I feel."

"Stop worrying," said Vinny. "This thing will be over with soon."

"One of my coworkers died," said Marshall.

"Shit man, who was it?" said Danny.

"It was that girl I told you about," said Marshall. He looked at Danny, to see if he remembered his story of indiscretion.

"Yes, I remember," Danny said. His voice held a dread that Marshall didn't understand.

"I can leave, if you two would like," said Vinny. "Then you don't have to talk in code all over my head like this."

"I'm sorry," said Marshall.

"Don't be," said Vinny. "I'm used to it. You two are worse than women." Vinny took her book and walked out of the room.

Danny looked after her, then when she was gone, he turned back to Marshall.

"That girl you got into it with got slammed?" asked Danny.

"Yes, she was beaten and left for dead. Looks like a robbery, no rape involved."

Danny was silent. His head dropped, and he buried his face in his hands. "No," he said. "No fuckin' way."

"What are you talking about? You didn't know Jessica."

"Okay man, was there a lot of blood at the scene?"

"Yes, Jessica bled a lot, but how did you know that?"

"You're gonna need something stronger than that beer when you hear what I saw today." Danny took a deep breath. "I found Chemin. She's staying with some woman named Rochelle."

"That's her annoying friend, but why is that upsetting?"

"And she hasn't been into work at that place—what's it?"

"Hallogent," said Marshall.

"Right. She ain't been there for a while. I followed her all day. She's seeing a shrink. Some woman doctor."

"I know about that. Figures she'd be going there a lot right now."

"There's more," said Danny. "I followed her back here from the shrink's office." Danny stopped a moment, as if he couldn't bring himself to say what was on his mind. "Chemin . . . she went into the backyard and burned some clothes on the barbecue."

Marshall almost dropped his beer. "No," he said. "You'd better not be fucking with me."

"I wouldn't kid you about something like that, man. There ain't nothing funny about this."

Marshall's head started spinning. He had to put the beer down for a second and compose himself. Jessica was dead on a half-assed robbery. A motive, but certainly a convenient one. And Chemin had caught him with Jessica. It would have been a simple thing to take a few days off, follow Jessica, then wait for her outside of her apartment and bash her pretty head in. In that instant, Marshall saw Chemin, her intelligent, calculating mind ticking, hiding in the shadows, cradling a heavy lead pipe. Then he saw her jump out into the light, and swing it at Jessica's frightened face.

"Chemin didn't do it," said Marshall.

"I want to believe that," said Danny. "But the shit don't look good, man. Why in the fuck was she burning them clothes?"

"I can find out," said Marshall. "Did she leave the ashes?"

"There wasn't nothing left of them clothes when she was finished. She washed out the grill."

"Chemin always washes it after we use it. That doesn't mean anything." Marshall said it more for himself than for Danny.

"I didn't say it did," said Danny. "Marsh, you gotta consider that she might have blown a gasket and killed that girl."

"You got a lot of nerve," said Marshall, standing up. "I live with that woman. I know her. Just because you would kill over something stupid, doesn't mean she would.''

Danny seemed hurt. He stood up and took a step toward Marshall. ''I know you think it's your fault. Maybe it is. But I'm your friend, and I'm not going to lie to you, man. And you're right. I'm a fuckin' psycho when it comes to love. If some guy was fucking my woman the first thing I'd think to do would be kill him. So maybe I know what the fuck I'm talking about here. Takes one to know one.''

''Danny . . . don't listen to me,'' said Marshall, trying to apologize. ''I got a lot of pressure on me these days.''

''I don't have pressure? I'm a goddamned monster according to the newspaper. The news had a cartoon of me with a dinosaur head on it.''

''We don't need to fight each other,'' said Marshall. And before he knew it, he was hugging Danny and patting him on the back. ''We'll get through this, I swear.''

''What you going to do?'' asked Danny. ''If Chemin did this, then she's gonna need some protection.''

''If she did it, I have to turn her in.''

''Are you sick? She was fucked up for a moment, you can't let her get locked away for that. Okay, I think maybe she did it. But that don't mean she should go to the joint.''

''Danny, the girl was twenty-three years old. She was innocent.''

''She tried to fuck somebody's husband. Shit happens.''

''That's not a legal defense in this state. I can't protect Chemin. That makes me just as guilty.''

''Okay, okay,'' said Danny. ''Listen to me here. I'm a cop, I admit I'm not the most stable muthafucka in the world, but I know how and why people kill—''

''I was in the marines with you,'' said Marshall. ''I shot men in that border incident.''

''That was different. We were a hundred yards away, firing in the dark. I'm talking about cold-blooded killing. Face-to-face. If Chemin did this, then she lost her damned mind, and if that's the case, then you can't let her go to jail.''

''The girl's family might not see the logic in that.''

''Yes, but they ain't you. Do you still want Chemin?''

''You know I do.''

''Then you gotta protect her.''

Marshall was tearing apart inside. Danny was right, but to protect a murderer was against everything he stood for. But he'd driven her to it, hadn't he? That was Danny's unstated point. *You did it.* If it wasn't for your weakness, none of this would have happened. Being a lawyer was a curse, he thought. It forced you to dissect the normal emotions of life and analyze them in the cold light of logic. Good and evil became just factors in an equation of decision, and death a consequence of reason.

"I don't know, Danny. I have to think about it." Marshall thought a moment, then: "I have to get to her."

"Let me do it," Danny said quickly. "You just think about what I said. Don't go off all crazy and shit. Think about it tonight. I'll find her and you can talk."

"Okay, man," said Marshall. "Okay."

Marshall went to bed that night with the unspeakable on his mind. Suddenly, he didn't care who killed Farrel Douglas. He didn't care who was assigned to be on the jury. The case was trivial to him. He might be married to a murderer. He kept trying to tell himself, his lawyer's mind, that there was another explanation, but it all made sense to him. The burned clothes, the robbery, which Chemin was smart enough to manufacture, even her shrink, a confessor who couldn't legally testify against her. It all made sense.

Marshall took two Tylenol PM and climbed into bed. He hoped the drug would stop the thunder in his head and help him sleep. He fell into a slumber, but his mind had no peace. It was filled with terrible images of Jessica covered in blood, and his wife locked away deep in prison.

33

....

Degree

Marshall walked into the courthouse the next day feeling worried. Normally, being in court made him feel better, but the trouble in his heart weighed down his mind. He debated asking for a continuance of the jury selection but knew Langworthy wasn't likely to grant it. And how would he ask anyway? *"Excuse me, Your Honor, can I have a personal day to find out if my wife committed a heinous murder? By the way, she killed a girl I almost fucked."* The absurdity of it almost brought a sick smile to his face.

The only good news he had was that they had found a link between Mbutu and Anthony Collier. They'd found a witness who was going to testify that he'd met Collier at a recruitment rally for the Brotherhood.

Marshall walked down the hallway and caught sight of the newest members of the jury pool being shuttled in. He glanced at them and walked on. It was never a good idea to engage them in any way before you saw them on voir dire. Suddenly, he stopped. He turned and looked at them again. Shock spun inside him, soon replaced by anger. There were about twenty people walking in, and about fifteen of them were black.

"Sonofabitch," Marshall whispered to himself. He rushed into the courtroom, where he found his team waiting. Rashad and his people were not there, and now he knew why. Marshall waved Ryder and the others into the hall just as the last of the new jury pool went into a door.

"This Kelly woman pulled one on us," said Marshall. "I just saw the new jury pool. They're almost all black."

"Impossible," said Ryder. "I read all the demos, the federal juries in this area are predominantly white."

"I know what I saw," said Marshall. "With so many blacks on the panel, surely a number of them will get in. We don't have enough challenges to get rid of them all, and even if we did, it's illegal to use them to exclude people on the basis of race."

"Jesus," said Roberta. "Do you think they could fix something like that?"

"You could if you bought off the clerk," said Walter. "Or if you just knew it was coming."

Marshall took a moment to think. Suddenly, he was back in the case and Chemin was forced into the bottom of his thoughts. Black jurors tended to be more liberal, especially if the defendant was black and he'd killed a man who was reviled in the black community. That made what he just saw very dangerous to his case. Many criminal cases are won during jury selection, well before one piece of evidence was entered.

Now letting the Chandler lady on the jury made sense. Kelly had set a trap. They gave Marshall a black juror so the defense could pack the jury with others who might not be as objective. They knew Langworthy well. The judge would think the government was trying to exclude black jurors, and he'd put them on despite objections.

"However Kelly knew, she knew," said Marshall. "We have to find a way to get out of this."

"Well, we can't object to the number of black people," said Ryder. "The judge would laugh at us."

"Not to mention the way it would look in the press," said Roberta.

"You know, just because they're black doesn't mean they'll be against us," said Ryder. "There are all kinds of black people."

"True," said Marshall. "But I'm black, and I know my people. We can't count on theoretical notions of humanity. The reality is black jurors tend to be biased in favor of the defense, especially in a case like this. We are more likely to believe in conspiracies, and more likely to give a defendant the benefit of the doubt."

"Reasonable doubt," added Walter ominously.

Marshall thought for a moment. This problem was practically joyous compared to things he could be thinking about. "I have an idea," said Marshall. "I'll talk with the judge."

"But you just said that won't work," said Walter.

"Don't worry," said Marshall. "I'm not going to actually say anything to him."

Marshall went into the judge's chambers and asked to speak with Langworthy. While he waited, Marshall wandered into the hallway by the room where the new jury pool was kept. This was risky, but if he knew Langworthy, he'd take the bait. Marshall waited until the judge ambled into the hallway. Suddenly, Marshall assumed a nervous look and walked quickly back to Langworthy.

"Your Honor," said Marshall. "I was wondering if you thought our selection would be over today?"

Langworthy looked at Marshall suspiciously. "I don't know," said the judge.

"Well, the government feels that we can end it today," said Marshall. He added a smile that was ever so slightly insincere.

"Why are you back here? You could have asked this in court."

"I—just wanted to see where your head was, Your Honor." He tried to sound as insincere as he could.

"My head is in the case, and you can find that out on the record. You may leave now."

Marshall thanked the judge and walked off. He waited by the chambers door to see if Langworthy would bite. Langworthy stood in the hallway for a second, thinking, then he walked over to the jury room and looked in. A troubled look washed over him. Marshall left as the judge turned and walked back his way.

Marshall went back into court to find Rashad, Leslie Reed, and April Kelly entering the courtroom. Marshall didn't think Rashad was the type to pull a stunt like stacking a jury pool. If Kelly was behind it, then she was worth every cent they paid her.

"What did you do?" asked Ryder.

"I rolled the dice," said Marshall. "If it works, we'll all be leaving soon. If not, get ready for hell."

Kelly looked happy as she sat behind Rashad and Leslie Reed. Soon, Mbutu was brought in.

Langworthy walked in and took the bench. He had an upset look on his face.

"Thank you all for coming," said Langworthy. "But there will be no session this morning."

Rashad and his people expressed shock. Kelly almost jumped out of her seat. She whispered frantically to Rashad.

Marshall saw his cue. He jumped up. "We have to finish today," said Marshall. "Our schedule is tight."

"I agree," said Rashad. "We would like to proceed."

"No," said Langworthy. "I don't feel it's in the best interest of this case. We are having trouble with the jury pool today. It will be discarded, and we'll resume this afternoon."

"I object, Your Honor," said Marshall.

"So do we," added Rashad. Kelly's face was red with frustration.

"This hearing is adjourned," said Langworthy. "And I'll see counsel in my chambers."

Langworthy walked out of the courtroom. Marshall and Rashad followed. Marshall heard Kelly curse behind him. In chambers, Langworthy reiterated his position.

"Well, can we know the nature of the problem?" asked Rashad.

"Yes," said Marshall. "I'd like to know too."

"I am not going to accuse anyone of anything at this point," said Langworthy. "But something is not right, and I will not jeopardize the objectivity of this case. I'll see you both this afternoon."

Marshall walked out of the judge's chambers elated. He watched as Rashad gave the bad news to Kelly.

"How did you do that?" asked Walter.

"I made Langworthy suspicious," said Marshall. "Just enough to get him to look at that stacked jury pool. I didn't show any anger about it, so he assumed that I was okay with it. This made him even more suspicious."

"I get it," said Roberta. "Why wouldn't a prosecutor be upset about a stacked jury? Because maybe he did it himself for some reason."

"Langworthy doesn't like us government types. So I knew he'd kick us out along with that bad pool."

"Great stuff," said Ryder. He sounded like a cheerleader. "So now what?"

"Now we come back this afternoon and finish selecting a fair jury."

Marshall and Rashad went back to it later that day, playing the chess match that is voir dire. At the end of the long day, they had a full jury and six alternates. The jury that would decide the fate of Mbutu was composed of seven men and five women, three of whom were black.

Marshall was happy. Kelly was not. She'd been outclassed and was pissed off about it. But it was far from over. Kelly would continue to try to manipulate the jury throughout the trial. It was a fact of life in the modern practice of law. A jury consultant stayed for the entire trial, watching the jurors react to everything from evidence to the color of the lawyers' suits and reporting back. It was not uncommon for jurors to be dismissed during trial and alternates picked to replace them.

Marshall accepted congratulations from his team as he walked back to his office. He was happy, but with each step he took, Jessica's murder came back to him. After a while, he was so upset that he ducked out of work early and went home.

He rolled along the Lodge Freeway watching cars zip by him. He glanced at his speedometer and noticed he was only doing about fifty. He guessed that he was stalling, hoping that going slowly would postpone the inevitable.

Once he got home, Marshall had a drink, something that was rare for him so early in the day. Danny had promised him that he'd get Chemin to come to the house and talk. He didn't know how Danny would do that, but he didn't care. He had to see her. He had to know the truth.

But what if she admitted it? he thought. What then? Would he turn her in, put the woman he loved in a cage for life? He didn't think he could do it, but he didn't see how he couldn't make her pay for what she had done.

The alcohol had made him light-headed, and soon he slipped into dark sleep. His mind was tortured with images of death and violence. He was awakened by the door opening. He sat up to see Chemin rushing in, looking upset. She saw him in the den getting up. She stopped in her tracks and turned to Danny.

"You goddamned liar! He's not hurt."

"Not on the outside," said Danny. "We have to talk."

"I'm leaving," said Chemin. "You two can play your game with someone else's life."

"Chemin, wait," said Marshall.

Chemin moved to walk away, but Danny cut her off.

"You'd better move, or I'll whip your ass," said Chemin. "I'm not afraid of you. I don't care how many defenseless men you beat. You will not hold me hostage."

"Then that's an ass whuppin' I'll have to take," said Danny. " 'Cause you ain't leaving."

"There won't be any fighting," said Marshall. "Chemin, Danny had to bring you here. I need to talk to you."

"About what? Did you do something else stupid?"

Marshall ignored the sting of her words. "You leave me, you don't call, and you ask why? How am I supposed to know if you're okay?"

"I'm fine, now can I go?"

"No," said Danny. "We have something to ask you."

"You are walking on some thin fucking ice, Danny," said Chemin. "I don't take orders from you." To Marshall, she said, "Get on with it so I can leave."

It was his wife in all her glory, he thought. He walked closer to her, and noticed for the first time that she was dressed in a business suit. Apparently, she'd gone back to work at Hallogent.

"Okay, Chemin," said Marshall. "Something bad happened."

"Marshall," Danny interrupted. "That's not what you want to say." To Chemin, he said, "The girl you caught him with is coming over here to talk this thing out. In fact, there she is." Danny pointed to a window.

Marshall was shocked. Not just because Danny exposed his knowledge of the incident, but also because he saw what his friend was doing. Jessica's death hadn't been publicized, so Chemin couldn't know about it unless she was involved. Now Marshall feared what his wife would say. No matter what he felt was right, he didn't want it to be true. His heart began to race the way it did before a jury foreman read a verdict.

Chemin didn't look toward the window. Instead, she focused on Marshall. "She's not coming here," she said angrily.

Marshall's knees grew weak. He felt like running, like taking her and running away so that no one could hear what she'd just said. Danny just stared at Chemin, as if he'd expected the answer. He was a cop, Marshall thought absently. He was used to getting confessions.

"Jesus," said Marshall. "Chemin—oh Jesus."

"Why isn't she coming here?" asked Danny accusatorially.

Chemin looked confused for a second. Her eyes went from Danny to Marshall, who looked like he wanted to cry.

"That bitch isn't setting foot in my house," she said. "What kind of shit are you two up to?"

"Jessica's dead." Marshall said. "She was murdered."

Chemin stared at her husband expressionless for a second. Danny just looked at her with his mean, accusing cop look.

Chemin looked genuinely surprised for a moment. "What am I supposed to say about that?" asked Chemin. "Am I supposed to feel sorry for her ass? Well, guess what? I don't."

"Where were you two nights ago?" asked Marshall.

Chemin's eyes sprang to life. Her face lifted with the sudden realization of what the two men meant by having her here.

"You think—damn both of you," said Chemin.

"Then how do you know that girl couldn't come here tonight?" asked Danny. "Why didn't you even look to see if she was coming up the walk?"

"Because I'm pissed off," said Chemin. "You invite that woman to my house and expect me to be happy about it?"

"Why did you burn those clothes today?" asked Marshall.

Chemin took on a shocked expression. "Are you spying on me, Marshall?"

"No, this is my house too," said Marshall.

"But you weren't here. How did you—" Chemin stopped, suddenly afraid of something. She looked sad, like a child caught in the act. "I am not doing this with you two. Whatever sick notion you have in your heads, you keep them there. I'm leaving." She walked to the door, pushing Danny aside.

Marshall ran and caught up to her outside the door. She turned and looked at him, and suddenly he knew what it meant to say someone had fire in their eyes. Chemin's eyes burned with emotion.

"Don't go," Marshall said.

"Marshall, what are you doing?" asked Chemin. "You fool around with some girl, then you spy on me and accuse me of killing her. This is beyond crazy."

"Look, I was wrong. What I did was wrong, but now I'm worried about you."

Chemin looked up at him, and he knew she could see the water in his eyes. Marshall was a strong man, too strong for his good sometimes, and if he was crying, Chemin knew that something serious was going on.

"I want to stay, but I can't," she said. "We'll end up in bed, and I'll forget about all the things you've done."

"I'll stay downstairs, anything you want," he begged. "Just please stay here with me tonight."

Chemin stood silent for a moment, and Marshall could almost hear her thinking. Despite his promise, he saw himself making love to her, rolling naked in their bed.

"I didn't hurt that girl," she said.

"I believe you," said Marshall. "Now come on back in."

"I can't. I have some things to sort out."

Chemin took a step away, and Marshall grabbed her, hugging her tight. It felt good, and for the briefest of moments, he was happy again. She responded, hugging him back, then gently pushed him away.

"I'll call you," she said.

She got in her car and drove away, not looking back at him. He watched her and wondered if he'd ever have her heart again. He felt dry and spent, as if someone had stolen his will and left him to die. He wiped his eyes dry.

"She did it," he heard Danny say from behind him.

Marshall turned and looked at Danny. He hated him for being so honest, for being so smart. He wanted to believe that Chemin didn't do it, but Danny wouldn't let him. And he was right. He was too in love to be reasonable about Chemin.

"We don't know that," said Marshall.

"You heard what she said. You saw what she did. She didn't turn to see if that girl was coming because she knew she was dead, Marshall."

"What is this, *Perry Mason*? Chemin could have just been shocked that Jessica was coming. And her explanation sounds plausible. She could have meant that Jessica wasn't coming because she would never let her in this house."

"You got it bad, brotha," said Danny. "I can maybe agree with some of that, but she's guilty of something. I could see it in her eyes. I've seen that look many times. The look of a person with something to hide. And what about the clothes?"

"I didn't ask her again," said Marshall a little sadly.

"I'd like to hear her explanation for that," said Danny. "Just heating up my underwear, honey. No, I'm sorry. She saw what she saw in your office, lost her mind, and wasted that poor girl."

"Will you please stop saying that?!" said Marshall. He tried to control himself. He didn't want to yell at Danny. "I know it looks bad, but I have to believe her. I have to."

"Then you agree with me," said Danny. "Don't say anything to anyone about this, protect her. Considering all that you know, you have to."

"I won't say anything, but not because I think she did it. I'll do it because I'm not sure. But now I have to find out. I have to know the truth."

Marshall went into his office and tried to work. He worked on his opening statement, knowing that it would set the tone for the trial. Trial.

He couldn't believe it was coming so soon. The immediacy of it suddenly caused him to grow anxious.

Marshall worked for hours, but the words wouldn't come. Finally he took another hit of Tylenol and went to sleep.

He spent a fitful night, running from the demons in his head and his heart. And somewhere in his mind, he wished that he could stay in that darkness forever.

34

....

House Call

Moses took another hit of the joint as the young girl slipped out of her clothes. He was taking a chance, but he couldn't waste all of his time out of prison worrying about lowlives like Dake, Nita, and Ted Walker.

The girl turned up the radio as she unbuttoned her blouse. The little motel clock radio squeaked out a rap tune that was a remake of an old Isley Brothers song. She caught the beat and moved her body to the song. He was pleased to see she was into her job.

Moses had found the girl walking along the street, looking tentatively at passing cars. She was a pro, but a recent one. She still had her looks and didn't seem like she'd rob your ass or cut your throat if you fell asleep too soon. She said her name was Donna, but it was probably a lie. She was about nineteen or so, and had a pretty face. Her body was round and curvy, the way a woman should be. He could not figure out why women were starving themselves trying to get thin. He found skinny women sick and unattractive. A woman should be full-bodied—not fat, but voluptuous.

Donna danced closer to him and took off her top, then her bra. Her breasts tumbled out. They were huge and real, he added in his mind. Only in these days would a man even have to make that consideration.

She walked over to him, still in her high heels, her breasts bouncing up and down. She straddled him. Her perfume was cheap, thick, and sweet. It made Moses more light-headed than the joint. There was something about cheap perfume that he loved.

Even before he'd gone to prison, he hadn't been with a woman for a while. A man shouldn't go without for too long. It makes you sharp and edgy at first, then you get unhinged and cranky. He needed this badly if he was to go on with his plan.

Moses gave her the joint. She took it and hungrily took a long drag. Then she pulled his pants off and knelt in front of him and pulled out a condom.

"Not yet," said Moses. "Gimme this first." He pointed to her mouth.

Donna backed off a little. She obviously didn't want any of that. She was a whore, but not a fool.

"Uh-uh, baby." She shook her head.

Moses smiled and pulled out a twenty-dollar bill and held it before her. Donna looked at it and considered the offer. Moses knew what she was thinking. It was almost as much money as she was about to get for having regular sex with him. But in the age of AIDS, she would be taking a chance. You could be putting a penis into your mouth or a loaded weapon. He watched her face. She probably had some kind of habit and had to weigh the risk of unprotected sex against the ever-present need for drugs. The money was too good to pass up. She took the bill, held it to the light, then she buried her face into his lap.

Moses took the joint back and smoked as he enjoyed Donna's technique. He wondered absently if Ted Walker's body had been found. If it had and it made the papers, Dake and Nita would run, and if they did, he might not ever catch them. He could try to turn some of his old crew, but it might be hard. Men were loyal to whoever was paying them at the moment.

Donna got up and wiggled out of her skirt. She had a gorgeous body that probably wouldn't last. In a few years, she would have worked so hard that she'd lose her looks. Her breasts would sag, and she'd waste away into a walking zombie spiraling down into the deepest regions of the underclass. But for now it was all good, he thought as she turned to let him see her.

"Beautiful," Moses said.

"Thank you," said Donna. She walked to him and started to straddle him again. Moses held her back, grabbing the condom.

"Now, I need it," he said.

Donna seemed insulted for a second. What was his problem? her eyes seemed to say. She got past the insult then put the condom on, and they started having sex.

The girl was indeed new to the game, Moses thought, because she seemed to enjoy the act. Old pros didn't feel anything when they did it. They might as well be getting a doctor's exam. But Donna was having a good ride. She moaned and wanted to be in several positions before it was over.

Moses let her use the shower, then he let her leave. She gave him a phone number, which he promptly threw away. A hooker's number wasn't usually good for more than a week. And even if it was good, he didn't want to see her again.

Moses dressed, making sure to cover his face as much as possible. Then he took some of Ted Walker's cash and left the motel.

He thought of hailing a cab but didn't want to be close to a driver. He opted for the bus, a place where people were afraid to look anyone in the face. He hopped the bus and took it to the near east side.

Moses watched the city pass in the darkness of the evening. The neighborhoods had pockets of rebirth that seemed to fight against the decay of time and neglect. He felt comfortable in the inner city. There were many terrible things within it, but it had spawned him, and so it was home. The city was like a drug, he thought. So bad for you, but so necessary to keep you going.

He got off the bus near Dequindre. He walked along a few streets, making sure his gun was ready. He was taking no chances. He was doing good so far and saw no reason to get sloppy.

Moses walked up to the little yellow house three blocks over and knocked on the door. Someone stirred inside. A shadow came closer to the door.

"Who is it?" asked a woman's voice.

"It's me," he said.

There was a noise that sounded like something falling, and then Moses heard the woman say, "Save me, Jesus."

After a moment, the door opened. A black woman about sixty or so stood there. She had gray hair and a face that looked as though it had seen a thousand dreams disappear. She stood in the doorway, sticking her head and upper torso out.

"She ain't here," said the woman.

"Mrs. Washington, I need to see her," said Moses.

"You heard me say she ain't here, didn't you?"

"Yes, but I know you. You can't lie to save your life."

Mrs. Washington shifted on her feet a little, as if acknowledging Moses' accusation. "Jesus in the morning, what have you done now?" she said.

"I had some trouble, but it was all a mistake."

"Ain't you done enough here? The girl was only a baby when you came around."

"Please, don't start that again," said Moses. "It's all old news."

"Not to God, it ain't. What you did was wrong, and you know it. Thank God no one knows about you and my Nessa. I don't like the police in my business."

"Can I see her, please?" said Moses. His voice was calm and pleading.

"Okay, but first I want you to pray with me."

"Pray?"

"Yes," said Mrs. Washington. "I may not have the answer to everything, but I do know this: Jesus saves. And if he can wash away the sins of the world, he can help a man like you. Now bow your head with me."

Moses didn't want to, but he knew Mrs. Washington would never let him in if he didn't. He closed his eyes as the old woman prayed.

"Heavenly Father, I ask You to heal this wretched man at my door. Look into his black heart and find the goodness that You put there. Let it grow, Lord, until it takes over and brings him back from the sinful hole he's in, back into Your grace. He was named after one of Your greatest prophets, but he has lost the faith. Give it back to him, Lord, so that he may find glory in Your kingdom one day. Amen."

"Amen," said Moses.

"Okay, wait here."

Mrs. Washington turned and closed the door, and as she did, Moses saw that she had a .38 in her hand. She was a religious woman, but a .38 would stop those the Bible couldn't.

Soon, he heard voices inside arguing. He looked around to see who might be watching, but there was no one. The street had several vacant lots filled with debris and the wreckage of what had stood there before. Other houses had cars in front of them, but looked as though no one would live in them. The windows were turbid apertures with curtains or sheets covering them like dark eyes filled with ruin.

Suddenly, the door opened, revealing a young black girl about eighteen. She was tall and striking. Her eyes were light brown and jumped

out against her darker skin. Her features were soft and classically beautiful. Her hair was done in long, thin braids that ended in a burst of curls.
Moses smiled at the girl, but the smile was not returned. She looked at
him with fear and hurt in her eyes.

"You shouldn't be here, Moses."

"How could I not come to see you, Nessa," he said.

"People are looking for you, the cops. I heard you busted out. Shoulda
known you was too smart to go to jail."

"Yeah, well, let them keep looking. I came to make sure you were all
right." He touched her face, and she grabbed his hand then pulled it
away gently.

"We're fine," said Nessa. She leaned her body in the doorway. "Everybody's okay, so if you're in a hurry, you can go now."

Moses could tell that she didn't mean it. Nessa could never resist him.
She was only sixteen when he saw her at a local store and chatted her
up. He knew she was young, but didn't know how young until it was too
late. He started having sex with her, and by the time he found out she
was a minor, he couldn't stop.

Nessa was a beauty, a little oasis in the hardness of the ghetto. He
wished he could be with her, make love to her, but that was impossible
now. Mrs. Washington would kill them both, and that was not much of
an exaggeration.

"You going to let me come in?" he asked.

"I don't know. I don't need trouble in my house. You gave me enough
of that already."

"Please, I'm only gonna stay a little while." Moses looked desperate.
If anyone who knew him could see him like this, they'd laugh. Hard-ass
Moses, groveling at the feet of some woman. "I brought you some
money." He pulled out a thick roll of bills.

"Where'd you get that?"

"It was a loan, from a friend. Take it."

"Moses, why don't you leave us alone?" Nessa asked. She looked up
at him with pain and affection in her eyes, the unmistakable look of a
woman in love.

"You know I can't do that," he said. "I still love you, girl.
Nothing can change that. Now, take this money and let me in to see
my son."

Nessa took the wad of cash and opened the door to the house. Moses stepped inside and saw a little one-year-old boy chasing a ball on the floor. The child turned and waddled his way to his mother.

"Come on, Kadhi," said Nessa.

She took the boy in her arms and passed him to his father. Moses took his son and held him tight. He looked into the boy's eyes and smiled.

"Daddy came a long way to see you," he said.

35

Postmortem

Marshall got to the office early and worked on his opening for trial. The lists were all in, motions done, and he could tell already that the case would come down to two pieces of evidence: ballistics and DNA. There were eyewitnesses, but that kind of testimony was not very important. Most people didn't understand that eyewitness testimony was notoriously unreliable and easily cross-examined and discredited. He thought about the Johnsons. Even if they had lived, they probably would have broken on cross when he got through with them.

He'd started the morning having breakfast with Danny, who was kind enough not to bring up the subject of Chemin being a murderer. Danny then left to attend a hearing with his attorney. He was going to try to be reinstated with pay. Marshall was kind enough not to tell him that he didn't have a snowball's chance.

Marshall decided that today he would get to the bottom of this mystery with Chemin. He could not do a trial with these terrible thoughts in his head.

He would need some facts on Jessica's death. The case had been put on hold by the FBI, but the locals were sure to have a file. He knew several people who could get him a case file if he needed it, including Tony Hill, the deputy chief. The only problem was they might ask why.

Marshall looked at his desk and realized that his life in the office had stopped during the case. Piles of unopened mail and court papers filled his in box. He sifted through it. Except for the court papers, most of it was interdepartmental crap, junk mail and the like. He gathered it up and tossed it into his trash can.

A powder blue envelope caught his eye. It was smaller than a standard envelope, and looked odd among all the other papers. Marshall fished it out of the trash and looked at the envelope, which was addressed to him. It had birds on the border and smelled of perfume. Then he saw the initials "J.C." in the return address corner.

"Jessica," he said aloud.

Marshall carefully opened the letter and took it out. His heart was racing as he looked at the date. It was written the very day she died.

Dear Marshall,

I know it's stupid to write this letter, but I feel I have to. My heart is not my own anymore. Since your wife saw us, I have been having the most terrible thoughts. I felt so bad for doing what I did that I went to see my pastor and confessed to him. He was angry with me, and made me pray with him for a half hour. I felt so much better when it was over.

But I still loved you.

I can't help but tell the truth, that's the only way I can get over this, you see. It's so damned pathetic to pine away for something that's not yours, but I swear I thought that she didn't want you anymore. I guess maybe it was just wishful thinking.

It's so hard to find a man like you these days. I guess I wanted to make sure that if you left her, I'd have a head start on all the other women out there (smile).

I had a dream about us last night. We were together, making love, I held you tight between my legs and whispered to you all the things I wanted from life. And you kept saying: "I'll be with you, always."

Marshall became embarrassed. This was a love letter written as some last attempt to get him. He was even more sick than he was before she died. "Was killed," he corrected. He wanted to throw the letter away, but he felt that he should read it out of respect. It was Jessica's last testament on earth. If only I had seen this, he thought. Maybe he could have saved her. *And Chemin* his mind added. She was lost too. He raised the letter back to his anguished face.

That was a silly dream, huh? I know it was stupid but it's how I feel about you, like you will take care of me if we could be together. Just so you won't worry, you should know that I put in for a transfer to L.A. It's some time off, but Agent Sommers said she can help me.

I wasn't going to write you, but I changed my mind because I thought you had come to the office today. Those CIA jerks were nosing around again, so we were all trying to make ourselves scarce. I took an early lunch and was walking out, when I heard your voice from behind a door. I heard your friend too, that white man who sounds like he's black. So I knocked on the door, and then the voices stopped. I called out your name, but no one answered. I went to lunch, and when I came back, the office was empty. I asked everyone if they had seen you, but no one had. I'm sorry if I stumbled on some secret meeting you had there, but your voice is so distinctive.

Well, this letter is getting long and I have to go home. Please don't hate me for what I did, and after I'm gone, please don't ever forget about me.

Love,

Jess

Marshall put the letter into his briefcase and stood. His mind was spinning, and he saw the letter shake in his hands. He'd been to FBI headquarters many times, but he'd never been there with Danny. So, if Jessica was right, how could she have heard his voice and Danny's? The only time Danny had even been in the building was—

When he was in his office.

Marshall sat back down in his chair. Fear filled his heart. Jessica had heard him and Danny, but what she had heard was a *recording* of them in his office. That meant there was a listening device somewhere in the office. He glanced around the room at the walls, looking for a camera. No, he thought. That would be too obvious. Too much trouble to put a camera in. You'd have to run the lines to a monitor without being detected. It was probably audio. That was more likely.

But why would his office be bugged? He thought of Jessica's letter. The "CIA jerks" as she called them were there. Van Ness, the happy-ass spook, and his pal, Easter, would be just the kind of guys to do something like this, he thought. But then there was also Sommers and the FBI, and yes, he thought, Nate and Toby.

The only answer was the Douglas case. He always felt that someone wanted to make sure he won this case. The Johnsons' deaths had never set well with him. Langworthy didn't make any sense because he was a liberal judge, but that might be a decoy. Even a liberal judge wouldn't spring a man who killed another judge if the evidence was airtight.

Still why? Douglas had been killed because he was a judge who—

Marshall stopped. Why had Douglas been killed? he asked himself. They all thought that it was because he was a conservative seen as a race traitor, but that was Mbutu's alleged motive. So, if Mbutu didn't kill Douglas, then whoever did had another reason. If Douglas was killed by someone else, that person had to be connected to powerful people, wealthy people, people with great resources.

Like the government.

A Supreme Court justice is like the president in that his vote can shake the foundations of society. And sometimes people don't want the foundation shaken. Now, he suspected everyone. Anyone involved in the case could be the culprit.

Suddenly, he realized that if Jessica had stumbled onto an illegal recording, then that was why she was killed that night. He felt a weight lift from his mind. Chemin was innocent. But if the killers had murdered Jessica just for hearing his voice, what would they do to him if he found out their identity?

He had to find the device, he told himself. That was the only way he could be sure he was right and flush out the spy. Marshall looked around the office and tried to remember where he was when Danny was there. He checked his desk and credenza, nothing. The FBI's new listening devices were so small that it could be anywhere. He went under his desk and inspected the underside.

If someone came in they would probably think that he'd lost it. Marshall got on his back and looked up at the desk. Still nothing. Then he took out the drawers one by one, carefully so as not to make any noise. Nothing. He stood up and looked up at the ceiling, but it was clean. He was not thinking right. He had to think like the killers behind all this. He walked to the front of his office and looked at the room. Where could a microphone be so as to catch a conversation no matter where you were?

In his vista, in the middle of the room, he saw the two bookshelves behind his desk. Slowly, he walked toward them. He checked them carefully. On the middle shelf near the back was a small silver microphone. It was a tiny thing, no bigger than a quarter. Because it was under a shelf and near the back, there was no way you would ever see it just getting a book or casually looking for something.

Marshall backed away from it. "Muthafucka," he whispered. What kind of trouble had he gotten himself into? His lawyer's mind quickly listed the crimes committed by putting the device in his office. Then he had a more disturbing thought. Whoever had done this probably had his indiscretion with Jessica and confrontation with Chemin on tape. He was enraged and embarrassed by the thought, but there were more pressing things to consider. The time had come to make an agressive move in this game.

He wrote out an opening for the case. This took an hour, but he waited to be sure no one suspected that it was a decoy. Ironically, the words came easily under this pressure. When he was finished, he got on the phone and started calling everyone.

Bob Ryder, Roberta, and Walter all filed in ten minutes later. Marshall told them that he wanted to practice an opening on them. He got up and paced before them; after a moment, he looked at the bookcase and went over to it and took down a book from the shelf with the microphone in it. He pretended to check a quote then put it back, looking curiously at the shelf and making sure they saw him looking. Then he finished the statement.

"So what do you think?" asked Marshall when he was finished.

"Not bad," said Bob Ryder. "But it should be longer."

"No way," said Walter. "A long opening makes a jury think you haven't pinpointed the issue."

"It needs more facts," said Roberta. "You should hit on the proof more, but otherwise, it's great."

Marshall watched them as they spoke. They all seemed calm, except Walter, who was his normal edgy self. It could be him, Marshall thought. Walter had a checkered past and a bad history in the office. He pondered Walter's substance abuse problems.

Marshall gave them all copies of the opening and told them to write out all of their suggestions for him. It was unorthodox, but he was sure they didn't know what was going on.

Later, Agent Sommers came in, and Marshall gave her a bullshit story about wanting tighter security on Mbutu. He felt that once the trial started his life might be in danger. Sommers seemed to buy it but showed no reaction when he seemed to notice something in the bookcase.

Agents Van Ness and Easter showed up around quitting time. Van Ness was his old happy self. Marshall told them that he wanted to make sure that Mbutu didn't have any radical connections that might make the trial dangerous. Van Ness agreed and said that they had already checked out the various antigovernment groups and so far found nothing. But he agreed that maybe they should look again. The last thing anyone wanted was an oversight that ended in a fatality.

They never flinched as he took a moment to straighten out the books on the shelf, not once, but twice. Marshall talked to them for a few more minutes then let the agents go and started to pack his briefcase.

He was about to leave when Nate Williams came in. Marshall had almost forgotten that he was on the list. Nate was his friend and mentor, and he felt bad deceiving him, but he told him the story about the stacked jury pool and how he suspected that Kelly had gotten to someone. Marshall made sure to go to the bookcase and notice something amiss. Nate showed no emotion. He didn't really expect Nate to show anything. He'd been in government for a long time and was a cool customer.

Nate said that he would look into the matter, then he left, saying that he was going home. But when Marshall walked out of his office, he heard Nate talking urgently to someone on the phone. Nate's door was open.

Marshall was excited and sad about this. Nate had found a reason not to go home, and it could be connected to the bug in Marshall's office. If Nate was reacting to Marshall's discovery of the microphone, it was foolish for him to have left his office door open. Marshall wanted to eavesdrop, but that was not part of the plan.

He walked out of the office but did not leave the building. He went down a floor and waited for a while, then he doubled back onto the U.S. attorney's floor and hid in an office across from his own.

He couldn't hide in his own office because his confrontation with the spy would be caught on audio. He waited and watched the office lights go out. Then he heard a noise from outside the room he was in. Marshall peeked out the door in time to see someone go into his office. He didn't get a good look, but the game was on, he thought. He'd wait until they came out, then confront them.

Then he realized that if someone came in he would be defenseless. If it were Sommers or Van Ness, he'd be at their mercy if they pulled a weapon. He was foolish. He was dealing with murderers, and here he was sitting in a dark room with nothing more than a briefcase to protect himself. Then he had an idea. There was a code for security that could be dialed from any phone. The guards would get the code and come to wherever the code originated from. Marshall took the phone in the office and got ready.

He heard noise across the hall. He quickly dialed the security code. He could hear footsteps. He had to catch the person before they got away. He quickly headed for the door.

Marshall flung open the door to the office he was hiding in and saw Roberta Shebbel stepping out of his office. She saw Marshall and was startled, letting out a little yell.

The two lawyers looked at each other for a moment, silent. Marshall stared at her with anger and accusation. He could not believe it. Straight-arrow Roberta, the confidante, was a spy.

"I've been waiting for you," Marshall said calmly.

"I left something—in your office," she said.

Roberta's words were fairly calm, but the look in her eyes betrayed that. It was a look of sheer terror.

"You're much too intelligent to think I'll believe that, Roberta," said Marshall.

Roberta was silent. She started to shake a little, she looked like someone about to go into shock.

"Marshall, I—I don't—" Roberta's mind stalled. She was a smart woman, and she'd put it all together. Marshall had set a trap, and she had been caught. Roberta's lip quivered, and she started to cry.

"How could you do this to me?" Marshall asked. "I thought you were my friend."

Roberta continued to break down, speechless. Suddenly, a security officer ran in. His hand was on his weapon, and he had a look of fear on his face. Marshall recognized Mike Phillips, a relatively new man in security. He was so young that he looked like a kid with a toy gun on his hip as he rounded a corner.

"Hey, Mike," said Marshall. "Sorry, man. This was a false alarm. I thought someone was in my office, so I hit the code. Turned out to be my good friend Roberta here."

Marshall walked over to Roberta and put an arm around her. The look on his face was friendly, but in his eyes, he knew she could see the look of anger and betrayal. "She's just having a little problem."

"Is everything okay?" Mike asked. He pulled his hand away from the gun.

"Yes," said Marshall. "You go back. Everything's good here."

"Okay, Mr. Jackson," said the guard. "But watch it. That code is serious."

"I will," said Marshall.

The guard walked off, talking into a radio. Marshall turned to Roberta, who was sobbing heavily now.

"I want to know everything," said Marshall. "Right now."

Marshall took Roberta out of the building over to Lafayette Coney Island, a hot dog joint downtown. It was late, and it was the only place he knew that would be open.

Marshall took Roberta to a table in the corner of the restaurant. She was calmer now but still shaken at being caught.

"So, what the fuck is going on?" asked Marshall.

"I don't know, Marshall" said Roberta. She was looking down in her chest, and her eyes were red.

"Don't you go soft on me," said Marshall. "I want to know who's bugging my office and why."

"I really don't know. It's all fucked now. Everything's fucked."

A waiter came by. He looked at Roberta and grew concerned.

"You okay, ma'am?" he asked.

"Yes," said Roberta. She pulled out some Kleenex.

"We'll have two coffees," said Marshall.

The waiter went off, glancing back at Roberta.

"Okay, Roberta," said Marshall. "If you won't tell me what I need to know, then I'm done. I'll go to Nate, and we'll have you investigated."

"They killed Jessica, didn't they?" she asked.

"Who is 'they'?" asked Marshall.

"I don't know, I swear." She started to cry again.

Marshall waited a moment for her to calm down. "Yes, I believe they killed Jessica," he said.

"I knew it. It was just too much of a coincidence."

"I think she found out about the recordings."

"Oh God, this is so awful. What am I going to do?" said Roberta.

"You're going to turn off the damned tears and tell me how you got into whatever this shit is." Marshall hated to see a woman cry, but Roberta was a traitor, and he had to know what she knew.

"Okay, okay," said Roberta. "I'm sorry."

The waiter came back with the coffee. Roberta took a sip without putting anything in it.

"Okay, I was seeing this man, a lawyer in the appellate division. You know him, Lance Young."

"Yes, he was disbarred. Had a gambling and drug problem, but I didn't know you two were seeing each other."

"Nobody did. We had a very discreet relationship." She sniffed a little. "Couldn't have anyone know he was fucking a fat girl." She laughed bitterly.

Marshall was mildly shocked. Roberta didn't curse often, in fact, he didn't think he'd ever heard her curse until now.

"So what did your relationship with Lance have to do with all this? I want you to start from the beginning and don't leave anything important out." He was treating her like a witness in prep for a trial or deposition. He had to. She was all over the place with her emotions and needed focus.

"Lance got into trouble," she started. "He owed money to some bad men. So, naturally he came to me for help. He always did. I knew what he was, but I was weak for him. Well, I didn't have the kind of money he needed. Lance was desperate. He'd been beaten and he was crying. He said they'd kill him. I couldn't stand seeing him like that. I was in love with him. You have to understand that."

Roberta stopped and took out another Kleenex. She had a wet pile of them now.

"I checked our recent cases, then I took the money from evidence control before they could check it for prints and all that other stuff they do."

Marshall remembered that a few months back, twenty thousand dollars turned up missing from evidence in a drug case. The defendant was freed and the money never recovered.

"Lance got the money," Roberta continued. "He gambled it and snorted it away. Then he got caught buying drugs and was disbarred. Not long after that he dumped me and went to Denver with another woman. After that I figured, what the hell, I was a dumb-ass woman in love. I thought I'd just stick that mistake in my little private closet where it would just turn into another skeleton, you know."

"But someone got to you. Who got you to spy on me and why?"

Roberta sniffed a little and blew into another Kleenex. "I got an anonymous letter one day that said how I stole the money and why. They said that they had evidence that I was the one."

"So, why didn't you come to me or Nate? Why not cut your losses, Roberta?"

"I was going to, Marshall, but—" She looked down into her coffee.

"Oh God, did you do drugs too? Did you spend the money on something?"

"Yes, I partied with Lance, but there was something worse than that. These people, whoever they are, sent me a copy of a video Lance and I made together—with another man."

Marshall was stunned. He was like most men. He never thought of a fat woman like Roberta as a sexual person. She had probably endured years of loneliness and rejection. She'd finally found a man but had gotten in way over her head.

"I didn't know he taped it," said Roberta. "Someone must have found it after Lance self-destructed. We had gotten so crazy. The other guy was one of Lance's drug connections."

She took a moment and wiped another tear from her face. "Do you know what it's like, Marshall? To be a woman who's not pretty or attractive? Fat. It's a death sentence for a woman my age. You haven't lived until you've seen the terror in the eyes of a blind date, or heard the whispers and laughing as you walk by people in a health spa. I don't blame anyone, it's just— The things about me that are good are not in my underwear, but that shouldn't doom me to a life without a man. All I wanted was somebody to be with. It's goddamned humanity, Marshall, didn't I deserve that?"

Marshall almost felt sorry for her. Roberta was a talented women, exceptional in fact, but he had to admit, she wouldn't be his first choice for a date. But that was not the issue. She'd committed several felonies and violated his privacy. He knew she was being blackmailed, bent to someone else's will, and what he was about to do was no better.

"What happened to Lance?" asked Marshall.

"He was found dead in Denver not long ago. Probably crossed the wrong people."

"So, this mysterious person told you to bug my office?"

"Yes, I kept getting these notes that told me what to do. They all came to my house. Never at work for some reason. I knew it was blackmail, but I just couldn't let that video get out. I just couldn't."

"Who do you think is behind this?" Now he was picking her brain. He knew she had to be thinking about her blackmailers and probably had some theories.

"Law enforcement," said Roberta. "FBI, CIA, maybe even someone from our office. I don't know what you're into Marshall, but someone's watching you."

"The only thing I'm into is my job. Do you have the letters? I want to see them."

"I kept them, but it's just regular paper from a laser printer. There's nothing you can get from it. Whoever's doing this is too smart."

"Okay, Roberta," said Marshall. "I want you to be cool and keep playing along."

Roberta lifted her head. "You're not going to turn me in?"

"I can't. This is bigger than you know. I'd tell you what I think is going on, but you're in enough trouble already."

"When I saw you go to that bookcase, I thought I'd piss my pants. I thought my life was over. I went home tonight and actually thought about killing myself."

"Roberta, I can't condone what you've done. But you're a good person and a good lawyer. You deserve better than this, but I can't let you out until I get to the bottom of this. More people may be hurt."

"So, why are they interested in you? Are you fixing cases or something?" she asked. "I heard you had that gunrunner cold on weapons charges and he got off."

Marshall was insulted, but it did make sense. As far as Roberta knew, the Douglas case had nothing to do with the bugging. "Langworthy did that," he said. "He gave the jury a fucked-up instruction that allowed them to spring Lewis Quince because of abuse by the cops. What they want from me is something else."

He didn't want to tell her any more than that. The one thing he couldn't do was give her information to trade to whoever was squeezing her.

"I'm gonna see if I can bring out our friend."

"What about the case?"

"We go on."

"Just like that. After all you know, we're going to continue?"

"Yes," said Marshall with determination. "I'm not going to stop this case and derail everything because of this. You—we're both in too deep now. Trial starts in a few days. Be ready with all your research and support."

"So, you still want me on the case?" She had a look of surprise on her face.

"Yes. I'm not judging you, Roberta, but I'm not saying you'll be clean on this, but if you help me, it might be easier for you when this is over."

Roberta thought about this. She tilted her head up a little, the way people do as if they are looking for divine inspiration.

"If I survive," she said.

Marshall didn't want to lie to her. She was smart enough to know that they were on very dangerous ground now. People were already dead and things were bound to get worse.

"Yes, if you survive—and me too."

36

. . . .

Original House

Marshall got up early the next morning. All night he thought of Roberta and her dirty tale of sex, blackmail, and regret. The seriousness of what it meant weighed heavily on his mind. The surveillance on him meant Mbutu might not be guilty. If that was true, then a bigger, more villainous force was at work.

He thought about who could benefit from Douglas's death. Reluctantly, he had to name Judge Bradbury, his old friend. He was in line to get Douglas's job and didn't like the dead man's politics. There might be radicals and subversives who didn't like Douglas, but none of them could bug his office. That was a government move. If it was the CIA or FBI, or the ever-elusive NSA, there could be a thousand reasons to kill Douglas. Who knew the kind of shit they were into?

He had to look beyond the obvious reasons. Everyone just assumed that Douglas was killed because of race-related issues. But that wasn't necessarily true. He remembered what he had told Danny about the racial overtones of his brutality case:

Race clouds people's minds, and while they're angry about it, someone can steal the world from you.

The first thing he'd do was check the crime again. If there was another shooter, then according to the ballistics report he could only have been in the same general area as Mbutu. The trajectories of the shots were close. They went over the scene carefully, but maybe their heads weren't in the right place. Then he had to work to find his brother. The FBI had an interstate manhunt going but so far had nothing. If they found Moses, Marshall would have to get to him first and make some kind of deal. The information in his brother's head might be the key to all this. If he could find out who really killed Douglas, then maybe he might flush them all out.

Before they kill me too.

The words slipped quietly into his head. And they were accurate. How long before the powers behind all this decided that he was dispensable too? Not long, he reasoned. So he had to get to it fast.

Marshall had a glass of orange juice and tried to read the paper. After a while, Danny and Vinny came downstairs and sat with him in the kitchen. Danny looked tired and upset. Marshall looked at his friend and saw the key to his plan. Danny was outside the law now and had no connections to the feds. But could he put his friend in harm's way like this? It didn't seem fair, although he knew that Danny would never refuse him.

Vinny grabbed a bagel and went off to work. Danny walked her out the door. He looked sad as she drove off. There was nothing worse than a man who wasn't making money, having his woman work, a woman who had been shot, at that. Danny walked back to the kitchen and sat with Marshall.

"Hey, man," he said.

"So, I take it your hearing didn't go well," said Marshall.

"No. I'm still out. And they're going to file a lawsuit against the city this week."

"It'll probably settle, but that won't solve your problem."

"I know that's right," said Danny. "And check this out, these muthafuckas want me to take a psychological exam."

"It's routine. In fact, it's a good sign. They might be looking for a way out of it."

"Not to me it ain't good. I ain't crazy. Fuck all of them in the ass." Danny grabbed a bagel and took a big bite.

"Good to see you're taking it well," said Marshall. "So, yesterday something happened to let me know that Chemin didn't have anything to do with Jessica's death."

"You had sex with her, didn't you?" asked Danny.

"No, and stop being so goddamned smart. I found out something, something big. And I'll need your help on it."

"Okay, it ain't like I got anything else to do these fuckin' days. So, what is it?"

Marshall wasn't sure his house wasn't bugged so he took Danny outside and told him everything he knew, then asked him to find Moses.

"Two guys and a fat chick? Man, that's some sick-ass shit, you know?"

"That's your reaction to a national conspiracy and four murders?"

"Sorry, man. This is a lot of shit to swallow, that's all. Look, I can get on your brother's trail today. There's a chance he's still around. A lot of lowlives don't feel comfortable in other cities. You grow up in shit and you like to stay around it."

"Aren't you going to say you're sorry about the things you thought about my wife?" asked Marshall.

"I would, but you still don't know for sure. Why did she burn those clothes?"

"I'll find out this morning. I'm meeting her for breakfast."

"That's cool, you two need to get your shit together. Whether she did it or not, I think you two should talk."

"I'll take that as a compliment. It's the best I'm gonna get from your sorry ass."

"You got that right," said Danny. He laughed.

Marshall walked into the Original Pancake House in Southfield and took a seat. The place was crowded as usual, but he managed to get a table near the back. He was meeting Chemin and didn't want to draw too much attention to himself.

Chemin walked in the restaurant ten minutes later. She was dressed in a nice suit. She looked good. Whenever she wasn't feeling right, she always dressed up to feel better. It had a different effect on Marshall. He saw her as he had the first time they met. Beautiful, sexy, and confident. He wanted to run to her, kiss her, and tell her that everything was okay. Chemin sat down and even managed a little smile.

"You look great," he said.

"Thanks," she said. "I got a lot of sleep last night."

"How's work?" asked Marshall.

"It's fine," said Chemin. "My boss went apeshit without me for a while, but it's cool."

"I want to apologize for what Danny and I did. It's the—" Marshall stopped. Chemin had heard about how hard his cases were too often. If he said it, the statement might damn him to hell in this meeting. "I'm upset about a lot of things. I got carried away."

"I guess I haven't been acting so stable lately."

A waitress came by, and they ordered. Chemin asked for something they didn't exactly have on the menu. She always liked to create her own food. The waitress was suitably annoyed.

"I want you to come home, Chemin. I'll do anything you want, just come back to me."

Her face turned serious, as if a shadow had come over it. She looked at him for a moment then looked down at the table.

"Don't you want to know about the clothes I burned?"

"I do, but I don't want to get into another fight about it. Neither of us have been acting like ourselves lately. I'm sure you had a good reason to do what you did."

"My psychologist told me to burn the clothes." She stopped for a second, as if what she was about to say was difficult. "They were maternity clothes."

Marshall expressed surprise at this. She wanted a baby so badly that she'd been planning it without him. "I see. So, how long had you been doing that?"

"Not long, but my doctor didn't think it was good to fool myself and plan for something that might not happen. So, it was kind of a ritual. I actually felt better after I did it." She smiled again.

Whatever doubts he'd had about her were now gone. His wife, this remarkable woman, had not been driven over the edge by him. She was still a great person, the love of his life, and he wanted her back.

"I guess a little wardrobe barbecue never hurt anyone. So, when are you coming home?"

"I'm not, Marshall. And don't get upset, just hear me out." She stopped and took a breath. She'd obviously planned what she was about to say. "I don't think you know what life is like for me. You'll still be able to have a family when you're sixty, but not me. A woman's child-bearing period is a small life within a life. I don't want mine to pass with regrets. I want children, I need them, and if you won't give them to me, I'll have to find a mate who can."

It was classic Chemin. Short, logical, and to the point. He was over-whelmed. She hadn't said the word *divorce* this time, but it was implicit in her statement. She wanted out. She was going to leave him after everything they'd meant to each other. She didn't mention his indiscretion with Jessica, and he thanked God for that.

"Okay, Chemin," said Marshall. "I'll do it. We'll have a kid. I'm ready."

She laughed a little. "You can be so sweet sometimes, you know. I know you mean it. But a baby is a lifetime commitment, Marshall. It's not the kind of decision you make on a whim, or to keep your wife with you. You have to want the baby. You have to want to put your life in second position. And make no mistake, that's just what you'll have to do."

"I can get there, I know I can," said Marshall. Even he could hear the pleading inside his words. There was a time when he would have never sounded so desperate, but he felt as if he were losing more than a wife and a marriage. He was losing a friend. He was losing his life.

"I need you there now," she said. "I talked to my mother about this and—"

"You did?" asked Marshall. He was suddenly ashamed of himself. He adored Chemin's mother, and the feeling was mutual. It hurt him to know that she might now think less of him.

"Yes, I did," Chemin continued.

"What did she say?" asked Marshall. Somehow he didn't think he really wanted to know.

"She was actually on your side," said Chemin. "She said that forcing a man to have kids was stupid and had never worked in the recorded history of mankind."

It was good to know that Chemin's mother agreed with him, but the essence of her statement still lent itself to a divorce.

Chemin looked at him with such compassion that he forgot all the pain he was feeling inside.

"And so?" asked Marshall.

"I agree with her. That's why I'm doing this. That's why we should separate."

They ate in silence then left. Marshall walked her to her car outside. The morning was cold, but the sun was out, causing the snowbanks to gleam with light. It was strangely beautiful. Chemin stopped by her car door and smiled at him.

"Don't be sad," she said. "Sometimes people just need to step back and agree that it isn't going to work."

"You're leaving me. What do you want me to do? You're not giving me a chance."

Chemin looked down at her feet for a second. It was the second time she had looked away. He knew this was big. She was not the kind of woman who was shy about anything she said or did.

"I know I'm a hard woman," she said. "But I'm sure I'm doing what's right for both of us. I was lucky to have a man like you, Marshall. I know most women would laugh at me for what I'm doing, but I can't be controlled by the forces of society, I have to be their master, otherwise, I'm a fool."

This was all too true of his wife. Her strength had caused her to turn away from everything that looked like weakness. And she didn't understand that her attitude might be construed as weakness itself.

She took a step to him and kissed him. Her face was warm, and she smelled like heaven. In that moment, he had everything he wanted. All his trouble and fear melted away, and he wished for a life without the terrible baggage of humanity. He hugged her tightly and didn't want to release her. She gently pushed him back.

"I'll see you," she said,

He didn't want to answer. To him, that would be an admission that it was over, and he couldn't believe that. Chemin got into the car, pulling her long legs inside. The car started up, and to him the engine sounded like thunder. Then she pulled away and rolled into the bright morning.

37

Habeas Corpus

As Marshall drove to Masonic Temple he kept seeing Chemin driving off in her car like the end of a sad movie. How did he blow it? he thought. Life was strange that way, it sneaked up on you and kicked you in the ass, and before you knew it, all you had were memories and regret. He thought that he would beat his family's curse. After all the trouble in his life, it seemed for a while as if he was going to dodge the bullet. But he'd been shot by fate and doomed to failure in his marriage.

He arrived at Masonic Temple and parked. He went inside and was soon standing on the stage where Douglas was shot. He looked up at the crawl space Mbutu had used. It was so small. How could anyone else have been up there with him? If the real killer had been too far away, the trajectories of the shots would have shown that the shots were beyond the margin of error.

Marshall checked the blueprints he'd gotten from the case file. Nothing. It was impossible for a second shooter to be there unless he was suspended in the air.

Marshall went up to the space itself. He took off his jacket and went inside. He lay down just as Mbutu must have and looked out of the hole that he used to shoot.

There was nothing smarter than a killer, he thought. When you commit the vilest of crimes, you brought to bear all of your power. Those left to catch you had to make due with ordinary smarts.

Marshall backed out of the crawl space. He had to go backward, and his hands and elbows hit the floor as he did. Suddenly, he stopped and started again. The sound of his body hitting the floor of the crawl space was weird, it was a round, airy sound, and then he understood.

It was hollow.

Marshall hit the floor and heard the wonderful sound again. That was how a second shooter could have been suspended under Mbutu. *He was under the floor.* Marshall tried to pull up the floorboards, but they wouldn't move. Nothing. What was the answer? He leaned against the wall. Suddenly his eyes widened. He went out of the room and checked the wall adjacent to the space that had been used. He hit the wall and heard the hollow sound again.

Marshall went back to building services and inquired about the wall. He was given another set of blueprints, an earlier set that showed an old ventilation system that had been abandoned back in the early 1970s. There was an air duct in the wall, and beneath all of the crawl spaces there was an area that was used for vents.

Marshall's heart raced as he went into the basement of the building. It was a cavernous place that was smelly and ancient. The head engineer, an amiable man named Darryl, showed him the old ducts.

After Darryl was gone, Marshall went to the duct that led to the area beneath the crawl spaces. It was huge. It had long been disconnected from any boiler or furnace. He looked inside into the blackness. Shining a flashlight inside, he saw handles in the side of the duct that must have been used for climbing. He took off his jacket, turned on a flashlight, and climbed up.

He went up past the seats on the floor, past the balcony, to the end. He climbed out and looked around. The duct had led under the spot where Mbutu would have been.

It was dark inside. Marshall felt around the front of the space. The killer had to have looked out of an opening and closed it back up. Marshall shined the light against the front of the space and saw that the vents had been covered up. Then the light caught something that looked like a small handle. Marshall grabbed it and pulled. An old vent panel slid to one side about a half foot. He looked through it and saw the stage.

"I got your ass," he whispered.

He climbed back down and cleaned himself off as best he could. He knew that he could go to Nate and Toby with this, but what would they do? If they couldn't be trusted, then that evidence was useless and maybe he would be too.

He had to have an airtight case. Only that would protect him and anyone else who was in danger. He had found his habeas corpus, the body of his crime in this mystery, but it would take more to convince others.

Whoever got into that second space had to have been there long before Mbutu got into his, maybe hours before. And he probably was there when they did the investigation, under the lab techs, breathing softly, waiting for them to leave. A patient man, a smart man, a very dangerous man.

Marshall went back to the office, excited about his discovery, but a little fearful of walking into an office he knew to be bugged.

He thought of Roberta. What if she had gone over the edge and confessed to someone? That could spoil everything.

He walked into his office and checked for the bug. It was still there. That meant Roberta was still on board. Marshall went into her office and found her there with a pile of books on her desk hard at work.

"Hi," she said almost like a child.

"Hey," said Marshall. "Can I talk to you for a moment?"

Roberta and Marshall walked out of the office to the lobby. Marshall didn't know if Roberta's office was bugged too, and he wasn't taking the chance. The lobby was quiet and peaceful. Outside, the smokers puffed happily away, like criminals banned from their offices.

"You okay?" he asked.

"Not really. I didn't sleep last night, and I've been on pins and needles all day."

"Just try to be cool. I'm on to something, and I think it might pan out. When it does, I'll need you to have a conversation with me on the bug, to flush these assholes out."

"What?" she said. "No way. I'm not getting into any cloak-and-dagger stuff."

"But you already have, Roberta," said Marshal. "Think about it."

She did, and said, "Okay. I'll try."

"And I want you to start carrying a gun."

"I can't do that. Guns scare me, Marshall."

"Getting killed should scare you more. Just do it. If you can't get one,

I'll get one for you, but you have to be smart about this. We're playing for big stakes here.''

''I can get a gun from my father. He tried to give me one last year.'' She looked defeated. This problem was making her do all the things she'd probably sworn she'd never do.

Marshall went back to his bugged office and worked on his opening statement. He felt exhilarated as he wrote, but he kept thinking of his wife driving away, the secret crawl space, and the ruthless man who had inhabited it.

38

Party Store

Danny pulled up his car by the little store called Brock's. It was what the locals called a party store, a little store by a residential neighborhood that had groceries but mostly sold beer and hard liquor. Many of the stores were owned by Chaldean merchants. The Chaldeans were Iraqi Christians, and many of them had immigrated to Detroit. Brock's store was black owned. Mo Brock had inherited the store from his father, Lucius, who was a community activist and former basketball player. Mo wasn't nearly as talented as his father, but he knew everything that went down in the 'hood.

Danny got out of his car and walked up to the three young black men standing on the corner. As he got closer, he could see that one of them was a girl, dressed like a boy. Danny smelled trouble. Enough time on the street had taught him to tell if a kid was good or bad, and these were definitely the latter.

"Wha'sup white boy?" said a tall kid with a green hat. "Hey, I think the hockey rink is thataway." The other two kids laughed.

"Which way is yo' fat-ass mama?" said Danny. He walked right up to Green Hat, whose friends moved closer to Danny, obviously intending to defend their friend.

Danny noticed that they made no comment about the way he talked. Within the inner city, he was welcome to be who he was. These kids had probably seen many whites who spoke like him. That made him feel a little better. He was always more comfortable around his own people.

"You don't need to be comin' 'round here with no bullshit. A mutha-fucka can get hurt like that," said Green Hat.

"If I was a muthafucka I guess I'd be scared, but since I'm not, fuck you."

Green Hat reached behind his back, but Danny already had his revolver out. He held it down in front of him. None of the kids even saw him reach for it. Danny's blood was pumping, and he had to admit he missed the danger of his work. These guys were lightweight, but he was enjoying the confrontation.

"Whatcha got behind yo' back, my brotha?" asked Danny "A piece of candy? A college diploma? Take it out so I can see it." Green Hat pulled out a knife. Danny laughed and put his gun away.

"What the fuck is wrong with you? You gon' slice some bacon or something? How you gonna kill somebody and get locked up in prison if all you gonna do is swing some little pigsticker like that? See, that's where you headed. Right to jail where some lifer who's been eating steak and pumping iron for ten years will drive a hole in your little ass big enough to park a car in."

"Later for you," said Green Hat. He put the knife away and walked off. The other two joined him. "You better watch yo' back 'round here," he said when he was a safe distance away.

"Why you fuckin' with them kids?" said Mo Brock from behind Danny.

Danny turned to see a little man about thirty. Mo had a small frame but a large head, just like his father. The Brocks were good people. Mo had taken over his father's community activism and was already helping to save lives in the neighborhoods.

"What are those kind of kids doing here?" asked Danny.

"I know they bad," said Mo, "but you gotta start somewhere with them. I let them come in and help out and in return I let them have soft drinks and food for free. By the time they figure out it's a job, I got them."

"I can't believe that works," said Danny. "Knocking heads is all they understand."

"That's cop talk. And if I didn't know you better, I'd say it was white man talk. Look at what banging heads got you, Danny. If I read the papers right, you shouldn't have those guns on you. You ain't a cop anymore."

"Not true," said Danny. "I just don't have a license to kick ass any-more. Now I gotta do it for free."

"There are better ways, you know."

"I haven't found those yet, but for you, Mo, I'll keep looking."

Mo laughed a little. "So, what can I do for you? I know you didn't come here to buy a forty."

"No, I'm looking for somebody. You probably know him. Moses. Moses Jackson."

"He's probably long gone by now, man. Be a fool to stick around here after bustin' out of jail."

Danny smiled a little. This was why he'd come to Mo. He knew every-thing that happened in the neighborhoods. The criminal's life was under those of normal people, a city within the city, and Mo was one of the many keepers of information.

"Yeah, but have you seen him?" Mo knew something, but even a good guy like him didn't like to talk to the cops. Danny would have to coax what he wanted out of him. He hated doing that. It was much easier to just slam his ass. But Mo was a good man, and you never messed with someone who was righteous.

"Nope, I ain't seen him," said Mo.

"Okay, Mo. I know you can't ruin your rep by giving up somebody, but Moses is bad news all the way around. Just give me a hint about what you know."

Mo thought it over carefully. He'd obviously spent a lot of time making sure the local kids would trust him. He didn't want to blow it by talking to a cop and having a finger pointed at him as the person who gave up a brother.

"I don't know much," said Mo. "Just that somebody who was selling guns was talking about him, about how he seen him in the city."

"His name," said Danny. There weren't many gunrunners in the city.

"Can't do that," said Mo. "That's all I know."

"I see. Just nod if you hear his name," said Danny. "Blue Jack?"

"Look, I told you, I'm not talking."

"Milton, Quince—"

"Sorry," he said. "Don't know 'em."

"Come on, Brock, cut me some slack."

"Sorry."

"Okay, what can I do for the name?" said Danny. "I know you have a price, what is it?"

Brock didn't have to think long. "I got a local kid named Eroy, Eroy Wilson. Bad customer. He's only eighteen, but he's already towering over the kids his age. He's into dope, thievin', extortion, all of that. And he's the real deal, a hard-ass muthafucka who'd cut you and watch the sun turn your blood brown while you died."

"So, he's giving you trouble?" asked Danny.

"No, he pretty much leaves me alone, but he's got something that belongs to me. Eroy is a basketball fan. I had this ball signed by the Piston championship team. Thomas, Dumars, Rodman, Salley, Mahorn, even the coach, Daly. The bastard stole it, but I can't prove it. Get it back, and I'll give you the name and a hundred bucks."

"Is that all?" said Danny. "Where is he?"

"Where he always is, on the basketball court 'round the corner."

"I'll be right back," said Danny. Then he headed up the block.

It was good to be back on the street, he thought. Even as a cop, he mostly rode around in a car, his feet not touching the hard concrete of the 'hood. This was better than riding shotgun with Vinny. This was real.

The neighborhood was a nice one. The houses were well kept, and there were not many cars on the streets, a sure sign that many of the people had jobs. It was a shame that even such a good place could be home to someone like Eroy Wilson.

Danny rounded a corner and saw the playground. Even though it was cold out, it was filled with kids playing, gambling, or just hanging out in big coats. A rap tune blasted from a nearby car.

In the middle of the action was Eroy, a muscular kid with a shaved head and dark glasses. He was fair-skinned and probably had a grandparent who was white, thought Danny.

All eyes were on the white man as he approached. Danny stopped short as Green Hat and his friends walked up. Green Hat had his hand in his coat. Danny kept walking.

Green Hat pulled a gun. "You still here," he said. "You must be a fool."

"Ray, put that shit away," said Eroy. "You know I don't allow that here."

"Eroy, he rode up on me waving his shit," said Ray. "Well, now I got mine." To Danny, he said, "You ain't so bad now, is you?"

Danny walked toward Ray. Ray raised the gun. Danny kept walking, not reaching for his weapons. Most of the kids in the street were just scared children at heart. He'd seen the cold-blooded type, but this kid was not one of them.

"You'd better stop," said Ray.

"He's crazy," said the girl who had been with Ray.

Danny kept walking, never taking his eyes off Ray's face. Danny got to Ray and walked right up on the barrel of the gun. His stomach pressed against the barrel. He could see Eroy better. Mo was right, he had the look of a killer in his eyes. He was a man who'd seen a lot of pain in his short life and had already accepted his fate on the street.

The weapon shook in Ray's hand slightly. It was hard to shoot a man. If he were still a cop, Danny would snatch the gun and beat the kid with it. But that kind of behavior had already gotten him into a lot of trouble. Maybe there were better ways, like Mo said.

"Go on, Ray," said Danny. "Buy your ticket to the penitentiary."

Eroy reached over and pulled Ray's gun down. "Get your ass back, Ray," he said. "Ain't nobody going to the joint." To Danny, he said, "Get on, before I change my mind."

"I got business with you," said Danny. "You got something that belongs to Mo. He wants it back, and I came to get it."

Eroy and his crew laughed. "You are? Well, I'll just give the shit to you."

"I'm not asking you to do that," said Danny. "I hear you like basketball. I'll play you for Mo's championship basketball."

More laughter from the crew. "Didn't you hear?" said Eroy. "White men can't jump."

"Then I guess you down then, right?" asked Danny,

"Okay, but what if I win? What do I get?"

Danny took out his guns. "These," he said.

"Nice," said Eroy, looking at the weapons. "Cool. Let's do it."

"I need to see the ball," said Danny.

Eroy nodded to Ray, who ran off and came back with the basketball. It was wrapped in plastic.

Danny and Eroy went to the court as the rest of the men on the playground made bets. Danny was nostalgic. This reminded him of so many days as a kid, not a care in the world. It was cold out and the court had frost on it, but it didn't matter. Basketball was a year-round sport in the city.

"Fifteen game," said Eroy. "Your ball."

Danny took the ball and drove to the basket. He went up for a shot and

Eroy pushed him. Danny fell down hard on the concrete. Eroy took the ball and easily made the basket.

"I forgot to tell you, these are street rules, big baby," said Eroy. His crew laughed and slapped five in the background.

Danny smiled. He had hoped that Eroy would do that. It was a long tradition on the street that the game could be played unfairly. It was called "hardball" when he was a kid. Whatever name it had now, Eroy had just made a mistake.

Danny got up and got on defense. Eroy drove in, his elbow out. He was slow, Danny thought, but strong. It would be hard to take him. He hit Danny with a shoulder and tried to drive around him. Danny stripped the ball from him, and as Eroy came back for it, he met Danny's shoulder. It caught him in the chest. Eroy fell on his ass. Danny drove around his opponent and easily made a layup.

Eroy smiled and tried to look amused. But Danny could tell he was pissed off. Eroy had probably been beating up on smaller kids all his life. He was not used to losing.

Danny took the ball and dribbled in. Eroy waited, his fists clenched. Danny stopped and took a shot, making it from long distance. There were no nets on the rim, so what would have been a "swish" was the ball soundlessly going through the rim.

Danny made two more shots, knowing that Eroy would have to play a closer defense. He did. Eroy went up to Danny and shoved him hard as he inbounded the ball. Danny kept his footing, then Eroy threw an elbow that caused Danny to lose the ball. Eroy grabbed it and drove to the basket, slamming the ball in.

The game continued as the two men beat each other down. Danny knew beating him was only half the battle. If he won, then he'd have to stop Eroy from reneging on the bet. But first things first, he thought.

After a while, Danny was one point away from winning. Both men were bruised and hurting, but they showed no sign of giving up. Danny took the ball and drove in. Eroy stuck out a foot and tripped him. Danny hit the ground hard. Eroy took the ball and tried to do a fancy slam dunk. He missed, and the ball flew into the air. Eroy grabbed it and tried to make a layup, but Danny had recovered. He blocked the shot, knocking it off the court. Eroy's crew reacted, cheering for Danny.

Eroy was upset and embarrassed. He glared at his crew, and they stopped cheering. Eroy got the ball and drove in again. This time

Danny made him earn his way to the basket, blocking him every step of the way. Eroy took a shot that missed. Danny got the ball and Eroy, sensing defeat, ran to attack him. He jumped on Danny as he shot the ball. Danny got the shot off, but Eroy fell on him with all his weight, knocking him to the ground. The shot bounced in anyway, and Danny won the game.

Danny got up, tired, hurt, and sweaty. Some of Eroy's crew clapped.

"Shut the fuck up!" Eroy screamed from the ground. He got up. To Danny he said: "You need to get out of here. And don't even think about taking that ball or them guns."

"You lost. I'm taking what's mine," said Danny.

Eroy threw a punch at Danny's face. Danny ducked to one side, easily dodging the blow. Then he responded by kicking out his foot into Eroy's abdomen. Eroy doubled over. Danny stepped closer and brought his knee up, while bringing Eroy's head down into it. Eroy straightened up from the blow. Then Danny spun around and caught him on the jaw with an elbow, which dropped him cold.

Danny turned and walked over to Ray, who held Mo's ball and the guns. Respect was something the kids understood. There was a good chance that Eroy's crew would shoot him, but there was just as good a chance that they'd respect Danny for winning and defending himself.

Danny got to Ray, who still had the gun under his coat. He waited a moment to give the kid a chance to play his hand. Ray didn't move. Danny stepped around him. Then, without a word, Danny took the ball and guns and walked off.

As he moved along the street, he was aware of the kids watching him. He wondered what they thought. Were they thinking of shooting him in the back and avenging their fallen hero? Or were they thinking about changing their way of life now that they'd seen Eroy bested on the court and beaten in life?

Mo was elated to get his ball back, but told Danny that he now had to watch his back for Eroy. Danny didn't think about it. He had business. Mo gave Danny a hundred bucks, and Danny would have normally turned it down, but he needed the cash right now.

Mo told Danny where he might find Lewis Quince. Danny committed it to memory, got into his car, and drove off.

The confrontation with Eroy had left him exhilarated. It was going to be hard to help Marshall and not get into trouble. The neighborhoods were not a place you went into softly.

He turned a corner and headed toward Gratiot. Quince was one of those people who operated under the radar of all things lawful and proper. To get to him, Danny knew he would have to get down and dirty. But since he'd volunteered to help Marshall, he'd felt like a cop again. Maybe dirt was just what he needed.

39

Trial/Event

The trial opened with a burst of energy that seemed to shake the court-house. TV cameras lined the perimeter of the court making the room seem smaller.

Outside, more media types filled the street. The court sketch artist drew pictures of TV reporters and gave them away to the delight of all. The somber, dignified days of court were gone. Now, important criminal trials were more pomp than procedure, more event than justice.

Marshall looked at the statue of Lady Justice with fear in his heart. The symbol of all he stood for seemed to taunt him as he waited to begin the trial.

He wondered what her eyes would look like without the blindfold. Would they be sad for the perversion that had befallen her cause, or would they burn like elemental fire, burning away the lies of lawyers and their clients to reveal the truth?

These were his thoughts as he was about to start a case against a man who might not be guilty. But he couldn't say anything about his suspicions without proof. Indeed, who would he tell them to? His misgivings were connected to all the people he could conceivably confide in.

More troubling was the fact that he was in possession of evidence that could exculpate Mbutu. It was his duty to give up those facts when they became evident. But what did he have, really? Conjecture, hunches, a bug in his office, and an air duct leading to a hollow floor. He'd be removed from the case, and likely fired from the department to boot.

And there was still the question of Mbutu. He had at least tried to kill Douglas and so was guilty of attempted murder, as well as assault and the attempted murder of Wendel Miller, who still had the only good slug lodged in his spine. But what did Mbutu want? If he knew there was a second shooter, then surely he knew he was innocent. Why not just say that and use it to embarrass the government? It was almost as though Mbutu wanted to go to jail.

Since he'd been incarcerated, Mbutu's popularity had grown. His organization, the Brotherhood, had gotten new members from all around the nation. Chapters had even started in some foreign countries.

Mbutu was set to publish a set of letters from the jailhouse in a month, like Martin Luther King Jr. and Mandela had done. Mbutu was probably feeling like a hero, and sooner or later, a talk with him was going to be essential to find the truth.

Roberta sat at the table with Marshall, looking as if she didn't have a care in the world. She was good at hiding her feelings; then again, she'd been doing it for a long time, he thought. Ryder and Walter seemed nervous by contrast. Walter wanted respect in the office, and this meant a lot to his career. For Ryder, the case meant a chance to move up in his already rarefied circle.

On the other side of the room, Mbutu sat looking sick and tired. As the case went on, he seemed to grow more and more feeble. The case was stressful, Marshall thought. And Mbutu was no longer a young man.

Marshall had gotten up early and exercised, as he always did on a trial day. Danny and Vinny kept the house feeling like a home, but even the presence of close friends couldn't replace the relationship he'd lost. He wondered what Chemin was doing. Was she as upset as he was? Or had she walked into a new life easily, making him a memory?

A bailiff called the court to order. "All rise. The United States District Court for Eastern District of Michigan is now in session. The Honorable Clark Langworthy presiding."

Judge Langworthy entered, carrying a load of books and papers. The gallery stood and grew quiet. Langworthy turned on his mike and got feedback. He seemed frustrated with all the electronic equipment in the court. He didn't want the media, but higher powers had intervened.

"United States versus Daishaya Ali Mbutu, also known as Deion Wilson," said the bailiff. "The defendant is charged with one count of first-degree murder, one count of attempted murder, criminal assault, assault with a deadly weapon, and possession of an illegal firearm.''

"Before we begin," said Langworthy, "I want to caution the media."

The TV reporters all seemed to become stiff at this statement.

"This is a trial, a court of law. The public may have a right to view our proceedings, but I will not tolerate tawdry displays of low-class journalism. Some of you may be insulted by that, but then again, only those dealing in low-class journalism would be insulted."

The gallery laughed, even some of the reporters thought it was funny.

"Bailiff, bring in the jury."

The bailiff opened a door and signaled the jury to come in. The twelve men and women and the alternates walked in and took their seats. Debra Gibson-Chandler had been chosen as foreperson. He was right about her, Marshall thought. She was a leader.

"All right," said Langworthy. "The jury has been seated. Counsel appearances?"

"Muhammad Rashad and Leslie Reed for the defendant," said Rashad.

"Marshall Jackson, Robert Ryder, Roberta Shebbel, and Walter Anderson for the United States."

"Let's begin with the opening statements. Mr. Rashad?"

Rashad stood and walked in front of the jury. He was wearing a white dashiki and a kente cloth hat. He looked like he'd been kicked right out of the 1970s, and yet there was an elegance to him that overrode the retro clothes. He had the face of a father, a mentor, someone you trusted.

"Ladies and gentlemen," began Rashad. "You are going to hear a lot of things in the case from the government. But they won't show you much of anything. They will say my client, a man who had given his life to service of his people, killed Farrel Douglas, but they won't show you how he did it. They will say DNA links him to the death, but they won't show you that it does. They will say bullets match a gun owned by my client, but they won't be able to prove it."

Rashad went on to tell all about Mbutu's community activism over the years. Then he recounted the facts, saying that Mbutu was nowhere near the place where the crime was committed and did not know Anthony Collier, the man who'd been killed as a conspirator.

". . . in life, people say a lot of things to us, don't they? But do we judge them by that? No, we judge them by what they do. In life, actions speak louder than words, and in court, proof speaks louder than allegation. Listen to what the government says then watch what they show you, and you will clearly see that my client is innocent.''

Rashad turned, as if to walk back toward his table, then stopped.

''I know what you're thinking,'' he continued. ''If my client didn't kill the justice, then who did? Well, people, someone had to pay for the death of a Supreme Court justice. Do you think America will ever let an assassination go unpunished? These are the people who still cling to the belief that Lee Harvey Oswald inflicted five gunshot wounds with one bullet. James Earl Ray went to his grave denying that he killed Martin Luther King Jr., and mystery and suspicion still surround the death of Abraham Lincoln. There is more to this case than the government will tell you. But as I said, don't listen to what they say. Consider what they prove to you—nothing.''

Rashad walked back to his table. Marshall felt a little pressure. The man was good. He had kept it short so as to make the jury believe it was simple, but he made it compelling, getting in his defense and setting the government up as purveyors of deception.

Normally, a government lawyer would counter with hard evidence and things you can touch. But Marshall had learned that emotion was the master of logic in the human heart and mind. Defense attorneys knew this too. He had to match Rashad with a plea to both sides of the brain.

''Farrel Douglas was an exceptional man,'' Marshall began, still sitting down. He rose slowly and made his way to the middle of the courtroom. ''He was born in poverty in Philadelphia and walked out of Harvard Law School at the top of his class. He was a man who personified everything we believe in this country. And he was murdered for those beliefs, killed by a man whose importance to his people had waned, whose beliefs were no longer popular.''

Marshall then went into a brief presentation of the facts surrounding Douglas's death. He kept it short, making sure it was easy to follow.

''To the defendant,'' Marshall continued, ''Farrel Douglas represented his demise as a leader and as a person. The defendant is no Oswald. We will prove that Daishaya Mbutu was at the murder scene, with the weapon that killed Farrel Douglas. We will present hard scientific evidence to prove it. Everything else is deception.''

Marshall sat back down feeling good about the opening, but guilty about himself. Had he just taken the first step toward injustice, or was he on a more noble path? It was hard to know which.

Marshall showed the jury the tape of the assassination. Rashad and Leslie had objected, but Langworthy had allowed the tape. What he didn't allow were most of the forensic pictures of Douglas's body. Marshall didn't see the difference, but it was Langworthy again trying to be Solomon, to help the defense and look as if he were impartial.

Marshall then called his first witness, Kevin Henderson, a former follower of Mbutu. Henderson was a postal worker and family man. He was a solid witness who had fallen out of favor with the Brotherhood as their views became more radical.

"State your name for the record, sir," said Marshall.

"Kevin Duane Henderson." Henderson was a tall, handsome man about forty or so. This always helped to sway a jury. Nice-looking people tell the truth.

"Are you known by any other names?"

"Omar Kahlil. That was my name when I was a member."

"You were a member of the Brotherhood, the defendant's organization?"

"Yes."

"Why did you leave?"

"Because Mbutu is crazy."

Rashad jumped up. "Objection, Your Honor."

"It's sustained," said Langworthy. "The jury will disregard the witness's characterization."

"Were there specific reasons of a philosophical nature that you left the organization?" Marshall asked.

"Yes," said Henderson. "I was upset that the Brotherhood's attacks were turning to other black people."

"Can you explain that for the jury?"

"The organization was supposed to be trying to free black people. Our enemy was the establishment. All of a sudden, all we did was jump on black leaders and criticize them."

"Were there any leaders in particular who came under fire?"

"Jesse Jackson, the NAACP, and of course Farrel Douglas."

"Of the leaders mentioned who got the most criticism?"

"Douglas. Mbutu was obsessed with him."

"Objection," said Rashad.

"Sustained."

"Mr. Henderson," said Marshall. "Do you know how Mr. Mbutu felt about the deceased, Farrel Douglas?"

"Yes. He said—"

"Hearsay, Your Honor," said Rashad.

Marshall expected this objection. Hearsay was basically the statement of one person offered to prove something in a case. In this instance, Henderson was offering statements about the defendant to prove he didn't like Douglas. Hearsay is also the one evidence rule that no lawyer completely understands.

Marshall looked at Roberta, who nodded. "These are admissions, Your Honor. And the defendant will get a chance to cross-examine this witness."

"Overruled. Go on, Mr. Jackson."

"Mr. Henderson, continue."

"Mbutu would always say how Douglas was a traitor to his people, that he represented the worst of black people and didn't deserve to live."

"Did he ever say he wanted to kill Farrel Douglas?"

"I renew my objection, Your Honor," said Rashad.

"And I renew my overruling," said Langworthy.

"Did he ever say he wanted to kill Farrel Douglas?" asked Marshall.

"Yes," said Henderson. "He said it a lot. Talked about how he'd like to see him publicly executed and shit like that."

"Watch your language," said Langworthy.

"Sorry, man," said Henderson. The gallery laughed.

"And did you know this man?" Marshall held up a picture of Anthony Collier, the man who'd been shot at the assassination.

"Yes, I did," said Henderson.

"Let the record reflect that the witness just identified a picture of Anthony Collier. Tell us where you know him from."

"I met him in 1995 at a rally for recruits for the Brotherhood."

"Did he join that day?"

"Yes he did."

"Did you see his picture in the newspaper after the assassination?"

"Yes."

"And what did you think when you saw it?"

"Your Honor," said Rashad. "This man's thoughts that day can't possibly be relevant."

"This witness knew the defendant and the alleged accomplice to the assassination," said Marshall. "Do I need to say any more?"

"Overruled," said Langworthy.

"Mr. Henderson again," said Marshall, "what did you think when you saw Anthony Collier in the newspaper after the assassination."

"I thought, Oh my God. He did it, Mbutu killed Farrel Douglas."

Marshall worked Henderson a little more, trying to shield the coming attacks by Rashad. He brought out Henderson's prior life of crime and his redemption in prison. He tried to leave Rashad nothing to ask.

"Mr. Henderson," began Rashad on cross-examination. "Weren't you dismissed from the Brotherhood for stealing?"

"No," said Henderson.

"Didn't you write several checks to yourself without permission?"

Henderson hesitated. Marshall was worried but tried not to look like it. He didn't know about this little matter. Henderson had obviously held out on him.

"I had permission," said Henderson.

"Mbutu was the only one who signed checks along with the treasurer. Were you the treasurer?"

"No, but—"

"Then the checks were not authorized, were they?"

"Look, man, everybody was allowed to sign checks, the place wasn't organized."

"You wrote five thousand dollars' worth of checks to yourself, isn't that right?"

"I don't know," said Henderson. He shifted in his seat.

He was buckling. Marshall needed to give him some time to think. "Your Honor," said Marshall. "This isn't relevant. The witness said that he signed the checks and that everyone did it."

"Overruled," said Langworthy.

"So," said Rashad. "Was it five thousand or not?"

"It was something like that," said Henderson.

"And what did you do with the money?"

"I spent it on this and that," said Henderson. "Clothes, food, you know."

"What about drugs?" said Rashad. "Didn't you also buy drugs?"

"Yeah, but I already said I was wrong in a lot of ways, but I changed all that."

"So, you stole money to buy drugs and you got kicked out, isn't that true?"

"It was not that simple."

"Okay," said Rashad. "About Mr. Collier. You say you met him at a Brotherhood rally?"

"That's right."

"Did you ever see Mr. Collier talk to Mr. Mbutu?"

"No."

"Did you introduce them?"

"No."

"So as far as you know, they didn't know each other."

"Yeah, I guess."

"Did you sign Collier up as a member?"

"No, that wasn't my job."

"But you said he signed up that day."

"Yes, I remember him signing up."

"But if you didn't sign him up, how do you know he did?"

"I guess maybe I don't, if you put it that way."

"One last thing. After you left the Brotherhood, did you ever say that you would 'get Mbutu'?"

"I might have said something like that, but it wasn't serious, man."

"Was it serious when you threatened his life?"

"I never did that."

"You didn't call his home and say that you would kill him?"

"If I said it, I didn't mean it."

"Maybe my client didn't mean it if he said he wanted Farrel Douglas dead."

"That's not a question, Your Honor," said Marshall.

"I withdraw it," said Rashad. "I'm done with this witness." He sat back down.

Marshall then called Bakaar Rasul, Mbutu's second in command. Rasul was a serious-looking man who wore flowing robes and carried a long wooden staff, which had been confiscated by security.

"State your name," said Marshall.

"I do not recognize the authority of this court to order me to do anything," said Rasul.

"I'm asking you to do it," said Marshall.

"I am Bakaar, Ali Khan Rasul. Son of Light."

"You are a follower of the defendant?"

"I object to the derogatory word *defendant*."

"Are you a follower of Mr. Mbutu?"

"Yes I am."

"In fact aren't you his second in command?"

"Yes, I am the keeper of knowledge and wisdom."

"And as such what are your duties?"

"I will not tell the secrets of my order to a slave like you."

"The witness will answer the questions or be held in contempt," said Langworthy.

"Contempt?" said Bakaar. "This whole so-called process is contemptible."

"Don't you speak to me that way, young man," said Langworthy.

"Your Honor," said Rashad. "I'm sure Bakaar will cooperate from this point on." Rashad stared at Bakaar with anger. Mbutu had a curious smile on his face. He should have been worried that Bakaar was embarrassing him and undermining his defense. But he wasn't. He seemed happy.

"What were your duties?" asked Marshall.

"I take your Fifth Amendment," said Rasul.

"You take the Fifth as to your job?"

Bakaar stood up in the witness stand. "This country has committed genocide on the black man, the original man. He has killed, castrated, and lynched us. He's injected us with the syphilis and the AIDS virus, poisoned our children, and now, he enlists men like you to help in his war—"

"Bailiffs, take this witness out!" said Langworthy. Two bailiffs went to Bakaar and took him out. Mbutu supporters cheered and applauded. Bakaar continued his rant all the way out of the courtroom. The TV cameras captured it all. Several reporters went toward the door.

"Bailiffs, close the court," said Langworthy. "Before you all go scrambling for your cell phones, I want to say that this outburst is to be ignored by the jury. Let nothing said by that last witness make you think less of the defendant or more of the government's case."

Marshall couldn't believe that Rashad had let Bakaar testify. Mbutu had probably overruled him. But these were just preliminary witnesses, anyway. He wanted to lay the foundation for Mbutu as an irrational and desperate man. He also wanted to see what Rashad and his team were made of. So far, they were competent, but not formidable.

Langworthy had seen enough for the day. He adjourned the case and let everyone go. The reporters literally stampeded to the doors. Marshall and his team filed out, refusing to make statements. Rashad held court with the media, dodging questions about his conspiracy defense.

"We did solid work today," said Ryder. "We tied him to Collier."

"That last guy was priceless," said Walter. "I know the jury thinks they're all nuts now."

"Maybe," said Marshall. "But we still have a long way to go. The real fight will be with our primary witnesses."

"Still no word on whether Mbutu will testify?" asked Ryder.

"No," said Marshall.

"I think it's just a ploy," said Walter. "He won't do it."

"Right," said Roberta. "Rashad wants to keep the possibility out there, but he won't let him testify. It's too risky."

Roberta was as keen as ever, despite her involvement in the dirty affairs behind the trial. She spoke the words without much passion, and Walter seemed to notice this. Their rivalry had gone cold, and he seemed a little sad about it.

They all went back to the office, where they received polite applause from the staff, who had obviously been watching on TV. Marshall felt happy for the first time in days. Then he turned to go into his office and the trouble fell back upon him. He walked back into the bugged office and sat at his desk.

40

Bounty

Danny watched as Quince sold the guns to the young boys. He'd been kicking around all day, waiting for a chance to snatch the sonofabitch. Lewis Quince talked with the two young black boys in the backyard of an old house. The yard was thick with weeds. An old garage was in the yard, but it was literally falling apart.

Danny was in the alley by the house next door. He hid behind an abandoned car, watching.

Quince was a devil, thought Danny. He sold guns to dealers and paranoid people living in the ghetto. He was putting death into the hands of people all over town.

Danny needed to get Quince alone. No one could see him take the man, or he might end up in even more hot water. And he could tell that Quince was not one to be taken lightly. He'd been popped by the feds, so if he got caught again, it was good-bye for twenty-five years. A man in that position will kill anyone.

He thought about what Vinny would say about all this. She would tell him to get his ass off the street, to stop being such a macho asshole, and do what's right for once. Vinny was a good woman, but she didn't understand how men were. They had to take chances, it was their nature. And Marshall was his friend.

Quince took a gun and placed a silencer on it. He fired into the old garage. All Danny heard was a muffled pop. The young boys smiled and slapped five. They pulled out a wad of cash and started counting out money to Quince.

Quince put the gun into his waistband. How many people had died by one of his guns, Danny thought. How many cops had taken one because of this man? Everyone reviled drug dealers for what they did, but men like Quince were worse. Many of the inner-city drug dealers were just kids, lost souls in a nation that no longer cared about its less fortunate. Quince could claim no such status. He was probably an educated man from a good family just looking for an easy way to some cash. People like him preyed on the underclass like a vulture, eating the carrion of hopelessness and despair.

Danny pulled his guns and walked quickly to the three men. He raised the Glock and aimed it at Quince. The revolver he put on one of the two kids.

"This muthafucka is mine," said Danny. "You two brothas walk away from his ass." He was ten yards or so away from them. He kept moving forward.

Quince froze. He searched Danny's face but did not recognize him. The two kids panicked. One of them dropped the money he was counting. Some of the bills blew away in the wind.

"Yo, we don't know this nigga," said one of the boys.

"Don't matter, just get away from his ass," said Danny. Five yards now, he slowed his approach. If he got too close, he wouldn't be able to keep an eye on all of them.

"Who the fuck are you?" asked Quince.

"You can call me shut the fuck up," said Danny.

"You can't be a cop. Where's your badge?" asked Quince.

"One more word, and I'll put one in your fuckin' head," said Danny. "Now, put your hands up and follow me."

Quince complied. Danny started to close the gap, when he heard the unmistakable sound of a gun being cocked behind him.

Marshall sat in his office with the door opened. It didn't really matter, but he felt less violated with an open door. He tried to go through his routine and forget about the device. He made a few calls and read over some case notes on the ballistics and DNA evidence. So far, it looked good.

He had done a good job in court, but his opening statement haunted him. He had indicted Mbutu in the official record without telling all that he knew. He had committed a crime today, and his more righteous self could not forget that. But he had done it for a good reason, he thought. If he revealed what he knew, the killers would surely go into hiding and start to cover their tracks. And that "covering" could mean more deaths. Right now, the killers' ignorance was all he had.

Roberta walked by his office door and stopped. She had an upset look on her face. She just stared at Marshall for a moment, then walked to the elevator. Marshall waited a minute, then followed.

In the lobby, he found Roberta in a corner pacing nervously. Marshall saw some of the TV reporters on the street doing taped reports. He went to Roberta, who was shaking.

"This was in my door at home this morning." She held out a piece of paper. On it was written:

GET RID OF THE BLACK JURORS

"Do you know when it was put there?" asked Marshall.

"No," said Roberta. "I didn't want to tell you until the trial session was over."

"The black jurors," said Marshall. "They're getting scared for some reason."

"So, this is about the case? I thought you were up to something, but they want you to blow the case."

"They want me to win the case, Roberta. Yes, I'm sorry I didn't tell you before, but I couldn't trust you."

"Great. Obstruction of justice, jury tampering. No, I can't take this anymore," said Roberta.

"Roberta, calm down. We have to figure out what to do about this."

"I want out of this, Marshall. Let's go to Nate and Sommers."

"How do we know they're not involved?"

"They can't be," said Roberta. "This is somebody outside of all this. I can't sleep, I can't do anything. I swear someone's watching my place."

"Just hold on," said Marshall. "I'm working on something."

"Look at me. I'm a mess. I can't wait. Every day I walk by Nate's office and his door looks like a confessional. If I go in now, maybe I'll just get suspended for five years or so."

"Roberta, you know that's not true. If you go in now, you'll be disbarred and jailed—and so will I. I haven't disclosed anything. I'm in this too, whether I like it or not."

Roberta looked at Marshall with a surprised expression. She had not thought of it that way until now. She had gotten her friend into her dilemma.

"Jesus," she said. "Marshall, I'm sorry. Maybe you can pretend that you just caught me."

"That will lead to other more embarrassing questions, and how do we know they won't say I helped you steal that money? No, it's too risky. Now, you go back upstairs and finish whatever you were doing, then go home and get some sleep. Do you have the gun I told you to get?"

"It's in my car."

"Good. Now go. I'm right behind you."

Roberta walked off. Marshall waited a few minutes, then went back to his office. He went back to work for a half hour or so before Walter came by.

"What's with the open door?"

"Just needed some air," said Marshall. He got up and walked to Walter. He didn't want to talk in his office. Marshall strolled about the bull pen with Walter.

"So, is Roberta okay?" asked Walter.

"I guess," said Marshall. "Why do you ask?"

"No reason. She was just acting strange."

"Really," said Marshall.

"I was coming by to give you the supplement on the DNA test when I heard her inside. She said something like, " 'Go to hell.' " Then she ran out of your office and headed down the stairs. And get this. There was no one in there with her."

"How long ago was that?" asked Marshall.

"It was a while, a half hour or so. Hey, I think maybe she was on your phone."

"Yes, probably," said Marshall calmly. "Let me go see if I can catch her."

Marshall got his things and went to the parking garage and drove away, headed to Roberta's condo. What was she doing? he thought. She'd obviously talked to the bug in his bookshelf. Had she told her blackmailers to go to hell to antagonize them? She had snapped, he reasoned. The pressure of the situation was too much for her. He remembered how shocked she looked when she realized that he was in as deep as she was legally. She had gotten herself into trouble, and the thought of dragging him in also was too much for her. He blamed himself. She was obviously not equipped to deal with the situation. And what he was doing was certainly not the smartest thing.

Marshall got on the Chrysler Freeway and hit the gas. Roberta lived in Troy, and he'd have to push it. He took out his cell phone and called her house. He listened as her answering machine came on.

He hesitated. He didn't want to leave an incriminating message of any kind.

"Roberta, Marshall. Look, call me at home this evening, okay? I need to ask you a question." He hung up the phone and punched the gas harder.

Suddenly, traffic slowed, then it stopped. It looked like an accident. He got over in the right lane to exit the freeway. An ambulance whizzed by on the shoulder.

It never failed, he thought. Whenever you were in a hurry this happened. Then, panic struck him. Marshall pulled his car on the shoulder and raced toward the accident ahead.

He stopped at the scene. There on the median was Roberta's car, a tangled mess of steel and glass. He looked for another car, but there wasn't one. It was a one-car accident.

Marshall jumped out of the car but was stopped by a police officer.

"What the hell do you think you're doing?" said the officer.

"U.S. attorney. The driver is my coworker." Marshall flashed his ID.

"Sorry, sir," said the cop. "I think she's gone."

"But the ambulance is right there."

"No, gone the other way. Dead. I think she's dead."

"Gimme them guns," said a voice from behind Danny.

Danny knew he had only a second to act. He dropped himself to the ground, turning at the same time. Behind him, he saw a fat kid holding a small .22. The kid fired but missed Danny. Quince and the other two kids hit the ground.

Danny fired the Glock, hitting the fat kid in the arm. The gun flew from his hand, and he yelled loudly. Danny got up to one knee and saw Quince with a gun in his hand, running out of the yard. Quince fired over his shoulder at Danny but missed.

Danny fired the revolver and hit a wooden post as Quince passed by it. Splinters flew into the air. Quince kept running.

Danny got up and ran behind him. Quince was at a car and ran to the driver's side. Danny fired both guns at the car, shattering the windshield and flattening one tire. He could have hit Quince, but unfortunately, he needed that bastard in good health. Quince ran away from the car and down the street. Danny ran behind him.

Quince ran to the corner and ducked into a vacant house. Danny got to the place and heard yelling inside. He went carefully inside and saw Quince holding a homeless man with his gun to the man's head. Several other homeless men cowered against the walls.

"Give it up," said Danny.

"Fuck you," said Quince. "I'll shoot his ass."

"You think I care about some homeless muthafucka? Go ahead, drop him if you want. Because in three seconds, I'm gonna shoot you no matter what."

Quince shoved the homeless man at Danny and ran. Quince fired a shot that went into a wall, blowing a big hole in it. Danny threw the homeless man aside, and ran after Quince.

In the back room, Quince was at a door that was boarded up. Danny entered the room and Quince fired several times at him. Danny fell to the floor in the next room, avoiding the blasts.

Danny heard Quince kick the door open and run outside. Danny followed and then heard a man groan. He stepped out the back door and saw Quince flat on his back. A tall, thin black man held Quince's gun. Danny stopped. The man looked to be one of the homeless squatters. Danny put his guns away. The homeless man walked toward him and raised Quince's gun.

"Take this," he said to Danny in a voice that was surprisingly soft. "We don't need trouble."

"What did you do to him?" asked Danny.

The tall homeless man raised a small baseball bat.

"Thanks, man. What's your name?"

"Gordon," said the man. "Please, don't come back here," said the man. "We're peaceful men, and we don't like to be disturbed."

The man spoke in an elegant manner, which didn't fit his dirty, ragged appearance. Many homeless men were merely unlucky people who were disconnected from life. This man had been educated in his former life and had not lost all of his polish.

"Fine," said Danny. "But he comes with me."

"You can put him in this," said the tall man, pointing to a shopping cart. Danny pulled out some handcuffs and put them on Quince. He had to get him to his car quickly before any police came in response to the shooting. He lifted Quince into an old shopping cart, and rolled him off.

*   *   *

Marshall sat in the intensive care waiting room with Ryder and Walter and Roberta's family. Roberta had survived the car crash but just barely. The cops said it was a hit-and-run of some type and were looking for the owner of the other vehicle, a black Chrysler.

Roberta was banged up pretty badly. Her legs and one arm were broken. Her internal organs were damaged, and she had already lost a kidney. The doctor's prognosis was not good.

Marshall begged the doctors to let him see her. They did, but only for a moment. She was in a coma and didn't know he was in the room. She lay on the bed, tubes and wires everywhere. It was a mess.

He was angry and scared. He could not let it go now, he reasoned. Whoever these people were, they were not going to kill and hurt people with impunity.

He went close to Roberta and promised her that he'd get the people who did this to her. And he said the words knowing that it meant putting himself in the line of fire.

Part 3

SUPREME JUSTICE

41

Delivery

Marshall stood across the room from Lewis Quince, who was tied to a chair in Marshall's basement. His workout equipment had been moved to make room for the hostage.

Danny sat on an old chair and drank a beer. He seemed surprisingly happy. He'd called Marshall's house and left a message, cheerfully telling him that he had found Quince. Danny then set up bringing Quince in.

Marshall left Roberta and her family at the hospital, but not before calling the U.S. marshal and persuading him to put a guard on Roberta. He was very unsure of things at this point and he wanted to insure her safety as much as he could. He hoped it would be enough.

Danny rolled up soon thereafter with Quince locked away in his trunk. Then they went and got Quince's car and parked it in a lot several miles from Marshall's home. Every so often, Quince would curse and slam his fist into the trunk lid. Danny would respond by hitting the brakes. They could hear Quince's body slam into the walls of the trunk.

They had returned to Marshall's house and took Quince inside. Danny had sent Vinny home, knowing that she didn't need to know what they were up to.

Marshall's head was spinning from Roberta's near-death accident and the events within the trial. He was still looking good to convict Mbutu for a crime he probably didn't commit, and now he and Danny were coconspirators in a kidnapping. Not bad for one week.

"We don't want to hurt you, Quince," said Marshall. "All we need is some information."

"Fuck you," said Quince. "You couldn't beat me on that case, so you send this black-talking white boy to kill me."

"If I wanted to kill you, you'd be dead," said Danny.

"All I want to know is where my brother went," said Marshall. "We got word that you saw him in the city."

Quince laughed. "Is that all? You snatch me for a piece of shit like him?"

"Then tell me, if it's no big deal," said Marshall.

"No," said Quince. "I got my ass kicked, and your boy here fucked up a perfectly good sale to some customers. I want to be compensated for my loss."

"You was sellin' guns to kids," said Danny. "Fuck you."

"Drug dealers," Quince corrected. "Fuck how old they are. They sell, and they all kill. That's my business. Deal with it."

"What do you want?" asked Marshall.

"Are you kiddin', Marsh?" asked Danny. "We can't pay this mutha-fucka. Let me beat it out of his sorry ass."

Marshall took Danny aside. He saw how pumped up Danny was. It was dangerous to let him loose. He took him into a corner, out of Quince's earshot.

"I have to get this thing going," said Marshall. "It's only a matter of time before the people who got Roberta figure out I know something."

"Yeah, but this guy is a—"

"I know what he is. Believe me, he'll end up in prison one day soon no matter what we do here today."

Danny thought about it. The need to get Quince was still very much in his eyes, but he seemed to accept Marshall's logic.

"All right," said Danny. "But I still say we should beat his ass."

Marshall smiled a little. Having a friend to do random violence was a good thing and sometimes amusing as well. He walked back over to Quince. "Okay, what do you want?"

"Three thousand," said Quince. "And I want a guarantee that if I'm ever picked up again, you'll let me off."

"I'll give you a thousand," said Marshall. "No guarantee if you catch a case, and if you don't take it, my man here gets to try it his way."

Quince contemplated the deal, checking Marshall's face for signs of lying. Marshall's expression was resolute and didn't waver under Quince's glare.

"Okay," said Quince. "Untie me from this damned thing."

"Tell us what we want to know first," said Marshall.

"I can think a lot better if my circulation comes back," said Quince.

Marshall untied Quince. Danny pulled his revolver and showed it to Quince as a reminder to behave.

"Okay," said Marshall. "Where is he?"

"He's holed up with a friend of his, a small-time dealer named Half over on the east side."

"Why do they call him Half?" asked Danny.

"Cause he's half black and a lot of other stuff," said Quince. "A mongrel, like you. He lives off Conant near Six Mile."

"I can find him easy," said Danny.

"Anything else?" said Marshall.

"Yeah," said Quince. "I think he's been up to his old tricks. He was following these two men, but he didn't know I was following him. They all went into a house in Rosedale Park, but only Moses came out."

"I'll check that," said Marshall.

"The money," said Quince.

"You can have it," said Marshall. "Or you can trade it for what we found in the trunk of your car."

"What the fuck is this?" asked Quince. "That wasn't part of the deal!"

"That's my point," said Marshall. "You want the grand, fine, but we keep the stash."

"Fuck that!" said Quince. He took a step toward Marshall, then heard the click of Danny's revolver and stopped. "Okay, you conned me. Fine. Just let me go."

"Okay by me," said Marshall. "Danny will blindfold you and drop you off. Your car is in a parking lot somewhere in the city."

"No way," said Quince.

"You don't think we're gonna let you know where we live, do you?" said Danny. "Let's go."

Danny blindfolded Quince and took him out. Marshall waited in the house until Danny came back. They had a lead, but Marshall wondered if they could get to Moses before things in the Douglas case got ugly. After an hour, Danny came back, still in good spirits.

"I knew you wouldn't pay that asshole," said Danny. "Now what?"

"We find Moses, and see what he knows."

"Somehow I don't see him cooperating freely," said Danny.

"Then we'll have to persuade him," said Marshall.

"Now you're talking my language," said Danny. "I've been wanting a piece of that bastard all my life."

Marshall went back to the hospital to see Roberta, but there was no change in her condition. Her family was still there, and Marshall wanted so badly to tell them what a good person she was despite what she had done. But all he did was give his sympathy again and leave.

He went back home and tried to sleep, but it didn't come. He tossed, turned, and padded back and forth to the bathroom all night.

The next day, he got up early and ate, watching the sun rise. It was something he and Chemin used to do on occasion when one of them couldn't sleep. This was his first time going it alone. He felt a deep sadness as the sun's rays shot across the horizon, and the world lit up around him.

Danny came downstairs a few hours later, and they set a plan. Danny would find Moses, and they would confront him together.

"And don't hurt him," said Marshall.

"I can't guarantee that," said Danny. "It's tough out there, you know what I'm sayin'?"

"Yes, I know what you're sayin'," said Marshall. "But I'm sayin' don't hurt the man. Just find him and come to me."

"Okay, but if he tries me, I can't be responsible for what happens."

"What does that shit mean?" asked Marshall. "Danny, you have got to see that you are always responsible for what you do. The world doesn't take doing harm out of your hands. You've got to be smart enough to avoid violence. Any fool can bulldoze his way through life. We have to be better than that."

"Damn, you sound like my old man," said Danny.

"I take that as a compliment. I'm sorry for lecturing you, but I'm prosecuting what could be an innocent man. And all because someone couldn't think of a nonviolent method to get Farrel Douglas out of their way."

"Okay, I'll avoid getting into it with him," said Danny. "What's up for you today?"

"Trial," said Marshall. "More witnesses are up today."

The friends said good-bye and Marshall went in to work. Everyone was concerned for Roberta and had taken up collections and the like. Marshall walked into his office and was surprised to see Toby and Nate already there.

"Sorry to barge in," said Toby.

"No problem," said Marshall. "What do I owe this to?"

"I came in for the witness today," said Toby. "The DNA evidence is paramount to our case."

"Toby and I are going to watch on the monitor," said Nate. "Her presence in court would be too disruptive."

"I heard about Ms. Shebbel," said Toby. "Terrible thing. Is she okay?"

"No," said Marshall. "She's banged up pretty bad. She's still in a coma."

"Will you need to replace her on the team?" asked Nate.

"No," said Marshall. "We can manage."

"Are you okay?" asked Toby. "If you want some time off, we'll understand."

Marshall regarded his superiors with a new suspicion. Had they come into his office out of concern, or was it a subtle message that they were still watching him? Marshall tried to discern what was in their minds, but he couldn't. Years of playing intragovernmental politics had made both of them unreadable.

"No, I'm fine," said Marshall. "Just been running hard lately. You know how it is."

"Yes, I do," said Toby. "I've been flying all around the country lately."

"Running for president," said Nate playfully.

"Stop it, Nathan," said Toby. "I'm getting enough of that shit back in D.C."

"I hate to throw you out," said Marshall, "but I'm due in court in just an hour."

"We understand," said Toby. "Nail it down. We need this one."

As Nate walked by Marshall, he reached into his jacket and pulled out a cigar in a plastic tube. He handed it to Marshall.

"What's this for, sir?" asked Marshall.

"I'm a grandpa. My daughter had a little girl last night."

"Congratulations, sir. What's her name?"

"Tia," said Nate. He was obviously proud.

"Yeah, he's an old man," said Toby, laughing.

Toby and Nate left and Marshall sat down at his desk. After a moment, he checked his bookcase for the bug. It was gone.

DNA is a powerful evidentiary tool in criminal procedure, but it is also delicate and susceptible to attack from a variety of avenues. The most critical of which was contamination.

Marshall had to make his proof in three stages. He had to show that the chain of custody of the DNA sample was unbroken. Then he had to show that the testing facility was competent and the procedure was uncontaminated. Finally, he had to show that these factors made the test results irrefutable.

The first part of the DNA testimony had gone smoothly. Marshall established an unbroken chain of custody from the crawl space to the FBI testing facility.

Leslie Reed did the cross-examination and was good but unable to show that any contamination of the hair sample had occurred. Marshall stole Leslie's thunder by bringing out the past scandals involving the FBI testing facility, then rehabilitated his own damage with an expert witness who proved that the facility is back on track and doing good work again.

It was the afternoon when Dr. John Belson took the witness stand. He was a man of fifty-seven, whose once blond hair had faded into a regal silver. Dr. Belson was overweight, but carried it well. He was an elegant dresser and looked like the epitome of credibility. Dr. Belson was the government's expert on DNA testing and had performed the test on Mbutu's hair.

Marshall established Belson as an expert witness, going over his education and experience. Belson was a pro and had authored two books on DNA testing, including all of the newer procedures.

"Doctor, can you tell us how the test in this case was conducted?" asked Marshall.

"Yes, I conducted a standard PCR test on a single strand of human hair."

"Can you explain the test, and please be as clear as possible."

"Well, basically the PCR test compares combinations of DNA traits. The sample is tested with results appearing on a test strip. This strip is matched to the one from the defendant. If it matches, we know the DNA is identical."

"And what is the accuracy of this test?"

"The chance that a match is an error is one in a hundred."

Marshall then went specifically through the test with Belson, letting the more technical terms flow. It was important to get the jury's head on straight before throwing the mumbo jumbo at them. In the jury room, only the common sense of the test would be remembered.

Marshall concluded his direct examination of Belson with the doctor testifying that Mbutu's hair and blood matched that of the sample taken from the crawl space and sat down. The testimony was tight, concise, and damning to the defense.

Leslie stood and looked at a stack of papers. Belson waited patiently for her to start.

"Why didn't you use the RFLP test, Doctor?"

"The sample was too small to use that test."

"And who made that call?"

"I did, pursuant to accepted scientific guidelines, of course."

"But another scientist might have decided on the more accurate RFLP test."

"He might, but he would have been wrong. The sample would have been deficient, and the test results would be useless."

"And the RFLP test is how accurate, Doctor?"

"Chance of error is one in a billion."

Leslie turned toward the jury and smiled slightly. "So, one in a hundred and one in a billion? Which one would you stake *your* life on, Doctor?"

"Objection," said Marshall.

"Sustained," said Langworthy. "Jury, please disregard the question."

"How about the mitochondrial DNA test? Why was that not used?"

Belson hesitated, and Marshall grew concerned. He could not object to such a general question, so Belson for a moment looked indecisive. The witness cleared his throat.

"Well, mitochondrial is new and relatively untested. Unlike most DNA testing, mitochondrial testing doesn't require a cell nucleus."

"And how does that affect the nature and quality of the test relative to the PCR test you used in this case?"

Marshall could see Leslie was on to something. She had that look when a lawyer was moving in for the kill.

"Well," said Belson, "mitochondrial is more useful and technically more accurate, but its accuracy is widely doubted in the scientific community."

"You're an expert, Doctor. Do you doubt it?"

"Yes, I have doubts about it. Mitochondrial testing needs to be worked on more before it can be as useful as the other two tests."

"You said the FBI had used the mitochondrial test. What were the results in the cases where it was used?"

"We had convictions in all the cases," said Belson.

"So, Doctor, again I ask why wasn't it used in my client's case?"

"Asked and answered," said Marshall.

"Overruled," said Langworthy. "Witness will respond."

"I chose the most accepted method," said Belson. "We only had the one small sample, and I didn't want to waste it on a test that could prove inaccurate, or too sophisticated for the sample. It was a professional judgment call. In the other cases we had bigger samples and so could afford to take the chance."

"Wasn't the government concerned that a more accurate test might show my client wasn't the owner of the DNA sample found at the scene?"

"No, of course not. A less accurate test doesn't help us."

"One in a billion versus one in a hundred, Doctor. Doesn't the difference in the ratio invite trouble?"

"Argumentative," said Marshall.

"Objection sustained," said Langworthy.

"May we approach?" asked Marshall.

"I'm almost done," said Leslie.

"I think it's important to talk about this now," said Marshall.

Langworthy paused, then: "Counsel approach."

Marshall could see Belson getting shaky and Leslie was on a roll. He wanted to cut her momentum and make sure Belson had a moment. Rashad and Bob Ryder joined Marshall and Leslie at the judge's bench.

"What is it, Mr. Jackson?" asked Langworthy.

"I'm concerned that we not confuse the jury with this scientific evidence."

"Nonsense," said Leslie. "They're doing fine."

"Dr. Belson has already thrown around a lot of terminology," said Marshall.

"But it was explained on direct," said Rashad.

"But the cross is undoing all of that without explanation," said Marshall. "I think it's a ploy to confuse the jury. The PCR test is supported by hundreds of cases. All this talk about other tests is not relevant."

"But you have redirect," said Langworthy.

"Then they are left with even more confusion," said Ryder. "I think we need some guidelines on her cross."

"Limits on cross fly into the face of the definition of cross-examination," said Leslie.

"Maybe," said Langworthy, "but I'm getting a little lost myself, Ms.

Reed. Go back to it, and be careful the jury doesn't get lost in your aggressiveness.''

They thanked the judge and returned. Marshall had not expected Langworthy to be on his side. He was just buying time, but now he had scored a minor victory.

"Sorry, Doctor," said Leslie. "Doctor, isn't PCR testing very susceptible to contamination?"

"I wouldn't use the term 'very susceptible'."

"What words would you use, Doctor?"

"PCR is a sensitive process, but if handled properly has a low risk of contamination."

"When you say 'sensitive', what do you mean?"

"PCR amplifies molecules for genetic matching. This ability may cause trouble. Again, only if the process isn't handled right."

"How does amplification cause trouble?"

"Well, if a contaminating molecule is present, it can be amplified and overwhelm the original sample."

"And what would that do to the results?"

"It would render them useless, flawed."

"So a match from the test would be inaccurate?"

"Yes."

"Nothing further," said Leslie.

Marshall did redirect, bolstering the PCR test, and verifying that the test on Mbutu's hair was proper and secure. Leslie waived recross.

"Well, I think this is a good point to stop," said Langworthy.

"We'd like to call our rebuttal witness, Your Honor," said Rashad.

"There is no such witness on the list," said Marshall.

"He is on the list," said Rashad. "It is Horace Parker, a worker at the FBI testing facility."

"This witness was called to testify about"—Marshall flipped through the list—"'filters in the test chamber. The defense had their stab at him."

"True," said Rashad. "But we now need him to rebut what we've just heard."

"I object," said Marshall. "This is not procedure." He was worried. Rashad and Leslie had just taken great pains to get information out of Belson regarding contamination, and now they wanted to switch the use of a witness. He felt doom racing at him. "I think the government should at least know what he's going to testify to."

"This witness has already testified as to the filters used to keep the test secure," said Rashad. "We need his testimony now to go along with our cross."

"I'll allow it," said Langworthy. "But if it looks like it's going nowhere, I'm stopping and going home."

The gallery laughed. Marshall sat and conferred with Ryder as the witness was called. Neither Ryder nor Walter knew what Rashad was up to.

Rashad established the witness, Horace Parker, as a maintenance worker at the FBI testing lab. Parker was about thirty-five and thin. He had a sincere, almost boyish face under thick black hair.

One of Parker's jobs was to change the filters that kept the air clean so that contamination would not occur. Parker testified that he had changed the filters in the lab on schedule and did a purity sweep of the room, and it all checked out. Rashad handed him an exhibit, a log showing the work Parker had done.

"So, Mr. Parker," said Rashad. "Is that your signature there verifying that the clean room was indeed clean?"

"Yes," said Parker.

Rashad's demeanor turned serious. He moved closer to Parker. "This report is a lie, isn't it? You never did the work described, did you?"

"Yes, I did," said Parker.

"No, Mr. Parker," said Rashad. "You forged this document. You missed your rotation in the lab that day."

"Objection," said Marshall. He rose out of his chair. He wanted desperately to stop what he knew was coming.

"No, Counsel," said Langworthy. "Overruled."

"Did you forge this document?" asked Rashad.

"No," said Parker. "That's crazy. All the work I did is in the log."

"Do you know who Katherine Martin is?"

Parker's face showed shock. He straightened his back and adjusted in his seat.

"Well, do you?" Rashad asked again.

"Your Honor," said Marshall.

"Quiet, Mr. Jackson," said Langworthy.

Marshall sat back down. The feeling of doom was now one of panic. Rashad obviously had an investigator on the case and had found something on Parker. The witness was nervous as hell and began to look down at his feet, a sign that something bad was imminent.

"Mr. Parker, are you going to answer me?" asked Rashad. "Do you know a woman by that name or not?"

"I do," said Parker. Then he put his face in his hands. "Shit," he said. "I knew this would happen." Parker just kept cursing and talking to himself.

"Watch the language, Mr. Parker," said the judge.

"Tell this jury why you're upset, Mr. Parker," said Rashad. "And remember, you've already perjured yourself."

Marshall now knew he was in deep shit. All he could do now was watch the testimony and hope the damage could be rectified.

"I got to work late, the day I signed that log. I'd been with Katherine all morning."

"This Katherine is your mistress?"

"Yes."

The gallery murmured, and Marshall could tell what was coming next.

"So, you didn't change the filter, did you?"

"No. I got in too late."

"So, what did you do to the room where our sample was tested?"

"I rigged the air quality computer to register that the room was clean before the test was done."

"So the air, the sample, could have been contaminated?"

"Yes."

The gallery almost erupted in one voice. Langworthy gaveled over the din. "Please," he said.

Rashad took a moment, enjoying the spectacle. Parker looked like he was about to pass out from stress. His arms and legs shook as he sat in the witness stand. Marshall seemed to be right with him. It was a disaster, and it wasn't over yet.

"A contaminant molecule could have been amplified in the test, couldn't it?" asked Rashad.

"Objection," said Marshall. "This witness is not an expert on DNA testing."

"I'll withdraw the question," said Rashad. "Mr. Parker, was the room clean under your guidelines when the sample in our case was tested?"

"No."

Marshall was reeling from what he'd just heard. He considered asking for a recess, but that would give the jury time to think about what they had just heard without any counterpoint of view.

He scrambled to get the data and questions that he'd used for Parker's direct testimony. He found them, then approached the witness.

"Mr. Parker," said Marshall. "Did anyone know about what you did that day?"

"Just me and Katherine and my friend Wally. I know that fucker told on me."

The crowd laughed, and the judge admonished Parker to refrain from cursing.

"But no one in the government knew, did they?"

"No."

Marshall had cleared his first hurdle. The government could not be accused of conspiracy now. They were innocent in this matter. Now, he had a more difficult procedure.

Marshall got Parker to tell the court that he'd been on his job for ten years and knew the procedures of the lab. He had also taken courses on the air filtration system. He had a college degree and seemed to be a fairly smart guy. Then Marshall had Parker orally dissect the parts of a filter, which he did with professional aplomb.

Rashad objected right where Marshall had hoped he would.

"This line of testimony is not relevant," said Rashad. "It's obvious that the government is hoping to confuse the issue."

"I move to have this witness admitted as an expert on the air filtration system of the lab," said Marshall.

"We object," said Rashad. "He's a janitor, nothing more."

"A person's professional status does not determine expertise," said Marshall. "The rules of evidence say all he needs is scientific, technical, or specialized knowledge. Mr. Parker has that."

"I would agree," said Langworthy. "The witness will be considered as an expert."

Rashad walked back to his table looking quizzically at Leslie Reed. Marshall continued. "How often are the filters changed in the lab?"

"We change them every other day. It's a rule." Parker was calmer now but still looked a little guilty.

"The filter you were supposed to change, how long had it been in the lab?"

"One day."

"So, it didn't have to be changed, did it?"

"No, it was a special order from my supervisor."

"So, if the filter was good, why did you rig the air controller?"

"I was scared, man. I was covering my—butt," said Parker, catching himself.

"Why didn't you just change the filter when you rigged the computer?"

"It takes a long time. You have to take it out, replace it, then test the air for an hour. I didn't have time."

"So, isn't it likely, in your expert opinion, that the filter performed its job as it was supposed to?"

"Yes."

Marshall was done. He had countered the bomb as much as he dared. He wanted to go on, but each second Parker was on the stand was a reminder that there might have been a blunder on their best piece of evidence.

"No more questions," said Marshall.

"Just one question," said Rashad. "Mr. Parker, in your expert opinion, isn't it just as likely that the filter may not have worked?"

"No," said Parker. "It probably worked."

"So why did you, the expert on filters, rig the computer? Didn't you do it because you knew the air was contaminated?"

"No, I was just scared," Parker said.

"Why should we believe you? You lied to your bosses, you forged a report, and you lied here today."

"Argumentative, Your Honor," said Marshall.

"No more questions," said Rashad. "We're done with him."

Parker walked off the witness stand as the crowd buzzed with excitement. Marshall felt weak. He could hardly move in his seat. He'd done a good job on Parker, but reasonable doubt loomed as a result of his mistake.

Marshall called Dr. Belson back and asked just one question.

"Doctor, knowing what you now know about the filters, would you say that the test was accurate?"

"Yes," said Dr. Belson.

Rashad didn't cross-examine Belson. He was too smart for that. Belson was a credible witness, and each question would reinforce the notion that the test was accurate. He'd hurt them with Parker and was not about to ruin it.

Langworthy dismissed the court, and the reporters swarmed around Rashad and Leslie Reed. Marshall and his team sneaked out through the judge's chambers. He was not about to make matters worse by getting grilled on camera. Toby and Nate were probably both hopping mad.

Marshall caught sight of Mbutu as he was led out. He should have been happy, but his face was solemn, as if Parker had not testified. Marshall wondered what was going on in his head. More urgently, he wondered what effect this would have on the conspiracy he felt existed beneath this case. Rashad may have dropped a bomb, but there might be a bigger explosion to come.

Marshall left the court, avoiding the rabid press. When he and his team got back to the office, Toby was on a rampage. She yelled, cursed, and stomped around the office accusing everyone of failure. She was justified. With the DNA tainted, they could not put Mbutu in the crawl space. That meant the case could go either way. The ballistic evidence was persuasive, but not conclusive.

Toby's wrath was great, but it eventually calmed. Bob Ryder looked like he was going to cry. The case was up for grabs now. Toby's faith was understandably shaken, but Marshall reminded her of the balance of their case against Mbutu, and this seemed to put her at ease.

Toby left Detroit. She went back to D.C. without any fanfare. Marshall understood what this meant. Toby would now distance herself from the case. If Marshall were to lose, she could not afford to be blamed for it. No longer would she appear in the newspapers when the case was mentioned or give quotes. The case was looking like a loser, and Toby was no one's loser.

Marshall dispatched Ryder and Walter to double-check the ballistic evidence. Marshall had two matters to resolve: he had to find a motive for killing Douglas, and he wanted to talk with Mbutu. He had to know why a man would allow himself to be prosecuted for a murder he didn't commit. Perhaps the resolution of one issue would shed light on the other.

Marshall called Rashad and made an appointment to see Mbutu. He then went to the databases and looked up all the decisions of Douglas. Then he went over his background again.

Douglas was a remarkable man. He was born in poverty but scraped his way into Harvard. He was a true conservative. He started as a Republican and had never looked back. He was not an opportunist who had switched parties. Douglas had always maintained a belief that less government was better, and that blacks didn't need special help to succeed.

Douglas's decisions were pretty routine. Since he'd become a judge, he had consistently decided cases on the conservative bent. There were lots of facts on the man, but it did not help Marshall with his problem.

Marshall checked his watch. It was time to talk to Mbutu. He prayed that he could get something out of him. At this point he was hoping for anything.

Mbutu looked like hell as he sat down across from Marshall. Marshall had already thought he was sick, but up close he was even worse. His skin looked pallid, and his eyes were littered with broken blood vessels. Rashad sat next to him and tried not to notice.

"Thanks for letting me come by," said Marshall.

"Get to it," said Mbutu. "I have an article to write for my newsletter."

"You don't look well," said Marshall.

"I'm fine," said Mbutu.

"He's under a lot of stress," said Rashad. "But he's as strong as an ox."

The two men had both just lied. Marshall saw them exchange quick looks, and Mbutu showed what was unmistakably fear. Marshall decided to press the point.

"No, you're not," said Marshall. "That's why I'm here, and you know it. This thing has gone far enough, and I'm ending it today."

"You got your ass kicked today and you can't stand it," said Mbutu. "Go on, spread your lies. See if I care."

"Be quiet," said Rashad. "He doesn't know anything. He's bluffing."

Marshall grew excited. He was on to something. Whatever they had been hiding had probably gotten out in prison, and they had no way of knowing who had informed him.

"If you want my cooperation, I'll need to know just why I should do it."

"Because you're black!" yelled Mbutu. "I am so tired of you kids getting these jobs, and forgetting about all of us who died so you could have them!"

"This interview is over," said Rashad.

"The disease is under control," said Mbutu.

"What disease?" said Marshall. He smiled at Rashad.

"Dammit, Daishaya," said Rashad. "Will you ever learn restraint?"

"Okay," said Marshall. "Now that I know he has a disease, I can make him take a physical to see if he's fit to stand trial. Then all of this will come out in the media. So, are you going to tell me what I want to know or will I publish your illness to all of your followers?"

"It's a rare, genetic disorder," said Rashad. "We had a doctor come to see him. He'll be fine for a while."

"You're dying?" said Marshall. "That's why you—" He stopped himself. The word *innocent* was on his tongue, but he didn't dare say it at this juncture. "Hiding," he said. "That's why you're hiding your illness."

"Our people need a wake-up call, Mr. Jackson," said Mbutu. "I'm here to do that. Since I've been in jail, our membership has doubled. Doubled. Chapters are forming in all the major states and some overseas. Activism will make a comeback because of me."

"So, you didn't have anything to lose when you murdered Douglas."

"You know he won't answer that," said Rashad. "Look, Marshall, you're a bright young man, but these matters are far above your head. We are battling for the soul of a people, not for the freedom of one man."

"If your client has information vital to my investigation, I want it right now," said Marshall.

"I don't know what you mean," said Rashad.

"He does," said Marshall. He looked directly into Mbutu's ravaged eyes. He wanted him to say it. He wanted Mbutu to say that he didn't fire the fatal shot, that someone else beat him to it. But Mbutu just looked away, unable to hold Marshall's glare.

"What is he talking about?" asked Rashad

"I want to go back to my cell," said Mbutu. He got up.

"Tell me!" yelled Marshall.

"Daishaya?" said Rashad. "What's going on?"

Mbutu had not let Rashad in on the secret. He had probably decided that he couldn't trust him not to expose a real conspiracy, because a lawyer would be happier with an imagined one.

Marshall at least had one answer to one of his two riddles now. Mbutu wanted to lose the case. He wanted to become an incarcerated martyr, a living testament to a new black activism.

"What are you two talking about?" Rashad demanded.

Marshall didn't answer. He left the conference room with Rashad yelling for an explanation.

42

. . . .

Delilah

The little drug house was doing a brisk business. Danny watched it from across the street. There were many things to hate in the city, but above all, Danny hated drug dealers. They were evil, he reasoned. Uncaring demons who murdered people over a lifetime.

Vinny had been upset when he told her what he and Marshall were up to. She did not like her man going out into the world getting into danger. She wanted him to concentrate on getting reinstated to the force. But it was out of his hands now. His lawyer, Victor Connerly, was on the case, and was waiting for the police panel to make a decision.

Danny noticed that there was not a lookout at the house. There was no guard outside, and no one in the windows. This was curious. Most houses had more than one lookout. But this was a small-time place. Half's rep on the street was that he was a nonviolent dealer, a man who was not a hard ass.

Danny went to the house and hit the back door hard and entered with both guns out in front. Several women were in the kitchen hard at work. They screamed and ran. Danny grabbed one of them, a girl with short dyed blond hair.

"Where's Half?" asked Danny.

"He's gone," said the girl.

"He was hiding a man named Moses. Where is he?"

"Moses?" said the woman. "Ain't nobody here by that name."

Danny moved into the dining room then the living room, taking the girl with him. Nothing. Danny went upstairs and only found a couple putting on their clothes and a kid asleep on a toilet.

Danny came back downstairs and found the place empty.

"What the fuck is going on here?" asked Danny.

"I ain't saying nothing to you. Go on and take me in," said the girl.

"I'm not a cop. I just need to talk to the man."

"Right. But you talkin' with guns."

Danny released the girl. "What's your name?" he asked.

"If you ain't no cop then fuck you." She started to walk toward the door. Danny cocked the 9mm.

"Just because I'm not wearing a badge, don't mean you can dis me," said Danny. The girl stopped in her tracks. "I need to talk to Half."

"Why?"

"You don't wanna know. Let's just say he could be in danger."

"Damn," said the girl. "I told that fool not to go after Delilah. He ain't got no idea what he doin'."

"Right," said Danny, playing along. "Half had no call to go after her, now I gotta find him before he gets himself hurt."

"Acey and them said Half sold them some bad shit, said Half would get her back when he replaced it. Half said no, so they snatched Delilah. They know she ain't right in the head, but they took her anyway."

"Where can I find Acey and Delilah?" asked Danny.

"They over on Arlington in a corner house with a red door. Half went over there with a gun."

Danny ran out of the house. He didn't have time to get the whole story. Drug feuds always ended with someone dead. And if Half was killed, he'd never find Moses.

Danny got to the house on Arlington. It was a nice-looking place with a flower garden in the front, and a freshly painted porch. This was no drug house. Someone here had a job and a purpose in life.

Being as quiet as he could, Danny walked to the alley and sneaked up to the house. He took out a gun. This Acey person had probably taken Half's woman hostage to secure payment of their debt. This was why he hated dealers. They put such a small value on life.

Danny peeked into a window. He saw one man holding a multiracial man who had to be Half. In a corner sat a little black girl who looked like she was in a trance. That had to be Delilah, thought Danny. The bastards had kidnapped a kid.

One of them was a short fat guy with wild hair. The other was of medium build with a shiny bald head. The fat guy held Half and the other waved a gun. Danny had to act fast. This Half guy was in over his head.

Danny was about to kick in the door, then stopped. He remembered that this was a respectable house, and there was a little girl in there who could be hurt. Just because the two punks inside were lowlives didn't mean that the owner of the house was a bad person.

He put away his guns and walked around to the front of the house. For once, he thought, his color might come in handy.

Danny pushed the doorbell. He heard muted voices. A moment later, the tall, bald kid answered the door. His evil demeanor was gone. Now he was a nice, respectable kid. Probably the game he played on his mom each day.

"Who is it?" the kid said from behind the door.

"Gas man," said Danny. "Need to read the meter." Most gas meters were still inside the house in the older neighborhoods. All Danny needed was for the door to open.

"Come back later," said the kid.

"Well, take this card and fill it out."

The kid opened the door. When it was slightly cracked, Danny slipped in the 9mm and shoved it into the stomach of the kid.

"Don't make a sound," he said.

Danny took the kid into the back room. His partner held a gun on Half. Delilah stood where she was before, in the corner, looking at the wall.

"Looks like we got us a situation here," said Danny.

The fat guy jerked around, taking the gun off Half.

"Who the fuck are you?" asked the fat kid.

"A friend of this man and that little girl. I came to get them, or I blow a hole in your boy here all over his nice mama's house."

"He owe me!" said the bald kid. "Let me go, or my man Blow will cap his ass and the girl."

"Yeah," said Blow, the fat kid. "Let Acey go, or I'll do it." He cocked the gun and placed it against Half's head.

"See, this is how shit gets started," said Danny. "I guess we'll just stay here like this until your moms comes back. Most folks get off work about five, five-thirty. If she catches the bus, she'll be here by six-thirty. If she got a car, then she'll be here by six. Let's let her decide.''

"Okay, okay," said Acey. "Blow, let the man go."

"Fuck that," said Blow. "You only out two hundred. I'm in for all my shit. How I'm gon' get it back?"

"Look, nigga, you can't be splatterin' brains all over my mama's floor!" said Acey.

"Well, I told you not to bring them here. Can't nobody do nothing in this house. Can't touch nothing, dumb-ass plastic all over the furniture and shit."

"Just 'cause I don't live in garbage like your family."

"You too damned old to be livin' with yo' mama anyway," said Blow. "That's the problem. You need to grow the fuck up."

Danny was at a loss as to what to do. The two friends were obviously not hard-core dealers, but they were stupid, which could make them even more dangerous.

Suddenly, Delilah moved. She started walking away from the corner and out the kitchen door into the dining room. Danny supposed that the arguing reminded her of bad times.

"Hey, little girl, get yo' ass back here," said Blow.

Blow moved the gun away from Half's head and swung it in the direction of Delilah. Danny pushed Acey between Delilah and the gun. Half grabbed at Blow, and the gun went off. Acey was hit in the arm. He fell to the floor. Half grabbed Blow and started hitting him in the face. Blow dropped the gun. Acey screamed as he fell. Danny quickly grabbed the loose weapon.

"Shit, shit. My mama's floor!" Acey grabbed at his wound.

Blow threw Half off of him and started to punch, but Danny trained his gun on the fat kid.

"Chill out, big boy," said Danny. "Mr. Half, take the girl and go outside."

Half left the room, scooped up the girl, and went out the door.

"I'm taking this gun with me. If anything happens to that man or that girl, the police will get it with a note saying where to find you two. God knows how many murders and robberies are on this bad boy."

"You shot me, you fat-ass muthafucka," yelled Acey from the floor.

"Stop crying, you little bitch," said Blow.

Acey kicked at Blow, who jumped back out of his way.

"I'm leaving now," said Danny. "Just remember what I said." To

43

Spike

Moses watched Dake and Nita's warehouse from two streets over. There were vacant lots on both streets, so he had a partially obstructed view of the place. It was early morning, and the sun had just come up. The air was chilly and a light frost had fallen. Most people were still asleep, but not thieves. They were just getting in from a long night's work.

A light truck and a moving van went inside the warehouse. They were tan and blue, as nondescript as you could get. Standard stuff for a crew. The vehicles looked new.

Tybo's was a legitimate business, specializing in wholesaling and delivering contractors' supplies. Dake and Nita had turned the owner, offering him a big profit for the use of part of his facility.

The warehouse was in a prime location. Nestled inside one of the worst neighborhoods in the city, no one would come looking for trouble without an army with him.

Dake and Nita had moved the hustling operation to a new level. Moses heard on the street that they'd stepped up high-tech thefts and abandoned low-end shit like clothes and cigarettes and the like. Too much trouble, too little return. A truck full of DVDs or computers was worth a lot more than a truck of filtered Camels.

In a strange way, Moses was proud of them. He'd trained both of them in the art and was glad to see that his lessons were not lost on them.

Still, they had to die.

How was the problem. The warehouse was guarded from all sides, and there were probably many more enforcers inside. Some of the faces looked new, so Moses didn't know if he could trust them or not. He was going to have to get to them whenever they came out. As a cold wind blew around him, he zipped his jacket higher and thought that maybe he might need some help on this one.

Moses spent most of the day watching the place. People came and went, but his prey had not shown their faces. He even saw a police cruiser come by, but to them Tybo's was just doing business as usual.

It was around five o'clock when Dake and Nita emerged from the warehouse. Dake was dressed all in black, a fashion statement he'd stolen from Moses. Nita was resplendent in a white coat. Her hair looked different, longer, and Moses thought absently that she had never been more attractive.

The couple made a beeline for a blue Town Car and got inside with two men. One of them was Wood, an enforcer Moses had hired. The other was a new man.

Moses quickly got into his car and followed them. Dake and Nita had been holed up in the warehouse most of the day. Ted Walker's body had been found by a maid service, and the story had hit page one. If they knew, they were scared, but for some reason, they had not jumped town. Either they had a major hustle coming, or they were just plain arrogant. Either way, they were in his sights now.

Moses followed the Town Car around town for most of the day. Dake and Nita apparently were taking time out to actually be human. They had lunch at a soul food restaurant, and shopped at Northland Mall. They looked happy, like a nice, well-to-do couple, thought Moses.

Suddenly, he grew angry. Their bliss reminded him of all he had lost because of them. The humiliation of the criminal process, the betrayal of Ted Walker, and the attempt on his life. All of it was their doing. It was now not enough to kill them. They had to suffer.

The Town Car cruised out of Detroit in the late afternoon and headed north to Royal Oak. There in the heart of suburbia, Dake and Nita went into a small, wood-framed house. The guards took positions in front and back. Wood, Moses' old friend, sat on the porch, listening to a portable CD player.

Moses parked his car several streets over and sneaked around to the back of the house. A dog barked loudly nearby. In the back of the house, he saw the other guard, a man with two earrings who sat on the stairs, eating a candy bar. Moses didn't know him.

Moses drew out his gun. The cheap silencer was still on it, but it was shot by now. The dog continued to bark. Moses looked over a few houses and saw the dog, a mutt straining at his rope, barking at the guard who was three houses away and across a wide alley.

Moses backtracked and went into the yard where the dog was. The animal was in a filthy backyard tied to a pole hammered in the ground. Next to him was a makeshift doghouse that had SPIKE written on it.

Spike saw Moses and started to bark at him. Moses went into the yard, making sure to keep low so the guard wouldn't see him. He pulled a rake from against the house and began to hit the pole to which Spike was tied. The mutt barked louder and growled. The pole loosened. Moses kept whacking at the pole until it leaned to one side. Spike, sensing freedom, pulled back hard on the rope, loosening the pole even further.

''Smart boy,'' said Moses to himself. ''Go get 'em.''

Moses crawled out of the yard and began to make his way closer to the man in the back of Dake and Nita's house.

The backdoor guard stood up suddenly as Spike jumped over the fence into the yard. The little dog growled and jumped at him, his teeth bared and his jaws snapping. The guard pulled his gun, then thought better of it and put it away. He grabbed a rock instead and walked closer to the dog.

The guard stepped away from the back porch and hit Spike with the rock. The dog yelped loudly and jumped back over the fence. He barked at the guard again. The guard ran toward Spike and chased him off back down the alley.

''Damned mutt-ass dog,'' said the guard.

The guard laughed and turned to go back to the porch. His eyes widened, and the last thing he saw was Moses swinging a shovel at his face.

Moses downed the man, splitting his head open with the spade. Moses looked around and saw no one in the area. He started to take the guard's gun, but left it. The cops would find it and know this was a case of criminals taking care of their own.

Moses pulled out his own gun, went to the house, and slipped inside. He crept through the kitchen, and heard noises from upstairs. He quickly went upstairs and soon heard the sounds of sex through a partially open bedroom door.

Inside the bedroom, he saw Dake and Nita on top of a bed. Nita was bent over, and Dake was behind her, thrusting and murmuring to the woman below him.

Moses watched for a second, his anger building. He thought of shooting them both, taking them out in the act, but that would in a way be a gift. Who wouldn't want to die fucking? Besides, he thought, he had to be quiet. He didn't want to engage Wood until he had subdued them.

"Don't stop on my account," said Moses. He walked in the room with the gun out in front.

Dake froze, his face registered terror. Nita broke the connection and rolled the bedsheets around her. They looked at Moses like he was a ghost, and he smiled like the devil himself. He quickly grabbed their weapons, then went back to the door.

"Okay," said Moses. "Now, finish it."

"Moses," said Dake. "Look, we can work this thing out . . ."

"Put it back in her and finish, or you both die," said Moses. "Just pretend like I'm dead, the way you wanted it to be."

"No," said Nita. "You crazy—"

Moses cocked the gun, and pointed it at Nita's chest. She trembled behind the flimsy sheet.

"Fine by me," said Moses. "You go first."

"Okay, okay," said Dake. "We'll do it." He went over to Nita nervously and pulled the covers away.

"No, he gonna shoot us anyway, fool," she said.

Dake pushed her hands away from the sheet, trying to push her on her back. Nita struggled, pushing him from her and kicking.

"Fuck her or die," said Moses. This was some sick shit, he thought, but it sure was funny to watch.

The couple struggled in the bed like two kids. Finally, Dake moved back from Nita, who was now frustrated and angry to the point of tears.

"It's just so hard to get a piece of ass," said Moses.

"We didn't know what happened to you," said Dake. He reached for his pants.

"Stop," said Moses. "I want y'all both naked. That way I know you ain't holding shit. Now, get out the bed and go downstairs."

"Come on, man," said Dake. "At least let us have some dignity."

"Where was my dignity?" asked Moses. "When I was chained like an animal in prison, or when that con tried to stick a shank in my ass."

"You so damned smart," Nita said to Dake.

"Shut up, woman," said Dake.

Moses walked them through the house and into the basement, where he had Nita tie up Dake with two extension cords. Then he tied her up. The hard plastic dug into their skin as they sat on the dirty floor. He stuffed rags in their mouths.

"Be right back," said Moses. "Don't move."

Then he went to the front door and opened it. There he saw Wood sitting, still listening to his music. Moses tapped Wood on the side of the head.

"What the—" Wood pulled the headphones away and jumped up. He was reaching for his gun when Moses showed Wood the gun he had.

"Shit," said Wood. "Moses, man—"

"Come on in and join the party," said Moses.

Moses took Wood's gun and led him into the basement where he saw Dake and Nita tied up on the floor. They'd spit out their gags, and groaned as they struggled with the cords on their limbs. Wood turned to Moses with anger and defiance in his eyes.

"Go on and do what you gotta do," said Wood. "After what you did to the crew, I don't care anymore."

"You hear that?" Moses said to Dake and Nita. "What *I* did to the crew. I knew you could only take my place with a lie, you piece of shit."

He kicked Dake hard in the ribs. Dake screamed. Wood made a motion toward Moses, but Moses turned the gun on him.

"Don't be foolish, Wood," said Moses. "It would break my heart to have to kill you. Now, what did these two lyin' muthafuckas tell you?"

"The truth," said Dake through his pain.

"You know what you did, nigga," said Wood. "Go on and do what you gotta do, or I'm gonna ram that gun up your ass." Wood took a step toward Moses. Moses would have to explain the situation to Wood or kill him.

"I hired you in the crew," said Moses. "I took your sorry behind right out of the joint and put money in your pockets and women on your dick. How can you believe these fools over me?"

"Don't listen to him, Wood," said Nita. "Take his ass down."

"Shut up!" yelled Moses to Nita. He kicked at her face but missed. Wood took another step, raising his fists.

"You turned on the crew after you killed LaShawn," said Wood. "Dake and Nita say you got popped by the cops and dropped on some of the crew. Rayvon, Larry, and PoPo got arrested in Sterling Heights right after you went down."

"That was a good one," said Moses to Dake. "Wood, LaShawn got popped for stealing from the crew. All that other shit was their doing.'' It would normally be easier to kill Wood, but he needed him to convince the crew that he was not dirty. Only with their help could he get out of town.

''Then why didn't you contact us?'' asked Wood.

''I couldn't call,'' said Moses. ''You know the rule, and no one ever came to the joint.''

''Bullshit,'' said Wood. ''Dake and Nita . . .'' Wood stopped, putting the pieces together in his thick head. ''They were the ones who went to see you all the time. They said you was in a police protective custody.''

''Lies,'' said Moses. ''I'd never turn on the crew. These two paid off my lawyer and hired a con to kill me. But as you can see, it's hard to kill a nigga, ain't it?''

Moses could see Wood's face change. Moses had to take a chance that his story was more believable than the lies Wood had been told.

''Why would I escape if I had a deal with the cops?'' asked Moses. He took out Wood's gun and tossed it to him. ''You got your piece back, you can shoot me if you don't believe what I said.''

Wood looked at the gun and the two people lying on the floor. Then he put the gun in his waistband.

''The crew should decide this,'' said Wood.

''The crew?'' asked Moses. ''I am the crew.''

''Not anymore,'' said Wood. ''If you tellin' the truth, then let your men decide.''

Moses didn't expect this. Dake's lie had been the basis for the new business, a business that was probably lucrative. No one wanted to give that up.

''No,'' said Moses. ''This ain't no trial. I made the crew, and they tried to steal it. I'm not going to prove myself.''

''You see?'' said Dake from the floor. ''He's full of shit. No respect. It's all about him. Wood, man, shoot him. Don't let him go back and take over our shit.''

Wood took a second to think. He was one of the brighter members of the crew. Always reading and trying to learn things. He'd been educated in the joint by a lifer and continued when he'd gotten out. ''If he sold us out,'' said Wood, ''why did he come back to get you?''

''Shit, he crazy,'' said Nita. ''That's why. He's out of his mind.''

''I'll go get Allan from outside,'' said Wood. ''Maybe he—''

''Allan's not coming,'' said Moses. ''He's gone. I didn't know him, or I wouldn't have done it.''

"He killed him," said Dake. "You see, he's dirty. Shoot him."

"It's up to you now, Wood," said Moses.

Wood looked at Moses, then at Dake and Nita on the floor. "I'll be upstairs after you finish," said Wood. He turned and walked back up the stairs.

Dake and Nita yelled and cursed as Wood ascended the stairs. Moses turned to the couple on the floor. Dake struggled with the cords. Nita just lay there, shaking her head.

"I knew it was a bad idea," she said. "I knew he wasn't smart enough to lead the crew."

"Shut up, you fucking bitch," said Dake.

"I understand him," said Moses. "But why you, Nita? I thought we were at least friends."

"Because you dropped me!" she yelled. "I was just another piece of ass to you. You fucked me, then went on to the next young girl. Couldn't you see how I felt? No, you didn't, because all you see is the next pussy opportunity." She cried, and Moses could see that it was real. He'd hurt Nita when he left her. She seemed like a stronger woman, but he had misjudged that.

"Shoot her so she'll shut the fuck up," said Dake. He laughed bitterly.

They were both out of it. Acceptance of death did strange things to the mind. Dake was almost delirious and Nita solemn and remorseful.

"*You* shut up," Moses said to Dake. Then he shot him in the head. His body jerked to one side, sliding him and Nita toward a wall. Blood and tissue showered the wall and Nita's nude body. She screamed and kicked, trying to get away from the dead man's corpse. Dake slumped over, his head falling to his chest.

Moses knelt next to Nita and put his gun under her chin. "I'm gonna do it quick, so you won't feel anything," he said. "I owe you that much."

Nita just cried and shook her head. Her body shook violently and she held her breath as Moses cocked the gun then pulled the trigger.

The gun clicked loudly as the hammer struck. The sound echoed off the brick walls of the basement.

Nita yelled and ducked her head down, and only a second later did she realize that she was still alive. She opened her eyes and saw Moses holding the gun's clip in his hand.

"Get up and put your damned clothes on," he said.

44

The Slaves

Marshall stood with Stephen Bradbury in the Museum of African American History on Woodward and Warren in the heart of Detroit's cultural center. The museum was a grand and opulent creation, a state-of-the-art facility showcasing the history of blacks in America. Marshall stood in the Core Exhibit, on a little bridge over statues of slaves. It was a beautiful and sad piece of art, a repugnant yet compelling reminder of the history of his people.

It was fitting that he looked into the sad faces of men in bondage, Marshall thought. He felt a little as they must have felt. He was trapped by the case and events of his life.

Bradbury was done with his Senate grilling and was now awaiting the vote. All the indicators said that he would make it and be the next black Supreme Court justice. Bradbury was happier than Marshall had ever seen him and looked much younger than his years.

"I'm glad you could come," said Marshall. "I just needed someone to talk to."

"I'm sorry about what happened with that witness," said Bradbury. "But you should know that there was nothing you could do. Muhammad Rashad is a great lawyer. He is thorough, and his attention to detail is nothing less than magnificent."

Marshall looked at one of the slaves who sat upright, his vacant eyes seemed to be sad. "When you worked for the Justice Department, did you ever break the rules?"

Bradbury looked concerned. "Marshall, are you in some kind of trouble?"

"No, I just—I want to know if you ever bent the rules on a case." He couldn't tell Bradbury what he was feeling, that he was conducting an underground investigation on his own case and his superiors didn't know anything about it. He thought he'd try to get an answer by asking a question close to the one he wanted to answer.

"Well," said Bradbury. "I never broke the law, if that's what you mean, but I did bend the rules here and there. Sometimes it's all you have."

"I guess so," said Marshall.

"Is this about the Douglas case?"

"Yes," said Marshall.

"Well, my advice is, don't do it," said Bradbury. His face took on a serious look. "You've come too far to take chances with your career. Play by the rules and your future will be assured."

Marshall took a moment to let his friend know that he was considering his advice. "Thank you. I needed to hear that. Hey, let's get out of here. These slaves are bringing me down." Marshall managed a laugh.

"Fine," said Bradbury. "I have to use the men's room. Then we can finish talking over lunch, okay?"

"Okay."

Bradbury walked off, and Marshall left the slaves and went farther into the Core Exhibit. The ceiling was lined with TV monitors showing various stages of black history.

"You look troubled, brother," said a woman.

Marshall turned to see a pretty black woman with a short Afro. She was in a lovely African dress and smiled radiantly at him.

"I am a little troubled," said Marshall.

"I'm Esaaki, a director here."

"I'm—"

"I know who you are," said Esaaki. "I hope you won't be upset if I say I am not rooting for you to win. Brother Mbutu is a good man."

"He murdered a man," said Marshall. "How do you root for that?"

"Look around you," said Esaaki. "It wouldn't be the first time someone was killed to advance a greater good."

"I'd argue with the use of those words," said Marshall.

"If you need anything, brother, you can ask at the front desk for me."

Marshall watched her walk away. She was a beautiful woman, and he couldn't help admiring that. She glided along the room, stopping to talk to a woman.

Suddenly Marshall's heart raced. Esaaki was talking with Debra Gibson-Chandler, the foreperson of his jury. Debra looked at him, and her eyes registered shock.

Marshall stepped off the little bridge and walked around the room. He didn't want to engage her by chance. It was totally improper. He made his way around the room, which was set up as a temporal history of blacks in America. Marshall circled around to the beginning of that history. He stopped as a long line of schoolchildren stopped to look at exhibits.

"I need to talk to you," said a voice.

Marshall turned to see Debra behind him. She looked scared.

"You know I can't speak with you," said Marshall.

"I've been threatened," said Debra.

Marshall quickly grabbed Debra and took her aside. "Look, this is wrong. You have to leave now," he said.

"I got a letter at my house that told me to resign the case or else," she said.

"Tell the judge," said Marshall.

"The note said if I did, I'd be sorry. It mentioned my children— by name."

"I can't help you," said Marshall. His heart was pounding.

"Ladies and gentlemen," said Esaaki's voice on a loudspeaker. "We are blessed to have noted attorney and activist Muhammad Rashad in our facility right now. If you'd like to meet him, he will be in the Core Exhibit, then later, in the gift shop. He'll be signing copies of his seminal book, *Defense of Life*."

"You have to go," said Marshall. "If Rashad sees us, we're both done."

"What do I do?" asked Debra.

Marshall could see the fear in the woman's eyes. She was terrified. What he did now would weigh heavily on his mind. He knew forces wanted to get rid of all the black jurors, and he couldn't let that happen.

Marshall saw Rashad and Leslie Reed wade into the room with a crowd of people. He pushed Debra around a corner to hide her.

"Don't say anything," he said. "Stay on the jury. Now, go!"

Debra turned and walked off quickly. Marshall heaved a sigh of relief after she was gone.

Bradbury returned a few minutes later. They walked out of the room, passing by Rashad and Leslie, who acknowledged them with mild surprise.

They left the building and had lunch at a little restaurant on Woodward. Bradbury told him all about the confirmation process and the power behind it. Marshall listened, trying to forget about his problems and share the joy of his old mentor's accomplishment. When they parted company, he actually felt a little better. At least someone's life was going well.

Marshall checked the time and went to his car and drove to meet Danny at his house. They were going to meet some woman who had a relationship with Moses in hopes that she might know where he was.

Marshall drove down the Lodge Freeway back uptown. Soon he was walking into his house. He found Danny inside putting together a handgun.

"Hey," said Danny.

"I'm ready," said Marshall.

Danny finished what he was doing. He pulled back the slide catch, and it snapped loudly. He nodded his head, looking at the weapon like a proud father.

"My lawyer called," said Danny. "I'm officially off the police force now." He sounded matter-of-fact about it.

"I'm sorry to hear that," said Marshall. "So, what happens next?"

"I find another line of work," said Danny. "And I try to keep Vinny from going nuts. Don't worry about it. Let's finish your thing."

"Okay," said Marshall. "I asked the judge for the day. After getting my ass kicked, I have my team locking down the ballistic evidence."

"You got your ass kicked?" asked Danny. "How?"

"Come on, I'll tell you."

Marshall and Danny left, and he told him about the DNA debacle as they proceeded to Nessa's house.

Marshall knocked on the door several times. Mrs. Washington came to the door and cracked it open.

"Hello," said Marshall.

"What is this, some kind of damned disguise?"

"Excuse me?" said Marshall.

Mrs. Washington opened the door all the way, then she raised her gun up to Marshall's chest.

"You heard me, Moses, is that a disguise you got on, and why are you wearin' it?"

Danny pulled his guns and trained them on the old lady.

"Drop it," he said.

"You drop yours," said Mrs. Washington.

Marshall held his hands up over his head. "Please, everyone, just be cool," he said. To Mrs. Washington, he said: "Ma'am, I'm Marshall Jackson, I'm Moses' brother, his twin brother."

"Bullshit," said Mrs. Washington.

Danny kept his eyes on the old lady, and Marshall knew that if she did anything wrong, he'd shoot her dead. Marshall stepped between Danny and the old lady.

"Marshall, move!" yelled Danny.

"No," said Marshall. "You are not going to shoot this woman, Danny. Ma'am, reach in my jacket pocket and take out my wallet. Inside, you'll find my driver's license and my U.S. attorney ID."

"U.S. attorney?" said Mrs. Washington.

"Mama, what are you doing?" said Nessa from inside the house.

"It's a man, says he's Moses' brother," said Mrs. Washington.

Nessa ran to the door. She surveyed the situation. Her face expressed surprise when she saw Marshall. Then, she took the gun from her mother.

"Mama, why do you answer the door without your glasses? You know you can't see good without them. That's not Moses."

Danny lowered his guns. Marshall lowered his hands and told Danny to put his weapons away. Danny did, but he mumbled to himself.

"I need to talk to you," said Marshall.

"You do look like him," said Nessa.

"I need to find my brother."

"I don't know where he is," said Nessa.

"Well, come on in," said Mrs. Washington. "It's cold out here."

Marshall and Danny entered. The house was clean and well furnished. Religious pictures lined the walls. Mrs. Washington still had up pictures of John F. Kennedy. Many older black people still thought of JFK as a great civil rights leader. Not far from JFK were Martin Luther King Jr. and Bobby Kennedy.

"Can I get you two something to drink?" asked Mrs. Washington.

"No, thanks," said Marshall.

"I'll take a beer," said Danny.

"No alcohol in this house," said Mrs. Washington. "I'll get you a pop." She walked off to the kitchen.

"Anything you could tell me would be good," said Marshall.

"Sorry," said Nessa. "I don't like to deal with Moses' business. I only tolerate him because of our son."

"Son?" said Marshall and Danny almost at the same time.

"He didn't tell you?" said Nessa. "That's right, you two don't get along. Wait here."

Nessa went into a bedroom and returned with Kadhi. Marshall's mouth almost hung open as he saw the little boy walk over to him. He could see his brother's features, his own features, in the face of the child. He thought about Chemin, and their broken marriage. The little boy ambled toward him, and he felt it, the wonder of life that can only be seen in a child.

"Say hello to your uncle, Kadhi," said Nessa.

"Kadhi?" said Marshall.

"It means leader," said Nessa. "That's what he's going to be one day."

Marshall was mesmerized by the child. He had lost everything dear to him because of his fear of making life, and here, right before his eyes, was a child fathered by his brother, Moses, a man who had made every bad choice in life. What did Moses have in him that he could be so courageous? He felt ashamed of himself.

"Can I hold him?" asked Marshall.

"Sure," said Nessa.

"Good-lookin' kid," said Danny.

"Thank you," said Nessa. "He's a good boy."

Marshall took the baby and held him tightly. The boy looked at him and smiled a little. Marshall's heart lifted, and he found himself getting a little emotional. He handed the child back to his mother.

"He's beautiful," said Marshall. "Just beautiful. Look, do you think I can come and visit him now and then?"

"Sure," said Nessa. "I mean, we are like family."

"Yes," said Marshall. "That's what I was thinking. Listen, if my brother comes back, and you find out anything, please give me a call." Marshall gave Nessa his card.

Nessa took the card and looked at it guiltily. "He's gonna kill me," she said.

"Why?" asked Marshall.

"Moses is back with his crew in a warehouse, Tybo's, over on the east side. It's not far from that car plant in Warren."

"I know the area," said Danny.

"Thank you," said Marshall.

"I'm glad to see my son has good people in his family. Maybe he'll grow up to be a lawyer too."

"Please call me, bring him over to my house," said Marshall.

"I will," said Nessa.

"Let's hit it," said Danny. "Time to do some damage."

"You're not going to hurt Moses, are you?" asked Nessa.

"I hope not," said Marshall, "but you know what he is."

"Yeah," said Nessa. "I know."

Danny and Marshall left the house. Marshall looked sad, and Danny noticed it.

"I know what you thinkin'," said Danny. "How could life give a kid to Moses and not you?"

"I'd rather not talk about it," said Marshall.

"He made the kid, but he's not a man," said Danny. "He's a scumbag because he's not there for the kid. And unless I miss my guess, that girl and her mama won't let Moses near his own son."

Danny was right, but Marshall still felt bad inside. Even in his foolish irresponsibility Moses had managed to hurt him.

"Let's go get his ass," said Marshall.

Moses walked around meeting the new men. Dake and Nita had only hired a few new people. Moses' old men were happy to see him. He had to admit that it was good to be back in the fold.

The owner of Tybo's was an old crook named Donald Tybolski. He stayed out of their way and let them have the back half of the place.

Wood told the new men who Moses was and what had happened. Some of them were skeptical, but they seemed to be cool about it. A hustler's biggest concern was the next hustle and how much money he was making.

Somewhere, Nita was on a Greyhound bus on her way out of the state. Moses had almost not let her go. Wood had advised against it, but Moses could not find a reason to kill her. Dake was gone, and there had been enough death behind this whole mess.

Since he'd come back, he discovered why Dake and Nita had not blown town. They had a big hustle coming down. One of their men had gotten inside an armored car company and persuaded his coworkers to help him pull a job. They were going to steal a truck filled with money on a currency transfer.

Dake and Nita had set up the armored car men with passage out of the country via Toronto. It was a good hustle, and Moses thought that when it was done, he would have enough cash to get out of town for good and set up shop in another state. Maybe California. It was wide open out there, and he could do well.

Danny and Marshall watched the warehouse as night fell on the city. They would have to make a move soon. When it got dark, the streets would be filled with people who could cause them trouble.

"We could call the cops and bust them up," said Danny.

"Moses won't go quietly," said Marshall. "He'd go away for good this time. He'd rather die first, and I have a feeling that if I go to the authorities, that's just what will happen. Dead, he's no good to us."

"Then how do we get to him?"

"We don't. This one's on me," said Marshall.

"You're kidding," said Danny.

"No," said Marshall. "He'll respect me coming right to him."

"He'll kill you and you know it."

"No, he won't. He's still my brother," said Marshall.

"He's a murderer," said Danny. "I'm your brother."

"I don't have a choice," said Marshall.

"If you're not out in a half hour, I come in and everybody in there is dead," said Danny.

"If I'm not out in a half hour, you go to the cops. Don't go in there. No use in both of us getting it."

Marshall left Danny and walked over to the warehouse. The building was a lot bigger than it looked as he got closer. The guards stopped him, and one of them, a short man with an Afro, pushed a gun into Marshall's stomach. The other was a muscular man with a thick beard.

"Damn," said the man with the beard. "Look at his face."

"I need to see my brother," said Marshall.

"Get the fuck out of here," said the short guard.

"No," said Marshall. "You can let me in, or you can kill your boss's brother. It's your choice."

The guards shared a look, then the short one ran inside. A moment later, Wood came out and took Marshall in. At the same time, several men ran outside and spread out.

Inside of Tybo's was dark in the front, but in the back, the place was alive with activity. Marshall walked over to his brother, who regarded Marshall as if he were back from the dead.

"You don't wanna live, do you?" said Moses. He face held wonder and disbelief.

"Tell me what you know about my case," said Marshall.

Moses laughed. "My men are checking to see if you brought the cops with you. If you did, it won't be a good night for you."

"What do you know about it?" asked Marshall. "A lot of people are dead because of the people behind all this."

"I don't know nothing," said Moses. "I was just shittin' you."

"Tell me who that man was. The one you helped steal the car. Give me his name and I'll leave," said Marshall.

Moses laughed loudly. "You said that like you actually have something to deal with. This is my land. It's not yours, with all them white people and stiff-ass judges. Here, you don't deal. I make the rules."

The warehouse door opened and Danny was brought in with three men holding guns on him.

"No cops, Moses, but we found this," said the short guard.

"They said they'd kill you," said Danny.

The guards took Danny and made him sit on a crate. One of them held both of Danny's guns. Danny didn't look the least bit scared, though. But Marshall couldn't endanger his friend. He had to get him out if he could.

"Let him go," said Marshall. "He's not in this."

"Oh, no," said Moses. "The wigger stays here. He's a fool, but he's too dangerous."

"I'm not leaving without the information," said Marshall.

"Okay," said Moses. "You came a long way to find me. I respect that. I'll fight you for it."

"What?" said Marshall.

"You heard me," said Moses. "You kick my ass and I'll tell you what you want to know. Just like the old days." Moses walked closer to Marshall and raised his fists.

"I'm not—"

Marshall didn't get a chance to finish. Moses threw a hook at his head and Marshall ducked it. Marshall raised his fists reflexively and threw off his coat. Moses' men cheered the fight and started to make bets.

Moses hit him with a hard right in the chest and backed Marshall up. All the fights they'd had as kids started to come back to him. Moses wasn't being childish, he wanted to beat him, make him pay for everything he believed Marshall had done to him. If he lost, he and Danny might not ever leave the warehouse alive.

Marshall connected a left hand to Moses' shoulder and followed with another punch that missed.

"Is that all you got?" asked Moses. "All that high livin' done made you soft."

Moses lunged at Marshall and hit him in the face. Marshall backed up and another blow landed in his stomach. Marshall doubled over and Moses kicked him hard in the side of the head. Marshall hit the ground. Moses tried to kick him again, but Marshall caught his foot, and yanked him off his feet. Both men scrambled to their feet. Moses faked a punch and Marshall jerked backward.

Moses laughed at Marshall. He was enjoying this silly game in front of his criminal friends.

Everything had come to this moment. His career, and maybe even his life, were in the hands of his brother, a man with no morals and fewer brains.

Marshall threw a wild punch and faked slipping. Moses took the opportunity to lunge at him. Marshall turned, pivoting on his heel, and hit Moses in the face. Moses staggered and raised his hands, but Marshall was on him, throwing punch after punch that connected. Moses backed up as his brother beat him. With each punch Marshall saw Moses' face as a kid, then he saw their father and mother and the life that had fallen to ruin.

Moses was in trouble, and he tried to run but fell down. Marshall fell on him, sitting on his chest and began to beat him mercilessly in the face. Blood flew from Moses' mouth, covering Marshall's hands and splattering his shirt. In the distance, Marshall heard Danny yelling, cheering him on. Suddenly, someone grabbed Marshall's hand.

Marshall looked up and saw Wood holding his bloody fist in one hand, and a gun in the other. Beneath him, Moses was unconscious and bloody.

"That's enough," said Wood.

Marshall got up and walked away from Moses, but not before he kicked him hard in the ribs. Wood pushed Marshall away.

"I want the information on my case," said Marshall.

"You need to leave before he wakes up," said Wood. "When he does, he'll kill you both."

"I'm not leaving without it," said Marshall.

Wood walked away as two men picked up Moses and took him to a chair. Marshall smiled a little. He'd finally beaten him. Danny walked over to Marshall and put a hand on his shoulder.

''You kick a lot of ass for a lawyer,'' he said. ''I thought you'd lost it.''

''We have to find out what he knows,'' said Marshall. ''If they refuse, we'll have to make a move on them.''

''You ain't said nothing but a word,'' said Danny. ''I'm ready. If I get my hands on one gun, I'll be able to get at least two of them before they know what's going on.''

Wood came back. ''I talked with some of the brothers. The man you asked about wanted us to steal a car for him. He killed one of our crew, a brother named Carlos. We tracked him to a motel he was staying at. His names was Charles, Charles Dolgen. He was a brother about forty or so. Now, go.''

''What did he look like?'' asked Marshall.

''I never saw the man,'' said Wood. ''You could wait for your brother to come to, but I wouldn't suggest it.''

''Gimme my shit,'' said Danny.

Wood nodded at another man, who tossed Danny his guns. Danny examined them and found that the bullets had been taken out.

''By the time you go to the cops, we'll all be gone,'' said Wood. ''So don't think about looking for us here.''

Marshall and Danny left the warehouse and got into their car.

''Mbutu didn't kill Douglas,'' said Marshall.

''Okay,'' said Danny. ''I say we find this Dolgen dude and bust his ass.''

''Moses was probably lucky he never found this Dolgen. If this man is the assassin, he's probably a professional killer who was most likely trained by the government. You don't just go and get someone like that and hope to live.''

''Then what?'' Danny looked disappointed.

''We check him out before we make a move.''

''You mean *I* check him out.''

''I know I'm asking a lot of you on this,'' asked Marshall.

''Okay,'' said Danny, ''but I want you to do me a favor.''

''What?''

''Start carrying your gun.''

Marshall didn't answer. He reached under the seat of his car and pulled out his gun.

''I'm way ahead of you,'' he said.

45

....

Magic Bullet

Marshall went home and parted company with Danny. Marshall had to get back to the trial. Danny's job was to find their mystery killer, Charles Dolgen.

Marshall went inside his house and found the message light on his machine blinking. He hit the button and passed all the telemarketers and such. He stopped at a message from Chemin.

"Hey," she said. "I'm just calling to see how you are. I heard about what happened in court. I'm sorry. I—uh—"

Marshall's spirits lifted at her voice. And she was searching for words. That made him even happier. Chemin was not a woman who was ever at a loss for something to say. If she were calling to say she'd filed divorce papers, she'd just say it. That meant she was hiding something. Maybe she was having second thoughts.

"I just wanted to see if you were okay. I'll call back. Bye."

The next message was from Bob Ryder. He was frantic, and Marshall could hear Walter in the background.

"Marshall, come to Mount Carmel hospital ASAP! Wendel Miller's been attacked. They're going in to get the bullet."

Marshall raced from the house. He got in his car and headed for the hospital, which was located on West Outer Drive. He chastised himself for being so slow. He should have seen this coming. With the DNA evidence questionable, the only thing left was the bullets. The only good one was lodged in Wendel Miller's spine. That made him forfeit.

Marshall got to the hospital and found Ryder, Walter, and Sommers there.

"Where the fuck have you been?" asked Ryder.

"I had business," said Marshall.

"Looks like you got the business," said Sommers.

Marshall realized that he was still banged up from his fight with Moses. He was bruised, and his clothes were torn.

"I had a little trouble on the street. So, what happened here?"

"Wendel Miller was accosted by two thugs at a restaurant," said Sommers. "They demanded money. When he refused, they attacked him."

"Is that the way he told it?" asked Marshall.

"No," said Sommers. "Miller is unconscious. We pieced that story together. All we know for sure is two men jumped him."

"They injured his back where the bullet is," said Ryder. "The bullet moved, so the doctors have to take it out." Ryder looked almost happy about these events.

Marshall sat down without another word. All he could do now was wait. But he already knew the outcome. The bullet the doctors were removing would match Mbutu's gun perfectly. That would put him in the crawl space and obviate the need for the DNA evidence. The killer, whoever he was, could not have meant to shoot Wendel Miller.

"I'm leaving," said Marshall. "Take the bullet to Serrus Kranet. Leave me a message at home when the results come in."

"It's the weekend, so we need to have a meeting before trial resumes on Monday," said Walter.

"I'll get back with you on that," said Marshall.

Ryder protested, but Marshall walked out. He had to get to the bottom of this before more people were hurt. Why hadn't they just killed Mbutu? he wondered. Like Oswald, he'd go to his grave with all the secrets. The answer had to lie in the real motive for killing Douglas. Mbutu needed to stay alive for some reason.

Marshall went back to the office. He took out the Douglas files he'd put together. He pored over the cases again, and this time he found something. Douglas's judicial record concerned mostly opinions involving individual rights. Marshall had been almost exclusively looking at those decisions. Again he was misguided by race and racial notions. Douglas could not have been killed for that reason. For better or worse, Americans were learning to live with one another.

Douglas's decisions on trade and business were altogether another matter. He was very liberal, or more to the point, protectionist. He had consistently voted against any business or trade measure that did not favor American workers.

Douglas's father was a steel worker who had been put out of work because the mill closed in favor of one overseas. Douglas's father had taken odd jobs and was finally killed when he was caught in a harvester on a farm where he was working. Douglas's family was thrown into poverty. Douglas had taken that pain with him to the land's highest court.

Marshall called a friend who worked for Congressman John Conyers and got a copy of the history of the Green-Dixon Trade Bill pending before the Supreme Court. The bill, if allowed to pass, would seriously hurt American workers. Moreover, the court had been divided five to four against the bill. Douglas had been the swing vote. With Douglas out of the way, the bill would pass.

"But they'd need Mbutu alive until that happened," Marshall whispered to himself. That was why Mbutu was not dead; they needed a spectacle to distract everyone while the plan was completed. After the bill passed muster, then Mbutu would have an untimely accident in prison, closing the matter for good.

He heard a noise. Marshall turned off the lights and took out his gun. He went to a corner of his office and waited. He heard voices, which seemed to be moving. He went closer to his door and pressed his ear up against the cold wood.

"How much longer?" asked a man.

"Not much," said another man. The voice sounded like Van Ness, the CIA agent, but he couldn't be sure. The other voice was not familiar.

"I'm tired of this shit."

"Just be cool. Come on."

They kept talking, but Marshall couldn't hear the rest. They left the hallway. Marshall waited a moment, then he left.

What were they doing? Marshall thought. Planting more bugs, or searching the offices?

Marshall got on the elevator on the twenty-third floor and pressed the lobby button. The car went down. He was nervous. He had to get out of the building without being seen by whoever the men were. At this point, if they saw him they might decide to cut their losses and take him out.

Suddenly, the elevator slowed. Marshall had not pressed a floor before the lobby, so someone on another floor must have stopped the car. He took out his gun and placed it behind his back. If it was an enemy, they'd have to fight to take him.

The elevator door opened, revealing an empty hallway on the nineteenth floor. No one was there. Marshall held the door as he stuck his head out and looked around. Nothing.

He let the doors start to close. As they did, he heard a door of an office open on the floor. The door lock clicked loudly. He heard footsteps coming his way, but before he could see anyone enter the hallway, the elevator doors closed tight and the car went down.

Marshall got to the lobby and checked with the guard. No one had come through that night, he said. Marshall quickly left the building and headed for his car. He drove home nervously, making sure he was not being followed. He got to his house and got out of his car.

He walked toward his house. Halfway up the walkway, about ten feet away, a tree on his lawn was struck by something. The bark splintered and flew into the air. Marshall heard a soft pop from behind him.

He hit the ground and rolled over behind the tree. The shot must have been taken with a silenced gun. He took out his weapon and peered from behind the tree. He didn't see anyone.

His time had run out. The forces behind Douglas's death had decided to get rid of him. Marshall scanned the area. If he took a random shot, he might hit a neighbor's house or car, or worse, it might go through a house and injure someone inside.

Another soft pop and the tree was hit again. Marshall thought he saw a flash from across the street. There was a house across from his owned by some people named Milliken. The Millikens had two rows of bushes in the front, perfect for a sniper.

Marshall looked at his house behind him. He could make a dash for it, but he'd be out in the open for a few seconds. Long enough for the sniper to take another shot at him.

A car rolled down the street, coming his way. Its headlights shined in the dimness. Marshall tried to get a look at the approaching vehicle but didn't dare stick his head out.

A dark figure ran from the bushes at the Milliken house and dashed down the street, going in the same direction as the car. Marshall stood up and trained his gun on the figure.

The sniper ran into the yard of a house four houses down from Marshall's. Marshall followed and saw the sniper jump over a fence and run into the yard of a house behind it. He followed, jumping the fence.

Marshall ran through the yard and onto the next street. He stopped. Nothing. He walked down the street, his gun out in front of him. There were cars on the street, but he could not see anyone inside.

A car sprang to life and barreled at him. The headlights were out but he could see one person inside. Marshall raised his gun but he didn't have a clear shot. He jumped out of the way as the car sped by. He fell to the ground as the car sped off.

"Shit," Marshall cursed.

Lights went on in a nearby house on the street. Marshall ran back the way he had come. The last thing he needed was a police investigation. Thank goodness he hadn't fired his weapon, he thought. A "shots fired" call would get a quick response in his neighborhood. He ran back to his own street and headed toward his house.

On the street he saw a man coming his way. Marshall raised his gun, then he saw it was Danny.

"Danny?" he said.

"It's me," said Danny.

Marshall lowered his gun and walked toward his friend. His heart was pumping hard, and his hand gripped the gun so tightly that it hurt.

"I saw you run after someone from my car," said Danny.

"Someone took a shot at me," said Marshall, "but he got away."

"We'd better get inside," said Danny.

Marshall filled Danny in on everything. Bob Ryder called soon thereafter and informed Marshall that the bullet had been recovered from Wendel Miller's spine and that it matched Mbutu's gun. Miller was still in the hospital, but he'd live and would probably not be paralyzed.

"You think it was that CIA guy?" asked Danny.

"I don't know," said Marshall. "So, what did you find?"

"Well, this Charles Dolgen guy is not a criminal," said Danny. "He was just an average Joe who lived on a farm out in the sticks," said Danny.

"Why are you speaking of him in the past tense?" asked Marshall.

"Because he's dead," said Danny. "The farm burned down with him inside of it."

"But it happened before Douglas was killed, didn't it?"

"Yeah," said Danny. "How did you know that?"

"That's our man. He used Dolgen's identity while he was working on killing Douglas. After he was done, he changed identities."

"Muthafucka's a ghost," said Danny. "We'll never find him if he can change his identities. If he can just disappear, he could be anywhere."

"Maybe we can get to him," said Marshall.

"How do we do that?" asked Danny.

"My wife," said Marshall.

46

Dead Men Walking

Chemin punched a series of numbers on the keypad of the computer called The Eye. The screen sprang to life.

Marshall had awakened her and begged her to help him out. She didn't protest and seemed genuinely glad to see him.

Marshall had to suffer Rochelle's terrible gaze while he waited for Chemin to put on clothes and leave with him. It was worth it, though. Rochelle hated that he still had part of Chemin's heart, and he relished making her watch him take her away.

Hallogent Corporation was located in a sprawling, high-tech tower downtown. Chemin's position as assistant vice president afforded her twenty-four-hour access to the company office.

Marshall had told Danny to go home and stay with Vinny. He didn't trust the safety factor at his own house after the sniper incident.

The computer room was huge, with banks of terminals set up in an oval. It looked like something out of a sci-fi movie. They were truly living in the information age.

Hallogent was a database facility, consulting firm, and think tank. Basically they gathered and sold information. They had contracts with the government as well as many foreign countries. Hallogent got data from everywhere, including the government, and sold it to anyone who could pay. They were like a defense contractor, serving a quasigovernmental function.

"So, can you tell me what I'm doing?" asked Chemin.

"I need to find someone," said Marshall.

"Who?"

"A man who supposedly died in a fire, but who is probably still alive."

"Insurance fraud?" asked Chemin.

"Maybe," said Marshall. "And something a lot worse."

The Eye's screen flashed the Hallogent logo.

"System online," said a computerized voice.

"Okay," said Chemin. "What's this guy's name?"

"Charles Dolgen. He died in a fire in Dundee, Michigan, several months ago."

Chemin typed in the information. Almost immediately, the screen flashed the news articles on the fire, obituary, and the estate of Joe Dolgen. In the corner, a red dot flashed.

"What's that dot mean?" asked Marshall.

"Anomaly," said Chemin. "Something's not right with this profile." Chemin hit more buttons and the screen flashed again. "The Social Security number is not his."

"I'm prosecuting an innocent man," said Marshall. "Mbutu was there, but someone else killed Douglas. Mbutu put himself in the case because he wants to be a martyr. This man, this Charles Dolgen, is a paid assassin, probably government trained."

Chemin didn't say a word, she typed in a code.

"Override," said The Eye.

"This Dolgen guy's Social Security number belongs to a woman named Alissa Bekhor. She died when she was nineteen in Bowling Green, Ohio," said Chemin.

Chemin kept working. The life of Charles Dolgen kept expanding. He had at least twenty aliases.

"He's a pro," said Marshall. "You can assume different identities by stealing Social Security numbers and the names of dead people. As long as the ID looks valid, you can do almost anything. I think this person we're looking for is a government agent using elaborate false identities to hide his true one. I'm sure Dolgen is not his name, it's just one of the fake identities we found."

"I can get him," said Chemin. "I'll have The Eye cross-reference all info and see if the lives he's stealing have a pattern."

She rapidly hit keys on the keyboard. Marshall was proud of her. He knew she loved her job but had no idea she was so good at it.

"There," said Chemin. "Our boy has an Ohio thing going on. Almost all of the stolen lives came from cities and towns in Ohio. Several others came from Michigan."

"So he's local. I have to find him."

Chemin had The Eye print a map of the Midwest. Danny then marked the cities Dolgen had stolen identities from in Michigan and Ohio.

"Got him," said Marshall.

"How?" asked Chemin.

"Don't you see? All the cities are either north or south of one major city."

"Toledo?" said Chemin. "Why would an assassin live in Toledo?"

"Because no one would think he would," said Marshall. "The government would teach its operatives to hide in places where smart-ass people like me would never look. Go where people are decent and normal and kill with impunity. 'Hiya doin' Fred, hi Martha,' " Marshall said, imitating a hick. "All the while he's got severed heads in his car. He's got to be there."

"But why would they use aliases from the same area? That's not so smart, is it?"

"If there's one thing I know about the government, it's that it likes to keep tabs on everything it does. What better way to keep track of assassins than to secure their false identities all in one geographic location? That way, if one of them ever got out of line, you could track him."

"This is where my tax dollars go?" Chemin said.

"Honey, now I need you to do this: track men in the Toledo area ages thirty to sixty who've served in the military."

"I can't," said Chemin. "Hallogent can only get to public data. I'd have to hack into a military computer to do that. I'm good, but not that good." She looked upset that she'd reached a dead end.

Marshall smiled at his wife. "I am," he said.

An hour later, Chemin was sitting at a terminal in the Justice Department's Information Systems Department. ISD was a bright shiny room done in mostly white. It was kept cold, probably because the huge computers ran constantly and needed to be cooled. The department was tightly run, so he'd have to be careful.

Chemin tapped on the keyboard rapidly. "There," she said, "we're in."

"We're only on security level six," said Marshall. "I have to get higher."

Chemin hit some keys. "Okay, it says security level nine, but we need a code."

"Try mine," said Marshall.

Chemin did, but the computer rejected it.

"Sorry," said Chemin.

"I'm only a seven," said Marshall. "We need another way in."

Suddenly, a box appeared on the computer terminal screen. It was counting down from one minute.

"Uh-oh," said Chemin. "The computer needs that code or in a minute it will shut down the system and probably send a warning to whoever watches security for this thing."

"If it does we're screwed," said Marshall. "Quick, type *N-A-T-E.*"

Chemin complied. The code was rejected.

There were forty seconds remaining.

Marshall tried to think. He knew Nate pretty well. What would his code be?

"We're running out of time, honey," said Chemin.

"Nate has a boat called *Juris.* Try that."

Chemin did. Nothing.

"Dammit," said Marshall. "We all change our codes a lot," said Marshall. "It could be anything."

"Twenty seconds," said Chemin.

"I got it. His new granddaughter. Try *T-I-A.*"

Chemin did, and the computer accepted the code.

"Bingo," said Chemin.

"Okay, now track men in the Toledo area ages thirty to sixty who've served in the military."

Chemin did and got over a thousand names.

"Now, the number in special forces, SEALs, Rangers, Green Berets."

Chemin executed the function. The list was down to seventy.

"Good," said Marshall. "Now, let's see how many of them have exited the country, let's say, over five times in the last five years."

"Why is that important?" asked Chemin.

"Killers travel."

Chemin executed the function, but the result was zero.

"Damn," said Marshall. "He probably travels under another set of aliases. How do I narrow the list?" Marshall thought for a moment. Chasing a man like Dolgen was not easy. This type of person spent his entire life eluding detection, flying under the radar of life. *Life?* Marshall thought.

"Chemin, let's see how many of these men are dead now."

Chemin executed the function.

The list narrowed to twenty men.

"Now how many were killed during military action?"

The list narrowed to fifteen.

"Okay," said Marshall, "here's the big one. To hide an identity, it's likely they would fake an assassin's death in battle, but if it were an authorized skirmish, that would leave too many questions. So, let's see how many of these men died in an accident, a fire, explosion, something unrelated to battle."

Chemin executed the function.

The list narrowed to three men.

"Reginald D. Barnes, Cyrril B. Thounter, and Zachary T. Williamson," said Marshall.

"Is your job always this exciting?" asked Chemin.

"Thank God, it's not," said Marshall. "Now we can find him."

"How?" asked Chemin. "I was following this pretty well until now."

"We use the date of death of each of these three men. Which of the false identities we found was the first one used?"

"That would be James Daniels in 1977."

"The use of the first false identity we found should coincide with the accidental death of the man we're looking for. You see, his exit into a shadow life was probably planned."

Chemin hit more keys on the computer, and soon a list of names popped up on the screen. The computer listed them in chronological order. The list ended with the death in 1977 of Cyrril Baker Thounter.

"That's him," said Marshall. "What can we get on him?"

Chemin went to work accessing as much as she could on the man.

"Thounter was born in 1957 in Mississippi. His parents died in a boating accident when he was ten. He went to live with his uncle, his mother's brother, in Cleveland after that."

"Cleveland," said Marshall. "You see, Ohio again."

"Thounter enlisted in the navy at sixteen," Chemin continued. "He lied on his application. He became a navy SEAL not long after that. Thounter was an expert marksman, scoring in the highest percentile of accuracy. He was trained to use a variety of weapons and also proficient in hand-to-hand combat. In the fall of 1977, Thounter was killed in a freak explosion in Saudi Arabia. Almost immediately thereafter, the first alias was used.

"So, how do you find him?" asked Chemin. "He's probably using another alias right now."

"This guy may be a ghost, but he has to be human sometime. Is his uncle still alive?"

Chemin did a check. "Yes, he is," said Chemin. "Robert Carson. He lives in Cleveland, but he was moved to a rest home in—"

"Toledo," Marshall finished.

"My goodness," said Chemin. "Carson is ninety-five."

"Good work," said Marshall. He gave her a kiss on the cheek.

"Yeah, I guess we make a pretty good team." She hesitated on the last part of the sentence, realizing what she had just said. Marshall wanted to broach the subject but didn't want to spoil the good mood they had going.

"Come on, I have to get you back," he said.

"I need to stop at the house to get some more clothes," she said. "I'm all out at Rochelle's."

"Fine," said Marshall. "No problem."

Marshall had Chemin print out all of the data he needed, then he took her back to their house. She went upstairs and packed a bag.

Marshall felt sad as she descended the stairs with a suitcase.

"You can stay, you know," he said.

"Is that really a good idea?" said Chemin. She looked at him with longing and fear in her eyes.

Her willingness to help him did not change the fact that they were at odds. But Chemin didn't know what he'd seen lately, what he felt and how he'd changed. Moses was probably not a good parent, but he had at least taken the leap, and if a man like Moses could become a parent, then so could he.

He decided to catch her off guard, the way she had done to him so often in the past. He took her in his arms and kissed her. Chemin did not resist. He started to take off her clothes, and though she protested, it was weak.

Soon they were both naked, lying in their bed. Marshall pulled himself up between her legs and felt her hand on his chest.

"Wait," she said.

Chemin reached over to the nightstand and pulled out a condom. She tore open the package and gave it to Marshall.

He took it from her and looked at it for a moment, then tossed it over his shoulder. They kissed as he pushed himself inside her.

Chemin clasped her arms down tightly around him, thrilled by what his action had meant. Marshall's mind was filled with the happiness of knowing that he had his wife back, and that they might be making more than just love.

47

....

Home

Danny's car roared down U.S. 23 into Ohio. It was the weekend, so the Douglas case was on hold. On Monday, Marshall would come into court with the bullet removed from Wendel Miller and send Mbutu to jail. At least, that was the plan someone had in mind. The more he thought about the sniper outside of his home, the more he believed that it was just a warning, that the man didn't want him dead.

Lake Erie poured into the Maumee River, and the little city of Toledo came into view. It was an unassuming town, but the vista was almost breathtaking.

"Nice-lookin' place," said Danny.

"We need to go through the city. The place we want is just outside Toledo proper."

Danny drove into the city and out of it in no time. Soon, he was turning into a place called Home, a name taken by the retirement community for obvious reasons.

"I wouldn't mind living here myself," said Danny.

"Yes, but it must cost a few dollars," said Marshall. "But I guess our boy is doing very well in his chosen profession."

They went inside and walked over to the receptionist, a young black woman about thirty or so.

"We want to see Robert Carson," said Marshall.

"Are you family?" asked the receptionist. Her name tag said DORA.

"We don't know," Marshall lied. "That's kinda why we want to see him."

"Sorry, but only known family can visit the members here," said Dora.

"But he might be my granddaddy," said Danny. "I've come a long-ass way to see him, and I'm not leaving until I do."

Dora's face registered mild shock at the sound of Danny's voice. Maybe an interracial affair had taken place. Marshall had to suppress a smile.

"Well, I guess it wouldn't hurt just to talk to him for a minute," said Dora. "But he's old, so don't go shocking him."

Robert Carson sat by the pool in a wheelchair. He looked good for his age as he sipped on a glass of lemonade. Danny and Marshall sat down next to him.

"Mr. Carson?" said Marshall.

"Who you?" said Carson. He was bald and had lost all of his teeth. His voice was scratchy but had lots of life in it. "Got a cigarette?" said Carson.

"No," said Marshall.

"How about you?" Marshall asked Danny.

"Naw," said Danny.

"Cigar, chewing tobacco, snuff?" asked Carson.

"Sorry," said Marshall.

"Damn," said Carson. He pulled out a little cigarette. It looked like it had been half smoked already.

"I thought you didn't have any smokes," said Danny.

"Never said that," said Carson. "Why smoke my stash when I can bum one from you?"

"Mr. Carson," said Marshall. "We're friends of your nephew, Cyrril. We want to talk to you for a moment."

"He don't got no friends," said Carson. "You two must be from the government. He gotta protect the president again?"

"Yes," said Marshall. "We need to find him."

Obviously, Thounter had told his uncle that he was some kind of high-ranking government man. A necessary lie to impress a man he probably loved.

"Let me see your ID," said Carson.

Marshall showed Carson his government ID. Carson squinted, then took another pull of his cigarette. "So, you know all about your nephew's job?"

"Sure," said Carson. "He's a Secret Service man. Travels on assignment for the State Department. Done won every medal there is. Took a bullet for George Bush, but the newspapers never got the story."

"Can you tell us where he lives?" asked Marshall.

"Don't know," said Carson. "Boy won't tell me where he lives, but you know that. He's gotta keep it secret."

"How can we get to him?" asked Danny. "It's important."

"You can wait," said Carson. "He'll be here any second. He's having lunch with me. Don't tell the boy I smoked. He'll go nuts."

Marshall looked around in panic. He couldn't let Thounter know he was here. "Mr. Carson, it's very important that your nephew not know we're here."

"Okay," said Carson. "But the boy won't like it."

Marshall and Danny got up and walked inside. They waited in a corner of the lobby for a half hour. Marshall was filled with so much energy, he could not keep still.

Soon, Thounter walked in. He was a lot smaller than Marshall had pictured him. Thounter was dark, about forty or so, and thickly muscled. His hair was cut in a buzz, and he had a beard and mustache. He walked with a straight militarylike strut, a remnant of his service days.

Thounter walked over to Carson and kissed the old man. Thounter smiled and sat down.

"Let's take him," said Danny.

"Too dangerous here," said Marshall. "Let's go back out and get into our car and follow him when he leaves."

"But that could be for hours," said Danny.

"No, it won't. Carson is going to tell him that men from the government are here, and Thounter will know that no government men are supposed to be here. He'll panic and run."

"But the old man gave his word," said Danny.

"Thounter is family," said Marshall. "He'll protect him first. Think about it, you take the kid in, raise him as your son, and he takes care of you in your old age. If I were him, I'd rat us out first thing."

Marshall and Danny went outside and got in their car. They pulled in next to a line of cars so as not to draw attention to themselves. Minutes later, Thounter ran into the lobby and angrily questioned Dora, the receptionist. Then he ran outside and looked around, then hopped into a blue Toyota and sped off.

Marshall and Danny followed Thounter into Toledo. It wasn't easy. Danny tried to stay behind other cars so that Thounter couldn't make them. They followed him into a little town called Blissfield outside of Toledo.

They had to keep a big distance behind him after he left the city. In such a rural area, Thounter would see them if they followed too closely. They took the chance of losing him, but it was preferable to being discovered.

Danny did lose Thounter after he took a left on a two-lane road. He cursed, then went back the way he had come and took a right. After fifteen minutes, they spotted a small house in the distance, with a car that looked like Thounter's Toyota.

The car was parked in a driveway of a nice little house with a picket fence on a dirt road called Season. The nearest house looked to be a quarter mile away or so. Thounter had a nice piece of land with no nosy neighbors to pry into his business.

Marshall and Danny parked up the road and waited for darkness. Then they walked the rest of the way.

"Look at this fuckin' place. It's like a goddamned postcard."

"Evil men always want to hide out in places of goodness. Maybe it gives them the illusion that they are not what they are."

"So, what's the game plan?" asked Danny.

"Well, if he thinks someone had made him," said Marshall, "he might run. He probably has some sort of escape scenario. So we have to move fast."

"I suppose we have to take him alive."

"I'd like to think we can, but somehow, I doubt it."

Cyrril Thounter quickly packed his bag. In the old days, he'd have several packed and ready to go. But he was getting old, he supposed. No one had made him since 1988, when he ran into an old friend in a mall and had to dispatch him in the parking lot before hitting his assassination mark and moving on.

He caught sight of his face in a mirror in his bedroom. He was indeed old. The forty-year-old man looked back at him, and he wondered what had happened to the kid who enlisted in the navy hoping to see the world.

After his parents died, he went to live with his Uncle Robert. His life was good, but the loss of his parents haunted him for six long years. He did poorly in school, couldn't score with girls, and generally didn't fit in. His Uncle Robert suggested the marines, but Thounter wanted to go into the navy. They traveled more.

They lied on his application and he got in. He excelled in marksman-ship, defeating experts in competition with handguns as well as rifles. It wasn't long before he was accepted in the navy SEALs, an honor that he didn't think he qualified for. But there was already a plan being laid out for him. A man named Colonel Folke came to him and told him of special work he could do for his country, work that necessitated his disappearance.

They rigged his death, then shipped him off to an island in the Pacific where he learned to be a trained assassin. Uncle Robert was devastated until he contacted him and let him in on the secret. For the next part of his life, he traveled the globe executing his "assignments," trading one identity for another.

Then one day, it all stopped. The program was halted, and he was turned out into the world without any usable skills. The government found better ways of getting rid of its enemies. With the cold war over, they could use economic and diplomatic means to destroy. It was ironic. He was a professional assassin, and he'd been downsized.

But it wasn't long before he had other clients, private ones who still needed someone skilled in the art form of causing unnatural death. Thounter took up his occupation, this time being paid handsomely for his services.

But today some strange men had come looking for him. They could be the government, he thought. That job on Justice Douglas was clean, but a government man would know that Mbutu guy was just another cleverly set-up patsy.

His first thought was to cash in his insurance policy. Since he'd gotten into private practice, he'd discovered the need to have insurance for his jobs. The people who hired him these days did not like loose ends, and the triggerman could always be seen as one. But before he got his Farrel Douglas insurance out, he would teach whoever had sent these men a lesson. They needed to know just who they were dealing with.

Thounter finished packing the bag. He went to his closet and opened the door. Inside, there were several guns, knives, and ammunition. Tools of the trade.

He reached past the weapons and took out a small black case. Inside, there were several driver's licenses, Social Security cards, and a thick stack of hundred-dollar bills. He took out a driver's license that had his face on it and the name Victor Raffelson. He put it in his wallet and took the money. He grabbed some explosives and stuffed them into a case.

Thounter then went into his basement and poured several cans of fuel on the floor. He had to torch the place and run. He could not leave any trace of his life here. Thounter threw a match in the gas and it ignited with a loud *Whoomp!*

He ascended the stairs quickly when he heard the sounds of movement above him. He showed no surprise. He had been expecting this. He knew the men would follow him and try to take him out. That's just what he would do. He just didn't expect them so soon. But they were here now, and that only meant he'd have to kill them a little sooner than he'd planned.

Marshall waited at the top of the stairs, hiding behind the doorjamb. He heard the footsteps of someone coming upstairs and he smelled the distinct odor of fire below.

Suddenly, three shots hit the door and the wall. Marshall had to back off. He was backing up when Thounter kicked the door open and leapt out of the doorway. Marshall could see the red glow of the fire below. Smoke was already starting to fill the house, billowing up from the basement.

Marshall backed out of the little kitchen as Thounter saw him and raised his gun. Thounter fired three quick shots. Marshall was astounded at how fast the shots came. The shots hit the kitchen wall, barely missing Marshall as he hit the floor in the dining room.

Thounter ran through the smoky room after Marshall, never seeing Danny crouched behind the refrigerator.

Marshall got to his feet. Thounter was in the kitchen and had to come back in to get Marshall. That was what Marshall was hoping for.

Marshall fired two shots into the kitchen doorway. Nothing. He knew he hadn't hit Thounter, but he was hoping that he would respond. The fire was in the kitchen now, and Thounter had to get out of there.

Thounter swung into the doorway and fired three more shots. Marshall rolled on the floor, pushing a table in front of him. But he still ended up within Thounter's view. Marshall raised his gun and saw the assassin aiming at him.

Suddenly, Danny appeared behind Thounter and grabbed him, forcing Thounter's arms to his side. Thounter's gun fired. Thounter yelled something.

Marshall quickly ran over to the two men and saw that Thounter had been shot in the leg by his own weapon. Thounter's gun had fallen to the floor. Marshall kicked the gun away.

Danny struggled with the assassin. Thounter dropped to one knee, throwing Danny off balance. He grabbed Danny by the head and threw him across the room. Thounter was strong, and even injured, he was formidable.

Without missing a beat, Thounter hit Marshall hard in the ribs and kicked his feet from beneath him. Marshall fell but managed to grab Thounter on his way down.

Thounter grabbed at Marshall's gun, and Marshall, sensing that he would lose the weapon, tossed it away. He had to keep the gun away or someone would die.

The fire was still in the kitchen, but it was starting to come into the dining room. The flames licked at the ceiling, turning it black. Smoke wafted in, pushing out precious air.

Marshall heaved Thounter from him, but the assassin got to his feet and leapt at Marshall, his foot out in front. Danny caught Thounter in midair, and slammed him into a wall. Thounter grunted hard. Danny was behind him, pinning him to the wall. The assassin rammed his elbow into Danny's side. Danny pulled his gun and put it to Thounter's head.

''No!'' Marshall yelled.

In Danny's moment of hesitation, Thounter grabbed at the gun and pushed it away from his head. The weapon discharged into a wall. Thounter raised his legs and pushed himself from the wall into Danny. Both men fell and hit the floor. Fire began to consume the room as the struggle continued.

Thounter grabbed Danny's arm and wedged it between the crook of his elbow. He was bending it backward, trying to break it. Danny yelled, dropping his gun. Thounter let Danny go then chased the weapon.

Marshall didn't have much time. If Thounter got the gun somebody was going to die. He grabbed a little marble statue from the floor. Thounter got Danny's gun and turned with it as Marshall swung the statue at the assassin's head.

Marshall hit him on the side of the head with the heavy statue. Thounter staggered, losing his footing for a second. He fired the gun randomly, missing Marshall and Danny. Marshall hit him on the jaw with his elbow and Thounter fell to his knees. Danny got to his knees and slammed a fist into Thounter's chin, and the assassin fell to one side, still holding the gun.

"That's one tough bastard," said Danny.

"Let's cuff him, quick," said Marshall.

Marshall took the weapon from Thounter. Then they took out handcuffs and cuffed Thounter's hands and feet. He was too dangerous a man to think he wouldn't resist if he recovered.

Danny found one of his guns, the Glock, and they moved into the front part of the house. Smoke was everywhere. Marshall felt heat beneath him. He looked down and saw smoke shooting from the wooden floor. Danny and Marshall dragged Thounter out of the dining room and into the living room. Marshall saw the front door and freedom. Suddenly, the door opened and two figures appeared.

"Nice job," said a man hidden in the darkness of the front of the house.

Danny raised his gun.

"No need for that," said Agent Van Ness as he stepped in. Easter was behind him, looking solemn.

"Don't lower your gun," Marshall said to Danny. To Van Ness he said: "What the hell are you doing here?"

"I don't think we have time to discuss it," said Van Ness. "Let's get out of here and I'll tell you."

"No," said Marshall. "Drop your weapon and back out of the house." Marshall choked a little.

"What?" said Van Ness. "Look, we were tracking the use of some special weapons in the Douglas case. You breached a security computer. Didn't you think we'd have a backup on a level-nine check?"

"Shut up and drop the guns," said Danny. "I'm not in the mood."

"Okay," said Van Ness. "Fine." He put his gun away and turned to Easter. "Put your weapon away, Phil."

Easter didn't move. He kept his gun on Marshall. Marshall could feel the soles of his shoes sticking to the floor as the fire below burned. Thounter's clothes were smoking where his body touched the floor. They had to get out soon.

"Phil, what's the matter with you?" asked Van Ness. "Come on—"

Agent Easter put his gun to Van Ness's head and shot him behind the ear. Van Ness fell to the ground, his smile faded into a look of shock as he died. Easter whipped his gun back on Marshall.

Danny fired at Easter as part of the floor dropped in a fiery crash behind him. Danny dropped his gun and fell to the floor next to Thounter.

Marshall jumped at Easter, grabbing Easter's hand with the gun in it.

Danny got to his feet and went to the fighting men. Easter's gun discharged into Danny's side, but Danny still managed to grab Easter and shove him across the room. Easter flew past Thounter's body and fell near the fiery hole in the living room.

"You okay?" Marshall asked Danny.

"Yeah, but I caught one."

Marshall grabbed Thounter and dragged him toward the front door. Suddenly, Thounter's body jerked, and he kicked out with both legs. Marshall was caught in the thigh and stumbled back into the front door. Danny stepped over to Thounter and kicked him in the head. The assassin passed out. Marshall grabbed Thounter's legs and pulled him toward the door.

A shot hit the door jamb.

Marshall and Danny turned to see Easter coming toward them firing a small gun.

Easter's clothes were smoking, and he looked like a demon as he came closer with the flames behind him. He aimed the gun at Marshall. Suddenly, the floor gave way under him. Easter fell backward through the hole, his body disappearing in a shaft of fire.

Marshall and Danny pulled Thounter from the house. Danny had caught a slug near the rib cage. He was bleeding and stumbled as they scrambled from the house. Marshall helped him, trying to support Danny and drag Thounter at the same time.

"I'm cool," said Danny. "I don't think it went in."

The air outside was sweet as Marshall and Danny pulled the assassin farther from the burning house. Danny's pants were turning dark with his blood.

Thounter coughed loudly. His eyes fluttered and he passed back out.

"Good," said Danny. "I didn't want to knock his ass out again."

They moved toward their car when Thounter's house exploded. A ball of flame shot out the side of the house and rose into the air.

Marshall and Danny almost lost their footing as a shockwave hit them. They moved farther away from the house, dragging Thounter toward the dirt road.

"What the fuck was that?" asked Danny.

"He must have had some kind of explosives in there," Marshall said.

They got to the dirt road and rested. Marshall checked Thounter. He was still out cold. A bruise filled with blood had risen on his head. They'd have to get him checked out soon.

"Hard day's work," said Danny. "Shit." He grabbed his side. "Hurts like hell."

Marshall and Danny took their captive to their car. He drove the car down Season Road as Thounter's house burned, driving black smoke high into the Ohio night.

48

Shadow Life

Marshall was apprehensive as he approached Agent Sommers's house. He'd left Thounter at FBI headquarters and dropped Danny at the hospital.

He wanted to check Easter's and Van Ness's offices, to see if he could find the blackmail material Easter had on Roberta, but it would be impossible at this point. The CIA was already locking down everything Easter and Van Ness had touched and questioning everyone they had contact with. If they had anything, it was lost to him.

He was operating without the aid of his superior, Nate Williams, but he had to. He was still unsure of Nate's involvement and didn't want to alert anyone who might be involved.

It was early in the morning, and Sommers was probably asleep. That was good because he'd wanted her a little off her game. Marshall walked up to Sommers's house, a nice little place tucked in the corner of a cul-de-sac in Southfield.

Chris Sommers answered the door in a silk robe. Her hair was pulled back, and even without makeup she looked good. He never thought of Sommers that way, her all-business attitude was completely asexual. She opened the door and stood halfway behind it, like a kid peeking at a grown-up.

"What the hell is this about that you couldn't call?" said Sommers.

She pulled the door all the way open to reveal that she had a gun behind the door. She lowered the gun, just as Marshall knew she would.

"It's about my case," said Marshall. "May I come in?"

"No, you may not," said Sommers. "Whatever this is can wait—"

Marshall raised a gun from under his coat. "I insist," he said. "Don't even think about it," he said as Sommers's hand jerked. "I'll take that." Marshall took the gun. "Now, get inside."

Marshall backed Sommers into her living room and made her take a seat. She was angry and nervous as he sat opposite her holding the gun.

"Whatever you've done, it can't be this bad," said Sommers.

"It's not about what I've done," said Marshall. "It's about you and your partners in this Douglas thing."

"Partners?" said Sommers. "What are you talking about?"

"I'm talking about the fact that Farrel Douglas was murdered by a paid assassin. That assassin is now in custody and he named you as a coconspirator."

"Bullshit!" Sommers stood up. "You put that gun down right now, dammit. I don't care what half-assed story you heard, I'm clean."

"The assassin's name is Cyrril Thounter, although he has many other aliases."

"No fuckin' way," said Sommers. "Take me in, I'll confront this liar, and you'll see." She was angry and defiant. It was genuine, and Marshall had all he needed to know.

"I bet I would," said Marshall. He tossed Sommers her gun back and lowered his own.

"What the fuck is going on, Marshall?" said Sommers.

"I just needed to know that I could trust you," he said. "I'm sorry, but this thing has got me spooked something awful."

"So, you were lying about Douglas?"

"No, that part's true. I've got the real killer. He's at FBI headquarters with one of your subordinates."

Sommers sat back down, looking confused. "Then what the hell was Mbutu doing?"

"I think he thought he was killing Douglas," said Marshall. "He went up there with that intent, but Thounter was already there, in a small space beneath him. I know. I saw it. Thounter fired the fatal shots, using bullets that wouldn't leave a trace."

"Chris, what's going—" said a man behind Marshall.

Marshall turned to see Bob Ryder dressed in a robe. Ryder expressed shock at seeing Marshall. That shock immediately turned into embarrassment. Marshall blushed and smiled at Ryder.

"Shit," said Ryder.

"It's okay, Bob," said Sommers. "You might as well hear this too."

"Marshall, I know how this looks," said Ryder. "Chris and I just found each other during the case."

"We're adults, Bob," said Sommers. "We don't have to explain ourselves."

"That's right," said Marshall. "Agent Sommers is a beautiful woman. Whose head wouldn't be turned?"

"Can we get back to business?" said Sommers. She was flattered but feeling a little embarrassed by the commentary.

Marshall filled Ryder in on the details, careful to leave out the parts about Roberta's indiscretions. Ryder and Sommers got dressed, and they all went down to FBI headquarters to see their suspect.

When they got inside, Ryder excused himself and walked off. He seemed embarrassed that Marshall had discovered his affair with Sommers. He went to watch the suspect in another room.

Cyrril Thounter sat in the little interrogation room staring at the wall. He'd been in the FBI holding facility all night and still had not said a word. His head was wrapped with a bandage and his left eye was red. His face was surprisingly calm, almost as if he were waiting for a traffic light to change. Behind him, two armed FBI men watched, their hands on their weapons.

Marshall was frustrated. Thounter was a rock, a man who was trained in discipline. He would outlast them all in a waiting game. Sooner or later they had to charge him, and when the system was invoked, he could hide behind the Fifth Amendment until the cows came home.

Marshall did know several things. Van Ness and Easter had been following the Douglas case because they suspected a government weapon, the disintegrating bullets called DH-9s, was used. Easter was part of the conspiracy, although his partner did not know how. It must have been Easter who killed the Johnsons and Jessica, and tried to kill Roberta as well. His partner, Van Ness, was innocent but had led Easter to Marshall and Danny.

"He still not talking?" asked Agent Sommers as she entered the room.

"Did you get him?" asked Marshall.

"Yep," said Sommers. She smiled at Thounter. "Bring him in."

The door opened, and Robert Carson was brought inside in his wheel-chair. Thounter's face turned angry. The old man smiled and waved at his nephew.

"Hey, boy," said Carson. "They told me you were on a special assignment."

Thounter leaned over to Marshall and whispered, "Get him out now, or I'll never tell you anything."

Marshall had Sommers take Carson out, but not before Carson asked to be wheeled over to Thounter so he could hug him. Thounter showed genuine emotion as the old man was wheeled out of the room.

"He can't know what I am," said Thounter. "It will kill him."

"This will all come out sooner or later," said Marshall. "Unless your uncle doesn't read or doesn't have a TV, he's going to find out. Question is, do you want to tell him, or do you want him to hear about it on the news? Now, tell me what I need to know. Who hired you to kill Farrel Douglas?"

"You sure you want to know?" said Thounter. "People always think they want to know things until they see it, then they want to crawl in a hole and die."

"Try me."

"First I want a few things," said Thounter.

"Immunity?" said Marshall.

"That's the easy part," said Thounter.

"I don't think you're in a position to be making a lot of demands," said Marshall.

Thounter smiled, the nasty little smile of a man who'd been living a shadow life, engaged in the occupation of killing since he was a boy. "Wait until you hear what I have to offer," he said.

"And what is that?" asked Marshall.

"This thing goes up high, real high. I always carry insurance on my jobs. I can prove everything."

"And for that you want to walk on a murder?"

"That's my offer," said Thounter.

"Fuck that," said Marshall. "We already have you on attempted murder and possession of illegal guns and explosives. That will keep you in prison for at least the rest of your life."

Thounter thought about this for a moment, then: "You drive a hard bargain," he said.

"You will do time for what you did," said Marshall. "The only thing I can promise is to make a recommendation that you don't get the needle.'' Marshall was referring to the death penalty imposed by lethal injection. He was giving him a chance at life in prison.

''So you let me live and that's a deal?'' Thounter laughed.

''I think that's a pretty good trade.''

Thounter leaned back in his chair. He was caught and seemed to know it. He was smart enough to understand that since they had him on legitimate charges, he'd have to act soon, or perhaps the deal he'd been offered would disappear.

''Okay,'' said Thounter. ''I want my deal in writing. Then there's a package you need to pick up.''

49

....

Closing

The courtroom buzzed as Marshall entered. He'd cleaned himself up as well as he could, but he still looked as if he'd been in a fight. Danny was in the back of the courtroom with Vinny and Chemin. Danny had come against Marshall's recommendation. Even though he was hurt, he did not want to miss out on the end of what he'd risked his life for.

The media had heard various rumors about something important happening in the case today. Marshall surmised that it was the ballistic evidence that had set tongues wagging.

Marshall told his team to fall back, that he wanted to do this alone. Walter didn't complain, but Ryder did. He wanted to share in the glory, but Marshall would not take no for an answer. He had broken the law and did not want to taint anyone else.

Marshall took a seat at his table. Mbutu still looked sickly but seemed in good spirits. Rashad walked over to Marshall with an inquisitive look on his face as a bailiff rolled in a TV monitor.

"Counselor, may I have a moment?" said Rashad.

"Sure," said Marshall.

"I'm curious about the rumors I've heard," said Rashad. "You have new ballistic evidence, conveniently available as soon as your DNA case falls apart. But I'd like to know about these rumors of the case ending today."

"It will end today," said Marshall. "And the bullet we recovered was fired by your client."

"You still have to prove that," said Rashad. "I will be asking for an adjournment so we can check the procedure under which you make the analysis."

"You won't need to do that," said Marshall.

"Isn't that for a judge to decide?" said Rashad.

"Not today," said Marshall.

"Okay, I see you want to speak in riddles. At least tell me what the TV is for. Are you going to force us to watch the killing again?"

"No," said Marshall. "We are going to watch the reason why there was a killing in the first place."

Toby Newhall and Nate Williams entered the courtroom and took a seat behind Marshall. There was a commotion within the ranks of the media as every camera in the place covered the couple as they sat down.

It had been difficult to get Toby to come. After the case started looking bad, she'd receded from the spotlight. But Marshall had informed her that the case was back on track, that she should be there in court to see him close it.

"Mr. Jackson, I hope for the sake of my jet lag that you make good on your promise," said Toby.

"I will," said Marshall.

"Is this about the new ballistic evidence?" asked Nate.

"Yes," said Marshall. "I wanted you both here to witness what I am about to do this morning."

"You don't look so good, Counselor," said Toby. "Have you been in an accident or something?"

"I'll explain it all in a moment," said Marshall.

The bailiff called the court to order. Langworthy entered and started the case.

"Mr. Jackson, is the government ready to proceed?"

"Yes, Your Honor," said Marshall.

Marshall then called Serrus Kranet and admitted the new ballistic tests, which proved that Mbutu's gun had shot Wendel Miller. Rashad requested a continuance, but it was denied. He tried to cross-examine Kranet, but the witness and the evidence held up. Finally, Marshall got to the matter he'd come for. With Mbutu firmly connected to the Wendel Miller shooting, it was time to close the case.

"I have another witness as to this matter," said Marshall. "I'd like to call Cyrril Thounter."

"We don't know this witness," said Rashad.

"He's not on the list," said Langworthy.

"He couldn't be," said Marshall. "We just found him last night. I remind the court of Mr. Rashad's surprise rebuttal witness to the DNA evidence."

"That witness was on the list, Your Honor," said Rashad.

Langworthy took a moment to think. He glanced around the courtroom, then: "I'll allow it," said Langworthy.

It was not an appropriate ruling, but Langworthy could sense that something special was going on. He saw the U.S. attorney for his district and the U.S. attorney general sitting just a few feet from him. He was not about to let procedure ruin the moment. "Mr. Rashad, you can have a continuance for your cross if you wish, but let's get the direct examination this morning. Mr. Jackson, what will this witness testify to?"

"The murder in this case," said Marshall.

Marshall signaled two FBI men, and Thounter entered, restrained in leg irons, and took the witness stand. The FBI men stayed close to Thounter on either side. Their side arms were on their hips, exposed instead of inside their jackets. Marshall was not taking any chances with a dangerous man like Thounter.

Toby and Nate looked dumbfounded as the assassin walked in and was sworn in.

"State your name," said Marshall.

"Cyrril Baker Thounter."

"Do you have any aliases?"

"Yes."

"How many?"

"About sixty or so."

The murmur in the court was loud. Langworthy gaveled to quiet them.

"In what profession do you use those aliases?" asked Marshall.

"I'm a paid assassin," said Thounter calmly.

"And did you shoot and kill Farrel Douglas?"

"Yes, I did."

The courtroom erupted in noise. The reporters headed for the door, but bailiffs stopped them.

"No!" yelled Mbutu. "He's lying!"

Rashad pushed Mbutu back in his seat and made him shut up. He'd just gotten an acquittal and didn't want to blow it.

"Sit down," said Langworthy. "Bailiffs, station yourself by the defendant. Mr. Jackson, continue."

Mbutu took his seat as a bailiff stood next to him.

"Tell the court how you planned the murder."

"I was told to set up a patsy for the kill," said Thounter. "I was given Mbutu's name and address. I started writing him angry letters railing against Douglas. Then I told him I had connections to people overseas who could help us kill him. He bought the whole thing. He never knew who I was. I used a false name, and I would only contact him by phone or letter. I planned the whole distraction, the man with the gun was used to break the security so Mbutu could get out of the building."

"Mr. Thounter, what kind of gun did you use to kill Farrel Douglas?"

"A Wagner .308WIN. It's a small, light, compact gun."

Marshall went to the evidence table and took Mbutu's gun and showed it to the court and then to Thounter.

"Is this the kind of gun you used?"

"Yes," said Thounter.

"Why did you use this particular gun?"

"Because I knew that Mr. Mbutu there had been given one just like it to kill Farrel Douglas."

"And how do you know that?"

"Because I sent it to him."

"And why was that done?"

"So that it would appear that he shot Douglas. I used special ammunition called DH-9s in the rifle. I got them from Phil Easter. DH-9s explode on impact, not leaving a slug that can be matched with accuracy. Mr. Mbutu had ordinary bullets, but they would tie him to the shooting."

"Why, Mr. Thounter?" asked Marshall. "Why not just let Mbutu do it?"

Thounter laughed. "The people I work for don't leave these things to amateurs. And as a matter of fact, Mbutu missed his target."

"Did you shoot Wendel Miller?"

"No. I was only after Douglas. I hit what I aim for."

"Now, Mr. Thounter," said Marshall. "Tell the court how you got to be so close to where Mbutu fired his shots."

Thounter adjusted in his seat. The FBI men on either side of him reacted, turning inward and placing their hands on their weapons. Marshall tensed, as did the entire courtroom. Someone gasped loudly. Finally, Thounter settled.

"Mr. Thounter?" said Marshall. "How did you get to be so close to where Mbutu fired his shots?"

"I used an old air duct that leads to an area under the crawl space that Mr. Mbutu occupied. I got there a month before the speech and prepared the area, making a sliding door out of an old vent cover that I could shoot out of. I knew the security procedures wouldn't start until three weeks before the target came. When Douglas came in, I was right under Mbutu, maybe only three feet away. I hit my target twice. I even scored a head shot with the second."

Thounter was cold, clinical, and proud of his deed. Marshall was chilled by his demeanor and suspected that everyone else was too.

"How did Mbutu get out of the building?"

"My employers somehow rigged the security team to leave the crawl space unattended. Mbutu was to pack the gun, run downstairs, and hand the weapon off to a man who would hand it off to another. Then one of Mbutu's men was to brandish a gun and take the security men on a chase while everyone else escaped. I simply climbed back down to the basement and walked out the back during the chase."

Marshall surveyed the stunned courtroom. Nate and Toby looked at him with anger. They were obviously upset at not being let in on all of this. Marshall turned back to his witness.

"Who hired you for this job?" asked Marshall.

"I was recruited by Phil Easter, a CIA agent I got to know doing some special government jobs."

"Was Easter the only CIA man involved?"

"No," said Thounter.

"For the record, Your Honor," said Marshall, "Phillip Easter was killed in the capture of this witness outside of Toledo after he killed his partner, Art Van Ness." To Thounter, Marshall said, "Did you know who Easter was working with?"

"Not then, but I found out."

"How?" asked Marshall.

"When I heard who the target was, I wanted double my usual fee. And I thought that I needed some insurance, so I followed Easter."

"And who were his contacts?"

"A couple of other CIA agents, several high-level lobbyists for these big companies. They wanted to stop some trade bill from passing. When Easter met a man, I'd follow him, and so on and so on.''

''And what did you find?''

''I ended up in D.C. following two senators, one from Pennsylvania and another from Georgia. They got a lot of money from these companies that wanted that trade bill defeated.''

Marshall stopped his examination and turned to Langworthy. ''Your Honor should know that right now, all of these men are being arrested in various states and the District of Columbia through a coordinated effort between the FBI, CIA, the U.S. marshal, and local law enforcement. The government believes that Farrel Douglas was killed to defeat the Dixon-Green Trade Bill, which would be worth billions of dollars to the interested parties.'' To Thounter he said, ''And what else did your investigation find?''

''I recorded a conversation between the senators. They talked about how to do the hit.''

''Mr. Thounter, do you have proof of this conversation?''

''Yes,'' said Thounter. ''I followed them using a directional mike attached to a high-end surveillance camera. It wasn't easy, because they kept moving. The picture is fuzzy, but you can tell who they are just fine.''

Marshall rolled the TV monitor.

''The government would like to submit this tape into evidence as government exhibit one hundred and fifty-three.''

Marshall hit a button on the VCR. Two men appeared on screen. They were both about fifty or so. One was dressed in a light trench coat, the other in a dark one. The men made small talk, then: ''I need some assurance of a conviction after the bad vote is eliminated,'' said the man in the light coat.

''No problem,'' said the other man. ''It's all taken care of.''

''This is goddamned unnecessary. The president is so obsessed with being liked that he can't see how he's hurting the country.''

''It's too bad we can't get to Douglas. He's just too inflexible on this issue. Attempts to influence him have failed.''

''A small price to pay for what we'll get.''

''Our DOJ contact wants assurances of the deal.''

''Send her the message not to worry. I can guarantee the number two spot on the ticket in the next election.''

''Then we're all set.''

"From today, this matter never happened."

"Agreed."

The men split up and walked away. The picture started to fade out. Marshall turned off the TV.

"Your Honor, I know this is unusual," said Marshall. "But I could not allow this court to be used to perpetrate this grand injustice. The plot to kill Farrel Douglas was undertaken for billions of corporate dollars and the ambitions of powerful people. I'm done with this witness."

"Any questions, Mr. Rashad?" asked the judge.

Rashad was much too smart to follow this examination with anything. "None," said Rashad.

Marshall walked over to Nate and Toby and stood before them as Thounter was led out of the courtroom.

"I'd like to call one last witness. And it doesn't give me any pleasure to do so."

Nate and Toby looked at Marshall as if he were the angel of death, huge, terrible, and there to take them. "I call the attorney general of the United States."

The courtroom erupted again. Toby stood and looked at Marshall with contempt.

"What the hell do you presume you are doing, Counselor?" said Toby. "None of this is authorized. It's over, right now."

"I'm the judge here," said Langworthy. "It's not over. Will you take the stand or not, Ms. Newhall?"

"I'll do no such thing," said Toby. "This is—"

"Helen, be quiet," said Nate Williams.

Toby looked at Nate with disbelief. "Nate, you don't believe—"

"The man in the tape said 'her' and 'DOJ.' The acronym for Department of Justice," said Marshall. He referred to an accomplice in the department who wanted to run for vice president," said Marshall. "Who else in Justice is even qualified but you?"

"This is crazy," said Toby. "I am the attorney general of the United States!"

"Your part in the conspiracy was to guarantee a conviction while they replaced Douglas. And you did a good job. Picking me as counsel, staying close to Nate, assuring a speedy trial. You've been the hand moving this case all along. In return, you'd ascend to high office. Now, for the last time, will you take the witness stand?"

Toby was silent. She looked around the courtroom as if she'd landed in the middle of fierce enemies.

"Your Honor," said Marshall. "I move to find her in contempt and place her under arrest."

"So ordered," said Langworthy.

Agent Sommers and two other government men went to Toby and took her into custody as the shocked gallery and media looked on. Nate just watched silently, his face a mask of hurt and disbelief.

The court calmed down and was eerily silent except for the sound of TV cameramen moving to get their shots as Toby was taken out of the courtroom and into the judge's chambers.

"The government will drop the charges of murder against the defendant, Your Honor," said Marshall. "However, he did conspire to kill Farrel Douglas, attempted to kill him, and his reckless disregard led him to wound Wendel Miller. We will press charges on those crimes in this case. The people rest."

Marshall walked back to his desk. Nate looked at him as if he had never seen him before.

"Well," said Langworthy. "I think that was a bellyful for one morning. Are you sure you don't have any cross-examination of any witness, Mr. Rashad?"

Rashad was about to answer, when Mbutu pulled his arm. Rashad looked at his client, and Mbutu shook his head solemnly.

"No, Your Honor," he said.

"Okay," said Langworthy. "For reasons that are obvious, I'm dropping the charge of murder against the defendant. I'm calling a recess until tomorrow. Court's adjourned." He gaveled loudly. It was drowned out by the voices of the gallery. The reporters rushed toward Marshall but were held at bay by the bailiffs.

Marshall told Walter to tell Chemin and Danny to wait for him. He told Ryder to speak to the press in his place. Ryder gladly accepted the offer.

Marshall walked toward the judge's chambers. He didn't want to talk to the media. He was tired and had just one additional matter to attend to. Suddenly, Nate was beside him, looking at him with anger.

"Marshall!" said Nate.

"I'm sorry, sir," said Marshall. "I couldn't tell you."

"That's unacceptable," said Nate. "When this is over, we'll talk about your performance."

"When this is over, sir," said Marshall, "I quit."

Nate was shocked. He searched Marshall's face to make sure he was serious. Marshall could see that his boss knew it was not a lie. Nate's face turned complacent.

"You don't mean that, do you?"

"You should go to see Toby," said Marshall. "I think she'll need a friend right now. I have an appointment with Judge Bradbury downstairs."

Marshall walked out of the courtroom with the press behind him, screaming his name.

50

Legacy

Marshall could hear the echoes of his heels clicking on the floor as he entered the chambers of Judge Stephen Bradbury. The sound was discordant, a contrast to the beauty of the dark wood and polished floors. He'd called and left word with Bradbury before he went to trial, saying that he wanted to talk to him.

Bradbury's chambers were empty. Since being nominated for Douglas's vacancy, he'd dropped out of the normal rotation of judging cases. His staff had taken this as a sign from God and took paid time off. The normal expanse of the place seemed even bigger without people in it.

Marshall entered Bradbury's office. It was dim inside. The blinds were drawn, and the lights turned down. Bradbury was sitting in his leather chair, holding a drink. A bottle of cognac sat on the desk.

Marshall walked up to the desk, and looked at his friend and mentor. Bradbury's normally alert eyes were red, his face sad and flushed. Marshall couldn't tell if it was from the alcohol, or if he'd been crying.

Bradbury had been watching the trial on TV. A color portable sat in the corner in pieces. It had been thrown against the wall.

"Did you know?" asked Marshall.

Bradbury didn't answer. He looked past Marshall, as if seeing some apparition behind him.

"I have to know," said Marshall. "I couldn't find anything to link you to the conspiracy, but it seems to me you're much too savvy about politics not to have known something was up. Toby and her people had to be sure that the new justice would vote their way.''

Bradbury stood up. He was a little unsteady on his feet, and Marshall noticed that the cognac bottle was about a third empty.

''After all the struggle of our people,'' said Bradbury. ''After all the death, pain, and misery we've suffered, we finally get to a position of power in this country, and they pick an Uncle Tom to represent us.''

''He was a man,'' said Marshall. ''He may have been misguided, but that's not a crime.''

''What do you know about it?'' said Bradbury. ''Your generation did nothing to advance our people. Did you march in front of murderers, did you run from attack dogs, and get knocked off your feet by high-pressure hoses? Do you know what that feels like? It's like getting hit by a car. I paid my dues, Marshall. I suffered for black people. I deserved to be on that Court!'' Bradbury sat back down.

''Don't you get it?'' said Marshall. ''Douglas wasn't killed because of his ideology, he was killed for money. In all your wisdom about who was the blackest black man, you forgot that America only cares about who's the richest man. So, I'm asking you again, *did you know*?''

Bradbury emptied his glass. Then he poured another and drank half of it.

''I didn't know anything, but I suspected. I knew that people were trying to squeeze Farrel on his vote on the trade bill. They didn't know he'd be liberal on that one issue. So when he was shot, I tried to deny that it was related, but in my heart I knew.''

''But you were not part of the conspiracy?''

''I'm a judge, not a politician. And it was clear from my record that I would vote the trade bill into law.''

''Why didn't you say something, Judge? Why didn't you come to me or Nate or anyone with you suspicions?'' Marshall voice had anger and sadness in it.

''Because I knew if I did, I'd never get to the Supreme Court. The powers that be would not like it if I started trouble. Don't you understand? I wanted the job, Marshall. I wanted it more than anything I've ever wanted. The Supreme Court is more than a judgeship. It's immortality.''

Marshall stared at the man whom he'd admired for so long. Bradbury had always been like a knight to him, a crusader for a noble purpose. Now he looked like a common criminal, a thief caught in the act.

"You were wrong, sir," said Marshall. "In a way, you have blood on your hands."

Bradbury didn't respond. He just downed the rest of his drink.

"You'll understand if I don't come when you're sworn in," said Marshall. Then he started to walk away.

"I'm not getting the nomination," said Bradbury from behind him.

Marshall turned around and saw that Bradbury had stood up again.

"The White House will pull my nomination now," said Bradbury. "I was recommended by Toby and all the people you've just had arrested. The president will not want to back a candidate with friends like that."

Marshall saw the logic in his words. With a scandal of this size, the president could not afford to get any dirt on himself.

"Some people would call that justice," said Marshall. He turned his back on Bradbury and walked out.

His footsteps echoed on the high walls of the chambers. All he could think about was the big mess the government had to clean up, and seeing his wife, who he was sure still loved him.

51

··

Ceremony

Marshall and Chemin watched proudly as Detective Danny Cavanaugh accepted his commission and gold shield. Normally there would be a whole class of detectives receiving the honor, but this was a special ceremony. Only Danny's family and a few friends were allowed to attend. Deputy Chief of Police Tony Hill conducted the ceremony in his spacious office. Outside, spring had come early in March, and the sun shone over a clear sky.

Danny's part in solving the Douglas conspiracy had made him a celebrity. Suddenly, the case against him was dropped and the messy brutality lawsuit quietly disappeared.

Danny was reinstated and given his dream, a detective's gold shield. He'd even managed to get his father's old number, a fact that made Danny's mother and father cry like babies.

Vinny was taking a desk job and going to law school at Wayne State University. Vinny's family stood in stony silence as Danny was sworn in. Marshall could see it in their eyes. They knew they were stuck with Danny forever.

Deputy Chief Hill presented Danny to polite applause. He and Marshall hugged. And Marshall saw mist in his friend's eyes, something he hadn't seen since he was a kid.

"I love you, man," Danny said into Marshall's ear.

"Same here," said Marshall. "Same here."

Danny's father made everyone wait for pictures. He'd gotten a new camera just for the occasion. They all stood together posing for photos commemorating the event.

All of the initial arrests had been made in the Douglas conspiracy. Toby was in custody, stripped of her office and turned in by her coconspirators. The president had gone on national TV to express his deep regret about the matter and to spin the embarrassing situation into a positive light.

Thounter was in protective custody, and his uncle, Robert Carson, had been offered a hundred thousand dollars to do an interview. Carson had refused. The old man was too heartbroken to talk about his disgraced nephew.

Roberta had come out of her coma and was making a slow, but steady, recovery. Marshall told Nate that Roberta had been instrumental in helping him solve the case, so Nate let Roberta get away with an unpaid suspension for a year from the office. She would not be disbarred or fired.

The CIA didn't care about Roberta, and Sommers made sure the FBI didn't either. Sommers had gotten a promotion and didn't mind throwing her new weight around. With Sommers's help, Marshall recovered the embarrassing tape of Roberta and the one of himself and Jessica. He destroyed them all.

Sommers ended her relationship with Ryder when the case was over. Ryder didn't seem to mind. He'd gone back to D.C., trying to distance himself from his old boss and keep his career going.

Bradbury withdrew his nomination for health reasons. At least, that was the official word. He retired from the bench, taking senior status. For Bradbury, it was the functional equivalent of being put out to pasture. His career was over.

Moses' men had been arrested in a sting operation involving an armored car. The local police had set them up to rob the car, and made six arrests. Wood, Moses' right-hand man, was shot and killed. Moses escaped during a gun battle and was still at large. With his crew destroyed, Marshall was sure that his brother was gone for good.

Marshall left his job at the U.S. attorney's office. Nate had begged him not to resign. But he was never going back. The cause of justice that he believed in so faithfully had been forever perverted in his mind.

He was getting job offers from all over the country. Law firms in New York, D.C., Chicago, and even one in London called and sent letters of inquiry. *Time* had put his face on the cover above the caption JUSTICE'S LAWYER. When all this settled down, he promised himself he'd look the offers over, and decide what he was going to do.

Danny was like a kid, and he hugged and kissed Vinny in front of her stunned family. Marshall promised himself he'd talk to Danny later and make sure he knew this was a gift not to be blown. For now, he'd leave him to his happiness.

"That's the luckiest man in the world," Marshall said to Chemin.

"I don't know," said Chemin. "You're pretty lucky too."

"That's right," said Marshall. "I still have you, don't I?" He kissed her as everyone started to file out.

Marshall looked out of the office's window and saw the old courthouse across downtown. Lady Justice was still there, watching over the city.

Justice was an ideal, a perfection of fairness, logic, and humanity, he thought. It was something that men aspired to, but never quite attained. Justice was flawless in its potential to function. It was men who were flawed in its execution.

He knew now what Lady Justice's eyes were like under the blindfold. They were not sad or angry, as he had first thought. Her eyes were clear, resolute, and determined that the scales she held would never be imbalanced.

Epilogue

Life

November.

   Marshall held his son in his arms for the first time as the nurses finished cleaning him off. He was eight pounds, but he seemed so small, so fragile. His little hands and feet moved without purpose, taking their first motions, like leaves quivering in the wind.

   Chemin lay on the operating table crying, but looking happier than she'd ever been.

   Marshall came to her with the child. He sat down and told his wife how much he loved her and how amazing it had been to witness the birth.

   Chemin laughed, then asked to hold her son. Marshall carefully placed the child in her arms. Chemin stroked his wrinkled face, not believing how beautiful he was. She held the baby to her chest and looked at him with such emotion that Marshall believed he was witnessing some kind of miracle.

   He regarded his family and knew in that instant that he'd done it. Despite his apprehension and fear, he was going to be okay. He had beaten the demon in his heart and his head. And if there was some answer to life's great question, he'd just taken the first step to finding it.